D0960341

ETERNA AND OMEGA

Tor Books by
LEANNA RENEE HIEBER

The Eterna Files
Strangely Beautiful
Eterna and Omega

ETERNA
AND
OMEGA

LEANNA RENEE HIEBER

TOR

A Tom Doherty Associates Book
NEW YORK

ETERNA AND OMEGA

Copyright © 2016 by Leanna Renee Hieber

A Tor Book
Published by Tom Doherty Associates, LLC
175 Fifth Avenue
New York, NY 10010

www.tor-forge.com

Tor® is a registered trademark of Tom Doherty Associates, LLC.

The Library of Congress Cataloging-in-Publication Data
is available upon request.

ISBN 978-0-7653-3675-0 (hardcover)
ISBN 978-1-4668-2926-8 (e-book)

Our books may be purchased in bulk for promotional, educational, or business use. Please contact your local bookseller or the Macmillan Corporate and Premium Sales Department at 1-800-221-7945, extension 5442, or by e-mail at MacmillanSpecialMarkets@macmillan.com.

First Edition: August 2016

Printed in the United States of America

0 9 8 7 6 5 4 3 2 1

ETERNA AND OMEGA

CHAPTER
ONE

New York City, 1882

The scene inside the Trinity Church graveyard in downtown Manhattan Island on this witching hour was dire, no matter if one could see the myriad ghosts gathered therein or not. A living woman shook on the ground, surrounded by a dead horde.

Louis Dupris, his phantom form floating beside the shaking body of his lover, Clara Templeton, was screaming at her, alongside the spectral spectrum of Manhattan. Not because she'd done anything wrong, but because she was unwittingly drawn into a far more dangerous situation than she could possibly have known. The ghosts were unable to impress this idea upon her, certainly not in her state.

An unkindness of ravens had gathered to add to the cacophony from the tops of a nearby tree that arched over Trinity's brownstone Gothic eaves and overlooked the graves. Everything dead and living lifted keening protest; wailing and squawking, these ravens as much harbingers as they were scavengers.

A dread power was about to unleash itself over England and America. This was dawning on those in the spirit world who remained attuned to the living. The two countries were woefully unprepared for the black tide that would rise like a biblical plague. Only in this case, the surge would be sent from devils, not from God.

But Clara, a Sensitive—a gifted, empathic medium—wasn't

in any state to help the spirits or herself, seeing as her ability came with the unfortunate side effect of seizures. Her dark blond waves of hair had shaken free of their pins, the cloak she'd worn over her black linen dress seemed to catch most of the dirt her limbs would be battering against, her high cheek-bones and distinct angles were tense and taut, her chattering teeth had bitten the inside of her cheek during the seizing, and blood dribbled down her fair chin.

Thankfully, a friend who had been told to mind her business didn't. Lavinia Kent, one of Clara's coworkers at the Eterna Commission, launched herself into the Trinity Church graveyard and, not seeing Louis or the ghostly retinue around her, rushed to Clara. She turned her on her side, taking her head in her hands and carefully slipping a fold of fabric from her skirt into Clara's chattering teeth, never minding the blood on her black gown.

Louis Dupris and the other spectral compatriots attempting to alert Clara were suddenly attuned to a new distraction.

Down Pearl Street, from the site of the Edison company's vast electricity-producing dynamos, came a terrible whine, a buzzing, terrifying roar. This electrical disturbance disrupted the plane of the dead; the subtle currents upon which they flowed and the various modern conveniences they could interrupt were trumped in a way they'd never experienced. The mild spark of a spirit was nothing compared to the surge of a great turbine.

Louis had noticed, in his fascinating new existence as a ghost, that sometimes he and his fellows could generate electricity—and that sometimes a current could put them out instead.

Clara roused to explosions of lightbulbs along one of Manhattan's most influential, wealthy streets. Coming to, she slowly focused on Lavinia. Louis, ever attentive to Clara's eyes from their various amorous encounters during his life, could see her senses returning. He knew they always came back in pieces.

"Vin . . . what . . . I . . ." Clara's tongue seemed thick and unwieldy.

"You're all right," her friend said gently. "I assume this place is too haunted for you to be in here for too long. Come, let's get you back home. I don't suppose you'll actually tell me what you were doing in here?"

"Official business," she mumbled and said no more, allowing Lavinia to help her up and gingerly walk with her as her body slowly began to respond normally to her mind's instructions. Louis knew, from having seen her through more than one of these episodes, that her mind would remain hazy and she'd collapse into a deep and deathlike sleep until morning.

But as he watched Lavinia supporting Clara's drooping weight and clumsy steps, Louis felt comforted that she would indeed be all right. Both women shuddered as he reached out to try to touch Clara's hair. At this, he was saddened, as it was likely from his own chill.

He floated away, feeling as lonely as a sentience could. If the loneliness of life was unbearable at times, the isolation of death was the stuff that drove specters to haunt the living for centuries. It was the sharpest of pains, impossible for his theorist's mind to quantify.

"I *have* to get through . . ." the ghost murmured to the night, wafting up a side street speckled with the occasional gas lamp. The constraints of the spirit world were chafing against his desire for clarity and forward motion, lulling him toward the stasis of a mere haunt. He was between worlds, a dangerous place for a man to be recalled to a mission.

"I know leaving her be, that's for the best, considering her condition, but I *need* to talk to her," Louis said anxiously, darting his translucent form back up Broadway. "The files, my work, is a *safeguard*. Not a danger, but a help, a breakthrough in localized magic. It wasn't the creation of the compound that was the killer, but the presences that came in after. Clara must understand. Surely something personal can connect us. Clara, love, I need you, and you need me more dead than alive to sort this all out. . . ." A gruesome but brilliant solution presented itself. "Something tactile. A tactile remembrance where I died . . . Her hair . . . Beautiful hair . . . To connect us . . ."

In his ghostly state, a helpful idea literally illuminated his grayscale form, and he blazed like a candle for a moment before returning to a ghostly default of *eisengrau,* the color behind one's eyes, a gray the epitome of that purgatorial space between awake and asleep.

"The medium!" he gasped, and thought hard about where he could find the specific woman who had communicated with him before. Unfortunately for them both, the moment in question had happened by force. Mediums and spirits were best met by welcoming relations.

He doubted she'd be happy to see him. He wasn't sure he'd be able to get through. But he had to try. Using a strange new sense that had come to him only in death, he tried reaching out a tendril of association, knowledge, and remembrance. Once a medium and a spirit spoke, an indelible channel connected them, a sluice one could slip through again if given the chance.

Floating amid the wind, time was as amorphous as his body in this state, a serious danger when time was of the essence and he was only essence at all. . . .

Fifth Avenue, finally. A fine stone town house with the most modern of Tiffany glass panels on either side of the carved wooden front door. There she was. He could sense the medium's radiance even from outside. He floated through beautifully leaded wisteria.

She was in the parlor having an evening cordial, but hardly

relaxed as one would hope at such a late hour, though Louis was relieved he wouldn't have to wake her. Sitting stiffly in plum-colored satin and starched lace, she remained alert and wary, as gifted as she was mysterious and elegant. He read her posture like a line of dialogue in a play.

With such chaos downtown, if she truly was as talented as those who had kidnapped her and forced that unfortunate séance had indicated, she likely knew the air was off, that New York was an unsettled creature awaking to find itself under threat of being caged . . .

Tall with dark brown–blond hair streaked with distinct swaths of gray, a woman in her mid-forties as striking as if she were in the bloom of youth, so did she command a space with imperious presence matched only by a glimmering vivacity. She outshone all the crystal in her home and the glass-beaded folds of her double-skirted Parisian gown, the rich plum color doing her fair skin fair service. While she commanded attention like a colonel an army, what Louis needed was hers.

That Louis's twin brother Andre had fled New York yet again was most inconvenient, the coward. While Andre had sworn he would tend to unsettled matters in New Orleans, the city of their birth, Louis knew all too well that Andre's reputation was for trouble, not reconciliation, so it may have been ill-advised. If he had remained in the city, Louis could make use of him, for his twin could hear *and* see him, even in his current state. The ability of both, due to their twin blood tie, proved a rare and useful talent.

"Hello . . ." Louis said feebly before chiding himself; this was no time for hesitancy. "Good Madame Medium. I know this is hardly custom in regard to communication, but it is an emergency," Louis stated.

The medium turned toward him, though she did not look

in his eyes or at his person, but past and through him. While she could perhaps sense his presence, she did not fix upon him. All he needed was for her to hear him, and to help.

* * * * *

Mrs. Evelyn Northe-Stewart was relaxing after a late dinner with her husband in their mahogany-paneled parlor filled with exotic, mystical souvenirs from around the world when the ghost first came to call. They were night people, she and Gareth, Mr. Stewart having to keep the hours of artists and the leisure classes, associated as he was with the new Metropolitan Museum of Art. For Evelyn's part, when one often convened with the dead—whether invited or not—one was relegated to the clock of an owl.

She wasn't one to "see" ghosts, and not always hear them either. But she never failed to feel them, and she felt this one first as a gust of cool breezes. Then came a strange twisting in her abdomen and an odd radiating vibration outward. The strength of it meant she had encountered this particular spirit before, that she was a previously established channel.

"Gareth, darling," she said to the mild-mannered man staring at her appreciatively, as he often did. She knew he still marveled that he had convinced her to marry him.

In a world that chided—if not hated—her for being a powerful woman and gifted Sensitive, finding a man like Gareth, who wanted her to be nothing more or less than her whole self, was a treasure worth more than the fortune her dear—similarly awestruck—late husband had left her. She had been lucky enough to procure one forward-minded husband, let alone a second, and she was as grateful of this as she was desirous for her sex to be afforded equality.

"Yes, dear," he replied, responding warmly to a broken reverie. Gareth was a peaceful soul; however, spirits unsettled his quietude.

"Don't you think you'd love a cigar in your study? I'm

getting a . . . premonition. And it doesn't seem to want company."

Gareth Stewart rose slowly, his fair face paling against his auburn beard. "Indeed . . ." He never knew what to say in cases such as this, so he simply left a room when it cooled degrees and the day turned from normal to paranormal. To each their worlds.

Once he exited, Evelyn gestured impatiently as she spoke. "I know you're here. Out with it!"

The ghost must have floated closer to her, for the feathers of the fascinator pinned into her coiffure wafted in the breeze of his spectral presence, tendrils kissing her forehead. The flames of the crystal-globed gas lamps on a small mahogany table beside her velvet settee flickered subtly.

"I need your help," the ghost said.

While pleading and desperate, after all she'd seen and weathered, she was a wisely wary woman, and suppliant tones alone were not enough to enlist her.

"You need help," she repeated, staring in his direction, changing the focus of her eyes in an attempt to see any differentiation in the line of flocked wallpaper, anything that might give an indication of his form. "Spirits always do."

"It's a matter of grave importance," he insisted. "I wouldn't bother you with trivialities, not after all we've been through. You might remember me . . ."

"Ah. Yes." She set her jaw and turned away from the spectral voice. "The twin. No wonder I can hear you so clearly, Mr. Dupris. You maintained the channel."

"Yes," he admitted ruefully. "I had to."

Her shoulder twitched beneath tailored layers of satin. "You know, that is hardly comfortable for us," she said through clenched teeth. "When you keep the channel open, it's like a cut on our skin never healed and is continuously exposed to the elements."

"No. I didn't know. I'm sorry. Truly." The spirit did seem contrite. At least this one was eloquent enough to comprehend in more than sentence fragments. Either she was gaining greater talents, or the ever mysterious spirit world was empowering this individual above all previous. "But I need any access I can afford," the ghost insisted. "You, Madame Medium, are at the core of all those who are important and critical in the times to come."

At this, the medium's eyes flashed a fierce warning. "If you want something of Clara—"

"I do," the ghost she knew to be Louis Dupris, Clara's secret lover, exclaimed, wafting before her face in a chill gust, and she turned, unwilling to truly face him, whether he was visible to her or not. Extended ghostly exposure was exhausting and made Evelyn feel plucked at as if she were a series of string instruments being played all at once.

The ghost would not be deterred. "You need to help me contact her."

"I will do nothing to upset her," Evelyn declared.

"This is beyond her," Louis countered. "You and she *must* understand what happened at the Eterna site on the terrible day I died. I am beginning to unravel what sabotaged us in that house. We were not alone when the disaster happened. I need someone to listen."

"I'm here now," Evelyn declared, exasperated. "We've a strong channel, don't squander it—"

"Our laboratory was invaded, Madame, by multiple *presences*. As my chemist partner Barnard and I combined the Eterna materials on that fateful day, our material must have been threatening to outside forces. One of our colleagues was courting something terrible. We didn't know . . ."

There was a long and terrible pause. Evelyn felt queasy. Such prolonged contact, with such clarity, was unprecedented. She now understood Clara's overwhelmed nature when it came to contact with the dead. Whatever she could take and save Clara from the brunt, she had to do. "More," she said quietly, gesturing toward the sound of his voice. "Tell me as much as you can."

Louis continued, his haunting voice deepening in sadness. "I didn't notice it until I returned to the brownstone after death, to find clues, trying to remember. The site had been a home, once, but Goldberg had gone mad, emptied the place of everything but our work. He was so odd, muttering things we could not understand . . ."

"Such as?" Evelyn closed her eyes. Perhaps she could focus on him better if she didn't try to look at the place she thought he occupied, just felt his draft.

"It was a language I didn't understand," Louis replied, frustration underpinning his every word. "We thought it was Yiddish, but now I'm not sure. I remembered having seen something very odd, right before everything went wrong. In the wall, carved in, was the outline of a door. And it sort of became one—a blank space, a void where there should have been substance. Dark entities stepped through. Shadow-like, devoid of light, the opposite . . . As if summoned. It happened right as the Eterna Compound turned into a noxious gas. I remember nothing after that."

"Entities. From a door. Carved in a wall . . ." Evelyn murmured. The room spun, and she could feel all the color drain from her cheeks. "My God . . ."

"What?" Louis countered in wary concern.

"It never really ended, did it?!" the medium said, her words a rasp, as if scrabbling for purchase in her throat. "The Society just went deeper underground . . . The network broader . . . Good God, we could've nipped it in the bud then, but now . . ."

She jumped to her feet and began to pace, looking down at the dark whorl of her plum skirts around the rich mahogany furnishings, the sumptuous deep tones of Tiffany sconces casting mottled, bruise-like patches of colored light onto her pale skin as she passed beneath them. For all her love of deep colors and magnetic shadows, at the moment she longed for blinding brightness to cast off any hint of darkness.

"You have . . . experience in such dealings?" Louis asked cautiously.

"Two years ago a demon tried to kill my friends," the medium replied gravely. "Part of an insane plot, something hellish and mad, and surely too similar to what you've described to be coincidence. And if so . . . then it would have made that whole dread business mere child's play. An exercise. A drill. A test for a coming apocalypse . . ."

"Whatever it is," the ghost insisted, "we have to stop the shadows before they wake."

"They've always been awake, Mr. Dupris," Evelyn snapped. "Devils never sleep. The trouble is that now, it seems they've multiplied."

"So will you help connect me to Clara?" Louis begged. "We've no time to waste. The devils are patient, but when moved, they seem to act with horrific, swift aptitude. They came upon my team the instant our work crested unto glory. We had wrought something of hope and honor when we were quashed by darkness."

Evelyn sighed and quit pacing. The dark satin whorl stilled and silenced. "I've no choice but to help. We'll need all hands on the proverbial spiritual deck."

"Thank you. There is an odd clarity in death that sharpens the grayscale of human morality. In the moments when I can keep focus, a feat itself, I see more clearly what's most valuable."

The medium turned again toward the direction of his voice. "What do you need from Clara?"

"As you know from the séance you were forced to undergo,

there remains a block between Clara and me. I cannot speak to her directly. Yet she alone understands the heart of the Eterna Commission and its properties enough to see it to a solution. Those shadows were threatened by what we made. It was a mortal protection, and they killed us for it."

"Clara's block is there to protect her. You know of her vulnerabilities, the senator guards her—"

"Of course I know that!" Louis cried. "One spirit alone does not overwhelm her, only when they cluster. I do *know* her, knew her"—Evelyn heard wrenching sorrow in his voice—"*well*, Mrs. Northe-Stewart. I knew her well and loved her with my whole heart."

The medium pursed her lips. "Then why did no one know?"

"Would I, a man with a most particular heritage, have been allowed to ask for her hand?" Louis countered bitterly. "Not to mention that Senator Bishop prohibited the Eterna researchers from contacting his ward."

"I am aware of the senator's rules," the medium said. "How did you meet, then?"

"At a soiree, early in my employment, before any trouble began. From first meeting in a quiet alcove, I was lost. Our rendezvous infrequent as we were both so careful . . . My heart was noble, I assure you, and a gentleman's boundaries were maintained. But all that is history. What I believe we created in that house was a Ward . . . Not a ward in need of a guardian but a Ward, in old magical terms—"

"A Ward of protection, yes, I am aware of the concept," Evelyn asserted.

"Someone, some*thing,* didn't want us to have it, and we need to know why. So now I beg you—obtain a lock of hair from my darling Clara," the spirit said, his chill directly at her ear, as if he didn't want her to miss one word of the vital details, "and take it to where I died. Localized magic is about connecting organic materials of life and death, and since I don't have a grave, I can only hope that the disaster site will serve, and that from there, I will be able to tell Clara more about the Warding."

"I hope you're right, Mr. Dupris." She was brilliantly conversant with him, but she couldn't be sure if that was instinct or literal translation from his plane to hers. "But I shan't be visiting your haunted house, or Clara, past midnight. This is the stuff of the morning, for safety's sake. Now leave me be lest you drive me to nightmares. Good night, Mr. Dupris, and I'll deal with you tomorrow. You can . . . waft yourself out." With a curt nod of her head, she exited the parlor.

Louis bowed after her, a formality even if she couldn't see him, calling a good night and thanks, and then, with what focus he had left, floated back onto dark Fifth Avenue, praying for dawn.

* * * * *

When Clara awoke the morning after any seizure, it was a sequence of putting herself back together, sense by sense, like restacking a deck of cards that had been thrown onto the floor and scattered.

For a woman who prized herself on relative control of her vast emotional and metaphysical scope, the loss of control in an epileptic seizure was the worst fate that she could imagine. She'd had to endure it since a séance she'd attended just as she was beginning to blossom into womanhood. Clara had expected that becoming an adult would change her abilities somehow but had not anticipated that becoming more sensitive would make her more susceptible to fits. Since the age of thirteen, vastly greater care had to be taken lest she be overtaxed and overtaken, as she had been at midnight in Trinity's sacred plot.

Every muscle of her body was screaming in pain. The clenching part of the seizure was always brutal and lingered on like a beating. Thankfully, this time she hadn't bitten off a chunk of her tongue; the cheek was bad enough.

When the thorough aches sharpened her senses enough to grasp the whole of herself, she noted was in her own bed, in the elegant little upstairs room that had been hers since she moved into the town house after her parents' deaths. Rupert Bishop had been a congressman then; now he was senator. But even then, he had made sure that his young ward had lacked nothing. He had seen to her education and given her leave to be and to express herself, to expand her mind. Most of all, to become the Spiritualist she and Bishop both felt she was born to be.

When she was only twelve years of age, it was her vision as expressed to grieving widow Mary Todd Lincoln that led to the creation of the Eterna Commission. Now, seventeen years later, she would have to be the one to end it, somehow. Too many people—not least her beloved Louis—had already died.

Lavinia. Thin memories returned like pale mist creeping over a dark expanse. Darling Vin had been her hero. That's how she'd gotten home. She didn't remember being helped into bed, but she must have put her in this muslin nightdress, as her best friend knew Clara would be mortified if Bishop had had to do it . . . What about Bishop . . . ?

As the last of the mists that enveloped her mind cleared, Clara realized her guardian was staring down at her, tall and imposing in fine charcoal shades of dress, his silver hair mussed, his elegant, noble face with its oft-furrowed brow knit more harshly than usual.

"Hello, Rupert . . ." she said cautiously. Did he know she'd stolen out to bury Eterna evidence in the Trinity Church graveyard? Clara decided playing innocent was the best tack. "What happened?" she said, widening her eyes and reaching for her guardian's hand.

"You've been asleep awhile. Longer than usual. I didn't see the seizure, but . . ." Bishop was about to step forward and grasp her outstretched hand when they were interrupted.

"There was quite an event," came a familiar female voice from the hall. The talented medium, Mrs. Evelyn Northe-Stewart, entered the room.

She was tall and striking, her once blond hair had gained streaks of classic silver, matching her with Bishop, her contemporary, ever dressed in the most magnificent finery straight from Paris's fashionably innovative minds.

Clara had long ago taken on Evelyn's style as inspiration, both in fashion and in furnishings, sure to tell her guardian that she, too, preferred her dresses Parisian and her surroundings entirely of the new Tiffany firm's provenance, seeing as the studio had just redecorated the White House.

Drinking in Evelyn's latest fashion was one of Clara's favorite pastimes, and today she did not disappoint in a champagne-colored bombazine day dress with a matching capped-sleeve jacket trimmed and accented with thin black ribbon.

"May we have a moment?" the medium said, turning to the senator. "Clara and I?"

"I . . . she . . . Clara just woke up," Bishop replied. The hesitation was unlike him, and while relations between her and her guardian had been strained of late, Clara's heart swelled that no discord could outweigh his infallible care for her.

"It's a personal matter, Rupert," Evelyn insisted, keeping her tone warm out of deference to his protective instincts. "I received a message that concerns her."

The senator's brow knit further. Giving Clara a worried look, he reluctantly left the room.

The medium turned to Clara gravely. "I had a visit from your Louis . . ." she began.

Clara swallowed hard.

Louis had awakened aspects of herself—mind, body, and heart—she had not experienced before. She had loved him truly for who he was, a passionate and energetic man of visions and spiritual gifts. Rupert Bishop held an old sway over her heart, one she never dared indulge, but Louis had helped her live more fully than she'd ever allowed. His death had been a hard and unexpected blow; that he still had a connection to her was a bittersweet comfort and a pang.

Evelyn, ever attentive and empathic, waited for Clara to meet her gaze again before continuing. "Louis was very insistent on gaining access to you. To talk to you."

The memory was sharp enough to make Clara close her eyes. Louis had often said if he could do only one thing in the world, it would be just to sit and talk to her. They both believed in Eterna's mission. Louis's commitment to Eterna was shaped at least in part by his desire to make his principles of spirituality and his Vodoun faith something science could champion.

She could not help but think back to their passionate discussions, often conducted while lounging about on the bed of his tiny flat near Union Square. Clara was all too willing to find reasons to excuse herself from work and dart uptown for a secret rendezvous. The weight of Evelyn's stare drew her away from the memories of her dead paramour.

Clara's body felt suddenly restless and caged by her condition. She shifted to sit upright, wincing as her arm and back muscles clenched again in a painful vise, but she refused Evelyn's help, as she needed her own movement to unlock them again. She cleared her throat and began cautiously.

"Louis wishes to speak to me . . . about us? Or was it . . . something of Eterna?"

"Eterna," Evelyn was quick to reply, moving closer to Clara and sitting on the edge of the bed. "He is learning, in the spectral realm, about what may have gone wrong at the site. Dark forces are afoot, having been granted entry by human avarice."

Clara thought of the disaster site and shuddered. "That would stand to reason, if reason can even apply there."

"Devilry has a peculiar reason to it, and a twisted logic. Louis believes dark presences that invaded the room treated the Eterna Compound as a threat."

When Clara had, daringly, visited the site of Louis's death, she had a terrible vision of looming beings . . . Perhaps the same presences Louis referred to. She had thought they were ghosts, but her time there had been so short, it was possible she had not perceived them as the threats they were. Her head wasn't nearly as clear as it needed to be, hadn't been since Louis's death.

She shook herself out of self-pity and stared at her dear friend and mentor with a ready ferocity.

"I said I would do this only with your permission," the regal woman stated. Clara nodded, hoping perceptive Evelyn would both note and trust her freshly steeled mettle.

"There is indeed more at work here than mere sentiment," Clara murmured. "I honestly don't know what I'm meant to do, with the commission, the research, the information . . . Perhaps Louis can help be my spiritual guide through the mess." She stared up at Evelyn plaintively. "I just hope I hold up. I have to. I can't let my condition get in the way. I wanted to be there for him, in life, to work with him." She clenched her fists. "I'll take what time with him I can get."

Shifting out of bed, swinging her legs down slowly, and then rising at a bent angle that made her feel older than her age, Clara winced again. Evelyn moved to assist her, but she waved her off. "No, thank you, I have to move eventually, and on my own, otherwise I can't shake loose what still wishes to clench and seize."

Clara moved to her vanity and withdrew a pair of small silver scissors from a top drawer. She looked into the mirror, her green-golden eyes staring past her somewhat haunted reflection, and snipped a lock of deep blond hair from her unkempt tresses. With a rough pull, she wrenched the clump free from the confines of her messy braid, looking alternately at the long streamer of hair in her hand and her somewhat mad-looking reflection.

Plucking a box of matches from her nightstand, Clara lit a taper, removed the candle from its holder, and tipped it above one end of the lock of her hair. Droplets of wax fell, sealing the hairs together.

Sitting back on the edge of the rumpled bed, Clara divided the strands and wove a thin braid, then sealed the second end. She blew out the candle and stared into the wisps of smoke for a moment as if she was hoping to read a message there.

"I hope this works," Clara said, and the tone in her own voice surprised her. Eterna had aged her beyond her twenty-nine years.

Evelyn nodded. "I can feel the tide of the city will darken, waking up old, terrible cases we thought we'd put to rest. We need to avail ourselves of any and all information. Thank you, Clara, for being willing—"

"It's the least I can do for his life," she murmured, worrying the end of the braid between her fingertips before finally passing it over to her mother figure and mentor. "I was never honest about him, I might as well attempt to honor him."

"I will try to do right by you both," Evelyn promised. The two Spiritualists held each other's weighty gaze.

"You'll find the key to that house in our offices," Clara stated. "In the top drawer of my desk. Thank you, Evelyn. Truly."

"Don't thank me yet," the elder woman said gravely. "We

may yet be dragged through hell and back." She stood and walked toward the door.

Clara stopped her with a plea. "Don't tell Rupert about Louis, please? About this return? It's a . . ."

Evelyn lifted a hand that fluttered in a gesture of understanding. "Sensitive subject, yes. But don't leave the poor man entirely in the dark," she insisted. Clara looked away, guilt twisting within her. The medium pressed a bit further, coming back into the room, close to Clara to take on a gentler tone. "You could have gone to Rupert with your love, Clara. Did it really have to be a secret? Do you not owe him more than that?" A look from Clara gave Evelyn pause. "I won't tell Rupert unless circumstances of safety require the knowledge. But I am telling you now that you *cannot* fight this fight without him."

"I will tell him, I promise."

Evelyn reached out and took Clara's hand. "You know I've always considered you family. Remember that. Brace yourself, Clara. You are strong, you mustn't forget it. Don't let your condition ever tell you otherwise, it's undermined your agency and your confidence for years. Get that back at all costs. What we're up against, if it's anything like what I've unfortunately been inured to, Lord help us all. The meek shall not inherit the earth unless we, the loud and bold, stop an onslaught of devilry."

Clara nodded. "I promise that, too. Strength. Now more than ever."

Evelyn squeezed her hand hard, then let go and exited the room with the calm grace uniquely hers. Clara hoped she would embody the same qualities as she aged. She wondered when to expect Louis and what their new connection might be like.

If Mrs. Northe-Stewart was successful, a new aspect of the

Eterna Commission would unfold, along with a new stage in her relationship with Louis.

She'd buried everything in the Trinity Church graveyard because she did not know what else to do, but she had to do *something*. Having dug a grave for all the Eterna material she had—all Louis's papers, all his mystical and imaginative work on talismanic, localized magic, and personal power tied to one's place on this earth—she had buried half her heart in that hole as well.

After loving him, feeling responsible for his death, being misled that he might actually be alive, only to find out he remained a spirit after all, could she bear this next shift to a kind of relationship she could hardly have predicted? She steeled herself just like she had done with feelings for Rupert Bishop so long ago, reinforcing the mausoleum doors of her emotions.

Sentiment cooled and hardened like a winter's grave. There was no time for a star-crossed love between forbidden planes of existence when preparing for further supernatural woe. Friend or foe was impossible to determine, British or American, living or dead. Clara hoped the spirit realm could make some sense out of whom to trust and what next to attend to.

CHAPTER
TWO

London, 1882

Harold Spire stared at paperwork. He despised paperwork.

Director of the Omega department of the secret new Special Branches of government, Spire was looking at shipping manifests that were innocuous at first glance. He and his co-worker, Rose Everhart, pored over them in silence, looking for a specific listing. This was tedious cleric's work, and they were doing it in a book-filled, file-laden closet.

This tiny space, literally tucked away inside the walls of Parliament, was Everhart's hidden office, which she still maintained even though Omega had its own facilities elsewhere in London. There were times when the raucous nature of other members of Omega made both Spire and Everhart yearn for quiet, and this was one of them.

They should, Spire thought, be investigating the blood-drenched compatriots of the late aristocrat, Mr. Francis Tourney, who had committed ritualistic murders. But as Spire was no longer a member of the Metropolitan Police and could not prove a connection between Tourney's infamy and the unnatural matters with which Omega was tasked, he and Miss Everhart had been consistently denied access to the case.

There had been nothing in the papers, either. That was for the best, Spire thought, as ridiculous, sensationalistic journalism would do nothing to help the police with their inquiries. Later in the day, Spire would meet with his old friend and partner, Captain Stuart Grange, to find out more.

He had to know. The horrors that Spire, Everhart, and Grange had seen in Tourney's basement: children's bodies, carved and marked, drained of blood and attached to strange wires; a woman's corpse hung in hideous mockery of faith and humanity . . . Tourney had not acted alone, that much was clear.

That Tourney was said to have been found reduced to pulp in his prison cell, the stone walls turned entirely crimson with his blood, was a great comfort to Spire, though it presented the police with no confession and little evidence to flush out the greater ring of insidious terror that Tourney represented.

There was real devilry in the world.

Why had the queen and Spire's direct supervisor, Lord Black, set him on this quest to find out when a handful of British corpses had been shipped to America? Why look for the dead when murderers sought the living?

Still, he preferred examining ledgers to the other task of the day: investigating a histrionic report of a headless horsemen outside London. The tedious tales of America's Washington Irving were not considered high art, far from it, more a childish, insecure need to overdramatically attribute an empire's worth of history to a sprawling, provincial, and unorganized country. It was an insult that an American legend had wormed its silly way into some old hag's mind out in Hampstead, where she should've been more worried about the ghosts of old highwaymen. If there were such things as ghosts.

Spire was grateful to be well clear of such nonsense. Mostly clear, rather.

For the dead men—British men of science—had been searching for immortality when they met an unknown end.

Harold Spire had been hired by Her Majesty herself to oversee the safety and administration of a select group of theorists, doctors, and scientists charged with investigating the cure for death on behalf of the Crown and before the

Americans. All of which, Spire thought, was as probable as ghosts and headless horsemen.

He missed his job as a rising officer of note in the ranks of the city's Metropolitan Police.

Dressed in a simple gray wool riding habit best suited for work, Rose Everhart slid a ledger toward him across the small wooden desk. She was a bloodhound with papers, ciphers, and patterns. A quiet, deep respect had grown between them in the weeks they'd worked together. She was the one reasonable, amenable thing in his damnable job.

"I inquired about the general height and build of the five scientists," Rose said quietly. "To general calculation, their weight would, roughly, collectively match the kilos and grams of these five rectangular cargo bins, which were accounted and stowed under the heading of "dry goods." Miss Everhart pointed out the entry, then handed Spire a separate paper where she had noted the approximate measures.

"Well done indeed, Miss Everhart. Now the question remains . . ."

"Who put the bodies of the scientists on that ship when no one from any of our departments knew a thing about where they'd gone?"

"This is our task for the day." Spire squinted at the ledger. "*Ax.* That's who stowed the bodies, that's the company monogram to ascertain."

"Should I check in at the Omega offices?" Everhart offered.

"They ought to be doing what I told them to," Spire countered, "preparing for New York City. Let them be. We're going to the dockyards."

Miss Everhart closed the ledger, placed the files of interest into a panel in the wall, stood, smoothed her skirts, and inclined her head, ready.

Spire marveled that he had been granted such a sure and capable colleague. In his years being partnered with various styles and personalities, all of them had been, of course, male. He tried not to differentiate her from his other teammates. That Rose was a woman couldn't be held against her any more than this modern age liked to remind the fairer sex that they were inferior under the law. Though on this point, women increasingly pushed against their various prisons in bold and subtle ways.

Spire was a man of equity, of meritocracy. Those who were worthy of what they could with their talents earn and ac- quire, then they should receive it, no matter gender or color or lineage. Many of the men making the rules of the world had nothing but blood and divine right to commend them, and in Spire's opinion, they were often the least worthy of the riches and powers lavished upon them. But not a word of that to his "betters," a word he would ground out through his teeth only if he absolutely had to.

Lord Black and the prime minister cherished Everhart, the relationships between them mysterious. That was the difficulty with her being a woman; in Spire's estimation, they only complicated matters. But it wasn't Miss Everhart's fault if powerful men were compelled by her. She was neither ugly nor beautiful; she was merely a person one wanted to have around, useful and intelligent—Spire's favorite qualities. She awaited him by the door, clearly unruffled by the prospect of visiting a part of London that respectable ladies would de- terminedly avoid: a cargo dock downriver.

Spire appreciated the companionable silences between him and Miss Everhart. The two members of Omega division each took in, in his or her own way, the peculiar and other- worldly jostling, sooty, steamy madness that was the London underground, still somewhat novel and incredible. The sights, sounds, and sensations of the journey were their own conver- sation.

They emerged from the tunnels and trekked a few streets

to a set of piers nestled where the river curved ever so gently. Spire was a fast walker. Everhart kept pace with him.

As they approached the small brick enclosure marked OFFICE at the head of the bustling pier, Everhart suddenly unbuttoned the smart collar of her riding habit, showcasing an elegant collarbone. From beneath the narrow rim of her hat, which was carefully pinned to a braided coiffure, she pulled loose a curl, letting it fall over her face more gamesomely than was her general attitude. Spire tried not to raise an eyebrow in surprise but was unsure of his success, as such a reaction had become a reflex since his assignment to Omega. Everhart's expression revealed nothing; she gestured that he lead on.

When Spire entered the office, a bell clanged at the door. A bespectacled clerk looked up from a well-worn desk where various nautical implements kept company amid ledger books and blotters.

"Sir, Madame?" He bobbed his head toward the two of them.

Spire flashed his Metropolitan badge. To most of London and its government, he appeared to have maintained an association to the force. Only three individuals in higher branches knew him to have any other rank, title, or duties.

"I'm here to inquire about a listing from a company abbreviated as *Ax* on a recent vessel," Spire said. "It was a direct journey to America."

The gaunt clerk whose dark hair was thinning kept an unreadable expression. "Might I ask what you are investigating? Merely a formality, sir, as I am sure you understand, and then I'll be happy to help you." The man readied a pen to take notes, which seemed odd to Spire. Usually it was he who took notes.

Spire noted that the manager's voice and face remained

entirely calm. However, at the mention of Ax, a man standing at the back of the room stared straight at Spire in abject fear. His clothes were those of the working poor, a sharp contrast to the neatly suited man at the desk; Spire guessed he was a deckhand. Their entrance had interrupted him in the act of pouring tea into a dirty cup. Now he shook his head, as if in warning, and wrung his hands a moment before setting down his teacup and shuffling out the rear door, looking woefully over his shoulder at Spire and Everhart as he went.

"Tom," Everhart whined suddenly, in a higher-pitched voice than usual, "you promised me a trip *on* a boat, not police work about a boat, you're such a spoilsport. I'm waiting outside, but you'd better be done soon, otherwise I'm not entertaining you further." She flounced out of the room.

Spire furrowed his brow. "Go on, then, good riddance," he called after her and rolled his eyes toward the clerk. "Women."

"Can't take them anywhere a day's work needs be done," the clerk said with a chuckle. Spire was quite sure, however, she was up to something useful indeed. "Now then," the man continued, "I am sorry that I can't offer you much information. Ax stands for the Apex Corporation. But I don't know their manifests offhand."

"How long has the Apex Corporation been working with your company?"

The man shrugged. "Several years."

"Always dry goods?"

The man thought a moment. "Sometimes liquids, basic things. Apex is, I'm told, in manufacturing." He leaned closer, genuinely interested. "Do you think there's something questionable at work?"

Spire shook his head. "My offices are trying to track some precious stones."

The man smiled suddenly. There was a distinctive sparkle that greed took when lighting up a man's eye. "Do tell. What kind?"

Bribable, Spire mused. It was his turn to shrug. "I can't disclose that any more than you can about the company that's done your dock a great favor." Spire gestured behind him. "Yours looks better than any other along the piers."

His smile remained. "We take pride in that, Mr. . . . ?"

Spire bowed his head curtly. "Good day, sir. If there's anything that comes to light about stolen . . . gems, please do let the Metropolitan Police know."

"And to whose attention, then, sir?"

"Tom Hamilton, Westminster."

He'd have to let Grange know of his new alias. He rotated several, and it was time for a change, especially in these new matters. He took Everhart's "Tom" and ran with it. Not that this clerk would follow up. He'd go scurrying off to report this "intrusion" and there would likely be further obfuscation.

Now what had Miss Everhart gotten up to?

He found her outside, alone, around the corner where a ship's prow jutted out and blocked anyone from view, awaiting him. Her blouse and collar were buttoned back up, errant curl no longer waving in the wind. When she spoke, her voice was again her own.

"My dramatic exit was an attempt to corral the deckhand." She gestured before her. "Across that battered masthead of a sea-weary nymph there, the deckhand stared at me wide-eyed, as if willing me to understand something he didn't dare speak. I pressed. The man trembled, saying if we were smart we wouldn't ask questions of that corporation. But I did get some information out of him."

"Very good work," Spire said earnestly. Miss Everhart

didn't rest on the pride of his praise, for a dark shadow fell over her face.

"If the poor man stays alive," she said ruefully. "It would seem secrecy is Apex's cardinal need, and anyone who questions this is summarily *dismissed* . . . Accidents are all too common around the docks."

"I see."

"Our friend, who refused to give a name," Everhart began, "lost his brother, who had gotten too curious, and then two more of his colleagues. He does not know exactly what happened save that the river took his brother after a dramatic fall and that his body has yet to be recovered."

"What dry goods or liquids could be so suspect?"

Everhart shuddered. "Dry goods as bodies, and liquids as embalming fluid, that's what. The brother wrote a harried note saying he'd seen frightful things in boxes, and the next day he was dead. The man says they're forbidden to open any of the boxes, only load them. But some, inevitably, fell, contents spilling.

"He said there were wild rumors of corpses alongside elaborate funereal supplies and enough chemical and electrical equipment to make Dr. Frankenstein weep, but nothing could be corroborated among the crew. The life expectancy of the deckhands staffing Apex ships appears perilously short, all of them plucked off streets, from workhouses or prisons with promise of pay and a hot meal."

"Easy to keep 'expendable' persons quiet," Spire muttered. "This sounds like the stuff of Tourney's ring. Is it fair to assume Apex is part of that? Does anyone from Apex ever deal directly with these docks? The one believable thing the clerk said is that he's never seen anyone in person. If he was frightened, he was good at acting the part of assuming it a legitimate company, shipping aboveboard goods."

They were walking away from the docks, Everhart lacing and unlacing her fingers in thought as she kept pace with Spire's bold stride.

"We must see if we can tie Tourney or any of the men on our mutual list to Apex. Since the bodies of our scientists are involved, that makes it a matter for Omega, not the Metropolitan, and we shall have fuller leverage," Everhart stated before her tone turned conciliatory. "Now I'm afraid we'll have to return to the offices, Mr. Spire. Our operatives require specificity in New York lest they . . . attract too much attention."

Spire sighed heavily. "Covert operations as envisioned by P. T. Barnum."

"Oh, don't encourage them." Everhart chuckled. "They'll go seek him out when they're in Manhattan."

"Maybe he'll trap them in his museum," Spire muttered.

"Oh, no, that burned down," Everhart replied. "Terrible affair. Whales and all."

"Can't say I'm surprised. Now, at the offices, Lord Black mentioned something about establishing his . . . war room?"

"Ah." Everhart chuckled and said no more. Spire wasn't sure what he was in for.

Why Spire, who considered himself a straightforward man, had been given the most flamboyant, odd company with which to conduct covert affairs, he'd never know.

"Underground again?" Spire asked.

"Don't suppose you'd care to walk? Too many people, too close, for my taste," Everhart replied.

"Couldn't agree more."

They spoke as they moved at a purposeful clip toward the Westminster precinct, Spire privately thrilled by a woman who could keep up with him in more ways than one. "So. Tourney," he stated. "It's all the unresolved gruesome details that gnaw at me. The sobering contrast to the absurdity of the Omega department. It isn't that I've any pity for Tourney, he deserved worse than being entirely torn to shreds."

"It's fitting, justice, really, but I hope vital secrets weren't dissolved along with his form," Everhart added. "I can't help but wonder if others might be targeted in the same way."

"The first one to interview, if he's not already dead, is that guilty chemist Stevens over in Whitechapel."

"I've asked for notes on Stevens, including the chemical compounds, from an associate of Lord Black, a solicitor named Knowles, a Spiritualist of standing in the community. Knowles reportedly has information on unseemly matters that affected Black's colleagues, such as Lord Denbury, whose troubles preceded these affairs. Do you think Apex could be transporting some of those chemist's compounds as dry goods?"

"Very possibly. From even the vaguest hints the clerk offered, Apex predates the Tourney murders. So it is likely a holding of the Master's Society, of which Tourney was surely a member."

"Or his murders were inspired by theirs. The dastardly hand of Beauregard Moriel lives on after his death," Everhart muttered. "The Society had been overtly instructed to take over key industrial and political holdings. We thought that must have ended with Moriel's execution and subsequent arrests and deaths of his followers."

"Tourney must represent the next generation, the new crop of believers."

"The heirs to hell itself."

They walked in chilled silence until the Gothic spires of Parliament appeared in the distance.

"I will meet you at the offices later," Spire said. "I've a meeting."

"As you wish." She turned away, then reconsidered and turned back. "Mr. Spire."

"Yes?"

"I wish to remain in England and not be sent to New York.
I'd best remain on task here, not participate in a flamboyant
chase to the Empire State." An expression of unease flickered
over her face, perhaps reflecting something she wasn't saying.

"It is good to have you here," Spire agreed. And it was.
Her presence was of consistent benefit. From his days on the
Metropolitan force, a partner was familiar comfort, and she
was the closest thing he could envision in the role. He desired
that in such strange currents. He found himself staring at her
a bit too long before adding, "Let the rest of the team attend
to demands overseas."

She seemed pleased at this and took her leave with a bob
of her brown-haired head, leaving Spire to catch a glimpse of
his former life.

* * * * *

There truly was, Spire thought, nothing better than the genuine, uncomplicated smile of a best mate in dark times. Grange
had been that man for Spire since their early schoolboy days.
But though they both sat with pints of ale at the pub they'd
chosen as today's personal fiefdom near the Palace of Westminster, there was no smile on Grange's face. Spire's friend
looked haunted and haggard.

"What's this?" Spire asked, shifting to sit more comfort-
ably on the wooden booth worn smooth from years of weight
and sliding fabrics from the backsides of innumerable cus-
tomers. "When I see that look, my friend, whatever day I've
had has gotten worse. I assume it is Tourney business keeping the unflappable Grange down?"

"The inability to get anywhere near what happened to the
bastard or anyone associated with him," the generally affable
man grumbled. "You want the bad news or the worse news?
Though I'm not sure which is which."

"Worse," Spire ground out, taking a long drink of brown ale.

"That Stevens chap, or those cleaning up the ring, burned his chemist shop to the ground, the one you interrogated him in. Looks like with him in it."

Spire sighed. "Conclusively in it?"

"Hard to tell in a fire. But my men said there was nothing left to salvage. I sent Phyfe to have a keen eye present."

"I don't suppose Stevens sent anything helpful to the post-box?"

"Not that I've received yet; the fire was just yesterday."

"Tom Hamilton is a new alias of mine as of today," Spire stated. "Everhart and I were down at the docks. Look into a company called Apex, shipping all kinds of foul materials, like the stuff of Tourney's cellar. We need to reopen what was done with Beauregard Moriel and the Master's Society—it is likely all related."

"Oh, that lot? Sick bastards," Grange grumbled. "We'll break open the files and look for parallels, and I'll set Phyfe to work on correlating with Apex."

"Now, the bad news?" Spire prompted, lifting his glass of ale in preparation for a long draught.

"I've *nothing* on what happened to Tourney. I appreciate keeping journalists out, but not letting police *in*? It's bad enough, your being taken off the department, but then, this block . . . It's as if a member of the royal family was killed with all the hush about it. Is there anything you can do from your new position?"

Spire snorted a mordant laugh. "I can't help open closed doors when I've been banned from the building. It may not be a royal, but it must be tied to the highest powers for security to be so tight. None of the guards are talking?"

"One is in Bedlam after what happened," Grange replied. "The other, found dead."

Spire's resulting sigh sounded more like a growl. "I'll make Black tell me *something*."

"We need to know how to protect the men on your interrogation list. Otherwise we've no incriminating evidence to plumb."

"Our job is supposed to be fighting crime and arresting criminals, not keeping criminals safe. The world has become an inverted joke," Spire spat before taking that long draught, slamming down an empty glass. "I'm sorry for all this."

"You have prided yourself on doing your job," Grange replied. "As have I. But we're now being told how to do it by those who do it worse or don't care. I've had it, Harold. Tell me you've a plan," Grange begged. "And *resources*. We need men we can trust." His expression shifted suddenly, something of softer concern. "Speaking of trust, how is Miss Everhart?"

Spire paused a moment. "Fine . . . why?"

"The fall, the incident at the carriage." Grange downed the last of his pint. "She's an asset, that Everhart, credit to her sex, and I hate that she was a target. It was so strange, that whole business. I've had nightmares about it, to tell you the truth."

Grange had always been a bit too sensitive for his own good. Though, Spire reminded himself, Grange was a good man who had never faced personal tragedy. It was kind of him to ask after Miss Everhart, and it made Spire wonder if he should have given her more thought and care himself. Maybe Grange had fallen for Everhart. Suddenly that notion made him even more uncomfortable. He felt the lines of his own scowl deepen.

"This impasse can't last," Grange murmured finally.

"We'll find ways around it. We always do." Spire rallied, but his voice sounded hollow to his own ears. He'd lost his innocence long ago, when he'd seen his mother's blood spilled onto the parlor floor, but he'd have liked to have kept the ability to inspire. The men drank another round, toasting to earlier days, simpler days, finer days, when the morality of the world didn't seem so precarious. When they had seen fewer dead bodies and unsolved crimes. When they believed they both were doing true good for the world and that the righteous outnumbered the wicked.

Spire had little sense anymore of what he was doing for whom, and toward what end. But before he engaged in another ritual—a long, brisk walk—the friends toasted last to rebuking limitation.

When he took to the streets like this, in a circuitous route, it was generally to purge himself of mental images of his mother's death. But since his discoveries of the ritualistic deaths in Tourney's cellars, images of those fresh horrors were superimposed upon the older ones. When his next allotment of funds arrived, he would invest in a hearty new pair of shoes. His sanity would need them.

By the time he reached the Omega offices, the exsanguinated corpses in his mind's eye had been replaced by more mundane sights: bustling, clattering London in all its vast splendor and squalor.

Their Millbank headquarters loomed before him, the onetime factory turned into spacious offices. It was a grand building but nondescript enough for Spire to feel confident in the covert nature within. He climbed the front stairs, and before he could insert his key into the hefty lock, the door was flung open with a distinct wrenching and then popping sound—but revealed no one.

Spire placed a hand on his breast pocket where a small pistol was a large comfort. The wide and empty foyer of brick and metal beams revealed no clue as to the door's automation.

However, there were sounds from the floors above that were distinct to his keen ears: metal on metal, small squeaks and pops. Was there some sort of mill or factory starting back up in this old industrial space? Slowly he stepped across the threshold onto the wide landing. The door closed behind him, accompanied by a little buzz. Spire whirled around and spotted an odd lever at the top of the thick door, with a wired contraption above that sported a clock and small roll of paper. An automatic door? Was that wise or necessary? He shuddered to think the man to whom he directly reported had so little care for security.

A moment after the door had swung closed behind him, there was a tapping noise and a tab of the paper rolled out. Spire reached out and viewed the protruding slip:

2pm entry—77kg

After this marking of time and weight, there was a small carbon imprint, a silhouette, *his* silhouette framed in the door, somehow. Likely that strange pop indicated an exposure that took in the door frame as if it were a crude light-sensitive imprint, just a silhouette, but enough for certain particulars, his hatless head, windblown hair, and the cut of his frock coat and trousers. Spire was conflicted—impressed and perturbed equally.

Spire followed the noise to the top floor. He opened the plain white door opposite Black's closed office door and, within, discovered that his circus had become a madhouse.

Guns lined the walls and a number of the members of Omega were examining them.

Across the room, Blakely, the short, nervous, excitable chemist and magician, was taking a rifle apart. That Blakely knew how to take a rifle apart and perhaps put it together again was a concept that awed and utterly terrified Spire, who deemed him too flighty for bullets.

The Wilsons, in their simple Cipher uniforms of black tunics, hoods, and leggings, were rappelling up and down the

high-ceilinged wall in tandem; the wire attached to the harnesses they wore over their costumes was so fine as to be
nearly invisible.

From various points horizontal to the floor, the smaller-
framed of the two otherwise neutrally clad bodies, Adira
Wilson, paused mid-rappel to throw an impressive sequence
of small silver blades at a target on the far wall. The speed
and precision were incredible, and Spire was reminded that
the Wilsons were infamous as international spies—and as an
epic cross-cultural love story—long before they'd turned sour
to foreign affairs, feigned their deaths, and took on this odd,
off-the-books employ thanks to Mr. Wilson's orphanage
mate Mr. Blakely. Spire surmised the Wilsons had talents he
might not even want to know, though he warmed to the idea
of utilizing Mrs. Wilson as a bodyguard.

Even Miss Everhart held an odd contraption, an electrical
device of some kind, judging by the thin thread of lightning
sparking around the ball that was cupped in her hands. A
Tesla coil, if Spire remembered correctly. Where her hair
wasn't pinned in place, it was standing up around her head.

Miss Knight, their resident flamboyant clairvoyant, who
was *very* fond of women, fondled a small pistol of a make
Spire had never seen as if it were a piece of fine jewelry. Spire
noted her utter, elegant assurance with the weapon, and
he uncomfortably realized his own biases about femininity
and the machinery of warfare and murder. So much of what
Spire had thought true of the world was upended by Omega.

What Lord Black hoped to accomplish with all of these
trappings was anyone's guess. Spire remembered Everhart
saying Black fancied himself a spy, an espionage enthusiast
who would take Spire's job if he could—oh, if only he
would—

Was that a coffin in the corner? Spire thought with disdain. Yes—upright against the wall, a red curtain partially

hiding it, stood a black casket with an ostentatious golden pyramid sporting an eye painted in the center, a Masonic symbol, of course, which made Spire roll his eyes at the theatrical mysticism heaped upon those ancient ranks.

No one noticed Spire for a good few minutes, making him newly skeptical of their abilities as spies and assassins. Where, also, was Black?

"Welcome to my war room!" Black declared, jumping out of the coffin as if on cue. Spire did not start, though his eye twitched a bit.

"Oh. I didn't scare you? That always scared everyone at parties," Black pouted. "You see, I used to have all of this in my home. But I am a generous man, and you fine talents shall benefit!" he declared triumphantly. "Peephole in the eye." Black grinned, tapping the golden pyramid. "That's how you surprise your prey . . ."

At the word "prey," Spire's eye twitched again, remembering how he'd been the butt of a circus act for Black's delight. "But not you, Mr. Spire!" the lord cried. "Steeled, Spire. That's why you're the man for the job!"

Spire's knees itched to dart back out onto the streets for a calming walk again, seeing as though he'd paced miles only to be harangued.

"I'll be steeled in my offices should anyone wish to join me," he replied.

Storming down the flights to his own office floor bright-lit by midday sun streaming through wide arched, curtained windows, his footsteps echoed through the otherwise silent space—until the rest of his team burst in behind him in a stream, chattering away.

Spire stalked to the circular central table. The others gathered around, and he started right in, eager to get something useful done. Lord Black brought up the rear of the group, and once the nobleman was within earshot, Spire launched into orders.

"In orchestrating the recovery of British bodies and arranging for you to question New York's Eterna Commission on the act, in addition to investigating the electrical oddity Lord Black added to the plate, I aim to remain in England while sending you operatives forth."

Instantly there was a murmuring outcry from everyone except, predictably, Rose Everhart. The Blakelys seemed offended and the Wilsons seemed baffled.

"Who shall lead the group if you stay behind, Mr. Spire?" Mr. Wilson asked finally.

"I'm not going, Spire." Lord Black waved a languid hand, leaning against a nearby table filled with various bottles from Blakely's alchemical arsenal. "So if you're not either, well . . ."

"I've no desire to abandon responsibility," Spire stated. "I'm better suited *here.*" Here in London, Spire thought to himself, where ghastly murders await a prescribed list of victims and nothing of "immortality" is rational or more important. "The dead scientists are dead," he added. "I personally would like to be sure a future crop remain protected."

"Your Metropolitan men have been trustworthy," Black countered. "Have a detail assigned."

"They are overtaxed with the Tourney affair." Spire leaned in Black's direction to remind the aristocrat. "Who is dead, you recall, by mysterious, gruesome circumstances *not* to be ignored."

"Let's have a word about all this," Black said, his war room delight having clearly sobered. Spire made for his door. "Not your office, mine," Black countered and stalked off toward the threshold, gesturing for Spire to follow. "Mine has far better liquor."

Spire turned to his team. "While none of you can announce a destination or purpose of your travel to anyone, do make sure no one goes looking for you and that all family and associates are summarily taken care of."

The rest of the team looked on in curiosity but did not press, instead moseyed to their desks, and Miss Everhart immediately to the telegraph machine. Spire shut the department door behind him before ascending the reverberate iron stairs behind Black, who held the door for Spire and closed it behind him.

"Speak freely, Mr. Spire," Black offered, gesturing for him to sit. Black moved to a sideboard to pour two helpings of what was likely bourbon worth Spire's whole salary. The nobleman slid the crystal snifter across the smooth, elaborately lacquered mahogany desk.

"I am torn between directives, and I do not wish my team to see hesitancy," Spire stated.

"Omega is your only directive. I thought that had been entirely clear from day one, when you met with the queen."

"The most gruesome sights and crimes of the age are not to be set aside," Spire insisted. "Your leads in the Tourney investigation secured his arrest." Spire leaned toward Black across his desk. "Why force me to stop now?"

"If you can prove Omega and Tourney have *direct* commonality," Black replied, "I can convince the queen to allow you broader scope. As it stands, I am directed to keep you very focused."

"I believe Francis Tourney had holdings in the Apex Corporation, the company that shipped the bodies of our scientists to New York."

"Well then, there you go!"

"Thank you, sir. Finally. That shouldn't have been hard, you know."

"I know, Mr. Spire," Black murmured. There came a distinct shift in him. The grand presence was suddenly just a tired man in a striped satin frock coat, seated at an overlarge desk.

"Lord Black," Spire pressed quietly, "Her Majesty hides aspects of Omega. I've been unable to visit the estate where the previous scientists had been living prior to being abducted. And though I am charged with their protection, I've not met any candidates for a new team save for the doctor, if you can call him that, Zhavia. Whether you, Lord Black, are complicit in this obfuscation, I cannot tell."

Black sighed. Spire was discomfited. Every time he and Lord Black had been together, the nobleman had been the picture of joy, mischief, and confidence. He was notoriously a charming dandy, the sort of personality that by all accounts should constantly grate on Spire's nerves. But, damn the man, he was insufferably likable.

It was clear, however, that today something was wearing upon this effervescent presence. Black took great care in responding.

"Obfuscation, no, not to my knowledge," he replied finally. "But things are afoot, Mr. Spire. I do confess I've bad news about the new scientists, my good man, and why you haven't met them."

Spire set his jaw. "Don't tell me we've lost more men?"

"I don't know," Black said wearily. "Possibly. There was supposed to be a fresh crop and I intended to bring them here to our Millbank offices as you requested, it prudent indeed to have them under your watch. I have been overruled."

"By?"

"Her Majesty. Before you ask, no, she gave no reason." Black offered a strained, ironic smile. "The new scientists are to be kept in the same manor the others disappeared from in the first place."

Spire blinked. "Lovely. That seems . . . *wholly* imprudent."

"I agree. But I was not given the opportunity to argue that point."

"*Lovely*. If neither of us is listened to—"

Lord Black held up a hand, his expression weary—the look of a man tired of being unheard. Spire knew the feeling well. For someone of such position and privilege to feel as helpless as Spire himself . . . the last of any remaining antagonism toward the lord vanished.

"Tell me, then, share with me what I *can* do," Spire said with a gentleness usually foreign to his nature. The extreme personalities that surrounded his new position had driven him to adopt varying tactics that taxed the range of his admittedly limited sentiments. "Give me leave and resources. I am driven to better this city. For Queen and Country. That is, truly, what I was born to do. But I can do nothing for any of those noble purposes under clouds of obfuscation and dangerous measures."

Spire feared that all the inefficiency stemmed from Her Majesty herself. If so, then he'd have to find a way—somehow—to be shifted back into his old position at the Metropolitan. And quickly, before the unfinished business of the Tourney case was cold as stone.

Spire shuddered as he thought about what the queen was after. Eternal life. He'd yet to meet a single soul in higher office he'd want to stay in for a next term, let alone forever . . . The true horror of "Eterna Pax Victoria" dawned on him in a sour ray of jaundiced light.

There was a soft click of shining leather boots upon the slate floor as Lord Black paced to and fro. The nobleman approached Spire, took his snifter, and refilled both glasses at the mahogany console table littered with various objects that by their appearance had likely been ferreted away from pyramids. Black returned Spire's snifter to him before taking a seat in his vast leather throne of a chair.

"I do worry about the Crown," Black murmured. "I know it's treasonous to say so."

Spire hesitated a moment longer, then dove in. "Treason is entirely contextual, sir. It camouflages to suit the surroundings. Good and evil are not so changeable. You hired me because you thought I did a good job in the Metropolitan Police. I was able to do so because I acted only with comprehensive information. I'll not risk my life or those placed under my purview carelessly or for a questionable cause. There has to be *morality* beneath it all. I will not pursue immortality or anything associated with it if there is not morality at the core. Nor should you, milord. Do not be persuaded to do anything but that which keeps mankind from regressing to animals."

This had an impact on Black.

"You're a good man, Spire," he said. "We're lucky—*I* am lucky—to have you. I'll do whatever I can to make sure this office is on the right side of what it was built for. You have my word, for what that's worth."

"A great deal, milord, and thank you," Spire said with a rare earnestness.

"I'd like to offer you proof of my word," Black added with a familiarly jovial grin, "but I fear you'll question the means."

Spire looked at him quizzically.

"That day at Buck House, I had you tested by a man who can gaze at the aura of a person and tell if he's doing right by humankind or ill. Whether he's on the side of the angels or the devils, let's say."

Spire recalled that horrid day, the day he'd gone from Tourney's cellar of nightmare to the splendor of Buckingham Palace. So that's what had been happening while he'd been stuck in that tiny room—his "aura" had been spied upon. Lovely.

"Whether you believe it or not, he deemed you right and honorable, Mr. Spire," Black said with a chuckle. "I'll have Lord Denbury keep a good eye on all of us, to make sure we remain so."

"By whose bias?" Spire countered.

"By that sweet, kind man's estimation," the nobleman said with an unmistakable fondness. "I am certain his bias is that of the godly. You'll see what I mean soon enough; I'm drawing him into our confidences. There's a parade Saturday, and I'll have him at our box when the queen passes by."

An aura reader to add to Omega's circus. Spire held back a sigh. But, he thought with some surprise, if Black had suspicions of the Crown itself, and that's why Denbury's eye was being called upon, this all could be labeled treason indeed. A new weight shifted in Spire's stomach.

"I've orders to give," Spire said, once the strained silence had grown uncomfortable. "If you'll excuse me, sir." He rose and bowed.

Black nodded and got to his feet, his exhaustion plain once more. "Lead on, my good man."

With Black on his heels, Spire opened his department door.

He heard a little *thwinging* sound that ended in a soft pop, then felt a distinct sting upon his forehead.

"Bull's-eye!" cried Mr. Blakely, theatrical ringmaster and chemical tinkerer, the arms of his aquamarine velvet frock coat flapping as if he were a tall, spindly waterfowl.

Spire stood stock-still and reached up to touch whatever it was that had landed upon his brow. Before he could remove the projectile, there was a cracking sound, followed by smoke that burst around Spire's face in an instant, gray and acrid. He doubled over, coughing, then spun around and went right back out, seeking clean air. He snatched the arrow-like object from his forehead and peered at it, crumpled in his shaking palm: a piece of broken balsa wood with little capsules attached.

"Really, Mr. Blakely, wouldn't the wall have been a wiser test subject than your superior?" Everhart said sharply from her post at the telegraph machine just inside the second-floor threshold.

Still gasping, Spire returned to the office as Blakely replied earnestly, "I need to know that it works on human skin in motion! The operative does have to have good aim, and I haven't yet accounted for wind—"

"You will *account*, Mr. Blakely," Spire hissed, after clearing his throat several times—acrid particles still clung to the inside of his nostrils and made his eyes water—for not coming within *many* feet of me, for the sanctity of your facial features, until you've proved that blasted thing of *vital* importance."

"Oh, rest assured, *mon capitane*, I'll—"

"Shut up, Blakely, and prepare to travel to New York City. Your steamer leaves tomorrow. And dress less . . . dramatically. I can hear that coat from across the room, it's so loud. Spies, Blakely, do not wear turquoise—"

Blakely gasped, utterly aghast. "It is *a-qua-ma-rine,* thank you very much!"

"We are here," Spire growled, "if any of you have the capacity to recall, to examine a plan of recovery of the bodies of our late scientists, learn what we can of Eterna's commission, and seize the man of electrical aberration known as Mosley." He squared his shoulders and took charge.

"Since you are a circus, I'm using you as such. Set yourself up as a small fair, tent and all, in whatever downtown space you can manage. If it's close to a governmental area, all the better. Present a Cipher invitation to your 'show' directly to the Eterna offices. We know from intelligence that Senator

Bishop and Miss Templeton spend part of their time investigating sham spiritualism and outrageous divination. Your performance should be irresistible to them."

He turned to Miss Knight, who nodded with a smile of understanding.

"Find out, by whatever clever discussion necessary, what they want and have done with our scientists. They may not be in possession of the dead bodies, but we need to rule them out. Be careful, as I don't know if they will seek retaliation for Brinkman's unconventional interrogation.

"As well, see what you can do to lure out Mr. Mosley. I'll wire every contact point for Brinkman I have, so he may make himself useful to you for a change."

"Apex, Mr. Spire," Miss Everhart prompted.

"Indeed. Keep all ears tuned for the Apex Corporation or ties to the Master's Society. Apex is the company responsible for shipping the bodies, which puts them on our watch list. The Master's Society precedes them and may be the inspiration, or directly responsible."

Spire turned to Black. "Now, have I your permission to send them all away and remain here in peace?"

"You do," Black said, hiding a chuckle.

"Might that be extended to me as well?" Everhart asked with careful nonchalance. "Do you really want to hear the PM whining if I'm entirely absent from Westminster?"

Lord Black shuddered. "God, no. Stay, Everhart."

"Thank you, milord."

For the first time all day, Spire took a calm breath and was able to relax his shoulders.

His respite was short-lived as an intruder appeared on the threshold of the offices—a petite red-blond woman wearing a deep red riding habit. Her sharp features and imperious air made her seem twice her size. She surveyed the room and its inhabitants, gave a single nod, as if they had passed inspection, then turned away and strode up the metal stairs to Black's top floor. "Let's see what all these offices look like, shall we?" she stated.

"Excuse me, miss?" Spire called after the newcomer as he stepped out onto the landing. "Who are you and how did you get in?"

"Why, hello there! Don't mind me, I've a way with doors," she replied, turning to stare down at him from the landing above. Out of the corner of his eye, Spire saw that Lord Black and Miss Everhart had come up close behind him at the second-floor landing.

"This is a restricted-access building, miss, you can't be here," Spire stated. "Can I help you?"

She offered the three who stood a landing below her a prim smile. Her small, sensible hat was cocked at a slight angle that was opposite from the tilt of her curious, scrutinizing gaze. "This is the Omega department, is it not?" Her accent was of good London breeding, but there was something a bit odd about it, as if it echoed.

Spire looked at Lord Black and didn't say another word. He'd let the man who said to defer insistent queries about the department take it from here. Spire knew the upper-class imperious type and he would let the gentry deal with it.

"No it isn't . . ." Lord Black said, rather unconvincingly.

"Oh, shut up, yes it is." The woman frowned, folding her arms. Black's mouth dropped open.

Spire wanted to put his face in his hands at what was *supposed* to be kept a government secret. Instead, he just scowled, watching the intruder as she descended again toward them, returning to the second floor to address them eye to eye.

"You are?" Black prompted.

The woman took a deep breath and replied on bit of a tear, her voice low, crisp, authoritative, and oddly echoing for so small a frame, and held their company in a bit of a thrall.

"I've many names, and to some I'm just a *visitor,* but you may call me Lizzie Marlowe of the Marlowe Trust. That should ring a bell with you, Lord Black. Seeing as you're a member of the House of Lords, you would know my family, and if I *do* recall, your uncle was set to do mine some favors that never arrived, and while I'm not here to call upon those at present, I am here to see what this department *begins* as. Taking notes, really, as what Omega could become if you're not very, very careful is very, very important."

With that, she swept down again to the front door.

Her bright eyes narrowed, as if she were a hawk that suddenly spied a mouse in a field, but in reverse, looking up rather than down at her prey. She pointed suddenly at Miss Everhart.

"You. It'll be up to you, my dear. You and Templeton, to keep the departments honest. Keep sharp. And do go to New York, will you?"

And with that, Lizzie Marlowe turned to the door, peered at the latches, clicked the lever so that it would lock upon her exit, and was gone.

Spire noticed with great discomfort that there was no read upon the paper ticker above the door that had been installed to track the time, weight, and silhouette of any visitor. The black paper read as if no one had been there at all.

Everyone was dumbstruck for a moment. The rest of the team had filed in silently behind Miss Everhart, and they were all looking at her expectantly.

After a long moment, a baffled Lord Black broke the silence. "Actually, I don't know any Marlowes at all. Aside from, you know, the playwright. And the Blacks don't owe them any favors . . . What in the *world* . . ." He stared at Miss Everhart, who had grown more pale than when the day began.

"Don't look at me," Everhart replied uneasily. "I haven't a

clue. But she said Templeton. Clara? She must be referring to Clara Templeton of New York's commission."

"Well, find out what she meant. We may need you in New York after all, Miss Everhart," Black stated.

Spire and Everhart sighed in unison.

Miss Knight was staring at the door with wide-eyed fascination. "I could not, for the life of me, get a read on that woman. And I'm fairly good with reading women if I do say so myself," she said, with a bit of entendre. "She reads almost as if she's a ghost, but far too corporeal. It isn't that she doesn't exist . . . but as if she exists too much . . . Whatever she is, she's not normal."

"Add her to our growing list of abnormal," Spire said through clenched teeth. "If you haven't noticed, Lord Black, your contraption there to register entrances and visitors is already broken. It recorded nothing, just then, and we all saw and heard that woman, so this wasn't a case for your secret ghostly department, but do something about the door."

"Go on," Black said to everyone else, shooing them away. "You leave at the crack of dawn. Carriages will be sent for each of you, be ready. Miss Everhart, I'll be sure there's a nurse sent to watch over your ill cousin until you are safely returned."

"Thank you, milord," Rose said, trying not to show her disappointment with this change.

"I'll be sure everyone's ticket envelopes have the address of the British safe house you'll be using in downtown Manhattan."

Black turned to Spire. "After the upcoming parade, perhaps we might corner Her Majesty at the palace and request audience." He spoke pointedly and earnestly. "To address your valid concerns. What do you say?"

Spire nodded. "Thank you, sir, for the effort."

* * * * *

"Is tonight the night, O'Rourke?" His Majesty, Beauregard Moriel, asked softly.

"It is, Majesty," the tall, scarred guard replied in a rumbling Irish lilt.

"Is my double chosen?"

"Yes, Your Majesty. The night watchman we've selected is roughly your proportions."

The dank, dark cell in the Royal Courts of Justice that no one knew existed held one small man, balding and beady-eyed, a person generally thought to be long dead by royal decree. He was wearing a fine deep burgundy suit that he'd had smuggled in to mark the auspicious occasion of his secret release.

"The man will likely scream quite like a pig, so we will have to account for that," Moriel stated.

"It is taken care of, Majesty," the guard assured him. "Chemicals were administered to the guards, so our path will be clear, and operatives are stationed near the exit for additional security. We're exiting via a rear alley and heading straight to Vieuxhelles, which has been prepared for you— all the wires, all the machinery. All tertiary operations can now continue from the estate, as Apex has shipped the appropriate products for each of the three ventures."

"O'Rourke, I am so pleased with you," Moriel cooed, reaching through the iron bars to clasp the man's wide palms. "Now. Are you ready to see how I summon my assistants?"

"Yes, Majesty," the guard replied earnestly, then continued warily, "provided the Summoned know I am your ally and don't think me the double. Can you promise me that?"

"Of course they won't mistake the wrong man," Moriel said. "My Summoned engage only upon my command, as it's my blood spilled that calls them. Blood is such a precious thing, and the Summoned love nothing more than wasting that which is precious. As my blood is *most* precious of all, they regard my sacrifice highly. The Summoned are diligent and loyal to me, considering the sustenance I've given them in the past and will give again as our world order nears."

Moriel turned to the wall, where he'd etched a distinct rectangular groove by diligent application of the end of a spoon through the months of his imprisonment.

"O'Rourke, my dear, do you happen to have a sharp knife?" Moriel asked nonchalantly. "I've a dull implement that will do, but I'd prefer not to be in quite so much pain when activating the corridor."

"Of course, Your Majesty," the man said, handing the blade between the bars.

Without a wince or a moment's hesitation, Moriel slashed his forearm. Blood burbled from the wound. A breath hissed between O'Rourke's teeth, but the Majesty remained unmoved. Drawing forth the Summoned was commonplace, as revealed by his forearm, which was scarred with cuts in varying lengths and stages of healing.

"The Summoned walk the dark path, O'Rourke. Some might call them demons, others use other words depending on their own traditions. As I believe in no God but Myself, all I know is that the Summoned are terribly useful and will be critical in reordering the world back into the old ways."

He used a finger to fill the rectangle he had carved into the wall with his blood. He caressed the top line, whispering to the stone, bidding the shadows and the darkest of matters to come forth, in tones a familiar paramour might use to call into a locked chamber where a sweetheart lay sleeping. This was not a courtship of rite and ritual but already an established marriage.

The wall rippled slightly as if it were liquid.

Two black silhouettes, forms of human spark and living energy in abject reverse, slipped from the spiritual halls of human choice and capacity. Moriel did not understand the exact properties of where the forces he summoned lived, if that's what their existence could be called, but it seemed they stepped out from between the world's moments, leaching from the corridors of time, where the soul in all its possibility moved between hope and misery. By the demons' influence in these corridors between life and death, black despair was bid to step into this imperfect world from the ranges of all that might be summoned, kind or malevolent. The vacuous forms turned to Moriel, as if listening.

"A man will take my place, here," Moriel murmured, "and, my dear friends, I need you to do the same to him as was done to our poor, devoted Mr. Tourney. Nothing left. Limb from limb. He's meant to be me, as I'm sure you realize. So be as thorough as you did in taking Tourney for your cause and turn these dank gray walls red. I love red. You'll have to come do up my estate once I'm finally home again! As always, thank you for your service, my devoted compatriots!"

Moriel turned to see O'Rourke shudder as he looked into the blackness that was those forms. O'Rourke, seeing that his reaction had been noted, made move to apologize, but Moriel held up a bloodstained hand.

"It *is* a particular absence, one that chills the soul if gazed upon too long," he said gently. "Even I have my limits. Now, my darling boy, set me free!"

O'Rourke took the key and began unwinding the chains that sealed the door of the makeshift cell. As he worked, he kept glancing at the figures; each time he did, the chains clattered a bit too loudly and the key rattled too tellingly in the lock. Finally, the gate swung open.

"After you, my friend." Moriel gestured the large man ahead, but O'Rourke bowed his head and retreated a step, gesturing in turn.

"Oh, no, no, after you, Your Majesty," he said, bowing

lower without taking his eyes off the hovering ink-black forms. "Your kingdom awaits."

After a slightly awkward pause, Moriel emerged from the cell. He paused on the threshold to look over his shoulder and give a little wave to the duet of coalesced malevolent mass within his erstwhile prison. Straightening his small frame, he strode confidently down the dark, dank hall, head held high, past two other guards. One was unconscious; the other looked dazed—evidence of the chemicals O'Rourke had mentioned.

The Majesty smiled, then stepped slightly to the side as a pair of men—one his own height and build, one much larger—passed through the corridor, heading for the cell Moriel had so recently abandoned. The smaller man was only half conscious, stumbling along and struggling in the other's grip. The taller guard bobbed his head to his master, and Moriel's smile grew when he saw the dark eyes of the possessed staring at him.

Not all the Summoned would take on a bodily possession to do their work, but many did, and it ensured greater service than shorter-term supplications and persuasions.

Moriel turned to watch the double enter the cell. As the door closed behind the pair, the Majesty heard a dim protest—apparently the man was rousing to his fate—then sounds of a struggle, punctuated by expletives.

The former captive began to walk away, listening with anticipation to what was happening behind him.

There came the most ungodly scream that ever man had rent.

The sound of crunching bones and the entirety of a body's fluids exploding outward, painting three cell walls and splashing through the bars to coat the corridor beyond.

O'Rourke clearly tried to hide a wave of panic and nausea, but Moriel noticed.

"Ah, the beautiful perfume of human fear," he said, breathing deep.

The guard and his protected charge stopped, just before opening the exterior gate. He glanced behind him, as if to make sure no Summoned silhouette had followed.

"Before we go any farther, it's been quite an experience with you, sir, and . . . but . . . I'd like some assurance, Mr. Moriel," O'Rourke stated. "Your Majesty," he added with deference. ". . . that all I have done, directed, and managed, which has been, please recall, a great deal, will be rewarded."

"Would I had money on my person, I would pay you handsomely," Moriel said with a sibilant sweetness.

"The pocket watch is quite nice," O'Rourke said. He placed another key to the next lock in the iron pad of the external gate but did not turn it, just stared at him.

Moriel assumed this man was desperate, for something, someone, some greed; men like him usually were and could easily be bought. Moriel's jaw tightened only slightly as he handed over the gold implement he'd had ferreted in along with his robes of release.

"I'm sorry if it has sentimental value, sir," the guard fumbled. "It's just . . ."

"Ah, no, no," Moriel reassured. "We all have needs. I took this from a paramour I left once . . . her kiss still tastes sweet upon my tongue, coppery, as I'd left her with a small stiletto blade slipped through corset bones to remember me by."

O'Rourke withheld another shudder as he escorted the Majesty to the waiting carriage beyond.

Majesty Moriel took a deep breath and stared up at what was unmistakably a glorious night sky, smoke of London's various industries and home fires wafting up into the atmosphere.

"England," he murmured in a quiet reverie. "America.

Beyond. It's time for your tables to turn. Everyone has their time and season. I think that's biblical."

"It is, Majesty."

"I was musing. I wasn't asking, O'Rourke."

"I'm sorry, Majesty."

"You should be, interrupting a regent in reverie. Goodness."

"It won't happen again, sir."

"Good. The Society will need you. Unfortunately, I've been running low on deputies—they're dropping like proverbial flies—so you'll be promoted. On with you, come to Vieuxhelles tomorrow midnight for the next indoctrinations."

"Yes, Your Majesty . . ." O'Rourke vanished quickly.

* * * * *

Rose was in one of her dream states. These strange, hazy incidents had begun after an attempt to recover a sample of the Eterna Compound. She had been knocked unconscious and for some days had felt drained of life. Since then, she had several times found herself gripped by visions.

Today she woke to see a woman sitting at the foot of her bed—the same Lizzie Marlowe who had visited the Omega division offices. Her light red hair was in a braid down her shoulder, and her searing gaze was fixed on Rose, who bolted upright. The interloper wore no hat or gloves, but clasped about the waist of her burgundy riding habit was a belt hung with strange instruments.

"The timetable," she said. "I sped up your timetable. Well, *I* didn't accelerate, I stay constant. The timetable itself sped, I am merely reacting to save my hide and yours."

Rose stared in silence.

"I was attempting to let the power of suggestion, and potent dreams, do the trick," the woman—Miss Marlowe—explained. "It usually does wonders. But I can't risk it."

"Who *are* you?"

The woman did not reply directly but gestured toward Rose's wrist. "I am sorry for the physical effects. I was going for more of a 'prophetic dream' result, but you and Clara both have such *wild* imaginations."

Rose gaped. "You mean you were the 'vampire'?"

The woman made a face. "*You* jumped to that conclusion." She shook her fair head with a laugh. "This silly, histrionic age. At least you have expanded your consciousness, and there are things you deem possible now that you hadn't previously. The world needs such minds now." She glanced at Rose's carpetbags against the wall. "You *are* going to New York, yes?"

"Not another word until you tell me who you are, whom you work for, and what all this is about," Rose declared, folding her arms.

The woman sighed. "I told you. I'm Lizzie Marlowe. Miss Templeton likes to call me the visitor, although I rather like 'Captain Marlowe,' assuming I live to tell that tale.

"Don't let your department become something it's not. You and Clara must stand up for what is right. A steadfast partnership. You'll see. She's been warned about you. Be warned about her. Wariness makes for good sisters."

In the next moment, Rose found herself alone. How that happened, she couldn't be sure.

* * * * *

The trip was long and Moriel was quite tired. Drawing out the Summoned took a great deal of concentration and life force. They were draining creatures, those black silhouettes, the absence of color, the vacuum of hope.

The sight of Vieuxhelles, his rightful home, cured all.

It was a crisp, bright night when His Majesty Beauregard Moriel entered his looming, sprawling, ivy-covered estate with a sigh, noting sadly that his palace was a bit worse for wear. Admittedly, the staff had been greatly reduced while he was "dead." He nearly jumped from the carriage and darted up the marble steps to the brass door knocker.

In response to the knocker's reverberate thunderclap, his steadfast butler opened the great door. An ancient creature, James had been with the Moriels since long before His Majesty was born.

"Good evening and welcome home, Your Majesty," James said with a familiar soft deference. "The estate has been prepared for you."

The butler escorted Moriel through the dusty, dark, cavernous foyer into the warmly lit grand sitting room, a sumptuous room that had always been his favorite. He basked in the glow of the golden objects that lined the walls and the luxurious furnishings. James lifted a golden crown from an ornate box and approached the waiting regent, the circlet trembling in his shaking hands.

Before Moriel's unfortunate stint in prison, this had been their daily routine; resuming the ritual was such a comfort. Moriel felt the gold settle into place on his brow. James had seated it perfectly. Crossing to a tall rosewood wardrobe, the eternal butler withdrew a fur-lined robe that he presented with the same slow ceremony, sliding it about Moriel's body.

This coronation had begun in his youth, and it always filled him with the same rush, both freeing and invigorating. He'd recommend it as a tonic for virility, were he not so loath to share the secrets of the diadem.

From the arched window, Moriel looked out over his land lit by the kind of moonlight that made wolves howl in delight. His beautiful land. His familial acreage, back in rightful hands.

Their estate had been taken, and the sin was Moriel's earliest life's mission to make right. A distant familial dispute two generations prior had escalated into an ugly affair that had disenfranchised the Moriel family from what was rightly theirs. The estate had been renamed Harcourt Hall, seized by the Wicke family and the Moriels erased from heraldry.

This had taken the gravest of tolls on his father, and Moriel vowed to make the usurpers pay. The whole ordeal nearly killed the entire disputed Moriel line, but Beauregard had won his hard-fought battle. The estate and holdings, all again in the hands it should be. If the seat of his kingdom hadn't passed down to him, would he not have become one of the wretched spirits his work bound to patchwork corpses, desperate specters built to undo the sanity of any commoner who looked upon them? He would have haunted the world forever if he did not have his rightful home.

There was one convenient, fated aspect to the usurpation that had so grieved his family. On all accounts and records, there was no Moriel, no Vieuxhelles, only a nondescript Harcourt Hall that was not for sale, and the owner remained unknown. The larger picture that titles, logbooks, and property records failed to show, due to a careful and thorough wiping of the Wicke line from the Empire, was that there were no Wickes anymore either ... Moriel had made painstakingly sure of that, having plotted since the age of ten various acts of poison, accidents and "unfortunate disappearances" that so plagued and cursed the usurping family.

So Vieuxhelles was conveniently off the proverbial map for the time being, and that suited Moriel's purpose grandly during this time of preparation.

There was of course the next conquest: lineage. He had tried valiantly to find a wife and an heir, but that, too, had been foiled by still further usurpers—that damned Denbury— but once his plans had unfurled, he would take as many wives as necessary until the line was assured.

"Tell me, James," Moriel said softly as he sipped tea, "whose house this is."

"It is your house, Your Majesty."

"And what will I do for this house?"

"You will find clever ways to annihilate anyone who tries to take this house from your family line, just as you did the traitors to your family."

"Thank you, James. Would you sit with me in a game of chess?"

"I shall do whatever you wish, Master."

James fetched a golden box. "I know, it's dusty," he said, brushing off the container, "but the last maid ran off screaming, claiming some kind of witchcraft was here."

"Truly, good help is impossible to find anymore," Moriel muttered mordantly. "Slavery or indentured servitude is far more efficient and reliable."

With shaking hands, the set was laid upon a marble-topped table at the divan, and Moriel launched into ode and reverie, his favorite music to accompany a good game of strategy.

"The systematic destruction of this age's industrial progress and the classes and uppity humans it created is ready to commence, James," Moriel stated. "Most of the products are in place."

"Very good, My Lord."

The contacts he had cultivated and coerced throughout the years had built a subtle set of detonation points across two continents. Once put into motion, they would inevitably change the course of the future and redistribute power back into the hands of those who should always have held it—the rulers and the aristocracies of old.

Never mind his line had been questioned, withered, beleaguered, set upon. He would restore lineage as power and, in doing so, set right so much of what had gone wrong when the barriers of society had been tumbled, creating a muddy sea of the unwashed. What had been termed the Industrial

Revolution was, to Moriel, a heinous crime. He hated revolutions. They were messy, rabble-roused affairs.

However, in order to return the world to its natural order, he would have to host a thorough counterrevolution, wreck the spinning top of an unborn future to preserve a more perfect past. He had enlisted the Summoned to help him in this cause, for this sort of rerouting of the human experience was impossible without the aid of the inhuman.

It wasn't that he hadn't tried asking for divine intervention. In his youth, he'd prayed to God to dismantle the injustice that was Parliament, a shouting, obnoxious group rule that accomplished nothing, a boorish, uncivilized mess. But despite Moriel's ardent prayer, God had not acted. The demons, in contrast, were on his side. They had such sense, those dear shadows.

"If I could only have the opportunity to lecture," he said somewhat dreamily, sitting back in the leather chair, sipping the finest of spiced teas flecked with a bit of gold leaf, relishing the taste of grandeur in his mouth. Surely the *right* kind of people would easily see his point of view. There were only two kinds of persons in this world: the common and the kingly. He'd appeal to the latter and demolish the former.

"Are my missives in order and has the corporation secured its holdings?"

"Yes, sir, but there have been so many deaths, sir . . ." James said worriedly.

"You've known Death to be my handmaiden since my youth, James." Moriel clucked disappointment.

"Of course, Your Majesty, I only say so because it leaves me unclear on who is your second-in-command now?"

Moriel thought for a moment. "Good question, James. I will have to appoint one."

He knocked over a rook with a wooden clunk and suddenly missed his improvised chessboard made from a rat he had disarticulated while in prison. The sound of striking bone on bone was a particular music to his ear. He contented himself he'd hear symphonies of the sort in the year to come.

CHAPTER

THREE

Connecting the dead to the living as if she were a telegraph wire was not the sort of errand Evelyn Northe-Stewart thought she'd be doing when she began the day. But the past few years had turned that way, with ever more paranormal threads woven into her daily experience so that they were now a seamless part of her life's fabric.

She alighted from her cab on Eleventh Street, instructed the driver to wait there, and walked down Fifth Avenue with a dark blond lock of hair dangling limply in her hand as if it were a dead rabbit hanging from the mouth of a dog.

Turning right onto Tenth Street, just a few doors in, distaste swept over Evelyn at the sight and the feel of the particular redbrick town house she paused in front of.

The exterior brownstone detailing around the windows had weathered poorly against the brick, discoloring the facade. It was as if a substance had oozed from the windows, the eyes of the house. It cried against its own mortar. The basement-level door was a shadowed maw under a plain arched portico, distinctly darker than the rest of the sunny, dappled lane to either side. To her senses, the address reeked of death and horror.

The metal door creaked open slowly when she turned the key, an agonizing sound that made her wince. Cautiously, the medium poked her head into the deep shadows of the interior hallway. After a long moment, she felt a cold draft on the back of her neck. She narrowed her eyes.

"Don't rush me, Mr. Dupris," Evelyn cautioned. "I don't take spaces like this lightly. You of all people should know better than to push."

"Many apologies," the ghost replied earnestly. "I am still learning to keep a civil distance between the living and the dead. Caught up in the currents of the spirit world, I bump quite accidentally into the solidity of the living."

"I don't suppose you've any ability to protect me in here? Are there malevolent presences within? I can still reach out to my dear exorcist friend Reverend Blessing. . . ."

"The place is no longer directly violent ground, though it holds a terrible echo of pain and cannot be endured for long periods," Louis explained.

"Clara said there were carvings on the second floor, something insidious. There is a chance the negative and malevolent energies of the house have increased."

"In which case," Louis said calmly, "I'll not ask you to stay longer than the moment of placing Clara's token upon my final corporeal resting place. Don't worry," he rushed a reassurance, "no remains are left to distress you. We were turned entirely to dust. I don't remember the event; I just appeared on the other side. God was kind to me in that regard. This will all be over soon."

Evelyn shuddered as she slipped into the house, keeping her boots quiet on the floor. Just because no one seemed to be there didn't mean presences were not, in fact, present. And if there was one thing she truly did not wish to wake, it was that which she thought she'd put to bed two years prior.

The residence had been fitted with gaslight, but the fixtures in the front entrance landing did not respond to Evelyn's touch. Reaching into the beaded reticule that was attached to her bodice, she withdrew a box of matches and stepped through the open pocket doors of the main parlor. A lantern hung on a peg beside the well-scorched fireplace, and she moved quickly to it and lit the wick.

The gifted Spiritualist attempted to study the room, holding the lantern at differing levels. Even the mirrored panel that brightened the lantern's light could not illuminate the room enough to relieve the gloom. An attempt to open the dark wood shutters revealed them to be nailed shut.

"Goldberg had grown paranoid about our work," Louis explained, "and sealed the windows to keep out any intruding gaze. He'd gone mad, really. We should have stopped him earlier, but he was always a quirky man. With such a kind heart as his, something, some force rotted his mind, as he'd never have sabotaged us willingly," he added with sad certainty.

"Explain to me what you need me to see here and where you need me to leave the lock," Evelyn urged.

"Ah, yes, the hair, Clara, right, yes, that's why . . . See, distract. I grow distract . . ." Louis said mournfully.

"Keep heart, brave spirit," Evelyn said gently. "Stay with me and this moment." She could feel the cool draft of the specter warm slightly. If there was one thing she knew about interactions with the dead, it was that firm encouragement produced results.

Evelyn examined the vague makeshift laboratory, stopping dead at the carved outline of a door upon the wall. The uneven gouge had been painted in a dark, rusted color . . . blood, surely.

"I know this after all," Evelyn murmured. "I know this hellacious magic. Damn it all, it did not die with that wretch Moriel. How does one kill a demon bent on misery? Woe to us all if this magic has grown. . . ." She tore out of the main room and raced up the stairs, swinging her lantern out before her.

On the second floor, rugs were pulled back in several places, revealing screaming inscriptions carved into the floorboards. Likely this was from Clara's inspection. The brave girl.

"Yes. This. It is as we feared." Evelyn's words were thick with worry, her body shaking. "The Master's Society was at work here." Panic nipped at her throat, threatened to cleave her stomach, but she pulled herself together. "At least the enemy is familiar. Is this England's doing? Their commission built to counter ours? Have they invited the devil in?"

"I know nothing of these particular black matters," Louis replied, "but the powers behind it stem not from man but from monsters, truly malevolent forces."

"Where did you fall, Mr. Dupris, if I may?"

"The last I can recall, I was on the ground floor," the ghost replied. "Trying to get to the door as I gasped my last breaths. I passed out, or so I thought, and then found myself running behind my brother Andre. I did not truly understand the change in my circumstances and corporeality until I realized could not feel the ground beneath my feet."

As Evelyn descended the stairs, she felt a weight growing about her feet, as if suddenly she were encased in stone.

She looked down and swallowed hard. There was a blackened spot upon the floor, as if flesh and bone had fused to the wood, turned coal black in the conflagration, and then vanished. The shape didn't even have the form of a man; Evelyn had walked past it without notice when entering the house.

To her horror, she realized that all the surfaces about her were finely coated with ash and dust. The idea that she was breathing in the poor men made her want to flee, but she owed it to them—to Louis—to be stronger than they'd have expected her sex to be.

"I suppose that is where it happened," the ghost replied with a slightly detached air. Evelyn attributed this to his profession. A scientist must, she thought, be able to set aside personal responses in order to facilitate his studies. "This is my grave site," Louis said musingly, sounding as though he stood directly above the charred mark.

"Shall I say prayers for you here, Mr. Dupris?"

"That would be very kind of you, but business first, matters of the spirit later. Leave the lock of hair, which we hope binds me tighter to this world, right here."

Evelyn Northe-Stewart had experienced much of death, but at a distance. She dealt with souls, not the sites and circumstances of death. Confronted now with the undeniable evidence of Louis's demise, she found herself frozen, unable to bend, Clara's love token dangling from her hand.

"My dear Madame Medium," Louis urged, "do not hesitate. I know this is hardly easy. But I am asking—begging—you . . ."

If she could have scrubbed the damned spot out, she would have. What a benefit to cleanse the floor and, in doing so, perhaps remove some of the guilt that she assumed dear Bishop and Clara had shouldered, knowing as they did what had occurred here.

"I would do anything to touch that hair once more . . ." the ghost said achingly.

It was too intimate a tone for even a medium to hear. Evelyn shook herself from her paralysis and laid the braided piece upon the floor.

Immediately, the air around her changed. A sudden breeze glanced off her ear and toyed with the fine hairs about her neck and arms. This specific sensory experience, she knew from opening the spirit world to hungry mortal hearts, was laden with possibility.

Perhaps, she thought with a surge of hope, the living twin could at last forgive; perhaps Clara could have closure; perhaps Louis could find peace once their duties were done and the devils dispatched.

The air turned sour. The lantern went out.

A set of distinct black shadows surrounded her.

"Get out," Louis ordered. "Now."

"Glad to." Evelyn ran to the front door and threw it open. She blinked at the sunlight for an instant, wondering at the lazy, sunlit street before them, the peaceful setting so at odds with the terror behind.

The medium—and the ghost with her—raced across the street and to the corner, where a cluster of carriages turned onto Fifth Avenue. The grand flow of traffic led all carts, carriages, pedestrians, and trolleys down through the Washington Square parade ground. The escapees paused in the shadow of the dark, beautiful Gothic-adorned Church of the Ascension to catch a breath.

Evelyn spoke firmly after a long moment. "Now. Let's see if Clara can accept your calling. Reach out only with considered caution, Mr. Dupris," she said warningly.

"Always with caution," he replied. "I know her state as well as any and helped her refine her spectral shielding. I'd like to think I will not trigger the same violences as have been visited upon her by other spirits, though I now share their form. I have never done anything but love her."

"Let's hope that's enough, Mr. Dupris," she stated.

Evelyn and the ghost headed back to her driver on West Eleventh Street. Settling herself inside, she felt a cool draft sweep through the closed door, rustling the fine curtains. The ghost would ride uptown with her.

"Those terrible silhouettes, Madame Northe-Stewart,"

Louis said mournfully. "Here in the spirit realm I can see light around life. And everything has a spark. But those . . . Devoid entirely. They are a nothingness born from death and live to kill. Is there anything so terrifying in all the world, in anything I have ever known, as that emptiness?"

The shudders Evelyn had been holding back out of pride and stiff paralysis now flowed freely up and down her corset-braced spine. That which frightens the dead is cause for terror indeed.

* * * * *

Clara had fallen asleep again after Evelyn left, though rest had been fitful since the incident at the Trinity Church graveyard, as full of imagery and of omen as her sensitive person could bear. Whether this was dream or vision was unclear, but the images were vivid, engaging all her senses, which usually signaled that what she was witnessing was real . . . or would be, in time.

A house was on fire. It stood at the end of a tree-lined lane. The tall, spindly trees were on fire, too, burning bushes reaching questing, gnarled branches to heaven.

Standing in shadow was a haunted-looking dark-haired woman in contemporary dress familiar in an old soul, past-life sort of way. Remembering nearly all of her past lives was one of Clara's gifts; she was sure she knew this woman but could not place her.

The woman raised one hand. Signaling for help? Or telling Clara to halt? Surely this person was the missing piece that the visitor had made such a fuss over.

The world was swaying . . . until Clara realized it was not the ground but her. She was swaying side to side as if her body were a fulcrum, attempting to balance weighty scales.

Clara looked down at herself. In one hand she held a large compass; the letters N, E, S, W glowed red-hot and the dial spun dizzyingly. In her other hand she held a golden chalice filled with a thick, dark liquid that smelled of pitch and copper. Script emblazoned across the mouth of the goblet read DEATH.

Murmurs sounded behind her, and Clara craned her neck to try to see what was making the noise. She was at the head of a great fan of her past selves. All were blindfolded and all held a chalice in each hand as if a strange personification of Justice. Each bemoaned choices made and cursed the blindness of Eterna Commission. She couldn't catch every incarnation's condemnation of her present life's focus, but the eighteenth-century ship captain she'd once been, a distinct, fine-featured man nearest her that bore enough of her essence to be clearly Clara but in a time prior said:

"Eternal life is meaningless if lived out in mankind's hell. The greater war is the one for the soul of the future. . . ."

Each of her was a figure like so many depictions of personified Justice, but on the scales of her own hands lay life and death . . . The iconography of Justice's infamous sword was present, too, only in the form of many swords, all broken and scattered at her various feet, iteration after iteration.

Could so many of her have gotten so much wrong for so long?

In each life she'd tried to take at least one particular injustice and right it. In the seventeenth century, it had been trying to make maps for safer travel along treacherous passages. In the eighteenth, the sea won again, and that life focused on creating more benevolent commerce than slavery for trade in France.

In Clara's present life, at age twelve, the pain of Mary Todd Lincoln, the need to heal the nation after the assassination of the man elected to lead in times of strife, had borne the Eterna Commission from her innocent mouth. Perhaps, however, it had awoken a greater, darker foe instead, happy to take that little girl's idealism and tear it to bloody shreds, replacing hope with horror.

If the fates would give her time, then perhaps the battle that needed fighting was just ahead. Each chalice, each body, bent and swayed with increasing violence and momentum until the contents of the cups spilled thick and scarlet onto the gray flagstones below the feet of the representative lives.

Another rumbling roar, like the shriek of harpies, accompanied a spire of flame that shot up from the ground, marking the boundaries of what looked like a large estate. A wave of acrid heat washed over Clara. Burning debris fell between her and the beckoning woman, and smoke and ash filled the air.

Clara woke from the nightmare, coughing and gasping for breath.

Before her hovered a transparent man in an open shirt, suspenders, and breeches. Were he not grayscale and floating an inch above her quilt, she might have thought him ready for work in his laboratory.

Louis Dupris, her wild chemist and poet-philosopher, whom she'd loved and lost. Her mind fumbled for purchase, even though she had been expecting this manifestation. She had asked for it, given permission, and this was no longer a dream.

Nothing could have prepared her to see his spirit so clearly. In his hand he held a silver lock of her hair, its color gone to ghostly grayscale, dead material connecting the dead to her. The sight of him was bittersweet, so different from the warm, vibrant man who, in his sure arms, made her feel that magic was not an unseen force but one at work in the human heart.

"Hello, Clara," he said, his voice still gamesome, but distant, and the sound and the movement of the phantasm's lips at a delay made for a jarring disconnect. "I've missed you."

Clara swallowed hard. "And I you, Louis."

"Thank you," he continued, his grayscale face brightening, "for permitting this."

"It's the least I can do to honor you," Clara said, steeling herself. She sensed ghosts and often heard them, but she saw them rarely, and never so clearly.

"It was your own forces that held me at bay, and for that I could not complain, as your shielding protects you admirably. But there is the matter of your . . . noise. You're very loud. Your aura, your presence—it's like one of the currents of Edison or Tesla. This made it near impossible for me to haunt you, though it drew me to you just as it did in life." He chuckled softly. "Even in death, I am not immune to your magnetism. I am so glad the lock of your hair did the trick and allowed me to cross these uncharted distances."

Clara blushed at his flattery but felt a wealth of burning questions rise from within. "You're *holding* my hair," she began. "I'm so curious about the physical properties of your world. . . ."

"I did not expect to be able to touch your hair, to hold it. But once Mrs. Northe-Stewart set it on the floorboards where I died, it came easily into my hand. We'll be learning about the strange ways of this world together, you and I . . ."

Clara blinked, trying not to think of the place where he died.

Louis continued as if floodgates of language were opened. "I wasn't sure it would work, but I've made great strides in tactile, localized magic. And here I am." He stared at her lovingly. "You're still a bit loud, darling." He gestured around her, as if to her person, her presence.

She stared at him, unsure what to say.

"Don't worry." He chuckled softly. "I doubt it's something you can adjust as if it were repositioning a hairpin. You're a force of nature, Clara. And I believe in the laboratory we created one. A force of nature. *That's* the Eterna Compound. It isn't what you think. In the end, the compound had nothing to do with immortality."

"What, then?"

"That's what I'm trying to find out. Something didn't want us to bring our compound to fruition."

"The British—"

"No. Not the British. Not any one person or government. But *entities*. Other forces of nature out there, hardly as pretty as you. As I died, I saw dark, terrible things. I wish someone had warned us like they warned Feizer."

"Who?"

"Bartholomew Feizer, his specialty was the mind. He was on leave in France. I never met him, but he sent a note saying hysterical women in his life, upon premonitions of disaster, demanded he not return. Turns out they were correct. Women are accused often of that, when they're really on to something—"

"Yes, *institutionalized* often, just for having intelligence, wisdom, psychic gifts, or, heaven forbid, any kind of romantic appetite." She growled through clenched teeth. "Where is that note, from Feizer?"

"Ash in the fireplace," Louis replied. "No matter, we didn't have enough time to heed the warning. We were dead within the next hour, at the hands of shadows straight from hell. Inky silhouettes manifested as if in reaction to our work. They struck against our work. Because, if you'll follow me, I think what we crafted is actually a *Ward*."

At this word, Louis's excitement built. When alive, he'd have flushed and his hazel eyes would have taken on a glow.

But now only an additional breeze burst from his transparent form. "That's what went wrong, and that's what you have to reproduce. *That's* why the spirits reacted in the Trinity lot; they were trying to tell you *not* to destroy our work. It's vital. It will stand as a wall between life and what killed us."

"I want to be very sure I understand what you mean by Ward, Louis. We've no room for misunderstanding."

"We had created a Ward inside a house that had already been tainted: the carvings on the upper floors, the 'door' carved into the downstairs wall. The space was neutral once, but not when we died. Goldberg used to be a reasonable man, but something got to him. He'd gone truly mad and we didn't see it. He let something into that place."

"Why couldn't you see it? None of the carvings? Was the change in him not obvious?" she prompted. Louis shook his incorporeal head.

"You've not been allowed to spend time around scientists, Clara. 'Mad,' to a scholar, theorist, scientist, is all relative. We all have—had—our quirks, odd notions and wild, sweeping moods. Goldberg was always a bit paranoid. The escalation, we assumed, was due to the stresses of his particular side of the research, working with living and dead tissue. It was rather gruesome, and at a critical point his mind went off the rails."

"Could there have been sabotage somehow?" Clara pressed. "From what I saw on the second floor hidden beneath carpets, the writings and scrawlings on the floor were similar to a case two years prior where a powder, an agent, was used to turn people's minds."

"Oh. Well, then, yes," Louis said, earnestly contemplative, "that would explain Goldberg's sudden shift."

"How do you *know* you created a Ward?" Clara continued. "What in the disaster tells you so? Shouldn't a Ward have stopped the horror, not encouraged it?"

"The forces that entered the room went right to the material, trying to snuff it out, strangle it, take it apart particle by particle. In a neutral space, the Ward would have the upper hand, but the darkness had it that day, due to the rituals. They took us with them in the exact same way. Strangled and plucked apart from life to dust."

Clara fought back tears. She had always had a keen streak of empathic gifts, and she could see and feel what he described as if it was happening to her, before her eyes, in the instant, in a terrible duality. And she still felt responsible, for having the Eterna idea in the first place. Louis knew that look, and he held up a transparent gray hand.

"No, Clara, I'll have none of that guilt. Let me rejoice in being here with you, in your bright contrast," the ghost said lovingly. She nodded, breathed deeply, and regained hawk-like focus on the luminous figure before her. "In life we are faced with profound moments of quiet loneliness," he stated, hovering at the edge of Clara's bed. "Those solitary, bleak moments are all the more extreme in death. To escape searing isolation, souls go rushing back into life again for another turn around the globe, bringing elder aches unto the next mewling existence, without any thought to that quiet corridor between life and death. So many souls bumble on, unaware of previous lives, eras, meaning, or purpose."

He wafted closer to her, engulfing her in chill. "But, God help us, those of us who know, remember . . . We dare to take the hand of another who shares the same bruises in the very same tissues of the soul. I don't know which, in the end, is more lonely—to see life and death alone, or in the company of very old souls. What a thrillingly terrible, inevitable, amazing cycle I see from this vantage point . . ."

Clara stared at him. Through him. "Oh, Louis . . ."

Before they could muse further, solid and shade, they

started at a sudden sound and movement as Senator Bishop flung wide Clara's bedroom door.

"Clara Templeton, who the devil are you talking to?" Bishop barked. He spotted Louis's floating form and cocked his head to the side. "Good God, a ghost. Is that . . . Mr. Dupris?"

Louis jumped—wafted—to his feet and bowed. "Senator. I assure you I was in no way disrespecting your ward."

Bishop clenched his jaw and pointedly looked away from Clara in her nightdress. "I take it you are here to report to Miss Templeton some matter of import regarding the Eterna disaster? I am sorry for your loss . . . of yourself."

"Thank you for your empathy, sir," the ghost said earnestly. "I'm very impressed that you can see and speak with me. It is a high caliber of talent indeed that can do such things."

"I'm not falsely modest, Mr. Dupris. I know I am very talented, but I'd say this exchange has more to do with your being a high-caliber spirit with a . . . very strong connection to us. I've never seen nor heard one so clearly."

"It is true, it is our collective connection. My brother, Andre, can also see and hear me," Louis said thoughtfully.

Clara blushed threefold, thinking of Andre, who had kissed her while pretending to be Louis, of her and Louis's more passionate encounters, and of the senator's talents, which always had her in a bit of awe.

The ghost abruptly looked pained, as if something tore at him. "I feel my brother's call upon me. Perhaps he got himself into trouble again." The ghost sighed. "If I can come again, I will. . . ." He stared longingly at Clara in a way that made her blush again.

He faded into the wall and was gone. Clara rose, went to her wardrobe, and pulled a quilted satin robe on over her nightdress, all the while ordering her thoughts in preparation for the conversation to come. She locked her emotions away, determined to focus on work and mission.

"Well?" Bishop asked with an edge.

"There's another force at work," she stated. "We've a far different enemy than we think."

Bishop stepped farther into the room, and she turned to face him. There was a long, tense moment as Clara watched him pour over all the things he could say, then seize upon the one thing he should ask. This decision process was hidden to most, under the veneer of his calm, politicking ways, inscrutable, but Clara had made a habit of cataloging his every expression, especially the ones that he took most care to hide.

"What happened the night of your last seizure?" he asked. "There are too many secrets here, Clara. I thought we were working on that."

"Eterna has always been complicated," Clara countered.

"That's not an answer."

"Secrets never are."

"Don't be coy. Why were you overcome? Lavinia tended to you but said she didn't know what you'd been doing. What did you do on your own to trigger a fit?"

"I was . . . trying to divest us of Eterna," Clara said sheepishly. "I . . . buried it all. Anything and everything I had."

Bishop's generally kind eyes, more worried of late than gentle, widened. "Buried it? Whatever for?"

"Because I thought everything—the silhouettes, the whole of the spirit world—was telling me to destroy it and by doing so make things right," she exclaimed. "I tried burning it all. I dug a little grave for the files and tried to strike a match, but it kept going out. And then Pearl Street exploded with that electrical fire."

Bishop scratched his head. "Yes. That is a whole other

matter. But the spirit world. Why did you listen to them when you know how a host affects you? Why did you act without, at least . . . consulting me?"

He was genuinely hurt by this.

"I'm sorry. I should have," Clara said. "I thought it was beyond us. It was the best I could do. The signals have been so mixed when my instincts used to be so clear . . . but with the new information—"

"In light of your ghostly lover here tonight, you mean?"

Clara barreled past the accusatory truth and her own blooming blush, blurting: "*Mr. Dupris* said he was trying to stop me, not encourage me. He blew out the match when I tried to burn the research."

"Stopping you, then?"

"Yes. Because what they made in that house was a *Ward*. The shadows that snuffed out their lives, in that already tainted house, were threatened by the protective magic and killed them for it. So it isn't the Eterna work or the Ward that was the danger; it was what was already inside."

Bishop's frown deepened. "I worry about your getting information from a ghost who may cause you an . . . episode."

Clara's eyes flashed. "Louis has not made me seize. Not even the first numbers on my safety countdown were triggered. I manage to commune at length with a spirit, for once in my adult life, without pain and humiliation, gain vital information, and you question it?"

Bishop came closer, wrestling with anger, she knew that expression well.

"Not only nice things want to speak with you, Clara," he stated. She stiffened, but he continued. "Had we not developed a system? I don't believe that you can be handled like a marionette to do evil's will, but hiding things from me is not your style. But then again, there was Mr. Dupris. Perhaps I don't know you at all, Clara Templeton."

Clara was hit by the onslaught of Bishop's emotions. Her empathic abilities felt how thick and unwieldy they were and how complicated for them both. She spoke very, very carefully.

"I cannot make a case for myself that is not indeed marred by a secrecy you would not have wished. I can do nothing to change that now but try to regain your confidence. To find that my generally accurate instincts acted in polar opposite to what Louis was trying to protect, while your trust in me has shattered, is devastating." She sighed, her tensed shoulders falling with the weight of exhaustion and unprocessed grief. Fussing with a cup and saucer, she poured milk into cold coffee. "I don't want to start over again. Am I no longer gifted? I don't want to live that way. Give me 'fits' over a life without *insight*. I could have burned their protective work that night, and they'd have died in vain for my lack of proper intuition."

Tears sprang to Clara's eyes and she screwed up her face to force them back, which only made them splash into the untouched coffee. She wasn't sure what she wanted from Bishop in the moment, but she didn't want him to be angry.

"We don't have to start over," Bishop began gently. Clara looked at him hopefully. "If it's a *Ward* that the lads made, then we'll make up the same kinds of compounds as we did in Salem, we'll build and prepare. You will resurrect what was paused by the Pearl Street explosion—and save that electrical mystery for another day—and we will attempt to find out *what* had you so convinced in your course of action."

"Yes . . ." She smiled. "Yes, Senator, very good, and thank you."

"Back to 'Senator' again?" He smiled wearily. "I can't keep track of when to be formal and when not, you'll have to tell me. . . ."

They stared at one another for a long moment. She was

trying to determine if that was some kind of invitation and if she wanted it to be one.

"I'll get dressed and start my day, *Rupert,*" she said, turning away so that he could not read her face. "I'll have no further supernatural phenomena making me feel an invalid. Either I take these forces on, or we give them the impression that they can take on me. I won't countenance it, and I know neither will you."

Bishop smiled then. "That's my Clara. I'll help you this time."

"You don't need to—"

"That wasn't an offer, it's an order, my dear," he said with a particular curt smile of finality that had so often punctuated her life. "We'll bring Lavinia to stay next to you in case of another fit. We'll resurrect those files and make them into magic. And this time, let's *try* not to keep secrets?" he asked hopefully. Clara nodded. It sounded like a wise promise impossible to fulfill. "So let's get to it, then, shall we?"

Clara stared at Bishop. "Now?"

"I'll . . ." Here he smirked a bit, as if hiding a delicious secret. Clara recognized this expression as the one he used when indulging the idea of Mesmerism. "Keep people away from the graveyard. If dark forces are amassing, let's not waste any more time than we already have. Whatever England's involvement, I think they must be off the mark. Let's get Louis's material back and see if we can resurrect what he recommends."

"Thank you, Rupert," she said quietly.

"For what?" he asked.

"For believing me, for believing Louis, and helping me now. You are so good to me."

He could stand in the way of so much. Instead, he facilitated. He truly did want the best for her and what they had undertaken. There was little altruism and general good nature in the world. She'd been lucky enough to be ensconced in it all her life, despite the tragedies that surrounded.

He smiled broadly at her praise.

"Besides, you don't let me be powerful nearly as much as I'd like." He tapped his temple. "My muscles need flexing."

Clara pursed her lips at him. It had been a long-running skirmish between them how much of his power of suggestion he would employ on others. He limited his own power vastly more than Clara thought he should, but—in a fond, playful way—he always blamed her for being the one holding him back. Seeing her expression only broadened his smile.

There was a time when Clara had felt she could share anything with her guardian. That was before she'd harbored any feelings for him, and long before she'd sealed those sentiments away like Montresor bricked up Fortunato in the nitre-filled caves of Poe's landmark story. The jingling bells of a flame of love sounded deep in her catacombs, and she looked hastily away, wondering if she could ever regain what had once been so innocent and pure but had become so complex and awkward in her adult life.

* * * * *

Digging things up in Trinity churchyard, a few streets northwest of their home and their offices, even in the light of day and after Bishop persuaded the groundskeeper to temporarily close it to other visitors, proved more difficult than Clara expected.

Once again her friend, the Eterna Commission's receptionist, Lavinia Kent, accompanied her, alert against any sign of a seizure. Though only two days had passed since the misguided burial, the ground had been tended, leveled, making it difficult to locate her diggings.

Clara couldn't let the energies of the graveyard derail her, as much as she adored the small brownstone Gothic chapel whose rich elegance she so enjoyed. She refused the attempts of past-life tendrils and wandering spirits to wrap around her senses. Focusing her core life force, she snapped it out from her person as if she were cracking a whip, erecting shielding boundaries, creating a modicum of spiritual and psychological safety.

A shudder consumed Clara, a sense memory of the seizure on this spot. For a sensitive, she was *too* sensitive, her gifts sometimes entirely counterproductive. No great revelations came from the fits, and she thought this a wasted opportunity. For what she suffered, she'd at least have hoped God spoke to her during paroxysms. All she got for it were raging headaches and bruises.

Clara knelt, lifting the light mauve skirts of her linen day dress to pool around her in a draping bell so as not to create a muddy mess of herself and removed her embroidered white gloves so as not to ruin them entirely. The trowel she took to the ground was plucked from the same carpetbag she'd brought everything in with in the first place.

In moments, she revealed the shallow pit of materials she had so hastily dumped, marked by dirt, damp, a bit of the ink ran on folded pages that had tumbled out from their folders.

"Not too much the worse for wear, thank God," she murmured.

All went back into the carpetbag; she'd sort it out at the office.

She stood, and with Lavinia close behind, left the churchyard. As she passed Bishop at the corner of Broadway and Wall Street, he fell into step beside her. Though the senator was a head taller than Clara, she always managed to keep up, it had been a point of pride even in her youth to do so. Poor Lavinia had to pick up the folds of her black crepe gown and trot after them.

The Eterna Commission offices on Pearl Street, near the

tip of the island, occupied the uppermost floors of a dark brick and brownstone edifice. The city records stored on the first floor gave the building its cover as a government bastion, shielding the commission's search for immortality and related supernatural matters.

The recent addition of security guards inside the front hall, iron bars, and a few clever trip wires, while unnerving and a reminder of Clara's kidnapping, gave the team a sense of increased safety about the building. Eterna's offices were as much home to her as the town house she shared with the senator down the street. They were a place of meaning, of a sacred purpose that had once been so clear and now was so muddied.

However, Clara wouldn't allow the building to carry that burden. This edifice represented a life far larger than what most women were afforded, a profession that suited her restless mind and the legacy of her past lives. She hoped to make her old adventurers and explorers proud by charting the waters of the spirit, mapping the sixth sense.

Making Louis's idea of a protective Ward created from sentiment and sediment a reality might be her great achievement in this life, provided they could put the pieces together while avoiding Louis's fate.

Once Rupert opened the new locks, Clara raced up the stairs.

"Remember the trip wire, Clara," Lavinia cautioned, taking her position behind her desk at the landing alcove, the tulle mourning veil of her black crepe hat trailing over a host of variously morbid curiosities upon the desk before draping to rest on a canopic jar.

"Right, trip wire. Thank you," she called halfway up the steps. "These new safety measures will take some getting used to, will they not?"

"Indeed," the other woman said cheerily, her bright disposition an amusing contrast to her melancholic wardrobe and fascinations. Clara had similar interests but hardly the fashion commitment.

Pausing on the landing to disable the trip wire that would lead to entrapment by rope, Clara then unlocked the wooden door of her top-floor office and swept in. She could feel the dramatic swing of her skirts as she moved about, lighting the stained-glass Tiffany lamps she so cherished: her jewel boxes of light, taking after Evelyn Northe-Stewart in thinking the whole world should be redone by their studios.

The rich hues illuminated several wooden desks and a slew of sacred talismans, many mounted on the room's plate glass windows. Clara immediately went to her rosewood beast of a desk with a bay window behind, and set down her bag. Here was her esoteric enclave built from ideas, stubbornness, and her guardian's fondness.

Bishop, a few steps behind, called to her from the landing. "Shall I work with you or fetch you a cup of coffee, Clara?"

"Both," Clara declared. He chuckled, and his footfalls retreated. The building was so quiet that she could hear the cups rattling, the maw of the coal stove clanking open.

She turned her attention to the papers she had retrieved from Trinity, spreading the material out on her desk. She plucked a thin-haired brush from a drawer filled with random implements such as Masonic tools she wasn't supposed to have or understand, a medium's séance bell, and vials of medicinal herbs used in folkloric magic.

This brush had been used to sweep debris from archaeological digs in Alexandria. New York was gaining impressive collections of that region's plunder. It had been given as a token to the senator, who passed it along to Clara, as he did any item he thought she might find interesting. Removing her gloves once more, she used the brush on the papers, dabbing at moist spots with blotting paper.

Clara traced her fingertips around the edges of the diary that held the key to Louis and Barnard's system. She and Bishop would have to put this to the test, see if they could recreate it multiple times, to protect multiple spaces. A successful Ward would need to be broadly applied.

She turned to the page of ingredients headed "The Heart of the Matter" in Louis's neat yet flowing script. He was an artist; his penmanship spoke of dreams and brilliance.

> The theory of Eterna in Spiritual Materialism is as simple as it is profound:
>> Seven ingredients are an ideal combination.
>> Separate: inert.
>> Combined: potentially the compound, and that which keeps this uniquely ours, American.
>> From these distinct, live cultures, the tether to a long life begins.
>> Herein are distinct examples of our localized compounds.

Several cities were used as examples; Clara and Bishop had already put Salem to the test in a spontaneous adventure of curiosity. The results had been inconclusive but encouraging.

They had yet to create the Ward for New York, but that *had* to be the next step, for Clara cared for her city as if it were an extension of herself.

> NEW YORK—The Economy and Engine of the Matter
> BASE MATERIALS:
>> Take from the most charged place of the city; where the striving meet the gods.

Soil of the harbor; cross—waters of the world.
Mix with the air of the center of the city.
Find haunts. Add item from scene.
ADDITIONAL CHARGED ITEMS:
Bone shards from Potter's fields.
Stone from Trinity churchyard.
A Wall Street dollar.
Final step: Burn elements collectively.

Rupert entered then, carrying two cups of coffee. He handed one to Clara before seating himself opposite her and helping her clean and organize the files.

"These are more of Barnard Smith's notes than I recall we had before," he said, pausing to sip his coffee.

"Yes, I got more of them from Columbia," Clara replied.

Bishop's familiar sigh spoke of his dislike for her doing things without telling him, but he did not pick a fight or complain, to Clara's great relief.

"Before us lies a precarious magic," Clara said softly. "Laid before us like an offering at an altar. Vital, specific keys to magic . . . What if we put it together incorrectly?"

"If Mr. Dupris has advised you to make these compounds as his papers instruct, then that is what we'll try," Bishop said, leaning toward her. "Together."

Her shoulders relaxed.

"It was never our job to save the world, Clara," he said calmly, adding, "It might just be that we have to cast a few magic spells in the right direction."

Clara smiled at his take.

Several cups of coffee later, Clara and Bishop had laid out the notes in as much of a chronological order as they could manage. The senator sat across the desk from Clara, examining the theoretical Wards pertaining to other cities and making notes in a small leather notebook of what to recommend to fellow statesmen if advising Wards as course of political action.

Clara had shifted into her musing spot, tucked into the bay window, layered mauve skirts bunched up around her like a cloud of fabric. Her eye kept resting on the New York Recipe. Testing the assembled Ward would be critical—it would mean seeing if it held up against evil. And that meant risk.

Although evil was entirely subjective, Clara was very good at sensing the tone or atmosphere of a person, place, or thing. The evil that wafted from the carvings in Mr. Goldberg's home, where the Eterna scientists had breathed their last, reeked of a particular bent, one she had sensed in a few cases nearly two years prior. Could she run an experiment in the tainted property from that older case to see if the Ward would be successful? There was no proof the case was related to what Louis endured, but Evelyn seemed to think so.

Franklin Fordham joined them in the offices, a gentle, noble-spirited man with useful powers of past insight. His psychometric touch Clara found of higher value to the team than the troubling pedestal he liked to place her upon.

"I'm glad to see you, Miss Templeton, I was worried hearing you'd had another *incident*. Downtown Manhattan is very haunted—increasingly, it seems, considering a constant influx of immigrants and deaths at countless new factories. You might want to take your walks uptown, where there is open space, cleaner air, and fewer ghosts."

She nodded as if he were saying something very sensible, got to her feet, and took a more formal seat at her desk. Lavinia swept into the room moments later in a flurry of black crepe, always dramatically herself.

"Your ladyship," she said, handing Clara a wire from the

telegraph office, bobbing her head, and retreating back down the stairs almost without pause.

Clara examined the missive.

DEAR TEAM,
ENGLAND FULL OF INTRIGUE. TEAM OF JACKS NEW
YORK BOUND. A ROVING FEW. TRAILED. OFFICES.
LOCALE VIA FORTHCOMING TELEGRAM. MURDERS
HERE RELATING TO SOCIETY. PARALLELS WITH
STEVENS OF EARLIER CASE. TRYING TO ASCERTAIN
GOVERNMENT DEPTH AND INVOLVEMENT. ACCUSA-
TORY TO US RE: BODIES OF THEIR COUNTER-TEAM.
US MOBILIZATION OF OFFENSES.

Clara sat with this news. It would seem things were about to get even more complicated.

"News from our Effie?" Bishop asked hopefully. She passed the telegram across the desk for the senator and Franklin to read. She hoped Effie hadn't had a difficult time of it, there.

Ephigenia Bixby's intrigue was doubled by her and her brother deciding to "pass" in hopes of better treatment from society. Clara and Bishop wished that was unnecessary—but that was easy for them to say. And so they simply reassured Effie and Fred that as far as Bishop and Clara were concerned, having lived as Quakers and fought for equality all their lives, the siblings were valued entirely for who they were and needn't make any other choice on their account.

Light skinned, with a dusting of dark freckles and dark eyes, Effie was a gifted field agent, efficient, autonomous, moving between races and classes with seemingly effortless skill. Clara admired her fiercely . . . and, ignorantly, coveted some of her freedom, as Bishop would never allow the same of her. She'd remarked upon that once to Effie.

Effie clucked her tongue at Clara's expression of envy and spoke with a bite. "Oh, no, people like you are too important to send out into the field; those with titles, standing, and lineage are seen and missed. I love my job, Miss Templeton, be assured. But my being 'unimportant' is a part of my success. My ambiguity and understanding of more than one social code, it all comes with a cost of feeling expendable in either world."

Clara had no idea what to say to any of that, but she didn't dare argue. Passing necessitated a complex double life. The Bixbys had seen pain and injustice in ways Clara had not, that was simple fact. They all had hope for a city that at its very best, if it held to principles and innovations, could reject cruelty, injustice, and systematic racial and cultural disenfranchisement. It was a hope for a distant future, perhaps. Clara wondered if it was any different in London.

Gazing down out her window onto the bustling waterfront beyond, she knew that New York had a very long way to go toward their hopes.

"Note a forthcoming telegram," Bishop stated. "She knows not to list direct sources of intelligence in one place. We should consider relocating our offices," he added. "Perhaps shift locations like our scientists did."

"Are any extra precautions enough if British agents are already en route to Manhattan?" Franklin asked.

Clara frowned. She liked this office. For years Eterna had gone almost entirely unremarked upon by the government, at least once the shock of Lincoln's assassination had waned. Each year, Bishop had seen that they were funded, but they went conveniently ignored. Recent events had made it clear that England found them of more interest than they'd hoped.

The important question now was how involved was

England in the unfolding evil. Was it their doing, or were they merely observing? To this, Effie offered no answers, and they didn't know how long it would be until they dealt with the Empire once more descending on their harbor.

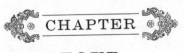
Andre Dupris abandoned the prospect of New Orleans before he even got to the great river that would have carried him home. He forsook the southbound call of the Mississippi and turned back toward the murky confluence of the Hudson and East Rivers.

Were all twins as opposite as him and Louis? Gentle Louis, fair and ardent in the understandings and practices of his mother's Vodoun principles of faith and transcendent supplication to *Bondye* and the *mystères*. Andre, a vastly more restless, complicated, unsatisfied man. During his travels in England, he had seduced more than one important English aristocrat of more than one gender. Lord Black, a friend of the variously offended, had offered him one path to redemption: Spy on what his devoted brother and Louis's Eterna Commission were up to back in the States.

Under the Eterna eaves, Andre had been exposed to a raw magic and horrific tragedy he'd never bargained for. He'd once considered himself fearless, capable of flouting all customs and circumstances. But now, he was terrified. He continually looked over his shoulders, convinced he was never alone even when he saw no one nearby. He sensed shadows watching him constantly . . . tracking him as he began his journey south.

So he retreated to New York because it had become the most familiar. Yes, there was an item Louis had stolen that he had hoped to return in person; Andre hoped the postal service would take good care of the sacred item in his stead.

Paranoid or not, valid or hallucinatory, the fact was Andre could feel presences watching him. His experience with his brother's ghost led him to think the newcomers were not of the same species. Something a great deal darker walked in the wake of Louis's death.

He never found his mother's Vodoun faith appealing. The idea of spiritual intercessors and losing oneself to song or rhythm, of giving over to anything but pleasure, wasn't his idea of how to *live*. Sensuality was Andre's patron saint. If he couldn't spend it, eat it, drink it, sleep in it, or kiss it, he counted it of little value.

Throughout their lives, the twin brothers had argued many times about who had gotten whom wrapped up in what. To himself, Andre had conceded that Louis was a "better man," but Andre always believed that he'd had more fun.

But right now, Andre was in crisis. Of faith, heart, and life itself. He stood at the rail of the ferry carrying him across the noisy Hudson River, uncertain of his next steps.

"Louis," he said, "tell me what to do. How can I help this situation? How can I shake the pall that hasn't left me since your death?"

"You called?" came a voice.

To Andre's great surprise, his brother floated before him, grayscale, slightly transparent, dressed in his solemn fashion—dark fabrics with none of Andre's brighter flair. He wore the clothes in which he had died, and Andre was end-lessly grateful that his brother's incorporeal body appeared to him whole and not desiccated.

"I did, Brother," Andre replied, shifting away from his fel-low passengers lest they think him mad, talking to the air.

Unmoved by the wind at the ferry's prow, Louis floated easily before him, the jagged, ever climbing, sooty, and scrabbling skyline of Manhattan visible through his brother's transparent gray forehead. "You can do that?" Andre asked, incredulous. "Come when called?"

His ghostly brother shrugged. "From what I understand of the laws of my transitional state, if the pull is strong enough, if the tie is blood, if the location has magnetism, I can be summoned. While others might need assistance to do so, I suspect you will always be able to draw me back. We have a deep bond, even if you never acknowledged it."

For a long moment the nearly identical faces stared at each other, solid to shade.

"I wish I'd let you know in life how much I appreciated you," Andre said quietly. "Respected you. Wanted to be like you, envied your peace . . . It's so unfair that you, the peaceful one, are now the restless ghost."

"I thought I absolved you of guilt, Brother," Louis said with a warm smile that brightened his charcoal features. "You've changed," he said, scrutinizing him, floating along after Andre as the ferry bumped against its west side docks and the passengers spilled out, teeming over lower Manhattan like a wave. Andre spoke softly as he strode onto the wooden pier that boomed with the tread of disembarking passengers.

"I have, dear brother," he agreed with weary contrition. "I accept all the complications of existence, of the mystical and spiritual."

"That is music to these dead ears," Louis exclaimed. "Oh, don't be sad," he added, with the gentle kindness that had been his way since boyhood. "Help heal what you can. Don't try to set me to rest until I've had the chance to do more work. I may be the only one who can solve certain mysteries due to ghostly access. I've never been more vital than now."

"I do want you to have peace, Brother," Andre murmured, "more than anything."

"Our destinies were always entwined. Any past selfishness of yours is redeemed by work you'll do to protect the world from deadly shadows." He paused, as if listening to a far-off voice. "I am needed elsewhere. For now, take up residence at my old apartment by Union Square. I'll haunt you there soon enough." With that, Louis vanished.

Andre sighed. His next task was crucial. He made his way to the nearest post office, nestled between grand-looking government buildings with their Federal colonnades, pulled out a dagger from his pocket wrapped in cloth, enclosed it in cardboard, and set to work on the letter that would accompany it.

My Dear Mademoiselle,

I am writing to return to you this piece, with apologies and hopes. My brother Louis took this from you and I am bid return it. Please don't curse him, or anything of the sort. You can rest assured that he has already met an untimely end, choked to death by forces I can only describe as evil. I would like to think better of you than a cruel smile and hope that, even if for a moment, you will share my grief.

While I may not be a believer in your Bondye or your mystères, I can tell good from bad. Something very bad killed my brother, who was a good man, the theft of this dagger notwithstanding.

On behalf of Louis, I know he regrets any pain he caused you. In no way did he intend to disrespect you or the tradition that this dagger represents, which I confess I know little of. In his last year on this globe, Louis discussed with me at great length how he despised the sensationalism with which Vodoun has been fetishized by white persons here in the North and by tourists in our beloved New Orleans. It's terribly uncivilized up here, for all their elite airs, and there is none of our beautiful Creole culture, at least none recognized as such.

Louis did not want your shared faith to be associated with any kind of violence or misunderstanding. If you can believe it, he was hoping that his work would help elevate Vodoun principles into scientific practices.

For my part, I believe he failed in that, but it was not for lack of trying. It was not his fault that their quest shifted from faith to "magic"—and then everything went (perhaps literally) to hell.

I hope this heals a rift.

It seems that for whatever remaining days I am afforded, I am meant to make wrongs right and smooth that which has been rent.

Louis visits me even now and advises me of a dark pall that is about to break across the country. He bids you take great care, to Ward and shield, to protect our cherished New Orleans. He is certain you can take care of her, and yourself, and all believers. He is very frightened. If a spirit is frightened, it's unsetting indeed, so take that for what you will and do act accordingly.

> *Sincerely,*
> *Andre Dupris*

He sealed the package, debated about including a return address, and decided he would, no longer wishing to live in hiding. The truth would all be out eventually.

Sending the item through an ornate golden-trimmed mail slot brought Andre a measure of peace that he hadn't felt in a very long time. Neither attempting reconciliation nor fixing messes was a usual element of his repertoire. He was sure the peace would not last, and he procured a bottle of bour-

bon before retiring to Louis's apartment. He best dealt with
spirits once he'd imbibed some.

* * * * *

O'Rourke was very nervous about Majesty Moriel's ruse. He
paced the dank hall in the back corridors of the Courts of
Justice, death ripe in the air, the crimson splatter of the de-
coy's blood bathing the stones behind him.

If the lie was not believed outright, he'd die in the spec-
tacularly gruesome way he could still note out of the corner
of his eye. He was in too deep, and spending time wondering
if he shouldn't have gotten in at all wasn't helpful at this
point. Only staying alive was.

There had been no way to win with a man like Moriel,
O'Rourke had known that right from the start. That he'd
been assigned to watch the man was mere fate. He couldn't
curse God for that. Having given up on the idea of a heavenly
father awhile back, he could only blame circumstance. And
damnable England. He could certainly blame England.

"Your Majesty . . ." O'Rourke bowed his large head.

"What's this I hear about an issue in these vaults?" came
the sharp voice of the empress.

The imperious round woman all in black was an inimitable, unmistakable presence, changing the focus of the shadowed hall as she moved swiftly through one of the Gothic
arched corridors of the Royal Courts of Justice, entering this
secret space. Just before she reached the place where the hall
narrowed as it led into the alcove outside the makeshift cell,
O'Rourke stepped forward and blocked her path. He was a
full two heads taller than the regent, yet she looked at him as
sternly and directly as if they were eye to eye.

"Out of my way," she ordered.

"I cannot let you pass, Your Majesty. Your see, it's . . .
there was some kind of . . . I don't know how to describe it,"
O'Rourke said.

"Try."

"It's . . . Moriel. Whatever evil he did, well, it seems to have caught up with him. This is no sight for your eyes, Your Majesty. Nor any man nor woman of any age . . ."

"I shall decide that for myself," the queen said curtly. She stepped forward and O'Rourke gave way. What he had concealed was immediately visible. The empress gasped and stared. From her sleeve she pulled a scented kerchief and covered her nose and mouth. When she spoke, he voice was slightly muffled. "Good God in heaven."

"Please, Your Majesty, come away from there, I cannot bear . . ." He trailed off.

It was a mistake ever to have fallen under Moriel's thrall, and he knew it now as he never had before. Seeing the rightful queen look bravely and unflinchingly at that offal . . . O'Rourke knew that Moriel would wish that kind of wretched sight upon the entire world.

"Well, at least it's justice," the queen said finally, turning away and gesturing for O'Rourke to follow her back into the broader stone corridor. "He was useless anyway, gave us nothing but a sense of misplaced devilry. I don't know why I kept him alive. We're no closer to immortality than those poor Americans in their own misguided search."

"Indeed, Your Majesty," O'Rourke said. He was tiring of the word "Majesty" and of bobbing his tall head to so many shorter, self-important folk. He wondered what, if anything, he could do to put a spoke in Moriel's gears. Perhaps the Metropolitan Police? "Pardon me, Your Majesty, but what should we *do* with this?"

The regent wrinkled her nose. "Clean it all up and burn the lot. Tell no one. Let it remain our business alone. It's good of you to keep this as hushed as you have. You're brave, Mister . . ."

"O'Rourke, Your Majesty. Jimmy O'Rourke."

"O'Rourke. You'll be commended for this."

"Thank you, Your Majesty, that is most kind of you," O'Rourke replied with a surge of desperation. "My struggling family, my little Bethany in particular, will truly appreciate it."

That was the God's honest truth. That's why he did anything. That's why it didn't matter what side Moriel was on as long as he paid out. There was a sick little girl at home whose lungs were ruined from all the factory fluff of cotton she'd breathed in since age seven when she'd started working. He'd do anything to give her a bit more ease for her last few years. Life was nothing but pain; he just wanted her not to go unto heaven in the throes of it.

"Do send a vague note to the palace alerting me that all of this is quietly gone," she declared.

"Of course, Your Majesty."

With a swift turn and swish of black bombazine and taffeta, the regent strode out as imperiously as she'd arrived. O'Rourke expected that she would, as usual, make her way quickly to a modest carriage, the average look of the conveyance ensuring her private comings and goings did not become city events.

Her footfalls faded and O'Rourke was left alone. The next shift wasn't due for another hour. More than enough time for him to think about his family. Bethany had gone to work without complaint and had worked rings around her older sister and brother. O'Rourke's son had been only twelve when he'd died at his munitions factory job. The family had barely finished mourning Joe when Beth got the cough, after only a year of work.

If immortality were real, O'Rourke thought, he'd steal it if he could and give it to his children. Just them. The rest of the world could rot in the hell it constantly created for itself. A hell where children didn't outlive their parents and there were no days of rest, no Sabbath and no Elysian fields.

If he could, he'd take them somewhere far away from the city, maybe, just maybe back to Ireland. They could work a quiet plot of land and let the rest of folk stew in their own miserable pot.

* * * * *

The Eterna team were stewing about England when Lavinia's "neutral" bell rang from below. Lavinia's particular gift was sensing intent, and three bells rang upstairs depending on what she determined downstairs: friendly, malevolent, or neutral. Upon hearing the bell, depending on her assessment, Clara then pressed a button indicating the caller could come up. Bishop rose and went to the threshold to press another button, a red knob on a newer fixture, and that disabled their fresh trip wire.

Everyone in the room stiffened as familiar company appeared at the open door. Franklin rose to his feet in a defensive posture, unsure what to expect.

Tall and handsome, with full lips and fair skin with a pale brown undertone, closely shorn brown hair, and hazel eyes whose gemlike quality was aged by dark circles ringing their hollows that bespoke ill rest, this man, Andre Dupris, had caused them all a good bit of strife.

Clara took small comfort in the fact he'd taken to wearing clothes that were not noticeably his dead brother's. Andre's style was livelier by nature, and he was dressed smartly in a russet frock coat, beige striped trousers, a black brocade waistcoat, and a golden cravat. To prove the contrast, behind Andre wafted his twin Louis, his somber grayscale not so different from the color scheme he'd worn in life. Identical in features, but so different in form and solidity.

"Dark forces are afoot," Andre stated, stepping into the room.

"You don't say," Bishop said, folding his arms. His black satin brocade frock coat sleeves sliding together offered a hiss of fabric to punctuate his statement.

Andre held up his hands in a supplicant gesture. "I haven't been the right kind of help. I'd like to be so now. I watched my brother for a very long time. I know something about it, and about what resulted. Let me help you recreate what will be useful."

Bishop, Clara, and Franklin exchanged looks. Bishop nodded. "All right." He waved Andre over to the table where everything was laid out.

Louis remained at the threshold. While Clara was fairly certain Andre was aware of his dead twin, and she could see Louis clearly, if Bishop had noticed the ghost, this time he did not make it obvious, and as she doubted Franklin had any idea, she did not call attention to him, though she could feel his ghostly gaze upon her, hot despite the chill he carried.

"Are we missing anything?" Bishop asked Andre as he perused the documents.

"That's the final draft here, for New York's Ward. At least for lower Manhattan. He thought the upper island might need something more tailored to their community. He went through several iterations."

"Have any samples been made up and stored anywhere?" Clara asked.

Andre shook his head. Out of the corner of her eye, Clara could see that Louis did, too.

"How can we test a protective Ward without inviting danger in again?" She paused, trying not to look at Louis's spectral form, which was staring at her lovingly. "But how can we *see* this is actually a Ward?"

"I've been musing about that, Clara," Louis said. "I'll discuss it with you."

Clara offered a slight nod of acknowledgment. Bishop's gaze flickered warily to the spirit, but the senator said nothing.

"Louis and I will scout for an appropriate testing site. And here . . ." He moved to Franklin's desk, which was far neater than Clara's nest, took pencil to an open notepad, and began to write. "I communicated with Lord Black via this telegraph connection. I don't know that what happened in that house of horrors had anything to do with England. England just wanted immortality; that was their sole focus. This darker ilk, I doubt you, or they, knew what they were bargaining for, what this might stir up."

He finished writing the information. Bishop nodded. "We'll wire our contact there, who will in turn offer us a read on Black and his department. Thank you. "

"I'm staying in Louis's old rooms at Union Square. I avail myself to your instructions and orders."

"By whose directive?" Clara asked. That he had lied and spied for England was known, that he still looked after his own interests first and foremost was best to assume.

Andre pierced Clara with his hazel gaze. It looked so similar to Louis in facial structure, but never had she seen such pain on Louis's dear face, not even as a spirit.

"Grief, my friends," he murmured. "By the directive of grief."

Clara just nodded and looked away. While she understood the grief, she did not wish to share in the empathy. Andre had made her uncomfortable enough impersonating Louis at first in trying to take advantage of the situation, and now he was living in his apartment . . . That place where she and Louis had shared as lively inspiration as they had passion. She wanted to be left alone while her stomach lurched.

"Good day," Andre offered.

"I will see you out, Mr. Dupris," Franklin said with an edge to his tone. "We've new security protocols going in and out of the building since we were all abducted."

"I noticed. Thank you."

The living men left but Louis remained, hovering outside the door, clasping phantom hands toward her. Clara dropped her gaze for a moment, and when she looked up, he was gone, without even a good-bye. Spirits could not be relied upon for courtesies.

Clara stared at her desk strewn with talismans, symbols of faiths and signifiers of deep mystical wisdom, its drawers full of papers, interviews, investigations, endless iterations of questions, not answers. She pressed a hand to the carved talismanic bird she wore below her chemise, against her skin, a token from Louis before his death. There was a hollowness inside her, below the pressure of that artful stone.

"I should have more to show for a life's work, Rupert," Clara said softly to the silver-haired senator.

He smiled gently. "My restless friend. Never satisfied, even when you've outpaced so many. What can we do but try, life after life, in hopes we may walk a bit taller in the next? Do you think heaven asks for a full report of each accomplishment achieved? If the angels see you doing your very best, dare we live in hope they might buffer you with a wing or a steadying hand, should you stumble? You're not expected to be a god. Relax and leave that to God." He picked up a file from her desk, brandishing it. "And keep looking for His presence in the least likely of places."

Clara smiled. "If there's paperwork in heaven, at least I can hope to be employed."

"Will you never learn the meaning of *rest,* my dear?" Bishop laughed. "Even when you've gone on to that 'sweet by and by'?"

Clara blinked up at the senator. "What has any meaning if it hasn't been worked for, *earned,* even in heaven? If I stop moving, how do I know where I'm going?"

Bishop chuckled again. "You are your own law of physics, Clara. I pity the day that your perpetual motion fails you."

She levied a knowing smile at her dear companion. "If it ever does, do send those angels you referenced, I may need a supported step."

He smiled. "Come, Clara, we have the list of ingredients for New York's Ward. Shall we attempt it? Or do you have a better idea?"

"You made a good ward of me," she said, enjoying the play upon the word. He grinned. She rose in a rustle of doubled skirts, smoothing out the layers and stays that always shifted and rearranged themselves when she moved; modern fashion was meant for women who did very little.

She went to a closet across the room, and from its dark interior pulled out a black leather doctor's bag, something they had procured from their last attempt at recreating Eterna research in Salem.

"Yes," Clara said brightly, striding toward the senator, "let's make a Ward."

They passed Franklin on the stairs and exchanged nods. Clara noticed that his eyes narrowed, clearly unhappy at being excluded from their mission. Though she and he had investigated many cases together, the spirit of the commission had always belonged to Clara and Bishop, who worked in special harmony, a music that had gotten admittedly more complicated through the years, but richer and more fascinating in tone and depth.

At the front hall, Lavinia beamed at them, looking up from a book on basic taxidermy.

"Miss Kent," Bishop stated, passing along Andre's wire instructions, "do send word to our Miss Bixby that, via this channel, she ought to invite Lord Black to diplomacy with our offices."

"That is wise, sir," Lavinia said. "I agree that England is not our enemy. If what I've been sensing is true, it's an old foe come back up from the depths, and we need allies, not spies." She shared a pained look with Clara, as Vin, too, had been a target of malevolent magic at that time; their whole office haunted in their own way.

"We're off to scare up some protections," Bishop assured the young woman. It was he who scouted her for employment after the torturous ordeal she survived made her ill fit for average society. Not that there ever had been anything average about Lavinia . . . or anyone in the office. Only a bastion of the odd could take on odds like these.

Once they were past the armed guards just inside the front door, to whom Bishop and Clara both nodded, the two walked up Pearl Street and turned toward the historic Bowling Green, angling up Broadway. It was a pleasant day for a stroll, but their quicker pace portrayed the urgency of their task.

"The 'charged' areas of the city are where we start," Bishop stated, rubbing his hands together in thought. "Where do you think to begin, Clara? We've a directive to find bone shards."

She gave it considerable thought. "Washington Square comes to mind first."

"I agree entirely," Bishop said, flagging a hansom and helping Clara up into it as he mused aloud, "Washington Square. The parade ground over the hangman's elm and potter's field. Ironic that New York placed celebratory fixtures above so many bones."

"Isn't that always the way?" Clara said, leaning back on the black leather cushion opposite him and bracing herself as they jostled up the artery of Manhattan. She stared out the carriage window for a while before breaking the silence.

"Look at the development, Rupert, goodness, the congestion and new construction. No longer is New York the backwater of earlier times. The city is moving upward, onward. "Washington Square sits caught between the old city and the new."

Disembarking at the redbrick Federal-style row of fine homes—some occupied by authors, artists, and reactionaries of note—the two walked at a slow pace under the first sets of trees and onto a demarked path across a wide swath of grass and dirt, a less tended area.

Clara took stock of the atmosphere, trying to ascertain the weight of bones beneath the surface as if trying to determine the shift in weather. "The air is volatile. Do you feel it?"

"Volatility? No," Bishop said, seeming to be tasting the breeze. "Creation, rather."

"It is an artistic enclave these days, is it not? This square?" She looked around her at the pleasant row houses that represented the first aims in sophisticated, side-by-side urban living.

"I've wanted to move here," Bishop replied.

"We'll have to move up eventually," Clara said. "Downtown has become so very crowded. I do love Pearl Street, but we should have moved a decade ago."

There was something about a fresh start that appealed to Clara. But if she and Bishop continued to live together, especially since she was obviously of age and had been for quite some time . . . Was the course obvious? She shook her head; this was not the time to think about those kinds of decisions.

They settled on a spot undergoing landscaping. Bishop scanned the ground with keen eyes that saw as much of another world as he did of this one. Clara did the same. They pointed to the same patch of earth simultaneously, as if their hands were dowsing rods and bones were water. Reaching into the doctor's bag to procure the trowel she'd used in the recent burial and unearthing, she never anticipated getting so much morbid use out of a gardening tool.

She poked at the earth surreptitiously. The occasional passerby remained undisturbed, as it merely looked like Clara had dropped something. Digging at a patch where soil had already been overturned midwork, she was able to sift bone shards out from the earth, as it had been only a couple of generations since the area had been used as a mass grave and executioner's plot.

Gathering as many vials of the shards as was easily attainable from shallow depths, Clara placed them in the doctor's bag, relieved the senator from his position as scout and mesmerist and, with a nod, they moved on.

The next items were divided between them to gather directly, though they accompanied one another on the errands as if they were the most normal and expected things of a day, like a trip to the post office or a merchant. Clara remarked upon this en route downtown once more.

"Talismans and Wards, the idea of a localized magic, is so natural to us, obvious, even, but if this works as viable protection against vile shadow, who else will take to this so easily? We can't be tasked to visit every city, to know its elements or what to gather. The continent is vast and the territories so very diverse . . ."

Bishop interrupted her worried reverie with the kind of calm, positive assurance that made him not only the most pleasant of companions but also one of the most likable men in Congress. Not an easy feat, to be a well-regarded politician.

"I've spent the entirety of my time as lawyer, congressman, and now senator taking stock of who my friends and allies really are. I'm well aware who is amenable to mysticism, spiritualism, and any discipline useful in a supernatural war."

"You've foreseen this? What happened to the researches,

the dark magic behind the forces that snuffed out their lives?"
Clara asked in a nearly accusatory manner, as if he should
have perhaps stopped something long ago.

"Of course not precisely, no, otherwise I'd have intervened. Clara, only a society that is as obsessed with death,
mysterious sciences, and mistaken piety as we are could
prompt such a backlash as what may be coming. The world
has gone looking for answers across the veil by whatever
means possible. What comes to answer those invitations often isn't a polite dinner guest. You know that.

"Why I stood by Eterna is that it is precisely *our* kind of
people—the ones who know the differences between what to
invite and what to banish—who should be asking the questions and discerning the invitations. You and I did not invite in
what ended up killing the team. An unstable mind did. Plenty
of other curious souls will submit similar calling cards out into
the void. If this Ward can protect the ignorant as well as innocent, I've taken painstaking stock of whom I can go to with the
solution we devise, so that it reaches amenable hands willing
to act for the sensible good of all, not the sensational few."

His surety was a balm, but perhaps it was still the pangs
of grief and guilt that could not settle Clara. It was good they
were active, as tasks were the only things that could keep her
calm.

For a set of dollars direct from the Stock Exchange itself,
Bishop took charge, as ladies were not allowed on the floor
of the grand building, and Clara knew his powers could subtly allow for a souvenir without much notice and awaited
him outside.

As New York's patron saint was currency, it was fitting for
its magic to include bills in a protective Ward, as the city and
its reigning powers had a habit of choosing money over
human beings. Here, the golden calf could offer its populace
some justice.

Last, but perhaps most vital, water from the harbor, life-blood of the city as it was. For this, Clara strolled down to an observation area at the Battery and hopped onto a small pier that docked a schooner meant to take ladies and school-children on leisurely sails. It was at present unmanned, and Bishop's mesmerism kept anyone curious from bothering the lady scooping harbor water into vials.

"Now then," Clara said, handing Bishop the doctor's bag and taking his proffered arm as they angled back toward Pearl Street.

Back at the Eterna offices, the guards were as silent as ever, Lavinia was buried in a new book about Egyptian funeral customs, and Franklin was out. Clara was glad to have the quiet upstairs, where she and the senator avoided placing things on her desk and opted for Fred Bixby's generally empty one, as his was as fastidious and organized as Clara's was chaotic.

Assembly was particular, painstaking, and full of emotion. And they did it all without saying a word. The weight of their old souls meant sometimes silence was best.

They used empty vials to mix the contents, and once Bishop had cut up the dollar bills into small pieces, they portioned out the contents of what they gathered into equal parts into the open tubes. Carefully parsing the ingredients, they made several combinations.

It occurred to Clara that what they were about was hardly scientific. The process was subjective and sentimental. And therein lay its power. Those looking at material assets had it all wrong. Louis didn't write "The Heart of the Matter" atop the page for nothing.

For all Louis's hope in making the reality of Eterna, that it might take his ancestor's beliefs and codify them in the annals of history for the sake of a more rigorous system exchanging witches for doctors—this was still all so personal.

How could one make the exceedingly personal into something scientific? She knew what the magic of home felt like. It would be different in any other space, sphere, or territory, and who was she to decide another area's magic?

In New York, they stood upon the grand history of the burning over.

In this century, everything had come into a stark contrast of progress and recidivism, of modernity outpacing human capacity to understand its momentum. The entirety of religion as the Western world knew it had fractured into myriad sects; warring parties or peaceable alliances, it was all a tangled, interwoven tapestry of faith and belief, of science and rumor, fashionable orders and obsession with secret knowledge. The desperate search to find answers to the age-old questions resurfacing every era.

Despite the fraught confusion of her era, Clara liked to think she knew better, that out of myriad denominational and secular camps, considering her empirical understanding of centuries of past lives, she might create a magic of general good, as broad as possible, bringing Louis's Warding system to life by cutting through noise and fear and working straightaway on heart and soul.

She went to her desk and drew out a small box of matches in a decorative silver tin and struck one, ready to light each vial and set up the awaited reaction.

Before they could complete the final step and burn the contents, waiting for the flash of otherworldly light that had accompanied their experimental Salem Ward, Franklin burst in to the offices with sobering news.

He eyed the lit match in her hand before he spoke. "There's been a fire uptown. It should be of interest to us," Franklin explained directly to Clara, "as a site you investigated during the Stevens issues years past. It's gone up in flames. The news from Centre Street depot says it was likely arson. I think we should look up that case—"

Clara blew out the match, and she and the senator said the surname in unison.

"*Stevens.* Of course," she said, darting to her desk and rummaging under what seemed like a haphazard stack, but she knew right where to look and held up the file in question. The similarities to the Goldberg property, the carvings and invitation to evil, were too glaring a parallel to be coincidence.

At the Stevens property, a chemical powder had been set to blow out into the city, rigged from within the building. This powder was a toxin that would make ordinary citizens mad, a diametrically inverting chemical agent that would turn the placid into the monstrous and make beasts of the benign for as long as the chemical remained in their system. The command was never released, thanks to a group of brave people, including Evelyn Northe-Stewart and Lavinia Kent, who had put a stop to it.

"Bring a few vials along, Clara," Bishop instructed. "If it's *that* property, we may have an opportunity to test a Ward in a dangerous place . . ."

Nodding, she put stoppers in three glass tubes and wrapped them in a handkerchief embroidered with primroses plucked from her center desk drawer. She placed the contents in her "work reticule," a wooden-edged box lined with velvet, reserved for carrying delicate but bulkier things while maintaining a ladylike appearance. Most useful, considering her position in society. Clara could not be seen to be working.

"Mr. Fordham, hold down the fort with Miss Kent. You know where we'll be if you need us, and we'll send a patrolman if we need you," Bishop said with the calm surety of leadership. Franklin nodded and it was obvious to Clara that he was biting his tongue at being left behind yet again. She could do nothing to change the dynamic. She and Bishop worked as partners and always had, even though Franklin was closer to her age and also gifted, and while Bishop had hired him to be the work partner his schedule in Congress couldn't reliably offer, nothing could match the synergy with which she and the senator managed their business.

* * * * *

After the great downtown fire of 1845, most buildings were required by law to be built primarily of brick and metal, to reduce the likelihood of fires razing whole blocks and neighborhoods. So the brick-based address, on Park Avenue just north of Grand Central Depot, was a contained blaze, but it burned black and hot. Crossing the wide street and pausing on the median, Clara could see the great-wheeled fire pumpers and attached hoses, firefighters doing their best to address the highest flames on the second floor.

A sudden thought alarmed Clara. She whipped a daintily embroidered handkerchief out of her buttoned sleeves and held it over her nose and mouth.

"Rupert, cover your nose and mouth. *Now.*"

He did, using his own, larger, white handkerchief. The tone she had used made him take orders without hesitation.

"The chemical agent utilized in earlier attacks may still be present in the building," Clara explained. "The flames may have sent it airborne. We can't know if it's inert or might still prove a maddening toxin to anyone nearby. Can you get the men to do the same as a precaution?"

"Very wise, Clara." Bishop strode to the captain of the fire brigade, and moments later his men began to find ways to cover their mouths and noses. Bishop returned to her side. "I suggested that from an earlier police case, there might be a poison in the air but gave few other details."

Clara turned at a tap upon her elbow and turned to find a familiar brown-skinned face looking up at her.

"Josiah!" Clara exclaimed. "Did Mr. Fordham send you here?"

"Yes, ma'am, he did," the boy replied. "I always check in with him after he meets with the policeman on beat. He told me to come see if you all would be needing anything."

"Hello, young man," Bishop said with a fond smile.

"Senator," Josiah replied, ducking his head.

"Did Franklin pay you downtown?" Clara asked. The boy thought a moment.

"Yes, ma'am, he did so, but thank you for asking."

Bishop fished in his pocket and handed a dollar to the boy. "That's for telling the truth rather than saying he hadn't," Bishop said. The boy blinked up at him, taking the dollar and tucking it carefully in his pocket.

"My gran's got what some call the gift. She can tell straight if anybody lies. If I'm not mistaken, you have the gift, too, Senator, sir, so I'd best not try my luck," he replied, getting a chuckle out of both Bishop and Clara. Fishing in the other pocket, Bishop handed over a quarter.

"And *that's* for being clever," he said as the young man beamed. "Stay close. I am sure I'll be wanting Evelyn's advice and I may need her to come 'round."

"Yes, sir, I'll be right here for you."

"You always are," Clara said with deep fondness.

Josiah lived in the Tenderloin, a neighborhood where the blood running in the streets wasn't just that of pigs or cattle. Injustice was a constant in the area, and Clara and Franklin were desperate to keep their favorite assistant busy, employed, and away from routine danger as much as possible. Josiah was reliable, quick, sharp, kind, and had lots of ears in different circles.

The boy didn't know all the secrets of Eterna, but he knew

enough to keep quiet. From a family lineage where gifts were understood, he kept his wits about him when it came to the paranormal. Clara had made Bishop promise he'd find steady employment for the lad when he was old enough; she disliked the idea of errand runners and wanted to make them fully staff instead.

A sunken-eyed, sallow-faced man, wearing a threadbare suit under a stained leather apron, his graying brown hair unkempt beneath a tattered cap, broke from the shadows of the neighboring building. He dashed through the cluster of onlookers and suddenly seized Clara by the arms, shaking her violently. She cried out in protest.

"You have to stop this," the man gasped. "Help me. Help yourselves! I thought it would end but it never ends . . . the cycle won't quit—"

Bishop pried the man off, and two patrolmen were instantly at his side to offer additional aid. The look of recognition on Bishop's face made Clara study her attacker's features, and in an instant, she placed him.

This tortured soul was "Doctor" Stevens himself—a self-taught purveyor of chemical "remedies" that healed nothing. The man looked like he hadn't slept in a year—and perhaps he hadn't. Held firmly by the two officers, Stevens stared pointedly at Clara. She'd last seen him at his trial, where she'd testified against him after what she'd seen inside the house in question: floor carved in grim, apocalyptic texts, and gadgets and powders everywhere, intent on harming the neighborhood.

"Is the city in further danger?" Clara demanded. "Will the old chemicals within spread with smoke?"

Stevens shook his head. "It doesn't survive water or fire. It's active when in the lungs. Listen to me. What's thought to be dead *cannot* be killed. The Society lives. Its tendrils have spread. The ivy is thick. They're into growing industries and will find ways to do as much damage as possible. I don't know what'll go first," Stevens exclaimed. "Possibly electric companies, highly volatile, the present 'war of the currents.'"

"What is this about?" Bishop asked, gesturing to the fire.

"I'm trying to take care of anything I was involved with," Stevens said plaintively. "Burn it all. I've not much time. The demons will come for me. I might not last the night. . . ."

At this, the senator turned to her. "Clara," he said slowly, an idea dawning, "him . . . he's how we test the Ward."

"Oh. Why, yes." The suggestion made complete sense to her.

Wide-eyed, Stevens said, "What is it? I'll do whatever you need. I've no hope nor shame left."

"It's your turn to be a test subject, Mr. Stevens," Bishop said with a grim smile.

"The sooner the better, then," Stevens replied mordantly.

Bishop turned to Josiah. "Reverend Blessing and Evelyn Northe-Stewart. Dispatch them straightaway to the inn southeast of Madison Square where you've sent associates before, please, my good young man."

Josiah nodded and was off like a shot. Bishop assured the officers they could return to their business. They did so silently, seemingly glad to be rid of the strange conversation. Clara groaned as a familiar presence strode up to her with an inappropriate directness, always managing to catch her, or perhaps waiting for the precise moment, when Bishop was not at her side.

"Why, Miss Templeton, if *you're* here, this is no ordinary fire." Peter Green, a mousy-haired investigative journalist, an annoyingly ardent admirer of Clara, and a royal thorn in Eterna's side approached in an obnoxious green plaid coat. "If I recall correctly, this has to do with an old case of yours . . ." Notebook in hand, he nodded at Stevens with obvious curiosity.

"You've a distressingly accurate memory of things I've

been involved with, Mr. Green, and as usual, I am not at liberty to discuss any particulars or insights," Clara retorted.

"Then set me loose on the trail of something interesting," Green replied.

"Women's suffrage," Clara countered. "Garment district fires. Slum overcrowding—"

Green made a face. "I don't work for the radical rags, Miss—"

"Since when is a basic human right and safety radical—"

"War of the currents," Stevens interrupted. "If threatening forces are infiltrating industry, as I believe they are, scouting for evil amid the most groundbreaking of technologies would be wise."

Clara glanced at Mr. Stevens and back to Green, noting that Bishop was striding back to their cluster, scowling at the presence of the unwanted.

"Mr. Green, how many times have I insisted that you not pester my ward—"

"We're just about to send him off in pursuit of something *interesting*," Clara interrupted. "He'll scout for anything particularly odd or infernal infiltrating this city's burgeoning electrical grid, won't you, Mr. Green? Give it time. I don't want to see you for a good long while, so dig deep and make yourself scarce but useful for a change."

Green set his jaw. Whether he would or wouldn't comply didn't matter, having him gone was the thing. In her years fending him off, he found her independence and the fact she held a job—beyond the acceptable female occupations of clerk, nurse, or teacher—a bit too fascinating and novel for her taste. She didn't want to be his journalistic model for the new woman. She just wanted to be herself, to live free, equal, and in pursuit of noble work without judgment.

"If you'll excuse us." Bishop led her and Stevens away from the frustrated Green.

"Mr. Stevens," Clara began as she and Bishop flanked their subject, walking away at a clip from the now controlled blaze, "tell us how you came to this terrible place, these dire acts, and what you expect of the night to come. You say you won't last the night. How so?"

"The Summoned are coming," Stevens warned, "and from what I understand, if you have turned on them, they will tear a body to smithereens."

Clara winced.

Stevens continued, "For those involved in Society business, to leave or defy it is certain death. It is only a matter of time for me, just like everyone on Tourney's list. The last of the ring were dying even as I left England to clean up my old mess here. Now that I accept death, any moment left of life I spend trying to mitigate my time in hell."

Clara glanced at Bishop, who nodded. She spoke carefully. "I've three Wards that we believe—we hope—can provide protection. But they can be useful only if released into a neutral space—one that hasn't been tainted by invitation to devilry."

"Unlike that damned spot I set fire to," Stevens said with a nod.

"Are there other properties to cleanse—I hope not all by arson?" Clara asked.

Stevens shook his head. "The police did a good job with that before. I don't think there are any further portals, but I wasn't the only operative and we never met as a group." He took a breath and spoke again, sounding almost like a professor giving a lecture. "You may remember from the trial, Moriel's Master's Society champions three types of mortal offenses: soul splitting, reanimation, and chemical alteration.

"These serve as 'offerings' to the shadows that Moriel summons from the depths. They also serve as weapons. That will be the next phase—full deployment of all three."

Clara held back a shudder. "Where?" she pressed.

"I'm not sure how widespread. I know London and New York are the chief targets, along with several other industrial cities. You're a senator, Mr. Bishop, you have to warn your colleagues."

"So it would seem," Bishop said grimly. "Tell me, is the British government involved in the Society, or is it its own entity?"

"I do not believe its acts are sanctioned by the Crown, though Society leaders were all aristocracy. I had very little contact with them when I was in England, just kept my head down and nodded to the occasional demon-possessed body spying on my shop."

Clara's few investigations had only scratched the surface of the issue. She wondered who in England might be feeling the same way—like a failure for not having seen the bigger picture.

They soon reached a merchant boardinghouse, a fine-looking brick edifice with brownstone detailing.

"Take a room there facing the street," the senator ordered. "My associates and I will be in the inn across the way," he added, waving at the building opposite.

"I will light a candle in a front window of whatever room I have taken," Stevens said.

Clara handed over the vials, clasping her hands over Stevens's. This simple kindness seemed to move him nearly to tears. Recalling Louis and Barnard's notes, she said, "It might be helpful to add something personal to one of the vials, something meaningful to you, since the dark forces seem re-lational . . ." He nodded. She kept her hands upon his, allow-ing a flow of her own life force to charge the items. "To active the Ward, light it afire."

Stevens laughed hollowly. "I shan't have any trouble with that."

"It should burn strangely," Clara explained. "That's the hope, an effervescence more than a flame."

Bishop added quietly, "While we will be nearby, I cannot promise we'll be able to help if there is an issue."

"This is my cross to bear, unfortunately," the tired man said with a sigh. "But I take it up willingly and will try to make something right of this if I live." He turned away, holding the vials as though they were sacred relics.

"We will pray for you," Bishop assured him.

Stevens turned at the stoop. "That's more than I deserve, sir, but I'm grateful."

They crossed busy Twenty-third Street to the grander, taller-storied building opposite, an angled stone's throw from Madison Square. A boutique inn rather than boardinghouse, the premises were more intimate than the bustle of one of the area's fine hotels, which would not have suited their purposes.

The hostess knew Bishop upon sight due to more recent business meetings conducted under the eaves of her tavern but had to put the pieces together on Clara.

"Senator, sir, and . . . Miss Templeton, it's been years, haven't you grown up beautiful! Business of the state or a bit of holiday?" the elder, round-cheeked woman said with a smile from beneath a wide lace bonnet.

"If I'm on holiday, Mrs. DeWitt, I'm loath to leave my house as I don't see the place enough," Bishop declared. "This is business. Is a suite looking out over Twenty-third Street available? With an adjoining room for Clara?"

"One just opened up," the innkeeper replied. "Any special requests?"

"Two additional associates of mine, Mrs. Evelyn Northe-Stewart and Reverend Blessing, are en route. Do let them in, their presence is most valued."

"Of course, Senator," Mrs. DeWitt said, handing him two keys.

The finely furnished second-floor rooms, connected by a door that Bishop unlocked and flung open, smelled of fresh flowers. Their white lace and damask fabric–covered furnishings stood in sharp contrast to the thoughts of dark, demonic shadows ready to descend upon their nearby test subject.

Clara looked out over the hectic cacophony that was Twenty-third Street and noted the lit candle in a window opposite, also on the second floor. "There he is."

A form was at the window. Was it a demon, or Stevens? She waved. He waved back.

"Clara," Bishop admonished, "don't let him know which *room* we're in—"

"He knows we're here, Rupert, and in a room that faces a window. There are only so many—"

"I don't want him running *directly* to you with a demon in tow. . . ."

"Then why did you call in Reverend Blessing, if we won't *try* to help Mr. Stevens?" Clara said, aghast at the thought. Bishop stared at her and after a long moment, sighed as he smiled.

"My heart. Always reminding me of the right thing to do, even when I'm doing what I think is best to protect you."

His smile drew one from her, which turned into a blush. She moved away and made a show of inspecting her room so that he didn't see her color.

It wasn't long before their friends arrived: Evelyn, whom Clara had seen so recently, and the fascinating Reverend Blessing, ever dressed in the black vestments and white cleric's collar of his Episcopalian faith. It had been a long while since they had met. Entering the room, the tall, dark-skinned man with hints of gray in his short black hair offered Clara a smile as big as his heart.

Evelyn had introduced them to the reverend; she'd met

him at various charity functions and they became allies in the Spiritualist community. A black priest who worked as a hospital and National Guard chaplain as well as substitute preacher in a diverse range of communities throughout the city, Blessing helped the others understand the communities that were not part of their elite world, and did so with love and impressive stores of patience. The reverend had been experiencing an increasing call toward exorcisms.

"Did Josiah come in with you?" Clara asked Evelyn.

"No, he had to wait out front," the older woman said with a deep scowl. "The woman at the door didn't even seem to want to let Reverend Blessing in, and insisted she had clearance to admit only two."

Clara donned Evelyn's scowl and darted downstairs immediately. Striding past Mrs. DeWitt, she opened the front door and found Josiah standing on the stoop. When he saw her, his face lit up. She gestured him in. He shook his head, his expression saying everything. The landlady must have made it very clear his kind were not welcome.

Using her body as a shield, Clara made a rude gesture toward DeWitt that the woman couldn't see. Josiah giggled— a sound Clara loved dearly—and hesitantly stepped over the threshold. She scooped up the skinny boy in her arms and gave him a smacking kiss on the cheek, at which he laughed outright before whining in protest.

"Aww, Miss Templeton, come now, what's that for?" he said, wiping his cheek but still grinning as she sat him down.

Out of the corner of her eye she could see DeWitt staring at them in horror; this gave her some distinct satisfaction.

"Because you're the most helpful, useful young man in the world. The senator and I consider you family and I want *everyone* to know it." She shot a pointed look at DeWitt. Josiah seemed somewhat stunned by her praise. Clara turned back to him and spoke more softly. "Now, if you would be so kind to finish off your work by telling Franklin everything that's happened today, and where we are should he need us, I would be most appreciative. He owes you double for all this back-and-forth."

"Yes, ma'am, thank you."

She put her hands on her knees to match his height, looking intently into his wide brown eyes. "You stay safe and take care out there, Joe. I do worry over you."

"Don't worry, Miss Templeton, Reverend gave me a special blessing!" he said with another big grin. He darted out the door and took off down the street, turning back once to wave, which Clara returned.

As Clara headed back upstairs, she saw that DeWitt was trying to pretend she hadn't been staring.

"New York City," Clara mused pointedly as she climbed the stairs, loud enough to be sure the proprietor heard every word. "Full of the most interesting people in all the whole world, and none so beautiful as every kind and race of child."

Entering the room upstairs, Clara found her associates deep in discussion.

The reverend punctuated Bishop's explanation of Wards with his declaration: "The Lord's weaponry has to be as varied as mankind's capacity to invent horrors." Rising to his feet, he drew an ornate silver dispenser from his breast pocket and cast a bit of holy water about the room.

They set a designated watch, but the night grew so very quiet that eventually they all drifted off where they sat.

* * * * *

The next morning, they awoke to pouring rain and a knock on the door. Mrs. DeWitt said, "There's a Mr. Stevens downstairs, asking to see you. Excitable man, I gave him a cup of tea to calm him."

Clara clapped her hands to her mouth, tears leaking immediately out her eyes.

"It worked!" she exclaimed. Bishop embraced Clara with a joyful laugh, then Blessing and Evelyn in turn before turning to address the increasingly disturbed proprietor.

"Thank you, madame," Bishop said as the foursome swept past, descending into the low-ceilinged, cozy pub on the first floor. Stevens sat glassy-eyed beside a lit hearth that was working to take the dampness off the wet air.

"Well. You survived!" Clara stated excitedly as everyone gathered around.

Reverend Blessing stepped near and, without a word, inspected Stevens closely. Clara knew Blessing was looking for signs of demonic possession. He'd seen enough of it in his day.

Stevens bore the scrutiny without shrinking, even allowing the reverend to peer into his eyes for longer than was comfortable. Finally, Blessing nodded and made the sign of a cross over the man. Stevens reacted as if he'd been dying of thirst and the clergyman had given him a drink of water.

Once they were all served—tea, strong coffee, and some sweet breads—Clara leaned in and said, "Do tell us what passed last night. Quietly, please."

"We've already made a stir with our mixed company," Blessing added in a murmur rather than his usually sonorous voice. "Let's not compound the issue with overheard discussions of demons." Evelyn and Bishop nodded in support, and all eyes turned to Stevens.

"The Wards. It's fascinating," Stevens whispered excitedly. "You're right about the need to make it personal, Miss Templeton, and thank you."

He took a deep breath and memory passed over his face like a black cloud. "The Summoned came for me. Deep, dark shadows, the stuff of true nightmares. The shadows are part of this work and always have been. But no one can truly be prepared when they come for you." He shuddered and stared into the fire for a long moment.

"Go on. This is vital, Mr. Stevens," Clara urged. "Truly vital."

He nodded and resumed with renewed vigor, obviously heartened by her encouragement. "Your initial Ward kept them at the foot of my bed, no closer, Miss Templeton, and there's a congratulations in that."

Clara looked around for Louis, to see if he heard the good news that his work was a lifesaving success, but her ghostly paramour was nowhere to be seen.

"But there was no banishment," Stevens continued. "A Ward is helpful in keeping danger at bay, surely, but what about banishment? As a child, I used to see ghosts. The more I told them to go away, the less they came, until one day I didn't see them anymore. Unfortunately, these dark forces are no ghosts. They need a force equal to their own, something to push back against.

"The trouble was finding *my* magic," he said, looking each of them in the eye, as if he was living for the very first time. "What could I call sacred and personal when everything had gone so dark and horrid?"

He showed them a small, ragged-edged daguerreotype of a woman. "My aunt, who raised me. She'd always been sickly, but she never made a worry over it, not a sound really, just suffered all her life in silence. When she died, I resolved to go into chemistry and see if I could make people's aches and pains go away. Then I was lured into the Society. I lost track of the reason for my work."

He indicated a torn edge of the remembrance. "I put the corner of Auntie's likeness into the second mixture Miss Templeton afforded me, along with a strand of my hair, and the whole of a pendant of St. Luke I'd been given as a child. I wasn't named for the saint, but Auntie insisted, 'Luke, you'll be the death of me, please wear this to protect you, you impetuous boy . . .'" Tears in his red-rimmed eyes spoke of ill health and strain.

"The chain broke long ago, but I always carried the medallion in my pocket. Because it meant something to her, it meant something to me. And who knows, maybe it's helped keep me alive thus far. I put that right into the vial. Lit it all up, as you said—the catalyzing power of fire I know well. I looked the Summoned in their nonexistent faces and said, 'No, I will not be taken.' And wouldn't you know it . . ."

Stevens, either a born storyteller or, like Ebenezer Scrooge, he was reborn unto a new personality after the most harrowing test, had his audience all leaning in and their teas and coffees gone cold.

"They hesitated, there," Stevens went on, "as if confused, clearly reluctant to be sent off. The vial lit up brighter than any fire. Once the contents had been reduced to ash,—save the saint, he of course weathered the elements without tarnish—I threw the contents at them and they vanished, as if I'd blown them out like a candle. Wisps of blackness, then nothing."

Everyone collectively took a breath.

"And then," Stevens continued, "I slept. I honest to God slept, for the first time in years. It's a miracle, whatever is up there in the heavens be praised."

"Indeed. I only hope this is a result we can repeat," Clara stated.

"How do we know you're telling the truth?" Bishop asked pointedly. Stevens stared at the senator with more earnestness than she'd ever seen, perhaps the expression of a man on the gallows suddenly reprieved.

"He is," Evelyn said firmly. "The spirits assure me." She

turned to Stevens. "Your Auntie Mim is proud of you. She forgives you for the candlesticks. She knows you were just trying to afford a nice gift for the girl, she's sorry it didn't work out."

Stevens burst into sobs. Evelyn blinked as if coming out of a reverie. Clara knew, from years attending séances with her and Bishop, that Evelyn was often unable to stop the spirits from using her to send messages. Everyone took to their cold tea and coffee until Stevens regained himself. Blessing offered his handkerchief, at which Stevens mumbled thanks.

"How can I next help?" the haunted man said suddenly. "I was prepared to die. And I am still, but if it is not my time yet, let me further your causes while I can."

This redemption helped Clara feel that her Eterna hadn't entirely done harm.

"Help us make more Wards," Clara said. "We'll need to place them all over New York, and people may have to learn to make their own, depending on how widely these 'Summoned' attempt to permeate."

"I should be happy to," Stevens said, "but I've no place to live at present. Everything I had belonged to the Society—"

"My mission includes rescuing animals," Blessing said. "I've a kennel uptown with a small shack on the property. If you are willing to look after the animals, particularly the dogs, you may live there. Help with the Wards, and, if there's any more of that dread toxin that you unleashed upon this city, you'd best make up a cure."

"Gladly," Stevens replied.

"Good, then, get to it. Thank you, Reverend," Bishop said, rising, handing a bill to the disapproving innkeeper who did well enough to keep quiet.

"I'll escort you to the place," Blessing said to Stevens. "I hope you like dogs. Between Henry Bergh and I, and our

ASPCA associates, we've rescued more than we can easily take care of ourselves."

"That will be a joy as well, Reverend," Stevens stated earnestly.

"Our associate will bring you the 'recipe' for the Wards," Bishop told him, "and you'll be responsible for collecting the necessary items. Depending on how many we'll need, you'll have help. You'll be checked upon regularly, if you even think—"

"As long as I live, you'll have my thanks, service, and loyalty," Stevens said.

* * * * *

Clara kept calling hours. Not because she was being courted or because she was so woven into the social fabric of New York society that she needed such formalities, but she did have a valued associate who preferred tea and sumptuous fabrics to the hard chairs and inconveniences of an office.

Years earlier, Mrs. Evelyn Northe-Stewart had explained, in a conversation over dinner, "Rupert, the girl needs calling hours. She needs a *semblance* of being a lady, of tending to the duties expected of her. That office you've put her up in is hardly conducive to the kind of talk ladies need to have to really get to the heart of matters. We need to be surrounded by lace and demure comforts, so that in a world owned by men, we appear inoffensive while we slowly and sweetly move to dominate."

This had made Bishop grin and his eyes light up. Clara had instituted the policy that week.

It was Evelyn who had been Clara's primary visitor in the years since. Clara had few acquaintances and fewer friends; the nature of her work and her epileptic condition kept society, and much of the rest of the world, at bay. And it was Evelyn who came to call the day after Stevens had gone off with

Blessing, with a familiar face in tow, a young woman displeased at having been brought along.

The housekeeper let Mrs. Northe-Stewart and her daughter-in-law into the fine parlor, where Clara had opened the curtains wide. It being another gray day, the light did not hurt her gold, delicate eyes as much as bright sun did. While Clara was hardly a shrinking violet, she was a "sensitive" in nearly every meaning of the word.

Clara greeted Evelyn and Lady Denbury warmly, the former, elegant and statuesque, always at the cutting edge of fashion, the latter, pretty, auburn haired, and dressed in similar finery, likely at the advice of her stepmother, helping a middle-class girl who had married above her station. The younger woman looked tired, and Clara doubted it was because of the young child at home. Natalie Whitby, Lady Denbury, displayed the kind of weariness that comes from nightmares and spiritual unrest.

The housekeeper brought them tea.

"How are you feeling, Clara?" Evelyn asked in her best maternal tone. "Have you had your . . . visitation?"

"I have." They hadn't had time to discuss Louis since the medium had connected his spirit to Clara. "It's been informative. Hard, but . . . carrying on Louis's work is what I am meant to do." She spoke circumspectly, for there were things Clara didn't feel comfortable saying to anyone other than Evelyn.

"There's much you may be meant to do, Miss Templeton," Lady Denbury said in an encouraging tone.

"Clara, please, Lady Denbury," Clara insisted, not for the first time.

"Natalie, then, Clara," the young woman replied, somewhat to Clara's surprise. Her voice shifted, becoming less personal. "I'm here because I'm having nightmares, and as you may recall—"

"They're portents," Clara said.

"Yes."

Clara readied herself for yet more difficult news. "Well. Do tell."

"I've had . . . visions . . . of a man . . . in a cell," the young woman said slowly, her cheeks flushing in frustration and shame. "Bear with me as I speak, I beg you. Selective Mutism no longer keeps my tongue in shackles . . . but . . . when speaking of the horror, I sometimes seize up."

"Oh, Natalie, how I understand," Clara assured her. "I seize up quite literally when surrounded by supernatural on-slaughts, I uniquely empathize. Continue when ready and comfortable. I am grateful you're here. I know you wanted nothing to do with this after your case was settled."

Lady Denbury nodded. She took a sip of tea and visibly collected her nerves, squaring her shoulders, her bright eyes sharpening with determination. When she continued, her speech was much more fluid.

"I didn't. And I hate that my husband remains in London. I hate that anything has been asked of him. But that's not your fault, Clara." She took another deep breath before con-tinuing,

"To the nightmare. I saw . . . Moriel, to be specific, the ringleader of the Master's Society. There were images of pure torture, along the lines of the experimentation we dealt with ourselves, but now burgeoning on an almost, I shudder to think, *industrial* scale. Moriel planted harrowing, horrid seeds and the trees of his work bear fruit of the highest evil."

"He is not dead, then?" Clara said, aghast. "Was Moriel not sentenced to death in England?"

"Perhaps he was, but we don't know for certain," Evelyn replied. "We all thought Stevens was done for, after all."

Looking older than her years, Lady Denbury shifted in her chair. "The beast's petty, personal motive against my husband has been supplanted by something far greater. My dream may not be literal, but that which Moriel woke gathers again. One can never truly kill evil, just displace it for a time." She leveled her gaze at Clara. "My telling you of this is the extent of my involvement. I cannot have the demons sniffing about me, my house, my husband or, Christ forbid, my child."

"Agreed, Natalie, entirely," Clara said. "Well, then. I've been feeling a burning need to go to London. This confirms it. When should I leave?"

"Don't act hastily," Evelyn cautioned.

"I'm not being hasty. When action is incited, when a chess piece is placed upon the board, why, if I make a countermove, am I hasty? You and Rupert—"

"Clara, it isn't only the timing. I've a caution for you."

Clara pursed her lips. "What else have I done?"

"Don't be so quick to be defensive," Evelyn scolded. "This is something I foresee. You are a captivating spirit, and people and forces are drawn to you. Be careful the company you keep."

The medium refilled her teacup, speaking in a measured tone that Clara could not ignore. "Every morning that God grants us, the universe offers a finite amount of energy. Every day is a choice in how vitality is utilized. Hope is measured against practicality, dreams pitted against fears, indulgences weighed against sacrifices. Love strains against loss. Every day our angels battle our demons.

"To rise to such challenges is a daily election, each day a new opportunity, and we must surround ourselves with fellow soldiers who make the decision to fly with us rather than entrench us deeper into a squelching pit."

Clara allowed this wisdom its appropriate breadth and space. After a moment, she sought further clarity. "Are there those around me now who seek to drag me down?"

"Perhaps. Those who may need more than you are able to give. Be careful of excess weight."

Clara nodded, unsure whom Evelyn might mean. The woman's message needed to be taken in and digested, like a hearty meal.

"London has its thrall," Evelyn added. "It is a captivating city. I adore it. But home is here." Her expression was far away, wrapped up in old memories that she did not disclose.

As the ladies sipped tea, Evelyn asked questions about her grandchild. Fighting the Society had resulted in a few romances and increased families, despite all its horror.

Clara knew with the same certainty of her past lives that she was not to have a child herself, similar to Evelyn. Sometimes those with gifts had to be different kinds of mothers to the world, in ways the world would not expect, and likely not often understand.

The women took their leave, and Clara read the notes she'd kept in a personal diary around the time of the Stevens trial, and notes on an earlier interview with Lady Denbury, then just a mere museum curator's daughter. It had been only a couple of years, but they felt like lifetimes past. She made some new notes about this recent talk.

That evening Clara nearly fell asleep at her writing desk at home, slumping over, so she shifted into bed, and it was the rare night when slumber took her swiftly, the moment she lay down. She was awoken only by the eerie, strange sounds of electrical surges from Edison's nearby power plant, and she hoped there wouldn't be another disaster on the street that night.

* * * * *

G. Brinkman—a man who went by many various names— awaited his current quarry on Pearl Street.

He had already advised Lord Black that this man might be of use as a weapon when the black tide of Master's Society terror was finally ready to pour forth from the floodgates that had been for years now merely experimental.

Brinkman liked to think he was at the center of all important goings-on. He'd had his hand, one way or another, in a great deal of the Empire's successes industrially and internationally. Not that it came with honors; his work was private, quiet. So then was his pain, loss, terror, and constraint. The Crown would never know or understand what drove him to the lengths he would have to go.

Electricity was of present interest to the Crown, who wished to make sure that electrical advancements were not solely the province of their upstart colony breeding so much innovation. However, the Crown was content that the progress was always tethered home, just like the first transatlantic cable bearing the first Morse code. Babe America would always reach out to Mother England. The Brooklyn Bridge would open on Queen Victoria's birthday next year. America wanted to show off, the rebellious youngster caught between trying to make its elders proud or jealous.

Brinkman's service had included speaking to the managers of every English electrical company and reporting anything out of the ordinary.

There were plenty of newfound "sciences" that inventors were keen to say would change the world. Brinkman believed electricity was one of the rare fads that actually might live up to their threats, and the man on the other side of this town house door knew all about it, could wield it, and had likely already killed with it.

Thin, gangly, boyish, with a struggling mustache and nondescript limp light brown hair, the man behind the glass of the front door looked younger than he reportedly was. Slowly he opened the door.

"What," he said flatly.

"Come with me, Mr. Mosley, if that even is your name, or

was it taken from Mosley Street after its first electrical lights?"

Mosley gave a thin-lipped, threatening smile. "I can hurt you without touching you."

"Current quicker than a bullet, is it, then?" Brinkman asked, gesturing to draw Mosley's attention to the gun in his rubber-gloved hand. "Is that an experiment you're willing to try?"

"What do you want?" Mosley asked, fear replacing bravado.

"Information. You're too valuable to kill, but I can wound something terrible. I suspect a metal bullet won't feel at all comfortable lodged in a body full of electricity. I am actually trying to help keep you out of the hands of those who would wish to do terrible things with your admittedly gruesome talents."

Defeated, Mosley said, "Come in, then, and say what you have to. At some point someone will see a man pointing a gun at a front door and trot over to the Centre Street police station. Keep the gun pointed if you must, but I'm not going with you anywhere. I don't let bullies tell me where to go."

Brinkman set his jaw and walked inside, closing the door behind him with a rattle of leaded glass and the thump of hard wood.

Mosley had backed down the hall, facing Brinkman, and stood before a tall rear window nearly his whole height, a wide, arched frame that looked onto a struggling and sad little plot where grass had been singed along paths he assumed were electrical wires. Backlit by a harsh sun, Brinkman could really see only the glint of the young man's eerie eyes, and so he raised his gun a bit, into a shaft of light, just as a reminder.

"What can you tell me about the New York City electrical grid and what might be trying to gain undue access to it?"

Mosley cocked his head to the side. "What can *you* tell me about the grid? And isn't it premature to call it something so organized, when it's anything but?"

"I thought I was coming to speak with the expert, so that's why I'm asking."

"I'd like to know where you heard that. My being 'the expert.'"

Brinkman could smell the man's paranoia from across the room. He shrugged casually. "I've my sources. There's someone at the Edison plant who seems keenly interested in you."

At the name "Edison," something flickered in the young man's eyes, a hunger, but he recovered a mask of indifference. "I am my own source," Mosley retorted.

"You'd be quite the prized experiment, you know," Brinkman said slowly, "if the wrong person—or *society*—got hold of you. There's a group I'm following that would *love* using you in theirs. They are actively looking for those like you—"

"There's no one like me!" the man cried.

Brinkman noticed a subtle movement, a shadow, at the window. Before he could say or do anything, a crashing sound came from behind the young man, and in a swift and terrifying motion, Mosley was seized, as if flown backward, through splintering glass and wood, into the arms of an enormous man in a long dark coat, his face broad and cruel, eyes no longer human but bloodshot with wide black irises.

The last thing Brinkman saw before he saw only the brick wall opposite the now broken arch, was Mosley's uncannily youthful face staring at him as his body was suddenly airborne, staring out as if Brinkman were no longer the enemy but his only source of help. And then he and his abductor were gone, spirited away with preternatural speed.

"Damn this whole business to eternal hell," Brinkman growled, spitting on the worn wooden floor strewn with broken glass.

He followed, carefully navigating the glass as he ducked his head behind the house to determine the course of escape. The rear courtyard, if one could call such a sad shaft that, was enclosed all in differing colored bricks from the various row houses or businesses, and only an open gate to an adjoining whitewashed brick edifice offered any clue as to where Mosley had been seized by the possessed body exhibiting such inhuman strength.

He darted off in pursuit.

He'd have to let the Society use young Mosley for their aims, now that he was in their possession. If he could figure out a way to make the young man into the kind of double agent he was, if that result wouldn't end up inevitable, it would be most valuable. In these matters, death begat death begat death, hate, and vengeance. In the end, would any of them be any better than the Society's aims, or would they all be transformed into demons in the process?

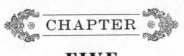

FIVE

Rose had hoped in some small way that Harold Spire might see his company off—well, see *her* off. But he did not, and for days into the voyage, the fact gnawed at her.

Why did she care? He had better things to do, and he was not a man of sentiment. But there was something about his respect and encouragement that helped Rose feel that someone else understood the value of her diligence and hard work, and didn't feel that her sex was a handicap. It was this that meant so much to her, she assured herself, not Spire's opinion of her *personally*.

Though he did not arrive to see them off, she had managed to slide a bit of simple code under his office door about a lead into the guards who had supposedly hanged Beauregard Moriel. Guards who didn't exist at all. It was a curious business, everything to do with Moriel, and it all rankled with foul mishandling. He'd want to know about it.

Rose had been looking forward to days with nothing to do but read, and had packed a few books in anticipation, but that ended up an unattainable luxury. There was no hiding the flamboyance of the Omega team, and so Spire had encouraged them to present themselves as a traveling theatrical troupe. Rose hesitated to use the word "circus," as she was rather averse to clowns, and there were, thankfully, no animals to oversee.

Early in the journey, Blakely tried to erect a tent in steerage.

It was soon realized that anchoring a tent not only would be inconvenient but also it could pose a serious structural threat to the ship. But the show most certainly went on, replete with the wirework that their infamous spies were, well, infamous for. They played to packed decks.

With most of these newly ardent admirers hailing from Ireland, Blakely and his faux wife, Miss Knight, were making immediate plans for a Dublin tour upon their return across the Atlantic, encouraged by the entire compartment.

The phrase "one more round" had made its rounds about the deck. However, there was no designated bar staff to make this dispensation—and indeed, *insistence*—of alcohol into a reality. There was grand cheer, at first, to this proclamation. Then there was the music and the singing. But then there was the question of said "round."

Mr. Wilson charmed his way into asking if a kind Russian clerk might see fit to offer up a personal store of vodka into a cask, cutting it all with water, and redistributing to a populous who was not used to fine liquor, thusly the expectations were low and the reward, he promised, would be high.

Who else had such privilege as that of a British citizen? Rose wondered as she watched this unfold, as they held the fate of a teetering crowd in their control, speeding on a man-made vessel created to part the seas of distance and bring the far-flung world close unto British control . . . The Ciphers were soon the life of the boat.

She asked herself how she could make this time useful, and it was the sight of a pyramid-shaped icon on a passerby's pack that made her think to question midshipmen about Apex, if any of them had worked for the company.

It became Rose's habit to make her way through the throng during Blakely and Knight's magic and spiritualism shows—Knight mixing legitimate psychic gifts with Blakely's flair for compounds, effects, smoke, and pyrotechnics. As

Rose wandered, she listened for conversations about London's wharves or shipping in general. Enough lewd comments had been hurled her way the first few times she did this, as she was seen as an unescorted female and thus fair game, that she asked Mr. Wilson to accompany her the next time.

Wilson showed an admirable glare and a curling fist to anyone who even looked at her wrong, making her task easier. Now she stopped before a young red-haired man whose last job, he said, had "frightened the holy ghost right out of me."

"I'm so sorry to interrupt," Rose began, taking the fine edge out of her voice to sound of his class, "but my cousin was killed working for a right nasty company with holdings on London docks. It's terrible. One has to have a job to live, but then when the job kills you . . ." she said, ending on a near sob.

The young man looked at her with plaintive eyes, as if he'd been hoping someone would understand. He nodded.

"It's why I'm on this ship, bought my ticket with the only money I had. I'm praying that my brother still lives in Boston. I haven't heard from him in many months, but what else could I do? That place was going to kill me."

"I wonder if it was the same company," Rose mused, taking a seat on the crowded bench beside him. Wilson stared down at them both with stern caution.

"I hesitate to say. The whole place is cursed," the young Irishman muttered, looking around as if speaking the word would smite him.

Shielding her gesture from anyone watching, Rose traced the letter "A" on her skirt. The man nodded vigorously. She put on an expression of relief and commiseration that wasn't entirely an act.

"What did you see? My cousin said he saw dry goods"— she leaned closer—"that was actually a *body*."

The man nodded again. "Strange fluids, lots of wires,

powders—I saw it all, more than I should have." He shuddered. "Far more than I should have."

"My cousin was shipping a lot to New York, before he 'fell overboard,'" Rose said, a hitch in her voice. "Do you know where everything was going? All to New York?"

"New York mostly, that's where I heard Apex was setting up offices and needing supplies and stock. But other cities, too, here and there, and up north of London, to an estate." He turned very white as he added in a whisper nearly drowned out by the raucous greeting Blakely's latest magic trick but chilling enough to carry: "It was a box of body parts that did me in. I know you're not supposed to look in the boxes, but someone has to put things in the boxes in the first place. I got stuck with that job one day. They told me the next day I'd be transferred to another department. *Transfer* in their eyes might be *terminate*, and I'd be the next body in a box. So I never went back."

"You were wise to get out, I wish Johnny had," Rose said mordantly. The young man glanced up at Mr. Wilson and respectfully tipped his hat.

"I am sorry for your loss, ma'am," the man said.

"Stay safe," Rose said encouragingly. "If your brother doesn't answer in Boston, New York has a lot of work. And if Apex is setting up offices there, it'd be best to alert authorities to their presence."

"You're going to New York, aren't ye? They may take to the testimony of an upstanding lady better than a paddy like m'self."

Rose winced at the slur and stared at him in empathy. "I will, sir. I'm not asking for your name because I know the kind of damage that company has done and I don't want to add to your fear. But I will alert New York authorities." Here she could speak truth, and her conviction seemed to ease the other's tension.

"You'd be doing heaven's work if so," he said, and turned back toward his empty steel pint with another bob of his cap.

"Thank you, Mr. Wilson," Rose said, as they returned to their crew.

"Pleasure, Miss Everhart. I appreciate watching you at work. You'd be better in the field than you think," he replied. Rose snorted. She had no wish do to more than gather information, sit with codes and ciphers, and bring a bit of justice to the world by thorough bookkeeping.

Making notes about the conversation to later share with Spire, she realized just how solitary a person she was. Life on a ship was her version of hell.

The sight of New York harbor was welcome after days of cramped quarters and endless din. Their tickets had been costly enough to exempt Rose and her Omega companions from the rabble of the downtown port system. Instead, first class was whisked efficiently through one of Manhattan's finest docks. The rest of the passengers would be routed back downtown into the fray.

In America, the differentiation of status was not about lineage but about assets. Accounts and holdings, not name. Yet this attitude created similar structures that separated people from each other and placed unspoken price tags on human value.

Rose let the show persons deal with their equipment and baggage while she took charge of her carpetbag—she had been a bit too paranoid to stow anything and therefore had packed lightly. Not that she had much to pack, regardless; her wardrobe, while as fine as she could afford, was limited and practical. Once all was in tow, the team made their way to the designated safe house, a nondescript four-story granite building. It resembled any number of the municipal buildings in the area and had been owned by England since before the revolution, though that fact was not widely known.

The third floor had been prepared for them thanks to Lord Black's connections with the British embassy. Rose had been given a key to a plain wooden side door that opened into an empty vestibule; an interior stair lead directly to their floor, enabling them to keep their own activities to themselves.

The teams took to their rooms and went soundly, gladly to sleep, for in the morning, it was showtime.

CHAPTER

SIX

Spire hadn't had much time to muse on his team being gone, Rose being the only one he really thought about. Lord Black had kept him preoccupied trying to gain access and details regarding Tourney's gruesome prison death, and they both found themselves blocked at many turns.

He took Rose's last bit of information directly to Lord Black, having found her note, wishing she'd had the chance to give it to him in person.

"Beauregard Moriel's guards who were supposedly over-seeing his hanging are two names that do not seem to exist," Spire stated, folding his arms before the nobleman.

"They do not appear in any court or police employment records. And before you tell me this doesn't have to do with Omega—"

"You're going to investigate what you want to, whether I put my foot down or not," Black retorted. "And the more I think about it, the more I think all of this stews in the same foul pot. Do you have any theories?"

"Was Moriel—animus for the Master's Society and Tourney's inspiration—really ever killed at all?"

"Who would have kept him alive?" Black asked quietly.

"The Crown?"

Lord Black sat at his desk with a sour look. After a long moment, he waved a hand. "Go. Talk to some guards. New-gate, Bedlam, Courts of Justice, wherever, I don't really care.

Come tomorrow to meet me at Westminster all the earlier, below the clock tower. From there, we'll make our way to the queen's parade."

"Yes, sir. And thank you."

Spending the rest of the day on what finally felt worthwhile, the only new information Spire received through talking with guards from varying palaces and courts all around the Westminster area was a freshly maddening rumor that there had been a *second* gruesome death of an indeterminate prisoner. Entirely unconfirmed and unsubstantiated, there was no identity to latch on to other than Spire's supposition it had been another Society member killed to prevent confession.

The next day, Lord Black appeared undaunted as he wove through the clusters of coats and bustles, parasols and raucous children in boaters and bows, Spire keeping up as best he could. It seemed everyone in London had turned out to see the queen.

Farther down the green there was a dais with bunting and elevated parade seating. *For the important folk,* Spire thought. He never was the parade type, this sort of thing raised his hackles.

They reached the area of seats reserved for nobility across from the dais. They had quite a view, give or take a few ostrich plumes on ostentatious hats.

Making his way toward them through the crowd was a dashing young fellow in a fine black brocade frock coat with charcoal trim, black silk top hat atop a mane of black hair, and a blue waistcoat that took nothing away from his piercing ice-blue eyes.

"Why, there's our aura reader now, Jonathon Whitby, Lord Denbury," Black shared with Spire. Spire's heart sank at the idea of adding another preposterous character to his paranormal charade of a department. He was saved from thinking up a pleasantry when a cheer went up from the crowd, indicating that the queen was approaching. All eyes went to the parade green.

Carried by the finest of white horses in an open gilt-trimmed, mahogany calash, its accordion roof back on this fine, brighter-than-usual London day, the queen, stately and dourly round-faced in her lavish black layers of eternal mourning accented by white lace, was seated alone. The queen's guards walked at either side of the tall, golden-rimmed wheels.

Spire's attention was captured by an intake of breath on the other side of Black. A wave of confusion and terror crossed Lord Denbury's face, like he'd seen a ghost. There was wild fear in his strikingly bright eyes.

Spire was just about to ask if he was feeling well, when Denbury turned to Black.

"Milord . . . this . . . city . . ." Denbury said, his voice slow and thick with dread. "There are so many auras . . . I know this must sound utterly mad, but you must believe me, this city has a grave problem. There are demons at work."

"How can you know?" Lord Black asked. "By aura? What shade do you see?"

The young man's haunted face twisted further, a grotesque masque of horror. "Oh . . . oh no . . ." he wailed softly. "I can't let this stand. Not from *her* . . . We're doomed. Doomed!" With shaking hands, he withdrew a small pistol from his breast pocket and aimed it at the queen.

Moving purely on instinct, Spire dove across Black to tackle the young man to the ground. Moving with alacrity, Black wrested the gun from Denbury's hand, pressing the safety and pocketing it. The crowd around them cried out at being jostled, but it seemed no one saw the gun.

Spire kept the nobleman pinned to the ground, but he gave no struggle. Black leaned down to exclaim angrily in his ear, "What the bloody hell do you think you're doing?"

"It's her . . . she has the aura of the demons," Denbury said, looking up from the ground, tears streaming from his striking eyes, his pain and distress palpable. "Lord Black, I promise you, I don't know why or how, but our queen is dealing with the devil!"

Spire helped the young man back to his feet but did not release a grip on one wrist. Glancing about, he was grateful that the throng was mesmerized by a particularly ostentatious presentation of carriages. Only a few concerned female faces, pinched in disapproval, were looking their way. He scowled back at them, and they turned away in a collective huff.

Denbury began pleading, "I am not wrong. You *must* ascertain why Her Majesty is thusly tainted. It is a matter of English life or death, milord. If the Society yet lives . . . Heaven help us all." He stared from Black to Spire, squinting at them. "The two of you remain clean and clear in your reads, neutral light. So whatever the queen has been involved with, it so far has not tainted you. But you'll become a target nonetheless for doing the queen's bidding. She's let something very dark near, perhaps into the palace itself. Root it out. Promise me." Denbury reached up with his free hand to shake Black's shoulder. "Promise me you won't take this lightly."

"I promise," Black replied. "Truly."

With a nod, Black indicated Spire should release the young lord's wrist.

The crowd shifted about them and, in a rustle of movement, a warm-toned woman with brown curls under a straw bonnet with ribbon and floral trims sidled up next to Spire. He paid no attention until she turned and light brown eyes stared right into his.

"You might want to tell me how much of your government is involved with something that drove an honorable man like Lord Denbury to such a length as attempted assassination," the woman stated quietly in Spire's ear, to his shock.

He tried to keep his expression calm, sure that if she made a dangerous move he could stop her with the knife he kept strapped to a forearm band.

The woman seemed to know he was considering his options, for she added, "Before you make a rash move, gentlemen . . . Lord Denbury here might have trained a pistol on the queen, but I've two trained on you, inside these dainty little pockets of mine. And yes, I am a good shot."

"Who are you?" Spire said quietly. That she was American was clear from her accent.

"Not all I seem," she replied matter-of-factly. She wasn't coy, she was on a mission.

"Do you work for the American Eterna Commission?" Spire asked softly, trying to memorize the pattern of freckles dusted across her face so he could later describe them to a sketch artist.

"Did your Omega department just send spies to New York?" she countered.

"Why did the Eterna Commission steal the bodies of British scientists?"

"Why does Omega think America had anything to do with that?" she scoffed. "There was no American plot against your scientists. Why did your operative steal property from the Eterna site?"

Spire frowned. "*That* operative acts on his own accord."

"I know you investigated Apex, but I've been looking deeper for names and holdings, speaking to those who are hired and discarded, used and manipulated, the possessed and puppets, the coworkers of the murdered, the chaff of your world," she said with a venom that spoke of personal investment.

The woman and Spire stared at one another. Lord Black, evidently captivated by the whole exchange, didn't say a word. Lord Denbury was squinting at the lady.

"Her aura is pure, gentlemen," the young noble said. "She doesn't work for the devil, that's for certain." His eerily ice-blue eyes clouded with concern as he leaned toward the interloper. "I see pain in your aura, my lady, having to do with you not being all that you seem. But a good soul lies within, that's clear."

The woman's expression softened for a moment at his kind tone, but she quickly recovered her steel.

"I'd find out what *her* aura portends," she said, indicating the queen, who had taken her place in the reviewing stand. "Then, if you want to play nice with America and sort this all out, I've been instructed to say you should. You're going to need our help."

The men had turned as one to look at their sovereign as the crowd cheered. When they turned back, the American was gone.

* * * * *

Effie Bixby enjoyed working on an international scope, though she was glad Senator Bishop had wired a handsome sum of money, because the information she had begun to discover—as if she were a grave robber with coffins yawning open before her—would generate some hearty telegrams. At nearly a dollar a word, given the exchange rate, these would be pricey communiqués.

Swift as they might be in these days of efficient steamers, she couldn't wait for the mail packets, not when so much of London, and perhaps New York, was like a powder keg in the basement of Parliament set to strike off a deadly explosion of horror.

From what Effie could see from poking about the hellish

rabbit hole that was the Apex Corporation, it seemed their sole export and import was terror. They exploited the disenfranchised of London and New York—in addition to a few other industrial cities across America—to keep it all quiet.

Her gauge of Black, Spire, and the presence of Lord Denbury, whose case files she had read last year in New York, was comforting, at least. She didn't think they wanted the world that the Master's Society or Apex had in mind. She thought her team might even like them, and they hers.

The key would be in determining who did want a world turned inside out, if these men would fight the *good* fight, and if her country would do the same.

* * * * *

While Lord Black found it difficult securing an audience with the queen, he could not in good faith continue in her service without confronting her. So he pressed his estimable charm to the hilt and won a very grudging few moments in an anterior receiving room.

Scowling and angry, the diminutive regent swept into view.

"Make this quick, Lord Black. I've not had time to recover from my appearance," she barked.

"Your Majesty, I have it on solid opinion that there is something very wrong. Not necessarily with you . . . but something around you is evil," Lord Black said carefully. At times like this he was very grateful for his famous neutrality, which kept him well liked in all spaces and class settings.

"Oh?" Her anger shifted to wary curiosity. "Whose opinion might that be?"

"A few of my psychics," he said, hedging his bets and protecting Denbury. "I believe there is something you have not told me, Your Majesty. I think it has something to do with that organization that Tourney ascribed to and with the execution of Beauregard Moriel, two years ago."

The queen looked uncomfortable.

"Ah. Yes. Well." The rustling of the queen's lavish black taffeta gown was suddenly loud in the strained silence as she attempted to find the right words. "I likely should have told you, the time line of that execution was . . . different to what everyone imagined. I did keep the man alive for a time."

Lord Black stared at her. "For a time?" he asked, incredulous.

"Well, he's no longer alive *now*; he was found torn to bits," she said, her petite frame shuddering, "just like Tourney."

Black swallowed hard. "But before that . . . he'd been alive this whole time. Where?"

"A secret cell. I thought he could shed light on immortality. That was the point of the stay of execution. I had his entire ring wiped out. At least I thought."

Lord Black curled his toes in his boots to keep from clenching his hands into fists. How long had the Society's operations continued due to that wretch's continued despicable presence upon this globe? It was all he could do to hold his tongue. There were things about him, his life, his heart, which the Master's Society would seek to destroy. As much as they threatened the world, they also threatened him. He strove to remember that his greatest strength was his unflappable calm, and so he sought it.

"Did you think you could not trust me with this information, Your Majesty?" He spoke gently, allowing concern to edge into his voice.

The regent sighed. "I haven't really known what to do this whole time. England has a responsibility, to her Empire, to be at the fore of every new development. How could I not see Moriel as a chance to turn an evil seed into something good for the Empire?" She stared up at him, an empress looking a bit helpless—not something Black wanted to see.

Denbury hadn't been wrong, seeing the reflection of evil in the queen's aura. The poor woman was guilty by association.

He could not think she'd meant genuine harm in keeping Moriel alive, but harm had been done nonetheless. He had been lied to outright, and he needed full leave to erase the damage.

A man of hope, deep in his heart, Black knew he could not ask a man like Spire to continue on in such a compromised atmosphere; he'd have a fit about the Moriel business. Denbury would be beside himself, possibly moved to new violence. The question was, would he tell them? Should he? He had to. They deserved the truth.

"You've *proof* of Moriel's death, Your Majesty?" Black asked.

"I saw firsthand. The gore . . ." She shuddered and turned as white as the lace around her neck.

"You weren't shielded from such horror, Your Majesty?"

"I had to be sure it was him," she insisted. "I wasn't proud of keeping him alive any more than you are. I had to take responsibility, I had to know. . . ."

"Understood, your highness." Black took a careful breath and continued, "With all due respect, you're sure it was Moriel?"

The queen was aghast at being questioned. "Who else could it be?"

"These men—Moriel, Tourney, and any of those associated with them—are terribly crafty. They stop at nothing; no human life besides their own is of value. One cannot tell what they might do, in time of need," Black explained.

The queen seemed unsure how to respond.

Black pressed her. "Did you have anyone see to the scene of Moriel's corpse?"

"I had the horror entirely cleaned up, of course," she replied, as if there had been no other option. "Why wouldn't I?"

Spire would have punched something if he had been

present, Black was sure. The queen would make a terrible policeman.

"No one is supposed to know he was alive to begin with," the queen said. "The entire country would be up in arms." She looked at him steadily, but he heard the weakness in her voice—she was justifying her actions to herself as much as to him. "You know I did not believe in his ideology. I merely thought some of his science might make *use* of his evil in a way."

"His ideology was woven into every way he sought to bend 'science' to his will, Your Majesty," Black responded. "If it were up to him, we'd lose any progress humanity has made in the past centuries and exist literally in the Dark Ages. Moriel and other unnoble nobles would hold the world on its knees."

As a nobleman, that nobility should be respected was a principle by which Lord Black most certainly lived, one that he benefited from. That Moriel and his like should live as feudalistic dictators was nothing short of laughable. That the queen had indulged this man's lunacy . . . It was inconceivable.

The queen's evident discomfort and embarrassment gave him all the permission he needed to continue his work with his team as he saw fit.

"Fix whatever it is that has been broken, Lord Black," she demanded. "And let's get back to a more positive task with greater hope."

"Greater hope, and less evil, indeed. Good day, Your Majesty."

* * * * *

Lord Black went straight to Spire's office at Omega headquarters, where he found Lord Denbury concluding the tale of his own entanglement with the Master's Society. The two men were a good deal into Spire's decanter of scotch and bowed their heads to Lord Black as he entered.

"My mother rejected Moriel as a suitor in their youth," Denbury explained, "so he swore a vendetta on my family. I admit that I and my associates dealing with the attacks all thought the Society business more a personal grudge than grand plan."

The fear of a larger web was evident on the young man's handsome face.

As Black came farther into the room, he could see Spire examining his expression, and without a word he got up and poured them all a drink.

"Out with it, milord, if you please," Spire stated, handing the nobleman his glass. Black took a stiff swig.

"Moriel was never executed," Black stated. He watched, pained for the boy, as the statement hit Lord Denbury like a bullet. "He died only recently, in the same manner as Tourney. At least, according to the queen. Whether she can be believed is certainly why you saw that aura, Lord Denbury, and for this news I am *grievously* sorry."

Lord Denbury, whom Black knew to be a scholar and a doctor, a young man who had devoted his life to helping others, looked utterly murderous. It grieved Black to see, as there was nothing so tragic to his mind as a kind, beautiful man driven to desperation. Like his dear Francis . . .

"Never. Executed . . ." Denbury's words were knife sharp. It seemed to take everything in his being not to hurl the snifter at the wall or crush it with his fist.

"I make no excuse for Her Majesty," Black continued. "She said she had hoped Moriel could shed light on immortality. I told her that knowledge from a source so polluted by evil is without virtue."

"Lord Black," Denbury said, seething, "if you wish me not to commit or commission gross acts of treason upon she who holds the scepter, please tell me you will fix this damnable error *immediately* and set the fumbling queen to rights."

Black stared into the man's arresting eyes.

"I pledge my life to it, Lord Denbury," he said firmly. "I truly do. If anything is left of the Master's Society, it will be done for once and for all."

Black turned to Spire. "To hell with anything but this directive, Mr. Spire."

"I'll drink to that," Spire said, lifting his glass. He turned to Lord Denbury. "For what it's worth, I, too, pledge my life to it, milord."

"Your pledge may not be a mere toast, gentlemen," Denbury said coldly. "It might be a promise heaven needs come collect, lest there be hell on earth."

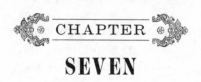

CHAPTER

SEVEN

The sun woke Clara, though she'd rather have lain in bed awhile. A shaft of light caught the third of the sample bottles of the Ward that she'd brought home after their adventure with Mr. Stevens. The refracted beam, thrown onto the cherrywood of her writing desk, glowed like an amplified piece of soul.

To be safe, after what had happened to the Eterna researchers, she shouldn't have any such elements in her home, lest they summon the forces that had turned the tide so horrifically on those men. She comforted herself with the fact the senator's house had not been made a ready path for evil—unlike the laboratory where Louis and his companions had met their fate—and was carefully Warded. Still, she told herself, these things should be stored at the office and she readied for her day.

Bishop had not been home, nor had he left a note or message with their housekeeper. Clara was still wondering what he was up to when she arrived at the office, bobbing her head once in greeting to Lavinia, who seemed utterly aghast, lost in the pages of a penny dreadful and could afford her friend only a little black-lace-gloved wave.

The guards were always so silent she nearly forgot about them sitting sentry near the door, but as she rounded the stairs she looked back to them, content to see that they were not interested in anything but exterior threats, their focus out the glass panes of the front windows.

Again, she nearly found herself bound up in rope but was able to disable the trip wire via a gas lamp fixture at the top of the office stairs before it was too late.

A telegram awaited her upstairs, lying on her desk atop the files all at different angles. Her stomach dropped as she read it, realizing that Rupert wouldn't soon be home or at the desk opposite her in the commission's office—one he had rarely occupied until lately. She hadn't realized until this moment how much she'd enjoyed having him across the room. . . .

C: LEFT ON OVERNIGHT TRAIN WEST TO SPEAK WITH AMENABLE FRIENDS. CONVINCING COLLEAGUES TO WARD THEIR DISTRICTS PROVING DIFFICULT. PRESS NY CONGRESSMEN: IMPLEMENT SECURITY SCREEN- INGS AT PORT OR INDUSTRY PER POTENTIAL THREATS, NOTE THE COMPANY APEX IF YOUR INSTINCT SO BIDS.

She groaned. If there was one thing she hated, it was politicking.

Glad she had worn one of her more businesslike dresses in folds of gray linen and black detailing, she needed to be elegant but serious. She needed to be considered a woman, not a frilly young thing, she didn't need to waste time on apparel— how much of a woman's day could be spent changing dresses?—but she did finish her look by affixing a small boater hat to the side of braids she piled atop her head with enough pins to withstand a storm, and took out her best pair of seed-pearl-adorned gloves. It would do neither her nor Bishop any good if she were not considered a consummate lady.

For the rest of the day, with the help of their diligent but bored driver, Leonard, Clara made the rounds of all the congressmen with whom Bishop had an even remotely cordial relationship.

Her first call, on Congressman Connor, was unfortunately indicative of how far she'd get with anyone.

"Well now, dear miss," said the portly man, who wore a suit more fine than his Fourth Ward district could possibly afford, "what might I be able to do for you?"

"Congressman, I am here on behalf of Senator Rupert Bishop to ask for your help in intervening on behalf of companies in your district that may have been infiltrated by a serious threat to national security."

The congressman made a face. "What threat is that? Why don't I know about it?"

"I'm afraid I am unable to discuss many of the details, at the senator's order," Clara said, aware that most politicians had no knowledge of the supernatural—nor any interest in it.

"Then I'm unable to authorize anything. I think Bishop's a fine man, but I don't put any of my men on any kind of payroll without just cause."

That was patently untrue. Tammany put countless men on countless pointless payrolls all over the city.

"Miss Templeton, tell the senator to come asking for things himself. If he wants something done in Washington, he can't send a girl to do his job."

"No, of course not, I don't suppose he can," she said with a distinct bite as she rose.

Clara thought of dear Emily Roebling, who, after her husband became ill, was left with the task of convincing both engineers and city officials of the needs of that glorious bridge that would someday connect Brooklyn and Manhattan. At a society function earlier in the year, they'd discussed being the go-between, a pendulum between sets of stubborn men, doubly dismissed. Clara was exceedingly tired of not being heard or seen. Only one man seemed to truly see her for herself—and he was dead and haunting her.

Stopping at a telegraph office not far from her own, she dismissed the driver, then shot off a message to Bishop at the usual Cincinnati hotel where he stayed when on business.

B: NO LUCK. TAKE CARE OF THEM YOURSELF. YOUR POWERS ARE THE ONLY WAY.

When Clara turned the corner onto Fifth Avenue again, a spot of yellow on the sidewalk caught her eye. Her hand went to her mouth at the sight of a small, unconscious songbird, with beautiful yellow, gray, and black detailing on its tiny body.

Clara had always been fond of birds. She'd identified every species that frequented Green-Wood Cemetery where the Templeton clan was buried. Birds were symbols of the spirit, of transcendence, of delicate beauty. She bent over the northern warbler, to see if she could help.

The little creature was dead.

Clara's frustrated, beleaguered heart quivered at this fresh assault. But she could not leave the poor darling there, so ignominiously on the sidewalk, unheeded by Manhattan's busy passersby.

She gently scooped the body into her gloved palm. It was so light, a magical little being. She wondered how it had died—perhaps it had flown senselessly against a window, the ever climbing skyscraper invading the territory of the winged. . . .

It was more than she could bear. Clara cried over the dead soul. Her larger task could wait; she had to bury the tiny singer. She crossed the street into the park. Her tears fell onto its bright feathers as she unbuttoned and slid off her right glove to scoop earth aside under a flowering bush. She set the nearly weightless body in the shallow grave and covered its bright plumage—how soft and delicate were the feathers—with honest brown dirt.

"May you sing joyously in heaven, you beautiful little thing," Clara whispered through tears, "watched over by Saint Francis forever."

If she wasn't careful, such would be the souls of New Yorkers, of northerners, southerners, all made equal in the end, leveled under the eyes of a vengeful violence, all of them little birds against windows. She felt as fragile as the warbler, yet she knew she had to be as strong as the building that had inadvertently struck it down.

Her walk back to her offices was a solemn funeral march for that lost bit of feathered song.

Clara let herself into the building with her new set of keys for the multiple locks. The guards, who knew her to be one of four allowed admittance whenever they pleased, did not get up to help her in. She was glad not to be made a fuss over, as it kept the building from attracting more interest should the guards be outside, though she had yet to determine whether their presence made her more or less nervous.

As she entered, the smaller of the two men, dark haired and dark eyed, handed her a bright white square envelope.

"This came through the mail slot," he explained, "A tall . . . flamboyant woman, in a bright teal dress, slipped it through. She didn't ask for entrance and I don't believe due to the angle of the windows she should have been able to see us, and yet she blew us both a kiss as if she knew we were there . . ." The young man's voice trembled a bit. The other guard, a stockier, paler gentleman, adjusted his collar and cleared his throat.

It was clear these guards hadn't been briefed, either by

Bishop or Lavinia, as to the psychic nature of those who might be drawn to this building, or perhaps they were merely in awe of finely dressed women. She thanked the men and walked away with the envelope, down the hall toward Lavinia, who was seemingly in the last nail-biting throes of her novel and so Clara did not disturb her friend.

Withdrawing the interior card as she climbed the stairs, impeccable penmanship loudly declared:

YOU ARE CORDIALLY INVITED TO
A PRESENTATION OF MAGIC,
DARING FEATS, FIRE, AND
CLAIRVOYANT SPIRITUALIST SPLENDOR!
PRESENTED BY THE WORLD-FAMOUS CIPHERS
Free today only at City Hall Park—High Noon
ALL ARE WELCOME.
MAY THE SPIRITS GUIDE YOU.

She turned right back around.

"I'll be at City Hall Park, Lavinia." Her friend jumped, made a sound of acknowledgment, and hurriedly turned a page. Clara chuckled, wishing she could still lose herself in wild fiction. While life entwined with the supernatural had deprived her of that pleasure, Clara was glad Lavinia refused to give it up. Tapping the invitation against her gloved hands, she bobbed her head to the guards and walked back out into the fine, bright day.

The invitation fell entirely under Clara's purview. Their offices were known to be "patrons" of the Spiritualist community, and this wasn't the first such advert left at the premises.

Most expeditions had turned up fakes and con artists. The real mediums and clairvoyants of the city knew that she, Bishop, Franklin, and Evelyn all had specific gifts of their own and would shut down those who didn't, quietly and without any fuss. Seeing for herself whether these Ciphers were legitimate or poseurs would be a nice break from the press of the Eterna Wards, her lingering grief, and the overall disappointments of the day. Even if the Ciphers were phonies, their show would likely be entertaining.

CHAPTER

EIGHT

The Ciphers set themselves up, red-and-white-striped tent and all, in City Hall Park, a grand plaza at the fore of the fine white municipal edifice, Federal styled with French flair, about a mile up the angling Broadway from the tip of Manhattan Island. The location was carefully selected so that the whole of the playing area rested over turf and soil while the place for the audience remained on the park's flagstones.

The Wilsons erected their elaborate pulley system, which would hold them airborne as they performed acts of strength and dexterity. Poles, staves, trick gloves, and chemical compounds were prepared for Blakely's various fire plays.

Outside the tent was a station with a table and crystal ball for Miss Knight. Dressed in a lavish turquoise gown and towering plumes—a veritable psychic peacock—she put on her own show for those waiting in line. She put out Blakely's top hat for donations, seeking, as ever, to keep herself "in the gowns to which I am accustomed."

Inside, deep in preparation, Blakely strutted about in shining black boots that added inches to his short frame and a red tailcoat. His silver ascot was adorned with a shining skull and crossbones that were mirrored in the buckle across the wide ribbon of his top hat. He tapped the silver tip of a black staff that was as tall as he was on the flagstones as he paced and periodically made flourishes in the air, practicing the choreography of his flamethrowing.

There were no seats for attendees, as Blakely intended to keep their shows short. If the Ciphers had been on a full tour, not on Omega's directives, they'd have brought along their musician, Samson, and perhaps an additional act or two. But the sea voyage, though brief, had made these four, the Wilsons and the Blakelys, so comfortable in this smaller dynamic that Rose was confident the audience would feel entertained.

Besides, the point of the show wasn't about the general spectators; their aim was to lure the Eterna Commission out of their offices.

Rose, having no specific task, and dressed in a plain blue wool skirt and cream shirtwaist with a smart blue double-breasted vest, blending into the city as the middle-class clerk she was, seated herself on a wooden box to study paperwork gathered thanks to Black's orders to the British embassy in New York. She scanned lists of various Manhattan companies and industries, looking for any reference to Apex. From what she could see of the Edison company, there was no direct involvement as of yet, though it had to be a matter of time. Electricity seemed a magical, strange property; the wiring that she'd seen attached to the bodies in Tourney's cellar showed that current was part of his ghastly process. Mary Shelley would be horrified.

Apex seemed to be focused at the moment on shipping, delivery, and warehousing—of, Rose assumed, the dead.

The long history in both America and England of "Burke and Hare" type of grave robbing—and, in some such cases, murder for profit—a riot over which had occurred on the very grounds where they now sat, had Rose wondering. Perhaps she needed to determine if Apex provided bodies to medical schools, but that would call for a different set of files, procured by a different set of staff at the British embassy.

The list of Cipher showtimes had been tacked to the exterior of the tent, but the word "free" had already drawn a crowd. Miss Knight was hard at work at divination. Some of what she said, Rose knew from her performances on the boat, would be true, but some perceptions she toyed with, for her own amusement or to shield listeners if necessary.

At long last, Blakely, once he was assured the Wilsons were in place, whipped back the tent flaps with a flourish and a huzzah, welcoming everyone with a deep bow and a wave of his top hat, admitting an excited audience. Rose watched the tent fill, studying their clothes and accessories. From finery to pauper's near rags, the diverse downtown population seemed out in force.

The Wilsons, entirely shrouded in black, mysterious and masked, clad in tight tunics and trousers, wore their leather harnesses like decorative armor. Soon the pulley system— new and more elaborate thanks to Lord Black's war room investments—would raise them into the air, and their astonishing performance would begin. Miss Knight came into the tent, looking a bit baffled, and stopped beside Rose.

"There's another tent being erected next to ours," the psychic said. "Don't you find that a bit odd?" Cocking her head, Rose could hear the murmurs of the crowd outside and the sound of hammering.

"Terribly odd indeed," she replied.

"Is it some kind of holiday we didn't know about?" Knight wondered.

Rose shrugged and walked to the entrance. Looking out, she saw the off-white canvas tent that had sprung up beside theirs.

"Any idea what their show is?" she asked Knight, who had followed her.

"The sign out front says 'Electricity Demonstration.'"

"Oh," Rose scoffed. How ironic. "That Thomas Edison. It

has to be Edison's men. I've heard of them doing things like this, putting on all kinds of outlandish displays, especially if there's something they can upstage. We provided just the bait. The man has exploded as many homes as he has lit them; nothing but a showman."

"Careful what you say about showmen," Blakely said as he came up to them and winked at Rose. "Never mind rivalry. It brings a far bigger crowd, so we'll get a good look at all kinds of New Yorkers today. Might even lure out some city officials."

He left her to take her own seat out of the way and bounded to the fore of the playing space.

Small, and often nervous in appearance, Blakely grew larger than life when he stepped into the role of ringmaster. He gathered everyone's attention with one strike of his staff on the resonant flagstone. At the impact, a spurt of sparking fire erupted from the upturned mouth of the silver skull that topped it. The crowd gasped in surprise, then applauded.

"Ladies and gentlemen of New York City! We are the Ciphers! From around the world, we bring you a range of delights: a bit of magic, a bit of mysticism from our dear Miss Knight. Wasn't she impressive, ladies and gentlemen, as she answered all your most important questions?" he boomed. A round of applause for their resident mystic. Knight was all too happy to curtsey and blow kisses.

"I am your host, Mr. B, and these"—he stepped aside to reveal the black-clad Wilsons—"are my Cipher seraphs! Ready to take veritable flight, they shall cast you into amazement as they soar to great heights and perform amazing feats!"

He pressed a lever on the pulley system, and the Wilsons rose in careful unison thanks to a weight lowering across the tent. When the acrobats were about four feet above the heads of the crowd, Blakely locked the pulleys into place. Miss

Knight struck a metal chime, an act she would repeat for each new pose, and the performance began.

The crowd was truly captivated by the Wilsons' graceful forms entwining artfully, forming living sculptures. There were *oohs* and *ahhs* aplenty.

Then there came a dreadful humming, whining noise. A crackling filled the air, and people started murmuring uncomfortably when any hair that was not constrained by braid or ribbon or hat, or kept in place by wax or pomade, began to rise from around ears and necks.

Rose heard a crack and a boom. The audience's concern grew more obvious—they shifted in place, spoke louder, began looking for the exit. A sizzle rose, sounding like it was hurtling toward them.

Many things happened at once: a flash of searing light; an even louder hum; the whole tent vibrated; and sparks shot from the wires of the Wilsons' pulley system. Rose heard a cry from above.

"Fall, Adira!" Mr. Wilson cried as he flipped the latch that kept the wires taut and secured to the safety system. Mrs. Wilson's smaller body plummeted down, accompanied by the *zing* of the wire, and hit the grass with a thud, limbs out in what Rose hoped was a practiced emergency-landing pose. Her wire released upon impact. Sparks crested and an arc of white-blue light shot along the wires, all the way up to where Mr. Wilson hung.

The screams in the tent were overshadowed by the aerialist's horrible shriek of agony as his body convulsed. Rose hoped desperately that he could reach his release latch. Blakely stretched his hand for the pulley lever, but a spark leaped from the metal. Rose heard the *zap* of electricity singe Blakely's hand. The ringmaster yelped in pain, and at last Mr. Wilson fell to earth—without the practiced grace of his wife. He hit the ground with a sickening thud, wisps of smoke rising from the top of his hood and the soles of his boots. Steps away, Mrs. Wilson struggled to get up, one shoulder slumping unnaturally.

The audience fled.

Adira cried out in Arabic, whipping off Mr. Wilson's hood. His skin was reddened as if burned, his eyes were closed, and he seemed unresponsive. Blakely rushed to their side. Rose and Knight stared at one another.

"Go see what's happening next door," Blakely barked.

The women moved swiftly, ducking into the next arena, which was packed with spectators.

Rose and Knight gasped in tandem at the horror that greeted them. Across a sea of bowlers and top hats, bonnets and feathers, on a raised stage platform, four bodies were laid out on metal tables that were raked slightly so their burdens could be seen by the crowd in full splendor.

"The bodies of the missing British scientists," Rose murmured. "They have to be."

All four were dressed in white linen coats and dark trousers, and matched the heights, weights, and general descriptions Rose had detailed. Strange markings covered any visible flesh: necks, cheeks, the tops of their hands. Large silver coins were laid over their eyes.

Each limb of every corpse was attached to a wire, and these, as if they were the reins of horses, were held by a trembling, scrawny young man with a thin mustache and mousy hair. He stood over the dead bodies like an uncertain angel of death, petrified by the crowd before him.

This creature under duress was not there of his own volition, of that Rose felt sure. Sweating profusely, he was dressed in an ill-fitting white coat, similar to those worn by the bodies, and a none too clean gray waistcoat, his perspiration-stained collar open and uneven at his throat.

This man may be the second part of their investigative mission, Rose thought. Perhaps this was the young Mr. Mosley, the citizen of the Crown so affected by electrical current that he had fled to America. Her heart lurched. All their quarry in one sickening display.

Pure but misplaced instinct had Rose on the brink of rushing forward when Miss Knight clamped a vise grip on her shoulder and pointed to a nearly invisible gap in the flaps of the tent. Rose glimpsed the glisten of an eye and the barrel of a rifle—pointed toward the crowd and roving as if ready for any excuse to fire.

She leaned back on her heels with a curse that was most unladylike.

Tearing her gaze away from the awful display to survey the crowd, she found herself staring a familiar face.

No. She didn't know that woman at all.

Yet she looked *very* familiar.

Her heart suddenly, inexplicably ached, as if she were staring at a lost relative found, a beloved misplaced item returned.

The woman across the tent was dark blond and angular, grand in her qualities despite being dressed in similar station to Rose. A working or traveling woman's charcoal linen dress with black piping accentuated the woman's tall lines topped at a distinct angle by a small straw hat with black ribbon pinned to upswept braids.

"Oh my," Knight said, following Rose's sight line. Knowing Knight's proclivities, at first Rose assumed her companion was attracted to the other woman, but the gravity of Knight's next words indicated otherwise. "She's the one."

"The one?" Rose asked, turning to Knight.

"The one I warned you about. The one who will be the death of you. It's *her*. She came to visit me outside the tent earlier, for a reading. I could tell she was trying to determine if I was legitimate. She gave me a name that I knew wasn't hers but shielded her real one from me. She's gifted."

* * * * *

"Ladies and gentlemen," the young man warbled, addressing the crowd as wires sparked around him. His voice displaying his frayed nerves, he spoke in monotone, as if scripted, but was a poor actor ill suited for the stage. "I am Mr. . . . Jack Mosley . . . I am very special. I am here on behalf of my"— he looked around nervously—"masters . . . to tell you . . . that you cannot avoid the coming monsters. . . ."

Rose felt sick, for her dead countrymen being made a display of, and Mosley, odd as he was, treated like a sideshow freak, and the unknown fate of their dear Mr. Wilson.

Continuing to sweat a flood, his eyes bulged out of his sockets as he cried, "Behold."

Mosley closed his eyes, and there was a buzzing surge through the wires.

The bodies before him shuddered and then, in a wretched and unnatural lurch, sat up. The crowd screamed. Women fainted. Men made declamatory statements. Rose and Knight froze, looking on in abject horror.

The woman Miss Knight had made infamous wore the exact expression Rose herself felt. There was a kinship there, undoubtedly, a mutual pain, as if the world should never have come to this. Tourney's cellar of horrors should not have been the presage for this kind of public display, and the woman in question seemed to hold a similar weight of responsibility and deeply personal conviction about the matter.

Yet isn't that just what the Ciphers had banked upon themselves, the comfort of theater to mask true intent? Were they any better for their ploys to lure the American team out into the open?

But what were they to do? Rose was now confident this wasn't the American team's doing, for this to have been a trick cooked up to mirror Tourney was a stretch. The character of the American team just didn't seem capable of so dark an act. She didn't know which, if any, of the American press would have gotten wind of the Tourney killings, as she and Spire had fought to keep the horrific mess from the sideshow-spectacle hands of the modern journalist. Yet here they were in quite the spectacle.

Who on earth could know, in this age of cunning sham spiritualists and gifted prestidigitators, that this was anything but a magic show? To the unwitting crowd, this was theater, not terror. The comfort of the former made the reality of the latter all the more pervasive and effective. Stage magic had made great innovative strides in craft and technology of prestige, and once this crowd learned the trick was on them, the whipping lash of fear would bind them up. . . .

What those putting on this kind of display wanted out of this she couldn't guess. Demonstration of power, certainly, drawing all operatives together.

The wires, the carved bodies—this was Master's Society inspired, of Tourney's like and the predecessor Moriel. It was tied into a greater picture. In the case of these scientists, Apex was involved, so it had grown from personal, private, and perverse ritual, fetish, and ungodly experiment for "science" into a corporate level of reach.

It had begun; the battering ram to the castle doors of civilization had struck. They were witness to it and at present helpless to stop it. If materials like what Apex shipped here went out to other port towns, how many of these displays might be happening in parks around America? England?

She doubted there were many Mosleys in the world, but with the increasing advent of electricity in many cities, who else might find themselves strangely adaptive to it, a new sense developing like one of Darwin's wonders as the species hurtled on toward the possibilities of its intelligent design?

Once the bodies sat fully upright from the surging force, their mouths sagged open, and in the instant, the world exploded in sensory assault. The resulting sound issuing from their black, swollen maws was an unholy scream like a steam engine, a boat's foghorn, and a thousand human voices shrieking all at once. It was the most terrible sound Rose could possibly imagine, and the entire assembled crowd winced and ducked, clapped hands to ears, and cried out in response.

Hands to her ears, when Rose fully opened her eyes again, she saw the world as she'd seen things when doubled. In visions awake and asleep since the accident and her losing consciousness, there was a second layer of sight upon the normal sense. She saw Mosley, still tethered in electrical currents to the bodies via the wires, but he was staring, mirroring the horror of his own audience, at the air around the four dead researchers, and in this shifted vision, Rose saw glimmering, transparent forms that had been made manifest in this display by the onset of the current and the waking, shuddering, animating bodies.

"My God, are those . . ."

"Ghosts? Yes, those are," Miss Knight murmured. "There isn't a more ghastly way to treat the dead than this. . . ."

Spirits, then, vaguely human forms that were luminous and transparent, wavering like heat from a horizon, an entire entourage of ghosts floated shackled to the bodies of their scientists. To have pitted such a display next to their tent could not be mere happenstance.

"I was a fool to think what I saw in Tourney's basement," Rose said numbly, grappling as the crowd was, with just what she was seeing, "with only the carved and wired bodies, was the worst of it ... To see them wake ... It undoes the mind. ..."

"And I think that's rather the point," Miss Knight replied ruefully.

The woman whom Rose had been so fixed upon, the one destined to be connected to her for better or worse, seemed deeply affected in a way different from those in the crowd with the stomach to keep watching, as if what was happening was having a dire physical effect upon her body. She seemed responsive more to the floating, phantasmagorical presences than to the hateful noise or sight of dead bodies shuddering to life. She was horrified in a different way, as if the ghosts were making her ill, and she rushed out of the tent. Rose wanted to follow, but Knight had a hand clamped upon her shoulder.

The crowd was quite truly beside itself, not knowing whether to stare or flee, many had fainted or run, many stood paralyzed.

"Enough!" Mosley cried in misery. "I can and will end this!" In a desperate, graceless move, he flapped his arms and shook the wires free, blood spurting from where the "plugs" had been latched into his arms.

Disconnected, the bodies of the scientists collapsed, thudding, sickly moist, against the metal tables. The hellish screaming of their yawning, blackened mouths stopped.

Mosley himself shrieked then, in agony and anger, arms flailing as if to set the tempo of a frenetic orchestra. A distinctly different whine tuned in the air, a threatening, cresting noise culminating as the corpses burst into roaring flame. Undoubtedly treated with something that accelerated flammability, they disintegrated rapidly. By the time the flames died down, most members of the audience had rightly fled the obscene spectacle.

Watching between the flames, through the smoke and the wavering heat, Rose saw Mosley turn toward the ghosts. He waved his arms once more, an unholy conductor drawing forth the first notes of a thundering overture. There was a cracking sound like that of a bullwhip, a surge of power and current. The spectral forms all blinked out in the same instant.

For a moment, Rose was glad that Spire was not present. He'd have been furious at all the ruckus and grotesque theatricality, especially considering his father. Whether or not he would have seen the ghosts, or believed that she had seen them, she couldn't know. Having freed himself with brute current, Mosley ran from the tent.

Compulsively, Rose took off after him, Knight behind her. Outside, Rose immediately noticed the blond woman steadying herself, one gloved hand gripping the back of a bench and another against a nearby tree, her breath heaving in difficult gasps. Rose rushed past her, Mosley in their sights ahead, and she soon lost track of Knight in the tumultuous throng behind her.

Suddenly, the blonde ran up beside and then ahead of her, still gasping but trying to reach out, crying out to the fleeing young man. "Wait, I know you! From Pearl Street! The surges there, please let me help you . . . My partners mean you no harm."

Partners . . . Perhaps the blonde was with the Eterna Commission. That would follow. Maybe this was even Clara Templeton herself—the files had contained no image of Eterna's leading lady. Considering this woman's age and particulars, she very well could be.

Rose was within arm's length of the woman now, preparing to call out to her, all cautions about her own health and safety—and prophecy—tossed aside. Clara Templeton—if this was she—was the missing piece. Allegiances between their two sides would serve them better, that's what the mysterious Miss Marlowe urged as she carried the pervasive whiff of the future with her in her mysterious rounds.

Hope of connection was interrupted by a threat—two men whom Rose spotted out of the corner of her eye. One wore plain work clothes and a fisherman's cap and carried a rifle, making him likely the gunman who had been keeping watch on the crowd. He fired at Mosley.

The slight man screamed and stumbled. Red blood bloomed on one shirtsleeve. In a raging fury, he flung the wounded arm up in the air. An arc of electricity soared from his hand, striking the rifle and zapping the gunman, who collapsed into a sizzling, singed heap on blood-spattered flagstones. Rose flinched at this, remembering what had happened to Mr. Wilson, pausing to pray that he might be all right. Had that been an attack or accident?

Mosley cried out again, and with a spurt of bright blood and a fresh smell of singed flesh, the bullet clattered onto the plaza stones, having been ejected by Mosley's self-current. He raced away, nearly getting run over by a trolley car before disappearing beyond Park Row's many newspaper buildings now buzzing with the activity of the day.

Rose and the blond woman stopped running, trying to catch their breath and staring after him. They turned to one another almost as if choreographed.

Before either could speak, long arms and black-gloved hands clamped over each woman's mouth and shoved them together, shoulder to shoulder.

A man's voice spoke close to Rose's ear in an upper-class London dialect. "Don't scream if either of you value your lives. Miss Templeton knows I do not make idle threats." *It* was *her,* Rose thought as their captor released his grip.

Both women whirled to face the man, who was clad all in black with a wide-rimmed black hat shielding his face, a man of shadow even in bright light.

"*You*," Clara Templeton spat hatefully. "If it isn't the *abductor*. What do you want now?"

"Mosley, of course. I'm sure he's heading home to Pearl Street. All he wants is to be left well enough alone.

"Call on him there," he said, addressing Miss Everhart, then rattled off the address, ending with, "Yes, I know who you are, I know who all of you are."

"You're Brinkman," Rose exclaimed. Clara whirled at the sound of her voice.

"You're English! From the British offices searching for Eterna," Clara exclaimed, looking at Rose warily.

"Did your Eterna Commission have anything to do with our scientists laid out like that, for a show? Injuring one of our agents?" Rose asked.

"We had nothing to do with these acts today," Clara retorted. "I was invited to the Cipher show by a direct invitation to my office."

"Ladies, please," the double agent said. "You've been pitted against each other by another foe, and while it would once have been advisable to make it appear that New York and London were still at odds, that theater is now pointless. Focus now on the Master's Society, an insidious organization bent on overturning the world order entirely, horror by horror. Those unfortunate researchers were killed in the Greenwich property where they'd been working. Killed by possessed society operatives, shipped here with the intent to have Mosley reanimate them. I merely engineered *where*, so you both could see for yourselves. The events will happen regardless; what we can do is try to use them to our advantage," the spy stated.

"How much of England supports the Master's Society? Is that what's been after our commission all along?"

"Not in the least—" Rose sputtered.

"Don't be so sure," Brinkman growled. "Both of you will

need to exorcise your respective governments of this non-sense lest they get lured—or forced—in. You will have to work together." Taking note of their obvious wariness, he added, "I've been planting the seeds of this for more than two years and in that time have survived more than two dozen attempts on my life. That I need you to do as I say is an understatement, and I don't mind punctuating it with gunfire."

"As if you give us any choice," Rose said. She turned to Clara. "Regardless of threats, and friend or no, I will say this, Miss Templeton, and at great risk." She lowered her voice. "You don't know me and have no reason whatsoever to trust me. But if you don't trust me, you may be the death of me."

The blonde blinked and looked concerned. "Well, that certainly has my attention. By what authority is this so?"

"By clairvoyance," Rose replied, keeping things deliberately vague.

"Your directive, Miss Everhart," Brinkman interjected icily before Clara could dig deeper in regard to sensitives, "is to get that dynamo on our side." He nodded after Mosley.

"Presuming we could possibly get him to trust us, what would we do with him?" Rose countered, fighting to keep her tone level, trying not to worry for Mr. Wilson. "My team is untrained to deal with someone of . . . such a nature. One of our operatives may have been killed by the display of his current, and I must return to my colleagues to assess the damage."

"He's more inclined to trust us than those who forced him into today's display. Appeal to his British heart. Offer protections against the Society. Remember, your enemies are the demons, but don't let the demons think you're building an army against them, lest they turn theirs against you before you're ready to fight."

As Rose shuddered at his use of "demon," the unpredictable

operative turned and fired a gun into a nearby tree, sending two ravens squawking angrily into the air and causing a wave of screams. Men and women ducked, parasols and top hats flying. The confusion made excellent cover for his disappearance. In the wake of his departure, the two women stared at one another, baffled.

"Will you sit with me a moment, Miss Everhart? I am unfortunately unwell," Clara asked, dazed. A wave of nausea must have struck the young woman, as she had to steady herself on Rose's shoulder.

"Yes, Miss Templeton." Rose led her to a small iron bench beneath a tall sycamore near the Federal-style City Hall, its Beaux-Arts detail and lovely white dome a more delicate architectural bastion amid surrounding sooty brownstones and cast-iron industrial facades.

"I suffer from epilepsy," Templeton explained. "And do call me Clara. When there are too many ghosts nearby, my body responds to their amassed sparks of life with a seizure. I've been fighting off a fit for the past hour. Thankfully, that Mosley fellow seemed to have driven off the tethered dead, but there's a bit of an after-effect."

Rose remembered her darting from the tent and read the struggle in her body now, saw the tension in her muscles and the occasional shudder as she tried to unknot them, causing rippling shivers all the way from the ribbons of her small straw hat down to the black trim of her skirts.

"Funny thing about you, though," Clara stated, breathing deep between words. "Your presence helps. It's as if I can breathe easier. Whatever you're doing, don't stop."

Rose shrugged. "I'm not doing a thing that I know of. But do call me Rose."

"Well . . . then, Rose. Where do we even begin?" Clara asked, trying to master a body fighting against her. "You say

I may do you harm, but I tell you that is not in my nature," she said with a weary but engaging smile.

Rose took a deep breath. "Let me first say, Clara, that our aims on your shores are simple: to recover the bodies of our scientists and lay hands on Mr. Mosley, a British citizen. I did not imagine those tasks would be entwined in such a terrible way."

"Those poor folk who are now reduced to ash—they were your team searching for immortality?" Clara asked. Rose nodded. "Our pursuits of the same yielded too similar a result . . ." She trailed off, seeming overcome with emotion.

Rose felt similarly moved, somehow at ease in tumultuous sentiments. She was scared by what had happened, grieving for her wounded colleague, and overwhelmed, but she did not feel judged, as if she sat beside a long lost family member who knew her well. How could that be? There was no connection between her and Miss Templeton.

"You cannot trust me yet any more than I can trust you. And I want to, despite the warnings," Rose stated.

Clara nodded. After a long moment she continued, "The Master's Society, with which today's demonstration appears to be correlated, has invented the strangest kind of . . . what's the word for it?"

"Terrorism?" Rose offered.

"Precisely."

"I've only heard that term referred to in terms of the French regime and the revolution's subsequent Reign of Terror," Rose mused, "but it seems apropos."

"It appears that via terrorism, this is the kind of world the Society wants—ruling through terror inspired not by guillotine but by reanimate bodies powered by ghostly retinue and gaping graves," Clara said mordantly, "specters, and all manner of supernatural threats we've been policing through the years but, when it comes to our office, always took second place to the search for immortality. I know you know about all that."

"Yes, I am a member of the Omega department, but do let me reassure you, Miss . . . Clara, that we had no direct say in what Brinkman would do. He's a bit of a . . ."

"Liability?"

"One might say that."

"Is he even trustworthy?" Clara posited. "How do you know his sending you after Mosley isn't a trap?"

"I'll bring along someone who is . . . gifted enough to assess the situation."

"Good. We need as many of the gifted as we can," Clara said, as if that were the most normal thing in the world. Rose nodded. "What's your gift?" Clara asked.

"Codes," Rose replied. "Although after I was hurt in an accident and then . . . accosted by a strange, insistent woman, I've been seeing the world differently. As if I've woken up to a world beyond our mortal one."

"That's very familiar. And don't worry, you *have* woken up, precisely. Most people have access to their sixth sense, but most don't wish to wake to it," Clara said supportively. She winced and tried to shake a clenched muscle in her forearm. "Pardon me. It takes a little bit until I'm fully clear. Usually I go right to sleep but I don't at present have that luxury."

"Don't let me keep you. I should be returning to find my colleague—"

"No, you're helping. The aftereffects are usually worse, and considering how many spirits were here, I should have already have gone into a full convulsion."

"That must be very frustrating in your line of work," Rose stated, "with your sensitivities, to have that kind of impediment."

"Oh, indeed," Clara murmured. "A Templeton curse . . ."

This sparked Rose's memory. That strange Marlowe woman had said the name Templeton.

"Do you know anything about a Lizzie Marlowe?" Rose asked. Clara looked blank. "Imperious woman, reddish hair, sharp featured. She mentioned your name, that we would have to make sure our departments didn't become something insidious."

The description of the woman seemed to ring a bell. "The visitor!" Clara exclaimed. "The visitor has a name?"

"Yes, she did say 'visitor', once, but she called herself Lizzie Marlowe after barging into our offices as if she owned the place."

"Sounds like her," Clara said with an exasperated laugh. "Ah! You must be the missing piece she referred to. That's it. Do you believe in lives past?"

Rose passed a hand over her hair, tucking errant brown strands from the ordeal back into the loose bun atop her head. "I didn't believe in much until this work, but now . . . Well, I am forced to believe in a great deal more."

"May I be forward?" Clara asked, piercing Rose with peculiarly gold-green eyes.

"Have we any choice but to be?"

"I think we've always been siblings. I've a sense of where those with whom I have an instant affinity fit, in worlds past. I know mine rather clearly. You've either been a sister or brother, nearly every time," Clara said, with mounting amazement as if she was seeing each iteration of possibility before her eyes. Perhaps she was. Rose was very moved by this.

"I was born a twin. The other died . . ." Rose trailed off. Clara nodded with a knowing smile. "I've always felt something missing . . ."

"I know. I've thought so, too. Been told so, even," Clara said. "Well, hello, then." Suddenly Clara embraced Rose.

Rose allowed the embrace and after a moment returned it. "Hello, old friend," she replied.

Clara pulled back, her hand still on Rose's shoulder. "So what's this about my being the death of you, then?"

"Perhaps our respective dangerous works coming together increases the threat for both of us."

Clara nodded. "Then we'll be twice as careful. I believe that warnings should be heeded, but I don't believe in a fixed destiny that ends only one way."

"Good," Rose agreed. There was a great relief in this.

"I was about to tell you where our offices are, but," Clara said with a slight edge, "you already know. Can you give that Brinkman orders to not be such a lunatic?"

"We already did," Rose countered. "Our director, Harold Spire, is a very sensible man. If I were a betting woman, I'd say you'd like him a great deal. He was afraid the issue of the kidnapping and the séance, when all Brinkman had been asked to do was gather information, would cause an international incident."

"You're lucky we're understanding folk interested in secrecy," Clara stated. Rose nodded. "So was your office responsible for any of today's madness?"

"Solely in the first tent."

"Agents of a secret department masquerading as mystical performers and talented acrobats?" Clara grinned. "That is rather clever."

Rose chuckled. "It's innovative, I suppose . . . to our poor director's chagrin."

"For my offices to trust yours, we'll need to know who and what in your government—as we'll have to ascertain in ours—has any involvement with the Master's Society, the force behind today's display, along with other tiers of supernatural terrorism. Come to my offices tomorrow, please. Top floor. Don't mind Lavinia, our receptionist, she'll have to get her own *read* on you."

"I won't mind," Rose said, the paranormal aspects of the work becoming part of the routine. "Now if you'll excuse me," Rose said, rising to her feet, smoothing her sensible skirts, they were very much two women of a set.

"Your colleague, by all means, I hope he is all right. Heading downtown, by chance?"

"Yes."

The women left the park and walked in as brisk a stride as their skirts would allow down busy, bustling Broadway that was still the epicenter of gossip, terrified declamations, and more than a few New Yorkers rousing from faints and vapors.

"You'll come tomorrow?" Clara asked. Rose nodded.

"If we don't stop what's going on," Clara added, "we'll all be the death of each other. It won't be by my direct hand. I hope whatever you can be sure of, in how *familiar* we feel. Sometimes instinctual trust is all I have to go on. The magic my team has been working on to keep the darknesses roused by events like today at bay is a very deeply personal one. We'll need all the connections we can get, not alienations."

Rose nodded. "That sounds heartening, at least, even if I don't really understand precisely what you mean by magic."

Clara smiled. "Magic doesn't need understanding. Not wholly. That's why it's *magic*. Someday I might know the science of it, but until then, well, let's call it something wondrous."

"Fair enough."

The women continued down toward Pearl Street, with New York all abuzz around them. The news of what had happened in the park was on the lips of every passerby, there were policemen and officials out and about on every walk and corner, but the ladies wove through dazed crowds with focused skill.

Clara stopped at Pearl and Whitehall and reached out to offer a comforting squeeze of her gloved hand on Rose's shoulder. "Good luck with your colleague. If I can be of help, let me know. It is good to meet you, Rose Everhart. And, I suppose, welcome home." She turned to walk away down Pearl Street.

Watching her until she disappeared around the bend of the street, Rose recalled the Edison power plant nearby and her directive to call upon the man who may have accidentally killed her colleague. She prayed, as she hurried down the block and around the corner to the entrance of the embassy's safe house, that she wasn't walking into the too-personal kiss of death.

As she came into the safe house parlor, a bland, boring room with a staid still-life painting, no windows, a plain brown carpet, and uncomfortable wooden chairs, Rose collapsed in the nearest one, utterly overwhelmed and exhausted by the tolls of the day. Blakely sat across the room, staring at the wall.

"Thank goodness you're safe," Knight murmured. She hoped their somber expressions didn't mean what she thought they did.

"Any luck out there? I'm so sorry I lost you, I was worried sick, but I had to . . ." The psychic trailed off, gesturing toward the closed door of the next room, tears falling from her dark eyes.

"We all did what we had to do," Rose replied. "By dire circumstance and force, I met both Clara Templeton and our agent Brinkman." She sighed, staring toward the closed door. "How is he?"

Blakely shook his head. Miss Knight put her face in her

hands. In that moment, Rose could hear Adira crying from the next room, mourning softly in Arabic.

"Oh, God." Rose slumped further, rubbed her eyes, and bit back a sob. "What do we do now?"

"Continue on," Blakely whispered. "It's what he'd want us to do. And take care of Adira."

Rose nodded, closing her eyes to block the sting of tears. She explained what all had happened, withholding the more personal past-life aspect from discussion.

"The key," Knight said after Rose finished, "will be to get this Mosley fellow on our side."

"It's clear what the Master's Society will do with him after today," Rose declared. "Scores of dead bodies waiting to be woken . . . he can give them all the charge those unhallowed bodies need to rise and connect the ghosts that trail those horrid bodies." She shuddered. "Brinkman gave me his address, on Pearl Street, saying we should go to him. Protect him."

"He's tailor-made to be exploited by their evil," Miss Knight added, rising to her feet. "I can find out why he is so angry and access his ability to trust. I can give him the closest thing he's ever had to a friend."

"If what you say is true," Blakely said bitterly, "could he not harm you like he did our dear Reggie?"

Knight moved behind Blakely's chair to kiss the nerve-racked man on his perspiring forehead.

"Trust me, darling. It's hardly the first time I've diffused a danger. We'll bring back results and make an ally out of a threat," Knight stated.

"Tend to Adira," Rose added. Blakely nodded obediently. "She needs comfort and safety, and make whatever arrangements need be made. Telegraph Mr. Spire and alert him to what happened."

"I shall."

"I should not tell Adira where we've gone, as the man we're to see is ostensibly responsible for her husband's death," Rose added.

Blakely nodded and the two women were off.

"Can you tell me what *you* saw in that tent, Miss Knight?" Rose asked as they walked toward the Pearl Street address, oddly, not far, she thought, from the Eterna offices. "I've never been one for second sight. But I believe I saw . . . spirits. Subtle forms somehow *attached* to the bodies of the dead scientists. Am I correct, or should Zhavia inspect me for further damage upon our return to England?"

"What you saw was entirely so," Miss Knight confirmed. "The bodies and spirits were bound to each other against the will of both dead parties. In effect, the bodies became banshees, magnifying the screams of tortured, enslaved spirits. Resulting in a weapon, a way to control a crowd by fear and sensory onslaught."

"Yes." Rose shuddered. "But Mosley banished the specters, yes? One moment they were hovering around the bodies, the next moment they blinked into nothingness."

"I cannot help but find that fascinating," Miss Knight said. "I have heard theories that ghosts are particularly able to affect electricity—and to be affected by it. I think Mosley sent a higher pulse of current that untethered the spirits, and I doubt he did that on command. I think he did that to free himself."

They did not bother to knock at the door of Mr. Mosley's modest town house—Miss Knight picked the lock of the wooden front door instead. The two women stood in the front hall, not far from the door, and called his name.

Disturbed to see that the back arch window was a gaping, broken hole, Rose could see they were not the first to have broken in. . . .

Waiting for a reply, Rose noticed that the house's carved

wood paneling needed to be dusted and polished, and the carpet runner in the entrance foyer was worn and dirty.

"Why are you people following me?" shouted an anguished voice from upstairs. "Am I at long last affecting Manhattan's patch-work electrical system to the point where you cannot ignore me any longer?"

"We don't want to hurt you," Knight called gently. "We saw what happened today, and as fellow British citizens, we would like to offer you another option."

Mosley sighed, a growling sound, poking his head down from around the banister. "I didn't choose to go down that path today. I was kidnapped and forced to send electricity into those . . . bodies. It was terrible."

"We know, truly we do," Rose added. "Those who forced you into that dread deed are whom we want to stop, believe us."

He peered at them. "You're not law enforcement. . . ."

"Who would send women and psychics to speak with you unless we understood just how special you were?" Rose offered.

"As if I should trust anyone, or anything . . ."

Miss Knight sighed. "Mr. Mosley, please." She walked down the entrance foyer toward him, looking at him on the stair above her. "Your heart is full of anger and bitterness—"

"What do you know of my heart?" he barked.

Miss Knight offered a half smile and stared into his eyes. "Enough to understand what it is like to live in this world entirely misunderstood. An aberration. A *freak*."

At the banister, she reached up and laid a gentle hand on his cheek.

"Don't—" He shrank away but could not evade her. At her touch, he fell silent and still.

Miss Knight's dark eyes fluttered. When concentrating, her eyes shifted to nearly black, frightening even to those who were intrigued by her gifts. She winced, then spoke with quiet gravity.

"I know you and your brother . . . Jack . . . were treated terribly. You took on his name out of deference . . . And I know what happened to your father. It wasn't a fireplace poker that did the damage. I'd have done the same thing in your shoes had I been there."

Mosley looked down at her in a mixture of awe and abject fear as he murmured, "How do you . . ."

Knight's black eyes flashed, showing a pain that Rose had only guessed at.

"Because I, too, am a freak, Mr. Mosley," she whispered. "That's how."

There was a long and uncomfortable silence.

"We are, honestly, here to help you," Rose began gently. "We do have ties to Her Majesty's government, but we do not work with the forces that you fear. We are tasked with rooting out the inexplicable. Help us help you."

"To do what? I won't be a sideshow trophy and I won't be your weapon," Mosley said angrily, pulling away from Knight and standing up. Rose could feel the hairs on her neck rise as the young man's charge electrified the room. "Too many people have been after me for that. I look out for myself, a lone agent of the lightning gods. I demand autonomy and respect."

"We respect that you could kill us right here and now," Miss Knight said, her moment of vulnerable commiseration gone. "But you won't, because for the first time in your entire life, you see in my eyes that I am telling you the truth. Because you can see that I do not wish to hurt, arraign, or experiment upon you. Whatever others have wanted to do to or with you, the Society will do worse."

"We've seen bodies and wires like that before," Rose added,

"in a dreadful English crime scene. Mechanical generation cannot compare with your power, so those who used you today would use you again." She leaned in to emphasize the point. "You'd power a thousand dead corpses attached to ten thousand dead spirits."

Mosley shuddered at this.

"With you living so close to Edison's dynamos, you are an ongoing risk and disaster—"

"You flatter me," Mosley sneered.

"Come home to England, Mr. Mosley," Rose offered. "Our offices will erase whatever past you please. But if you accept this help, help us in turn by rooting out your attackers wherever they may lurk. Protect the force your body claims as your own. It is for light, not for harm, and not for reviving the dead."

He stood on the front stair, facing them. "Indeed."

"Protect yourself against those who took advantage of you today," Miss Knight said with an edge. "Because of them, one of our operatives was killed today."

"I'm . . . sorry for your loss," Mosley said haltingly, as if empathy were entirely new to him.

"Thank you. We strange, sensitive, burdened, gifted persons have to look out for one another, do we not?" she said softly. It was the first time Rose thought that her colleague might have had a more difficult life than she'd ever let on.

"I . . . never thought so," Mosley said, "before." There was a long, pained pause. "How can I get home?"

"Papers will be under your door by midnight," Rose replied, "along with a steamer ticket and directions to a safe house in North London. Should you not report there, we will have cause to come find you."

"Indeed," he murmured. "Well, then, ladies. Do see yourselves out. . . ." With that, he withdrew up the stairs. Only then did the charge of the current dissipate and the small hairs all over Rose's body return to rest.

"Good day," Rose stated, and she and Knight quickly took their leave lest they be driven out by a surge.

NINE

Utterly drained after her strained, strange day, Clara went home to await Rupert, as he never traveled to speak with colleagues for longer than three days, and his stabilizing presence would be helpful in returning her still clenched body to peace after so near a seizure.

Awaiting him in the parlor, she allowed herself to drift off on the divan. Her unsteady rest was filled with dark, vision-like dreams of epic proportions. Perhaps Lady Denbury had left a bit of her dream prophecy gift behind after her last visit.

In this scene, she stood alone at the center of the Bowling Green, the apex of Manhattan Island's fraught, violent history, the heart of its colonized commerce. Ghosts of the Lenape tribe, brutally driven from the land first by the Dutch, floated about the perimeter of the park where she stood with a candle in one hand and a Ward in a glass vial in the other. Louis was not with her, though she heard the faint murmuring of spirits. Shadows moved at a distance. Closer.

The shadows began to march. First one or two, floating down Broadway. Then more, pouring from the side streets onto that angled old thoroughfare like floating rats, silent and entirely opaque, cut out of purest darkness and bleak lifelessness.

Back in the first days of researching Louis's death, she'd seen a host of shadowy silhouettes in the disaster site. She'd mistaken them for the ghosts of the dead scientists, and when they told her to destroy the files, she didn't realize they were the enemy.

They'd been trying to trick her all along, and now they were coming for her.

She stood all alone at the tip of one of the most powerful islands of the world, with no power but herself, with a dread horde making its way toward her. The shadows stopped just outside the green's wrought-iron fence, a spiked perimeter dating to the Revolutionary War. In those days, the king's crowns had been ripped from the tops of the finials; their iron pickets were still jagged, a century later.

The darkness hovered. The spirits wafted back, terrified of violence anew. Clara held tight to her light. The presences threatened to close in but were held back by one lit candle, one glass vial of personal protection, and one small prayer of hope.

How long could her own magic, or anyone who hoped to build and maintain a Ward, hold back this wretched, teeming horde?

The sound of the front door opening and closing roused her from her nightmare. She opened her eyes to see the senator standing on the parlor threshold. The room was dark; the sun had set, and she'd slept longer than she intended.

Clara groggily blinked up at Bishop. "You're late."

"Did we have an engagement?" he asked blankly.

"You're usually home by this hour on a day you return," Clara said wearily, sitting up and rubbing her eyes.

"I didn't wire—"

"You're never gone on meetings longer than three days. You have encouraged me to stay aware of your patterns so I can remind you when you work too hard. I know these are extenuating circumstances, but still."

The senator smiled. "So I have, and asked you to remind me of it when I bristle at being questioned. I'm sorry I'm late."

"So? Tell me, then. What kept you?"

He examined her as he crossed the room. "You look tired. Care to share why?" Bishop asked, moving to the samovar and pouring a cup of tea. Clara realized that during his journey from door to table, he had picked up her cup, which he was now refilling. He returned her cup and took a seat on the settee.

"It was a day that tried faith," she began, then, distracted, said, "I don't even know where to start. This city is in grave danger, and you look as if you've taken healing waters. What different states we are in . . ."

Their quiet housekeeper moved about the room, setting out a plate of small sandwiches and a snifter of liquor at the senator's disposal. He thanked her warmly before turning back to Clara.

"I am particularly invigorated after a talk with young Spiritualists being raised in the tradition," Bishop began eagerly. "Flexible senses, grade-schoolers, what a thrill. Nothing like a mind that hasn't had all its doors hammered shut with the nails of limitation nor the foundations of its imagination poured over with the tar of complacency."

Wishing she could see past the dark visions that had beset her, she pushed back. "How can you look into youthful eyes and tell those souls to hope and dream, to feel, to be a *sensitive* when the insensitive world will do its best to swallow them up? If not swallowed whole, then the darkening world will nip up parts of them, one by one, their flexible brains and bodies will harden to loss and pain and being told they cannot do, or be, or want, due to what they look like, their sex, their class, their hearts . . ."

"Clara, where is this coming from?" he asked softly. "I've known you to have melancholic tendencies, but you're not usually so bleak—"

"Today I saw the dead come back to life. Dead bodies, electrocuted, it was terrible . . ."

"Where did this happen?"

"City Hall Park, in a 'demonstration' by Master's Society operatives rising from the dead to haunt our world. Rupert . . . seeing a body shudder like that, convulse . . ." She stared up at him, overwhelmed. "Is that how I look when I seize? It's so horrid."

Bishop moved to sit next to her. He placed a tentative hand on her knee and, when she did not draw away, squeezed it in comfort. He was ever careful and gentlemanly when he touched her.

"I wouldn't know," he replied. "I focus on trying to keep you safe, not what you look like during the episode," he added warmly. She smiled as if this were a particular balm. "Did you seize today?"

"Nearly so. It seems impossible to describe this surreal day. I saw a man become a dynamo, the man I've seen cause the Pearl Street disturbances. During the event I met a soul sister whom I might endanger by no fault of my own. Her friend may have died during the incident. Tonight in dreams I saw a world where human dignity and imagination will be aborted, snuffed out by a lightless, sightless cloud."

She turned to Bishop, and her voice sounded tortured to her own ears. "How can you give young sensitives hope on the best of days, let alone when we stand on the precipice of a nightmarish world . . . ?"

Bishop stared deeply into her eyes. "Because I can't school children in suicide, Clara," he replied. "I must school them in empowerment. How else to diffuse the stifling storm clouds of the present and the future?"

Nodding slowly, Clara allowed this to be no argument, knowing he believed in his spiritual saplings down to the roots and admiring the quality. But creeping, needling, crawling unease had eroded the optimism and confidence that she usually held as dear as she did her guardian.

"Let me unpack. Then we'll go out for dinner, anywhere you like." He kissed her on the head and went upstairs.

Although she didn't want to be left alone with her melancholy, there was a memory trying to get out, something that required her focus. Something about Louis forced itself forward for review.

"What is it like to hide part of who you are, as you do?" Clara once asked Louis, the memory as fresh as if it were yesterday.

"Difficult. Complicated. Different for everyone, depending on their circumstances. A shame. An injustice," Louis murmured. Clara nodded at her lover in empathy. "What's it like to not be taken seriously because of your sex, disbelieved because of your gifts?" he countered.

Clara smiled at this; his ability to bring disparate sides together into peers was one of his great gifts.

"Ah," Louis said, mirroring her smile. "See, bridge building. If what was up here," he said softly, caressing her forehead with his fingertips, "was the basis for all judgment, merit, love . . . and not the color of my ancestor's skin or the notions of gendered roles, we'd truly be free. I don't want to be confined to bodies, Clara. I want to be animate energy. That is what I want in Eterna. That is how we can transcend. To discard the trappings, to live in truths. Raw, soul truth."

That's what Clara put into the Ward that made it work, when she'd clasped hands over Stevens's and put force into that vial, energy that held the demons back. The same proved true with Stevens, his truth leading to the banishment of those shadows. This renewed her fastidious attention to the work ahead, the Warding process. That's what her dreams supported.

Chemistry was not Clara's forte, but enforcing ideas by heart and mind was the key. She longed to share with him that she truly understood what he meant by the energy of the soul as an active, protective force. It had been some time since she'd seen Louis's spirit, and she missed the opportunity to commend him.

Over dinner, at the Astor, in a velvet-curtained alcove glittering with gaslight and crystal, she told Bishop all the details of the City Hall Park disaster, coming face-to-face with Brinkman, the new contact that was Rose Everhart and what that connection to her department might offer. Bishop was regretful he'd not been able to help shield her in the park but was proud of her fortitude and efforts.

Back home after dinner, turning to address the senator at the pocket doors of the parlor, she opened her mouth to ask if he might sit with her further, over a cordial, but he did not pause with her and instead walked past, continuing upstairs to his study. This stung strangely. A discomfiting sensation swept over her; Clara thought it was the onset of one of her senses blinking out one by one, a symptom of a possible oncoming spasm, and stepped onto the landing, thinking instead she might call up to him for help.

Unease grew in her stomach, blossoming like a diseased flower. She rushed upstairs, bursting in upon Rupert in his study. He looked up at her over his spectacles, raising one eyebrow in inquiry.

Once she was standing there, looking at him, she had no idea what had caused such a wave of concern. Horrified, she realized it was just a simple pang of loneliness. After he'd been away on business, she was not yet ready to be separated from his familiar and bolstering presence quite so soon . . . Had she allowed herself to become so emotionally compartmentalized that the natural urge to ask for company was taken as a dire emergency?

"Whatever premonition you just had that has you looking tortured," Bishop said with a little laugh, "well, it wasn't about me. I'm here, I'm safe." He smiled. "Though I'm flattered you thought of me . . . Are you feeling any better? You look a bit drawn."

She shook her head. "No. I . . . should . . . try to rest."

"Yes, do," Bishop said.

"Good night," she murmured and rushed out, embarrassed not because of anything he'd done but by the conflict between an assumed frailty and the necessity of community. She deemed it frail to need someone, yet community was the cornerstone of humanity.

It was either ironic or a bit psychic of him, then, to call out down the hall after her, "I'll be here if you need me. . . ."

He hoped to be needed; she was growing weary of loneliness. But how could two adults navigating an emerging peerage address "need" and still maintain intrinsic, equitable strength?

She flounced upon her bed, her aching head in her hands. The only sound other than her breathing was the ticking of the grandfather clock in the corner of her room—an heirloom from the old Templeton house. She had placed it in her room as if through that piece her family would be with her, watching over her proudly, even though her parents' souls had gone on to what she hoped was an Elysian place so long ago. Until now, she'd never thought of the massive clock as ticking up to an apocalypse, but it was hard to retract the notion.

A burst of cool air, accompanied by a visible ripple in the atmosphere of the room and a gray-white flickering in the corner of her eye, made Clara jump to a sitting position.

"Hello, love," she said to the entering ghost. "I'm trying to get used to your startling me."

"I'm so sorry, my dove," Louis replied.

"I'm glad of your presence nonetheless. Eterna and everything around it has become something entirely different from what I thought."

"Yes! It's so much more complicated!" Louis cried. "It isn't just about the Ward keeping the demons out. It's about souls, it's about reanimated bodies. I don't know how to help with those things. I'm afraid Warding won't be enough to address all these facets . . ."

"So you saw what happened today?" Clara asked.

"I did. It was terrible. I tried to shield you but could be of no help in the tumult. I couldn't get your attention and you nearly seized again. . . ." The ghost sighed, floating to and fro about her room, as anxious as Clara, making her lace-trimmed white curtains billow in his breeze. Their moods always had reflected immediately upon the other.

"Rupert is suspicious of my taking advice from you," Clara confessed. "In our work as mediums, we tried to keep detachment—"

Louis sighed. "He's worried I'll worsen your 'fits.' I am sure he wishes to banish me. Exorcise me. And perhaps that would be for the best." The ghost looked at the floor he floated above. "We can hardly be lovers."

"We never knew if we had a future. You said it yourself. You wanted to return to New Orleans. I will never leave New York. Your present state notwithstanding, our futures were forever separate—"

"You'll go where your heart leads, Clara," Louis said softly. "Let it . . ."

Clara said nothing, as she wasn't sure what . . . or where he meant. She was a woman of instinct. But when it came to her heart, instinct became mystery.

"How is the state of things out there?" Clara gestured outside, uptown, pointedly shifting focus.

"Dire. I've been appearing anyplace I have a tie, New Orleans being one. There is something off in the air wherever I go. Your Bishop is going to have to convince Congress, and quickly. With his powers of mesmerism—"

"Powers that he is *never* comfortable using on a group. He's highly—"

"Clara, do you understand the severity of this? What you saw in the park is just one instance of a maelstrom. You'll see. By now other events will have been reported in local southern papers, and news will travel quickly north."

"What will?"

"Entire graveyards in Louisiana have been disturbed. Like they . . . rose up at once, in energy and, in some cases, exhumations, a raw unsettling as if tremors of the ground were opening up graves. Some spirits were present, much like that spectral host gathered at the Trinity lot. Everything in the spirit world is awake and alert, and I believe practitioners of any faith, ritual, or sensitivity must feel it, too. I should keep an eye on Andre, of course . . . I hope he's safe. He intervened on my behalf to send back a dagger I'd taken as a proof of interest and loyalty to your Bishop. I hope there aren't any cursing rages turned on him instead of me."

Clara swallowed at the multiple discomforts. Bringing up Andre, and Louis had a way of saying "your Bishop" that always made a certain locked, fossilized sentiment deep in her heart shift with a sudden reanimate life. But she couldn't get lost in all that.

Before Clara could ask for further details about Andre's personal missions and what he was actually doing for Eterna rather than taking up space, Louis continued.

"Concurrent with this gruesome exhumation it seems there have been a few of what could only be described as 'industrial accidents,' costing lives and altering the products and means of production."

"Related to the graveyard incidents?" she asked, trying to get her mind around places of eternal rest and places of industry as similarly targeted when it seemed such a polarity.

"Effie said that in England, industry is targeted, and assumes here as well."

"That's what Bishop needs to address as a national call to Wards—"

"I doubt a Ward could have stopped the reanimation today, or an industrial accident, can it?"

"Warding is one of the initiatives to keep the shadows at bay. The spirits tell me that everything going on has a similar taste. Sour and sulfuric. Pure malevolence. That's what we have to stop from crossing our mental and physical borders." The look on Louis's near-transparent face made Clara feel even worse. "This is just the preface," he said mordantly. A spirit's melancholy was the most desolate breed one could fathom. "I am sorry I had no sense of this while I lived, Clara, else I'd have shifted my work away from bodily immortality and toward the protection of the immortal soul."

"I suppose this is the same work, after all, just changing for the needs at hand," Clara stated. "And you've no need to apologize, Louis. I pray apologies every day to heaven for your death."

"I suppose we must absolve one another, then," Louis said gently.

"Yes, let's," Clara said with a smile.

"I'll return with anything helpful. I need to check on Andre. I don't know what he's been up to, and if I'm not careful, he'll be lost to drink. . . ." With that, the ghost departed. Clara felt the warmth that came in the absence of his draft as an odd reversal, an aching opposite, as she'd grown so fond of having him near in any capacity, alive or dead.

Indulging in the sentiment of missing him for a moment, she curled up under her covers and was soon asleep.

* * * * *

The next morning, up in the offices, while Clara was torn between making coffee or tea—the weightier matters on her mind made the simplest decisions seem impossible—Franklin entered with wires and a newspaper.

"I read the account of yesterday's madness in the *Tribune*. I'm sorry I wasn't there for you, it sounded dreadful," Franklin said, setting the papers down before Clara.

"You were out doing what our mission demands. How can I fault you for that?" Clara said. The senator came in on Franklin's heels and handed Clara a cup of coffee, settling at least that unimportant dilemma.

Thanking the senator for the beverage, Clara realized sheepishly she had been far too preoccupied with her own dealings to have any idea what Franklin had been up to. Thankfully, he had news and elaborated.

"I went upstate, investigating what happened to Justice Allen," Franklin stated, holding up his hand to indicate he'd used his visionary psychometric gift to see the past. "You recall, Senator, that Allen hired Goldberg for the team? Well, whatever got to Goldberg somehow got to him, too. The researcher invited the shadows into Allen's house, just as he had at the laboratory. Similar ritualistic carvings there as well. The judge went swiftly mad, which explains his sudden demise."

Bishop nodded, his expression grim.

"We have to make sure that any contacts we have in real estate scour their workforce, owners, and construction foremen, and examine their buildings closely," Bishop stated. "We can't have any more buildings becoming portals inviting in darkness like that. Fred Bixby can be our bloodhound of deeds and titles, then Evelyn and Reverend Blessing can examine any property that formerly belonged to the Society, to be safe. If Stevens doesn't yet have an antidote for his chaotic poison, bid him make one."

Franklin nodded, taking notes.

"Perhaps I could commune with Louis, to see if he might speak to the ghost of Bernard Smith, the chemist whose offices at Columbia we visited," Clara offered, "to further Stevens's work against the demons."

"Does Smith haunt you, too?" Bishop asked with a quirked eyebrow. "You did take his things and bury them, so he might have cause."

Clara pursed her lips. "I *thought* I was doing right by that." She folded her arms. "And no, he does not haunt me. Does every man you forbid me to meet in life also have the same prohibition to haunt me in death?" she queried, her words at a bit too sharp.

Bishop stepped forward, leveling his gaze. "I have the right to know about the people in your life, Clara, as your guardian."

"You know I'm too old to have a guardian."

A deeply uncomfortable Franklin coughed from across the room, his face reddening at his desk. "Excuse me, Senator, Miss Templeton . . ."

They both whirled to him and he sat back, as if the force of their energies had physically pushed him. It was only then that Clara realized how many of her mannerisms and reactions mirrored her guardian's, and this only irritated her further, glaring at Franklin as a convenient target.

"The work of late is . . . firing up the both of you. . . . You're not usually volatile," Franklin stated. "And we cautioned, due to the toxins, the Wards, all the forces swirling about. . . . Do take care in how you're treating one another."

Bishop's tensed shoulders suddenly relaxed. "Yes, yes, my good man, you are entirely correct. We must be the control in this experiment. We must be sure none of us have been tainted, let none of the darkness creep in on us like a virus. It is good of you to bring up the concern."

Clara just scowled, her face flushed, at her desk. She didn't need any extra stimulus to make her fiery. She had plenty of kindling on her own.

"Should I go, then," Franklin said, the tension in the room clearly making him feel unwelcome, "and meet with Mrs. Northe-Stewart, the reverend, and of course Stevens, to see what other areas might be infiltrated or tainted and to demand an antidote for his altering chemical?"

"Yes, do, and copy down the recipe and concept of the Wards to have in hand, look into making more. Make that Andre Dupris help you. I doubt his brother's work is the only recipe that would prove effective; other areas of the city might do well using different items critical to neighborhood identity. Evelyn will understand best. While I'd like to trust Stevens, I simply cannot."

Franklin nodded and exited. His growing discomfort around Clara and Bishop made Clara wonder what kind of energy or undercurrent they two were projecting.

"What's the news?" Rupert urged, gesturing toward the papers Franklin had brought in.

Clara stared with wide-eyed dread at the headlines.

New York:

CITY PLAGUED BY REANIMATE DEAD.
ELECTRICAL HORROR AND RISEN BODIES
IN CITY HALL PARK

Boston:

COUNTLESS DEAD BODIES DISAPPEAR IN ONGOING
RESURRECTIONIST RING HORRORS

New Orleans:

SATAN'S LABORATORY MANUFACTURES DRUG
OF INSANITY AND UNLEASHES HELL IN
THE UNFORTUNATE WARDS;
SPECTRAL DISTURBANCES ROCK EVERY CEMETERY

"An unraveling has begun," Clara murmured.

She recalled a prophetic vision she'd had concurrent to Louis's death: the British armada sweeping into New York harbor to reclaim New England and beyond.

"We can't let it come to war," Clara murmured. "I trust Rose Everhart, Rupert. We must make the Society, not England, our true enemy. We need direct confirmation of the Master's Society's relations with the British government, as a British invention from the start. We must be sure who is on our side."

"Effie will come through for us," Bishop replied. "Clever as ever, she hit the ground running from the start."

Clara smiled, glad to see a brilliant woman being acknowledged as such. How rare his simple, unbiased acceptance of quality work regardless of gender was in this city, in this age, and among his peers.

"Rupert, if the Society has their way," Clara stated, her eyes falling again on all the headlines, "the world will invert. Nightmare will be empire. We have to counter this very broadly. We must mobilize a widespread response, even from those who do not believe in the magic. Warding, as *demanded* from the highest channels, must be the rule."

Bishop stared at her. After a long moment, he sighed. "I'll talk to Capitol Hill."

"Not just politician by politician like you've been doing these past few days," she countered. "Not just to your friends in the Congress. You need the *whole stage.*"

"Yes, Clara." He sighed again, mopping his noble brow with a white pocket handkerchief. "I'll speak to the *whole* assembled House and Senate."

"Not just speak, Rupert," she urged gently. "I know you don't like to use your powers, but you're dallying at this point. If I could do it for you, I would have already—"

"I *understand,* Clara," Bishop stated firmly, keeping her

gaze. "I'll hold absolute thrall and delay no further. And you'll come with me to be sure it's done properly."

Clara breathed a sigh of relief. "I will. Thank you. I'll soon meet with Rose Everhart and explain that she must insist that England Ward itself."

"I'll . . . make arrangements now . . ." he said, looking at Clara, and for one moment, he appeared more vulnerable than she'd ever seen him. The unflappable senator showed just a moment of fear, and this small crack in his stalwart facade moved Clara deeply.

"Rupert," she said gently, rising to her feet, moving toward him a step. "I know you don't like employing your talents on so wide a scale, you don't like what it does to you—the effects it creates, the perspective it distorts. You told me long ago you had to be careful not to become the villain such powers could easily sway you to be. I'm here to tell you, you couldn't be that villain if you tried. It simply isn't in you . . . You're too noble and too wise. Don't fear your gifts. They were made, if nothing else, for this purpose, for these dark days."

Bishop stared at her, a tear at the corner of one eye. "Why, you grand woman. With such a rousing vote of confidence as that, what indeed do I have to fear?"

He kept staring at her for another long moment before he swept his greatcoat and top hat on and bounded down the stairs, seemingly with a bit of a spring in his step, off to make preparations for Washington. Too old to be seen as merely his ward, she thought, but now, a grand woman? Her cheeks couldn't help but bloom into a bit of a blush, thankfully after he was well clear of the office.

For all that Bishop had done to provide guardianship to Clara, she wanted to do the same for the sake of balance, for his mortal soul and sanity. In addition, she wanted to be sure England did the right thing for its own people, too, as soon as possible.

* * * * *

Rose walked east along Pearl Street, heading for the offices of the Eterna Commission, already composing in her mind the long wire she would have to send to Spire in London, updating him on their progress so far. It was a good thing she had sufficient funds to cover the expense, provided by Lord Black. She wondered what Black and Spire were doing—while it was their job to keep Spire informed, as director of Omega division, he owed her no similar courtesy. With a bit of surprise, she realized she missed her conversations with Spire, her walks with him. She missed *him*.

There had been an odd sort of bond between Rose and Spire from the moment he had tracked her down in her secret secretarial office inside the very walls of Parliament. She couldn't put a label on the connection, but it had grown in the time she and Spire had worked together.

Approaching 61 Pearl Street, Rose set her musings aside, focusing instead on the excitement of her coming meeting with Clara Templeton. Rose had spent much of her life feeling like she was living for two people. The death of her twin had haunted her dearly; she worried at the loss of that kinship as if it were a phantom familial limb. Somehow Clara Templeton had, in the instant of their meeting, eased that endless ache.

The brownstone that housed the Eterna Commission looked fairly ordinary. Rose knocked. A redhead all in black let her in, past two uniformed guards sitting silent sentry inside the door. The woman in mourning examined her warily for a very long time before going to a row of rope pulls and pulling on a center rope. Upstairs, a bell clanged pleasantly.

"All the way up," the woman stated. A dramatic air about her made her seem like more than a mere keeper of the door, and Rose felt she'd been scrutinized in a way that surpassed mere judgment of appearance or character. It seemed the

American team as a whole was gifted, not just isolated persons.

As she climbed the thickly carpeted stair, Rose kept one gloved hand on the carved cherrywood banister. On the top floor, an open door enabled a room lit by stained glass to beckon like the sanctuary of a small chapel.

Entering, Rose saw Clara Templeton standing at a desk, poised in what looked like an act of prayer over an open doctor's bag. She was dressed in a simple utilitarian blue skirt with stripes of ribbon at the hem, a high-collared cream-colored shirtwaist, and a blue silk scarf weighted down by a large black-and-white cameo at her throat.

Before the doctor's bag sat a row of glass vials filled with silt, stone, and paper. To Rose's right, a wide bay window looked out at a skyline that purportedly grew ever taller by the day. She wondered how long it would be before Clara lost her view of the harbor, before this little building itself made way for something newer.

The countless pendants and tokens, talismans and sacred symbols that hung against the glass captivated Rose, whose burgeoning knowledge of and access to a world beyond the mundane made her stare at them with awe and reverence.

"Hello, Sister," Clara said with a beaming smile. The word and expression warmed and disarmed Rose. "Come and sit. Let me explain something England must adopt. Whether your government has it out for mine or not, you simply must understand protections."

"How can you . . . be so comfortable saying 'sister'?" Rose asked quietly.

"Awareness of my past lives lets me see that our paths have always been connected," Clara replied matter-of-factly. "The most natural thing in the world is to welcome someone home. There's a profound power in doing so." She did not linger in sentimentality but instead gestured to the materials before her.

"I have come to think, working on these Wards, that the localized magic is made even more powerful by the energies of identity, pride, and personal fortitude through the ages. Here, let me show you what Louis Dupris . . ." At this, her voice caught, and Rose recalled the details Brinkman had given Omega of the forced séance where it was revealed that Clara and Louis had been lovers. "What Louis created, along with his colleagues."

Clara showed Rose the ingredient list and properties of localized magic for the few cities they had from the files, explaining how the search for immortality had led Louis and other researchers to consider the spirit and strength of local tradition and custom. How the purpose of the Eterna Compound had shifted to a way to protect a person's life from demonic interruption rather than extend it.

"Why are you showing me this?" Rose asked bluntly.

The blond woman smiled again. "This is knowledge I'd give to anyone, truly, friend or foe. The knowledge of the personal divine I hold as a sacred right for all. What you do with it is your own business."

Rose nodded her agreement. "Do I have your permission to explain this to Lord Black and my director, Harold Spire? Spire will not believe any *magic,* but Black will, and Spire will obey Black's orders regardless of his own beliefs. If we state it as a way of drawing out Master's Society operatives, Spire will be utterly amenable, as he hates the Society as a sworn enemy."

"Yes, do. Senator Bishop will soon be in Washington to convince our federal lawmakers to root out Master's Society interference in industrial sectors and to directly instruct the adoption of Warding as a systematic protection. I will be with him to assist in the matter." Clara then came close, to stare at

Rose with an unsettling scrutiny. "Do *you* trust this magic?" she asked. "It will very much help if you do."

Rose thought about this for a long moment, considered the expansion of her senses that had occurred since the attack in London. "If you'd asked me that a year ago, I would have flatly said no. But as you well know, the more one sees, the more one must expand the mind and adapt . . . or perish."

She continued, "The current terrorism seems to aim to curtail such expansions and adaptations, seeking a reversion of human progress. Still, the members of the Master's Society seem to always underestimate hope, peace, love and, most of all, human momentum and will."

Clara's fair, angular face lit up with compelling magnetism. "Then let it be fitting that we, the underestimated women of the world, carry on this fight."

The ladies smiled at each other, feeling hope rise. If Rose wasn't imagining things, the assembled Wards on Clara's desk glowed brighter.

A brown-haired man in his thirties entered the office, walking with a slight limp. Since Clara seemed unsurprised by his appearance, Rose assumed he must be one of her colleagues. He took off his black top hat and bobbed his head toward the women.

As Clara introduced him, Rose took note of the man's neatly trimmed beard, basic brown wool waistcoat and trousers, and dark brown frock coat. "Franklin Fordham, meet Rose Everhart of London's Omega department."

Fordham bowed, though he couldn't help but look at Rose a bit warily. She couldn't blame him.

"Miss Templeton has been very helpful, showing me how we must be trusted allies," Rose assured.

"What's the news from uptown?" Clara asked. "Is Stevens behaving himself with Blessing's dogs?"

"Entirely so. He is spending every waking hour making

Wards at astonishing speeds. He does appear, dare I say, 're-formed.' And I can assure you of this because he regularly lets me touch his hand for veracity."

When Rose looked confused, Clara explained, "Franklin is a psychometric. Do you have one on your team?"

Rose thought of the files in the cellars of Kensington, which detailed all manner of paranormal gifts. "Someone who can touch an object or person and see the past? No. Not that I know of, although our team doctor does seem the type. I'll have to ask him."

"It's terribly useful," Clara said. Franklin beamed, and it was clear he idolized Clara. Rose understood the sentiment. There was a charming, otherworldly surety about Clara that Rose envied. Rose felt that between her own oft-praised qualities of diligence, moderation, and loyalty and Clara's effervescent, pragmatic mysticism, they were a whole, complementary, unit. How could Clara possibly be a danger to her?

Fordham said, "Andre Dupris is, surprisingly, already on hand, gathering materials for the Wards. He said Louis told him he'd be most useful in this capacity, and with his brother's ghostly guidance, he is writing letters to contacts in New Orleans, sharing information and warnings. Reverend Blessing is doing the same within his various communities and fellow exorcists—" Franklin paused, smiled, and said to Rose, "Not that there's a guild of them or anything, but they do know who gets asked onto various dreadful details."

"We're preparing for a storm, Rose," Clara stated. "My team will seek to demonproof our city as best our ragtag little army can. If there's any possibility that the Master's Society is still fully operational, you must do the same in London." A thought occurred to her.

Clara went to her desk—the disorganized nature of it made Rose feel a little ill just looking at it, but the woman's delicate, ungloved fingers danced over envelopes and file folders until she seized something and thrust it in Rose's lap.

"Would this be of use to you? This is my personal file on what I gathered on the Master's Society two years ago. It may have names your team should investigate if you haven't already. Oh"—she snatched another paper off the top of the mess and added it to the stack—"and I wrote out a copy of our New York Wards to use as a template for your team to consider a similar strategy in London."

"Thank you, this will be most useful indeed. I'll come again with any news or directives," Rose said, rising. "Mr. Fordham." She bobbed her head. He rose, bowed, and went back to writing his report of the day.

Rose returned to the embassy's safe house to prepare a wire of all this information.

Adira met Rose in the operations room and quietly sat down next to her. Rose paused what she was writing to take in the beautiful deep-olive-skinned woman before her, who was quiet, composed, a very long black head scarf draped more fully over her person than tucked into the more Western-style dresses she usually wore. She appeared a shell of her regal self, but was calm and collected. Her strength was inspiring.

"I wish to return Reginald's body to England. With the scientists dead, no bodies to recover as they were . . . all burned up . . . and with Mr. Mosley's papers given, with the American offices cooperative . . . what keeps us here?"

"Nothing," Rose replied. "We should return home and protect our own before it's too late. Only people like us are quite prepared to disseminate precautions properly."

Adira nodded and shut herself away again, the weight of grief heavy in the room. If there was sorrow to be borne, it best be borne at home.

* * * * *

Spire had planned, that day, to introduce Stuart Grange to
the solicitor, a Mr. Bertram Knowles, so that Grange could
begin searching properties held by Apex or the Master's Society. When he arrived at his office to find the lengthy wire to
decode, courtesy of Miss Everhart, his plans, as so often happened at Omega, changed.

The message, once deciphered and transcribed, read:

America implementing Wards to combat supernatural attacks. Ward recipe follows. Change ingredients to suit
England. Not your forte, enlist Dr. Z. Expediency advised. Root out M. Soc. sympathizers in government. Attacks may mirror American targets. Warn loved ones to
avoid public spaces, hold to personal protections.

If chemical and electrical attacks are planned, they will
target theaters and public gatherings. Society loves a good
"show," see notes on Nathaniel Veil case. Bishop to mesmerize Congress to insist on Warding. England needs follow.

Mosley recruited, given papers, return ticket, safe
house instructions. Bodies of scientists burned; irrecov-
erable. A wishes to return with R's body. All requesting
permission to return home to address society.

He swiftly sent a reply of assent, struggling to come to
terms with the fact that he'd lost Mr. Wilson before really
getting much of a chance to work with the famed assassin
and spy. It was tragic and senseless, and the death made
Spire feel helplessly angry.

In terms of the Warding, he'd have to do his best. Rose
didn't advise anything lightly, understood his skepticism, and
so this was likely a matter of formality of what Lord Black
would additionally expect of their team.

The "recipe" Rose included was a list of New York rele-
vant items and an explanation that Wards would have to be

adapted to suit the specifics of London on principles devised by the Eterna scientists before their deaths.

Spire, a bit baffled, looked up all the meanings of the word "Ward" and bit back a groan at the notion of that list of ingredients providing "magical protection."

Who in the world would help him begin to sort this out? Ah, Miss Everhart had already thought of that. *Dr.* Z—Zhavia, that quirky madman, likely not even a qualified doctor.

Upstairs, Spire found the arched door of Lord Black's office sitting open. The nobleman waved him in without looking up from his correspondences, thin wire-framed reading glasses on his aquiline nose.

"Word from Miss Everhart." Spire slid the transcript across Lord Black's lavish desk.

Black read the whole of it, then removed the glasses to look up at Spire, who hadn't taken the liberty or initiative to make himself comfortable.

"Yes, bring them back, especially after Reginald . . ." Lord Black's voice caught. "Horrid. So horrid and unexpected . . ." He collected himself before continuing. "I'm going to ask the Americans for their help," Black stated. "If Bishop has to mesmerize his Congress, I'm sure we'll need something like that in Parliament, or they'll never listen."

"I'm not so sure about *that*," Spire countered. "But having the Eterna team here can't help but be useful. And if they aren't trustworthy, we have the advantage of being on our own soil."

"If things worsen, they will worsen here most drastically. If that wretch Moriel is still alive—"

"It's my hunch that he is," Spire offered. "I'll presently be instructing my Metropolitan contacts to keep a close eye on public spaces, theaters, and anywhere Apex has touched." Spire realized that this would mean having to see his father, theaters having been a previous target. "I will get Mr. Zhavia on the 'Wards'"—he couldn't help neglecting the man's questionable title or saying the word *Ward* with distaste—"straightaway."

Back downstairs and left entirely, blessedly, to his own devices, Spire wrote a note to Grange, warning him of potential attacks and promising more details soon, before locating the file on Nathaniel Veil, a popular London actor who appeared in wild Gothic dramas and was an unfortunate devotee of Spire's father. Two years prior, Veil's theatrical audience, at a New York event, had been tormented by temporary insanity thanks to a powdered toxin. Though major injuries were reported, the group had suffered no reported casualties. It was the chemist Stevens who had reportedly made the toxin, before being extradited, as Moriel had been, back to England. With the details of the cases in mind, he set off across the Lambeth Bridge toward a downtrodden section of the South Bank.

His destination was a run-down tenement filled with rich smells, a haze of smoke, and foreign languages from Slavic and Russian inhabitants. It never ceased to amaze Spire how many different worlds lived side by side in London's heart; one section of a street could represent any number of native lands as London proved a refuge or last resort for some of the world's populace.

After the sound of slippered footsteps on the other side of the door, the glint of the peephole was darkened by a peering eye.

"Mr. Spire!" Zhavia said in heavily accented English, clucking his tongue and flinging the door open. Spire had never seen the man dressed as anything but a wizard from old fairy tale books and today was no exception.

The elder, energetic man sported a sweeping blue velvet robe tied with a gold cord, and his long dark hair infused with silver shocks was worn down around his long, silvering beard. He was short, and yet his distinct character made him larger than life.

"Mr. Zhavia, I need your help," Spire said, stepping into the dark book-filled flat lit by candles in leaded-glass lanterns and steeped in an array of scents that Spire's keen nose recognized as tea, incense, sage, and some kind of meat stew.

"Anytime, Mr. Spire," the doctor said genially, his wide black eyes glittering as if his own sockets were two of the candlelit lanterns in the place. "I am of your department. This is my job; I am daunted by nothing."

"Well, that's a relief to hear, really. I am not"—Spire cleared his throat—"*comfortable* with my latest task. We have been asked to create a 'Ward' on behalf of England. Does the word make sense to you?"

"A Ward? Oh, yes, of course." Zhavia eagerly took the paper Spire was holding out to him and read it closely, humming all the while. "Very necessary things, Wards. Critical." He moved his hand in a graceful, dance-like gesture, watching the tendons move and murmuring in Russian. After a moment, the little man said, "What lovely mystic cooked this up?"

"It comes from the American Eterna Commission. It has supposedly been tested on their populace. I have seen no proof."

"Seeing proof and feeling proof." Zhavia poked Spire in the forehead and then in the stomach, and the former policeman managed not to growl or flinch. "Two different proofs, but don't take one as valued over the other."

Spire set his jaw. "We have no guarantee that this is not another trap like what happened to my team on Longacre."

"Oh, no," he said, waving a curled hand, "this is different. There, Longacre was tainted by the dark forces that have tried to turn these very nice, lovely little things into their precise opposite. That was the whole trouble at that rendezvous." Zhavia tapped the paper. "This is smart, simple, good. How much do you need? I assume you'd like me to make it?"

"Yes, please, if you would," Spire said, grateful for the man's enthusiasm, even if the sanity underpinning it was highly questionable. Spire was just following orders. If he was about to host America's Eterna Commission, he had to at least entertain their directives, even if he couldn't allow himself to trust them. "As for quantity, the whole city is what needs protection, I doubt to a man, but at least a representative population."

Zhavia made a whistling sound. "How much time do I have?"

"I am under the impression as quick as you can."

"Indeed. Do I have permission to enlist help?"

Spire thought carefully to craft a reply that in no way incriminated the Crown. "We are limiting involvement only to trusted contacts who have worked against Society aims before. So . . . yes, as we're asking for a large quantity, you've permission, but be utterly circumspect in your associates and let our offices know everyone involved. Is this clear?"

Zhavia nodded. "Quite, sir."

"There's a solicitor named Knowles who dealt with the Moriel affair before it went to trial, I've included his location herein." Spire gestured to the Ward document. "Lord Black at this very moment is out trying to ascertain where in the world the Crown's secret ghost patrol regiment might be hiding; that's a pet project of his. But he'll be readily available to any of your needs, especially as he is far more of a . . . *believer*. Lord Denbury will prove your most valuable resource of all. Go easy on the poor chap; he's been through more than his fair share as a victim of the Society from the start."

"Much appreciated. I'll get right to work, Mr. Spire, and bring everything to your offices. Do I have leave to work there? If I am making many . . ." He gestured around his small flat.

"There won't be the room here. Quite. The basement level

of the department offices is reserved for researchers, so please avail yourself. Lord Black will give you access and a carriage will be sent for you. Would you like a security detail of any kind? I'll not take my assets lightly."

"No." Zhavia looked up toward the heavens and made another graceful gesture, as if casting a spell. "I've a significant"— he smiled enigmatically—"how did you say . . . *security detail,* which has kept me alive thus far."

"Suit yourself. If you change your mind, call on Stuart Grange at the Metropolitan Police's Westminster precinct if you can't find me."

"Thank you, Mr. Spire." Zhavia placed a warm hand on Spire's forehead. "You don't have to believe anything to still be able to do the right thing."

To Spire's surprise, this was actually a comfort. "Thank you," he said.

Zhavia suddenly looked horrified. "Oh! I forgot to make you tea! Forgive me."

Spire exhaled slowly, relieved it was nothing worse. "Least of my worries, Zhavia, truly. I've got to go persuade my mad father to protect his own business. Which I doubt will get me anywhere but a headache."

"Ah, well!" Zhavia bounded up with spry agility and shuffled off to a cabinet. Spire heard the clinking of glass before the man returned and bid Spire hold out his hand. He placed two small white tablets in Spire's outstretched palm.

"For the headache," he said with a smile.

"Thank you . . . *Doctor.*"

* * * * *

Spire had only one relation to warn—his father, with whom he was not on the best of terms. At least his father was a creature of habit, easily located at the small Covent Garden stage where he'd trod moldering boards for the last three decades to varying degrees of melodramatic, sensationalized success. To Spire's abhorrence, that success had peaked after Spire's mother had been killed by a violent intruder. The case had never been solved thanks to bungling, incompetent law enforcement. The event—and his father's embrace of his enlarged audiences, even though they were driven by morbid curiosity—spurred both Harold's estrangement from his father and his mission to become a policeman.

Spire stood for a moment in the dim foyer just inside the theater doors, where red-globed gaslights at half-light cast long shadows, exaggerating Gothic arches and rococo flourishes, the lobby as much a stage set as the theater itself. He grimaced at the theatrical poster for the present production:

THIS WEEKEND ONLY!
An Eighth Wonder of the Dramatic World by Victor Spire, inimitable author of *The Northernmost Castle*!
PRESENTING A STORY OF PASSION AND POISON!
OF REVENGE, RUINATION, AND LARGE REPTILES:

THE DEADLY DAMSEL IN DISTRESS:

ONE IMPERILED BUT CONNIVING WOMAN!
THREE MEN!
WHO . . . WILL . . . SURVIVE???!!!

An advert for the following month's fare was posted across the lobby. Spire audibly moaned at the second shrieking announcement:

IF YOU THOUGHT
VICTOR SPIRE'S *The Northernmost Castle* WAS A DRAMATIC PINNACLE, WE BRING YOU ALL THE MOUNTAINS ALL AT ONCE—JUST YOU WAIT.

ANNOUNCING
AN AMALGAM OF VILLAINY
IN ITS MOST GRUESOMELY PASSIONATE!
FEATURING SWORDFIGHTS, MAGIC HELMETS,
AND POSSIBLY VAMPYRES:

LADY, WHERE, O WHERE, ART THY HERO?!:

ONE DASHING BUT DASTARDLY VILLAIN!
THREE WOMEN!
WHO . . . LASTS . . . THE NIGHT???!!!

Could Spire blame the Master's Society for targeting a place
like this? It seemed to play right into their overdramatic,
seedy hands.

The eccentric box keeper, wearing a brightly colored caf-
tan and a turban stuck with ostrich feathers, turned the corner. Startled to find Spire standing there, she began making
overly affected noises and fanning herself.

After suffering through a long moment of her feigned pal-
pitations, Spire finally said, "I need to see my father, please."

The woman "recovered" immediately and led Spire through
the peeling, gaudily painted orchestra doors into the darkened two-hundred-seat theater that reliably sat only half that
number.

Victor Spire was rehearsing against the solitary ghost light,
creeping back and forth across the stage in an overdone,
painful display of scenery chewing. He wore a long black
cape and a too-tight tailcoat trimmed in red baubles that
flashed with every exaggerated step. His hands were held
out, fingers splayed as if they were claws; he flexed them
repeatedly, like some sort of strange reptile. Clearly he was to
play the "dastardly villain."

The box keeper turned away in a huff, leaving Harold the

sole audience. "Father, it's me." His sure voice echoed through the space's brilliant acoustics. "I need you to be aware of a group that may be targeting theaters and public spaces for dramatic displays of hideous evil. Things . . . *more* terrible than what you're presenting. This place would regrettably make the perfect candidate to launch a spectacle."

The elder Spire gave no sign that he had heard his son speak. He scurried across the stage on his toes, clawed hands held up close as if he were now some sort of nocturnal mammal.

"Father, are you listening to me? Evil will target your theater! It was done to Nathaniel Veil. A chemical compound was released on his followers; it may be as easily done to you!"

The name of a theatrical rival stopped Victor Spire dead in his exaggerated tracks. "Veil." The actor snorted and made a sour face. "That *childe* imitator!"

"Mr. Veil was extraordinarily helpful to the authorities when he was targeted in New York. You could be as well," Spire said, doubting that his father even cared.

A dismissive sound came from the stage. The elder Spire waved one hand before resuming his high stepping, this time with a few dastardly "ahas!" punctuating the ever-so-artful verisimilitude.

"Let me know if anything or anyone out of the ordinary turns up. Though how you'd discern that, I've no clue. Good day, Father," Harold Spire said, then turned and began to exit, confident that he had done his duty. Frankly, he couldn't care less if this audience and actors turned to monsters; no one might know any different.

"You know, Harold," his father called out to him in a plaintive voice that was not affected nor theatrical, just the sound of a tired, pained old man. Spire stopped but did not turn around. "Sometimes one has to mimic the darkness, imitate it, so that it doesn't come lurking about. It's camouflage, really. I've always hoped you could understand that . . ."

He wasn't sure he could understand, but he did not fight back. With no further word, he exited the darkened space. This explanation, or justification, was at least some measure of relief, as his father's seemingly impenetrable oblivion had been the chief source of strife between them.

The fact that Miss Everhart would soon again be returned to him was the bright spot in his near future. Thinking of what befell poor Mr. Wilson, he resolved not to let her go off on further field missions. People he could trust and tolerate were few indeed, and he had no desire to lose the very best of them.

TEN

Good Sir,

It is strange circumstances indeed that press me to request of you trust, action, service, and—dare I ask?—friendship.

You've not been inclined to trust my operatives, and for that I cannot blame you. In my defence, not all operatives have acted under my orders or in best judgement. I regret the misunderstanding that resulted.

I am humbled, I am desperate. London's way of life, whatever virtue it possesses, and indeed, the very survival of the Empire, may rest on whether or not you help.

Your Templeton and my Everhart have conferred as colleagues, and I understand you are to convince your Congress, by mesmeric means I am keen to see demonstrated, that drastic measures of protection must be implemented.

Eager to discuss our situation, perhaps over a stiff drink, I pledge to assuage any lingering ills. If the Ward you have developed to keep the Master's Society at bay as well as an antidote to chemical toxins are indeed a realities and not fiction created to throw England off—for all our sakes, I beg, no games—my parliamentary colleagues will require the same sort of persuasion.

The tragedies you have incurred across the ocean

are pending here. All hell could break loose. Help me avoid unnecessary death and destruction. Please let me know when I may employ your considerable talents. I, and my country, will be in your debt, and I look forward to hosting you and any travelling companions at my estate in Knightsbridge. I await your reply, post haste.

Sincerely,
Lord Black

P.S. I do hope you'll enjoy the case of sherry I've taken the liberty of having sent to your address. I have it on good authority that it's your favourite.

Bishop passed the transcribed wire to Clara. They had been preparing for their trip to the District of Columbia when the fat envelope had arrived at the Eterna offices, carried by a Western Union messenger. The very size of the telegraphed message was impressive—it would have cost Lord Black a pretty penny to send.

"What do you think?" Bishop asked.

"Hard to gauge the trustworthy in a letter written in dire necessity."

"Try," Bishop barked. Clara started, and he moderated his tone. "I need your instincts now more than ever, Clara. Don't be afraid of being wrong about something or someone; don't strive for neutrality. What do you think? Help the man or no?"

"I don't think we have a choice. I trust Everhart. But we have to convince the District of Columbia first."

That would prove as difficult a task as anything.

"Pack for both trips. We leave for London immediately upon finishing in Washington," Bishop said to Clara before turning to Franklin. "Mr. Fordham, I'm going to have to leave you and Reverend Blessing in charge of Stevens. Enlist Fred Bixby in any kind of record searches you need. I know he'll want any updates from his sister, so keep him well informed.

"In addition, I must have, tonight, as much as Stevens has of the antidote for his chaotic toxin. We'll take it to England; you and the others can help him make more for New York. Remember, your heart must be invested in the process, whether you are making Wards or the antidote."

"Yes, sir, be safe, the both of you," Franklin said, masking his own emotion, and was off, a man of duty above all else.

Clara embraced Lavinia long and hard at the first-floor landing as she and Bishop moved to exit the offices for what would be an indefinite time.

"You take care of the gentlemen, my dear," Clara bid her friend softly, affectionately patting the black lace epaulet on her friend's shoulder. "Offer them insights only *you* can see. Your perspective is vital."

"Only if you promise to do the same," Lavinia countered.

Clara smiled. "Promise."

* * * * *

That night as Clara packed for the trips, she reached into her mind for any clues to help her present situation. Had she ever, in any of her iterations, encountered such a dark enemy as this? Was there comfort, not to mention advice, somewhere in any of her pasts?

Squinting her eyes, like the day in Central Park when the visitor had bid her open her eyes to all her past lives, she sank to the floor in a pool of mauve skirts, bustling and boning, and lay back and stared up at the floral-patterned moldings of her ceiling, trying to glimpse even an angle of one of those lives, for a clue she may have missed along the way.

"Clara, what are you doing?" came a voice behind her.

The visitor. Clara knew what she sounded and felt like without even turning to look.

"I'm seeking help and perspective," she replied, keeping her floor vantage point, as there was something strangely calming about it. "What's the point of remembering one's past lives if they can't help? You're Marlowe, correct? Rose said so. It's strange to think of you as a person and not just a figment of my imagination."

The visitor came closer and peered down at Clara, who blinked up at her, refusing to stand on any kind of ceremony for such a creature who came in unannounced.

"You once told me I'm the center of the storm," Clara stated, "and to be worthy of the squall. I've tried to be worthy *every* life, through every storm. I'm trying to see my way. . . ."

"My dear girl." The visitor, Lizzie, smiled down at her. "The storm is not a separate, external torture that loses you at sea and washes you up on some remote beach. The storm has never been outside your control. The storm is *of* you. Once you see your tasks from the perspective of a maelstrom, what may stop you?"

Clara sat up finally. "You comfort someone like you've a hand on a rudder."

"Well, I do consider myself a captain. But that's for another day. The darknesses you're facing frankly can't compete with the sheer life force of a creature like you. *Use* that. Confuse them. Stop the demons' dread press of death by the volume of your *life*. I think you'll see what I mean when it's time to become *all* of you."

With that, she was gone again, leaving the same disconcerting sense of altered time in her wake.

* * * * *

Clara readied notes, one to be left in her offices for Lavinia's information, a wire to alert Effie Bixby, and a final and perhaps most important note to be dropped at the embassy for Rose and her colleagues, detailing when she and Bishop would be presenting before Congress and attending to Lord Black's request should they wish to escort and assist them. Clara suggested the Omega team watch Senator Bishop in action, then all travel together to London. There was no sense in not trying to act as a cohesive team. Their Lord Black was asking for help, and neither she nor Bishop sensed a trap. At least, not an Omega trap.

Franklin's psychometry unfortunately didn't work off wire transcripts. If there had been time to send a full letter, he could have examined the veracity or view of the person writing the letter to judge his character, but the distinct source of author versus telegraph operator severed the connection required for his talents.

After Franklin hadn't been able to fight for the state in the Civil War, a loss of duty he'd been unable to forgive himself for, regardless of physical impediment, heading up the tasks on the home front suited him. Everyone in Eterna and Omega offices was focused now, in a way that the amorphous search for immortality alone never rendered fruitful specificity.

Clara was about to ready a note to Evelyn when an instinct fluttered across her thoughts, and she smiled and put the gilt-edged paper back in her writing desk.

There was a wafting, cold draft, and Louis appeared suddenly at her side, causing Clara a mild shudder but not a start.

"I'll be with you, Clara," the ghost stated gently, "for as much of this journey as I can be, here however I can help. Due to my tether to the living world being stronger for Andre's presence, especially on foreign soil where my spirit has no tie, he too will travel to Washington and on to London. To be of similar service."

"That's all well and good," Clara said, staring the ghost straight in his transparent eyes, "But I'm . . . not comfortable with his traveling *with* us. After what happened . . ."

Impersonating Louis was something she doubted she could ever forgive Andre for. It was an egregious indiscretion, and she would not have her comfort compromised on the trip when it was her confidence that the magic required.

"Of course, I both agree and understand. He likes to travel alone anyway and always has."

"Then I'll see you both in Washington. Good night and thank you for the help, Louis," she said warmly, and she didn't know what else to do but blow the specter a kiss as he faded into the wall.

As Clara packed a few simple dresses, skirts and shirt-waists, workable things, disallowing even the thought of finery, as there was no pleasure in this business, their town house doorbell rang, followed by a large dragging sound and business at the door.

Stepping out onto the landing, she descended to hear Bishop and Evelyn mid-conversation and smiled broadly.

"Please tell me you've told Gareth, and Natalie, about this decision," Bishop demanded.

"I don't ask permission of my husband but I'm not *rude* about it, Rupert. Goodness, of course I alerted him! Natalie is horrified by the trip, naturally, but she's made me swear not to let her Jonathon out of my sight and I've instructions to bring him back with me. She'll allow herself to be distracted by the new wardrobe and gifts I left in my grandbaby's nursery as a surprise."

"Evelyn, you've a *family* now, you don't have to—"

"You *dare* to think you don't need me? Are you not family?" Evelyn scoffed.

"Clearly, I shouldn't dare think, my beloved friend,"

Bishop replied, bemused exasperation and deep fondness in his tone. The two of them sensed and turned to Clara at the landing in concert.

"I knew you'd turn up," Clara said, tapping her temple. "And thank God for it, my favorite medium!"

"I'm going to make sure your congressmen do what they are told," Evelyn declared. "And then, I'm not leaving England until I know everyone in that horrible Society is good and dead and incapable of reanimation!"

Everyone was focused indeed.

* * * * *

Bishop was grateful that his abilities of mesmerism had first manifested in concert with his Spiritualist teachings, when the throes of boyhood had been cast off for the responsibilities of adulthood and his career was well under way. He hated to think what use he might have put mesmerism to before he'd learned the necessary qualities of temperance, patience, and justice.

For Bishop, mesmerism was the ability to bring a person or persons under his thrall and persuade them unto whatever aim he thought was best for them.

For *them*.

Not for *him*.

This was the most vital of distinctions.

Only in extreme circumstances had he ever used this power. Much as he wished to mesmerize the world into equality and sensible justice, that was not what he had been called to do. He knew the ability was as much a danger as a gift, and that kind of guiding of minds was rightfully the province of a divinity, not a fallible mortal.

He'd spent the entire train ride to the District of Columbia deep in meditative thought, silently gathering up power and thrall as if it were a stream behind a dam, ready to be burst open upon Capitol Hill. Clara did not once for a moment disturb him, only offered a supportive smile whenever he turned her way. She kept the deep, contemplative silence that was so comfortable between them, a quality that spoke of their old, familiar souls.

Evelyn had chosen to travel in her own compartment, similarly wishing for peace. With deep sensitivity often came a penchant for solitude. Leaving luggage at the station, the three strolled onto the grand Mall as a quiet, confident team, and within a matter of an hour, the operation was under way.

* * * * *

Bishop managed to call a special session of Congress together—to be entirely honest, he'd mesmerized the vice president into calling a special session—in the Capitol building's grand Senate Chamber. In a matter of hours, the space filled with restless men in fine black frock coats and satin top hats, toting ubiquitous cigars of the most expensive quality.

Many stared at Bishop with contempt, particularly the Democrats, unhappy at having been called away from their dalliances or respites on a matter they clearly doubted was an emergency despite the strange occurrences reported in a few city papers. Not all senators were present, as Congress was between sessions, but enough were accessible that Bishop felt he had a quorum.

At this point, whether they believed him or not didn't matter. Bishop would tell them exactly what to do, whom to trust, and they would do it, not to honor his dear, dead Mr. Lincoln, or the grand, progressive ideals of the Republican Party, not for partisan gain, but so that the devils could not win.

There was no time for any margin of error or pride.

He climbed atop his own Senate desk to see them all more easily and to ensure that his voice would reach every corner of the great room.

"Gentlemen, I have gathered you here today to address a

dire threat. A complete coup, an entire overthrow of our way of life and freedoms, may be at hand. An evil organization, the Master's Society, has taken aim at this country's ideals, using supernatural means to terrorize and injure our population, targeting industry and perverting the dead. You need but look to newspaper reports in New York, Boston, and New Orleans to know I speak the truth."

Bishop felt he owed these men an explanation, in the hope that even though they'd have only a hazy recollection of these proceedings, they could know in their hearts they were doing the right thing. This conviction would bolster the hold of his mesmerism as well.

"Our great cities will be held hostage unless we act now. Protective Wards are being created in New York, and similar compounds will need to be created across our nation's industrial centers. Look to your local Spiritualists, mediums, healers, and ask for their help Warding your cities. My New York office stands ready to advise you.

"This is not witchcraft and superstition. This is life and death, angels and devils. This is not about belief in anything but the love of mankind and the places you call home.

"We recently bled and died together as a war-torn country. Let us not have another war. If we do not fight this good fight, our entire world will be overthrown.

"England faces this same threat, and we must be allies with our former governess, uniting with her now in a mutual struggle.

"What say you, will you Ward your wards?" Bishop cried, and the air around him crackled. The fine silk of his black frock coat buffeted his frame as if there were a breeze, and the crowd leaned in, rapt, his presence and thrall holding all breath.

"Shall we submit to darkness, or shall we protect against it? Do you rise to this challenge, my Congress?"

"We do," they chorused, not in a droning trance, but genuinely moved.

Bishop stepped down from the New York delegation desk to a smattering of applause. With careful deliberation, as if lifting the bow off of the strings of a violin at the conclusion to a beautiful serenade, he broke his hold over his fellows.

"As you were, gentlemen," he said quietly.

Within moments, everyone began to speak as they roused from their reverie. At Bishop's direction, they would think what they were about to do was as much their idea as his. Men formed a line to shake his hand and congratulate him and ask if there was anything else that they could do for the cause.

He looked at the gallery above. Clara was staring at him, smiling broadly, her bright green-gold eyes wide and her face flushed. Bishop in part hoped she had not been caught in the same thrall as his fellow legislators, and in part he did.

Now that the lawmakers were persuaded toward protection, the remaining members of the Eterna Commission would help disseminate Wards locally and submit other city recipes from Louis and Barnard's files to their designated locales. It would take time, but all the affected cities would soon have an aid to stem the tide and then reverse it.

Soon he'd have to repeat this little trick in London, with their infamous Parliament. While he sincerely hoped the British would be as amenable to his preternatural persuasion as his congressional colleagues, something told Bishop he had a certain advantage on home soil. It was, after all, part of the magic.

Seeking courage, he glanced back up at the gallery, to Clara. She nodded. He was convinced she was sharing his thoughts.

Clara wasn't alone in the galley. A few paces off stood Andre Dupris, who carried a parcel of Wards, with the pale grayscale ghost of his brother floating between Andre and Clara. To Clara's left, Evelyn Northe-Stewart was applauding Bishop's performance.

The woman to Clara's right, to whom she was speaking knowingly, Bishop assumed must be Rose Everhart. This likely meant that the three people beside her—a small, nervous-looking man, a tall, black-eyed woman in a bright gown that seemed too flashy for day wear, and a darker-skinned woman in a head scarf whose expression reflected profound grief—were the other Omega operatives.

Though Bishop had extended the invitation to Washington, he, Clara, and Evelyn had left New York without awaiting Omega's reply, so he was most pleased to see them, warmed by this show of trust. A full team indeed, watching him perform. If the British contingent had shown up in solidarity, it meant they had faith in their former colony after all, and his confidence was thoroughly bolstered. Time for a trip to merry old England to do all of this again, hoping for the best.

* * * * *

For their journey, Bishop and Rose had between them decided on the fastest ship, not caring about fine accommodations. Space was small, spirits were cordial—and the trip offered opportunities for further intermingling and bonding.

Rose continued to relate to Clara as her missing sister, feeling that old ache of something lost finally assuaged.

"With you," Rose said to Clara as they sipped tea on the upper deck on a crisp morning, "the life I had chosen, a lonely life of work and solitude, now feels more full; there are possibilities ahead."

"I've chosen the very same life," Clara replied. "We are twins indeed, in so many ways. We see the world in much the same way. Whatever sent my soul to America, it was because we were meant to become greater separately than we would have been had we been together all along. I have to believe that."

"I agree."

"Twins are like that," Louis murmured, hovering near.

Rose noticed Clara glancing at a patch of air that looked as if light was caught in some sort of gauze or film. She asked, "Forgive me, Clara, but I *must* ask. Are you communing with a ghost? I see the faintest irregularity in the air just there and feel a bit of a chill."

"Yes, Louis is here," Clara replied, gesturing to the air beside her. "Louis, Rose Everhart, my age-old sibling, Rose, Louis Dupris, my . . . muse."

Rose was glad she was matter-of-fact about ghosts and in fact treated them as if they were alive, simply with different particulars. Somehow Clara made it all seem perfectly normal, which was in itself a gift.

When Louis was not around, Clara told Rose of their relationship and alluded to a certain aching and unresolved strain between her and Bishop. Now and then Rose would say something about Spire, and Clara would look at her knowingly. Having a friend, a true kindred spirit—not just her distracted relation who was more like an empty body than a confidante—made Rose feel buoyed.

She'd deliberately turned away from what society prized about women in an effort to stake out her own territory, but here was proof that she didn't have to forsake sisterhood. Clara's example perhaps meant that she didn't have to give up entirely on the idea of male companionship either. Clara bucked convention and societal traps and still made room for caring, however much of a loss Louis had been and a complication Bishop might be. A more full life . . . Provided they stopped the shadows.

Rose, ever adept at listening in, enjoyed Evelyn Northe-Stewart and Miss Knight as they compared notes on clairvoyance. Knight was exceedingly keen to learn further mesmerism techniques from Bishop.

Andre and Blakely basically drank themselves complacent, with Louis hovering in rotation between his twin and Clara.

Only Adira Wilson held herself apart; she mourned in her bunk, reading holy texts and keeping a silent fast while her husband lay cold in the cargo bay in a slim airtight metal coffin provided by the embassy. Reginald had converted to Islam for her—she had sacrificed so much to be with him, he would not ask for her faith in addition. Now she would bury him in accordance with their shared beliefs, in a plot of land watched over by the small cottage in the north of England they'd bought to retire to.

Now and then Miss Knight or Rose would check on her and be sure she at least had some water.

Conversations covered any moment the company had— good, bad, normal, or paranormal—that might bear relevance to tasks ahead, thickening a web of shared experience so the shadows could not slip through. Rose hoped Mr. Spire, reigning skeptic, would deign to see this kind of shielding as vital as any physical retaining wall. If nothing else, she would try to be the one thing he could believe in.

* * * * *

Spire, with Lords Black and Denbury in tow, met Eterna and Omega at King's Cross, where the whole motley lot was assembled after having docked at Southampton and taken the train into the corporation of London.

The teams stepped onto the main platform at the loud, luminous steam-filled hub, the morning oddly bright as rare sun cut distinct shafts through glass panes into the grand, smoky station. Spire was glad Miss Everhart's eye was on him like a hawk the moment her boot made contact with stone and floorboard. They nodded at one another, and Spire's ongoing irritation at being wedged impossibly between fact and phantasm eased at the sight of his compatriot.

Introductions were made, with tipped hats, and gloves

meeting gloves in firm or delicate shakes of hand. Once the obligatory pleasantries passed—only Lord Denbury lingered at Mrs. Northe-Stewart's side to inquire eagerly after his wife and child—Spire separated everyone into designated groups with immediate goals.

Spire's intent was to get as many people on task as efficiently as possible. For his part, he wanted nothing to do with the Wards, though he was admittedly curious about Senator Bishop's mesmerism. Spire was as dubious about mesmerism as a particular *power* as he was about Warding, but he felt that an enigmatic, persuasive personality could indeed have an effect on an audience and was worth some consideration.

"Mr. Andre Dupris," Spire said, "since you were aware of your brother's work and then continued on with Mr. Stevens, you'll please follow Lord Denbury here." He gestured the two to stand side by side.

The haunted young lord looked the tall Creole up and down, noting, Spire assumed, his aura.

"He's stable and loyal enough to bring to Dr. Zhavia," Denbury said. "We'll continue to produce as many Wards as possible, substituting English parameters for the ones you used in New York. I understand the man already has a mass assembled." His youthful face had aged, and his tone made it clear that he was weary and desperate to be done with the business. Spire understood that well enough.

Andre Dupris gestured to the air to his right. "My brother will come along to help, unless you specifically object to the presence of a ghost."

Denbury's expression did not change, nor did he look at the spot where Louis supposedly floated. "They've saved my life many a time, ghosts," the young lord said matter-of-factly. "He is most welcome." Denbury led the living and dead brothers away to a carriage.

Spire tried to keep a neutral expression during this distressingly casual conversation about specters, but he could see Everhart holding back a smile so perhaps he hadn't been able to hide distaste.

The Omega field team banded together to help Mrs. Wilson and the train officials unload the steel casket from the cargo car. Before joining them, Everhart said to Spire, "If you're taking Bishop to Parliament, I'll come assist you there. Utilize my office if you need; its passages would be of use to any of your guards or men." She passed him a key.

"Thank you, Miss Everhart, and welcome home," Spire said with a small smile.

She smiled back and strode off to help her associates so that Mrs. Wilson, clad in black from head scarf to boot, did not have to trouble herself with the many painful logistics of death.

Only Lord Black stood apart, and now Spire waved him over to the Americans, privately surprised that the senator, his ward, and their best medium were so composed, courteous, fashionable and, if he had to bet on it, relatively sane. His bias against Americans as loud, inelegant, and generally troublesome evidently had run deeper than he'd thought.

"Lord Black has brought his largest carriage," Spire stated, "so we may strategize together en route to Parliament."

Black led the group out of the station to a four-horse carriage awaiting them at a side portico. Spire brought up the rear of the group and thus was last to enter and see that a man was already seated inside the cab. The medium, Mrs. Northe-Stewart, gasped in palpable recognition at the sight of him.

The black-clad, black-haired man—streaked with premature gray—might have been handsome at one point, but he looked like hell made flesh at present. He held a pair of pistols, aimed at Black and Spire.

"Gabriel Brinkman, what in God's name are you doing?!" Northe-Stewart admonished.

So here he was, Spire thought angrily, the mysterious man himself.

"I am not sure I will last the night," Brinkman growled. "So listen hard and quick. I am a brilliant man with nothing to lose, and there is nothing so dangerous."

"We are listening, Mr. Brinkman," Lord Black said quietly.

Spire examined how the man held his weapons, to see if there was a way of blocking or deflecting the aim. He'd just have to draw his own, hidden up his sleeve. But only at the right moment . . .

"I have not done as either of you have ordered, Lord Black, Mr. Spire," Brinkman stated. "For that I am truly sorry. I have, for the sake of the life of my beloved son, made deals with devils. My son's life has been forsaken regardless, and soon I will forfeit my own, but not until I push hell itself back to its infernal depths."

Brinkman's desperation was palpable.

"Moriel took my boy," the man continued. "He . . . was . . . the most precious thing to me in all the world, after his mother . . ." Brinkman trailed off, eyes watering. To Spire, making sense out of Brinkman fell into place. The agent continued, "None of you have children."

"I do," Mrs. Northe-Stewart, growled. "My Natalie and Denbury, my grandchild, and for their sake—"

"For their sake—" Brinkman overpowered her, his tone rising dangerously, "I expect you to stop the Society's initiatives. I did my best as a double agent, trying to keep them guessing during their first assaults. My son was returned to me, but as a shell, a husk. His soul had been ripped apart from his body, replaced with something ungodly. I never did believe in God, but I most certainly believe in evil; it's living in my boy. I have given up hope that he can ever be returned

unto himself." Almost to himself, Brinkman added, "I've searched everywhere for the canvas that might contain his soul and found nothing."

"We will do everything in our power to—" Lord Black began, only to be cut off by the wave of a pistol barrel.

"Their rituals," Brinkman said in a growl. "Never recreate them, you will only summon more demons. This is not child's play. Stopping the possessed and the dread shadows requires knowledge of their preferences, rites, powers, and predilections. I do not have faith that the populace at large will be able to battle these forces—"

"We don't expect them to. That's why we're here, to help," Clara said, her voice holding an edge for all this man had done to her team.

Turning to Bishop, Brinkman said, "You're going to convince Parliament the same way you did Congress, yes, Senator?"

"I am," Bishop said, impressing Spire with the confidence he exuded.

"I've been long 'assigned' as a Society double agent," Brinkman explained, "and my next orders are to spread Stevens's chaos powder onto the floor of the House of Commons so that the members would all go berserk."

"I'll gather my Metropolitan men to intercept," Spire stated.

"I doubt you can be prepared in time." Brinkman smiled, a ghastly sight. "But a little terror on the Commons floor might work to your advantage. . . ."

With that, in the next instant, the elusive man had opened the carriage as it rounded a slow turn, levied himself down in a nimble jump, and was off like a shot, Spire drawing the pistol from his sleeve and pointing it out the window, but Black closed the swinging door instead.

Everyone sat in silence a moment before Mrs. Northe-Stewart offered a disturbingly matter-of-fact explanation.

"Well, then, we've no time to waste. Lord Black, Mr. Spire, there will be three prongs of initiatives in play," she began. "Some of which you have had experiences with already. If the experiments are similar, you will find first attacks upon souls, ripping them from bodies to serve as shells for demon inhabitation. Then reanimate bodies, powered by the dead whose body parts are collectively tied to the patchwork corpse. And last, via a powder that renders an entire change in a person from docile to violent, as Mr. Brinkman is describing, you will see this launched upon Parliament. The Master's Society wishes to overturn the world order into his hands by devilry and chaos. There is good news that Mr. Stevens is repentant and under our employ and gave us a significant store of antidote for the violent toxin. We can dose the MPs."

Spire was focused upon what Brinkman had said about advantage. "Is the toxin lethal?"

"Only if they harm themselves or others," Miss Templeton replied. "So your men will need to safeguard those who can't be helped."

"Brinkman may be right that these men will be more apt to listen to you, Senator, if the threat is real to them," Black said, seeming loath to agree with their unhinged operative.

The company was startled as the composed medium suddenly pounded her gloved fist on her satin-clad knee. "What good are these gifts with such blind and massive holes?" Northe-Stewart exclaimed. "I should have foreseen the scope of all this years ago! I *know* things." Spire noted the pain across the whole of her stately body. Miss Templeton reached out to take her hand.

Spire could not understand this medium's gifts, but he did understand her agony. Every time he hadn't solved a crime, caught a killer, overturned every stone, missed something that after the fact seemed obvious, he grieved and nearly tortured himself over it. No matter how many cases he had tried or won, it never felt enough. There was always something more he could have done.

"These terrible matters put up walls," Lord Black reassured. "I've been misled and lied to all along. We cannot blame ourselves," he said gently. "At some point these devils seem to turn on 'their own,' and we can hope they do so quickly."

Spire turned to the nobleman. "Lord Black? If you want enough of my men to cover and attend to even a fraction of the hundreds of MPs who might be present, I need three hours and permission to say whatever I please to convince them. I was head skeptic of a team of skeptics. You can't ask my men to join this cause out of *belief;* we'll have to ask them to do their jobs as protectors of the peace and leave it at that."

"Three hours, Mr. Spire, you have them," Black granted. "And yes, your judgment remains yours, thank you. Say whatever will get the job done."

Spire nodded and turned to the Eterna Commission. "Which of the American team feels confident in administering Stevens's antidote?"

"I can, and I will," Clara Templeton volunteered. "I also advise, as we have enough of the treatment for your men, that they take it beforehand, as their keeping their cool is more important than anyone else, save ourselves. Senator Bishop will need to keep the subjects in thrall. Evelyn will need to read the room for threats and liars. I should be the tactician with the antidote, and Miss Everhart will help me." Miss Templeton spoke with the kind of unflinching due process Spire admired, a quality that reminded him entirely of Miss Everhart. Those two must have got on well during the journey, like long-lost sisters. He hoped Everhart was doing all right assisting Mrs. Wilson; he looked forward to speaking with her.

"Good. So we'll assemble the masses and see what sorts out." One by one, Lord Black took in the rest of his company, clapping his hands together in the tense cab. "Well? We've got to give Mr. Spire three hours. Let's take your trunks to my home, my footmen will have the lot taken care of. We'll take a moment of well-earned rest, then it is off to Parliament to rejoin Miss Everhart, await good Mr. Spire's readiness, and see what kind of a scare those poor bastards are in for!"

Clara was very taken by the understated grandeur of Lord Black's fine Knightsbridge home, a neoclassical-style building with bright openness, simple lines and arches, wide spaces, an inordinate amount of verdant ivy in small ceramic pots, and white-paneled walls. She was glad to sit for a moment with a fresh cup of tea on a sumptuous divan in a large parlor where a set of French doors showcased a verdant rear garden.

They were tended to by the most pleasant, and handsome, of butlers, a man who treated the lord of the manor with a fond fastidiousness that spoke of a closer bond than she'd have expected from an office traditionally groomed to be detached, quiet, and unseen. But Lord Black was a man of warmth and of equalizing. He made no one feel out of place or station.

The guest room assigned her was white paneled, dressed in blue silk curtains trimmed with wispy lace, and bedclothes of the same, the upper walls lined with flocked wallpaper in floral patterns. She longed to lie down on the bed a moment and rest from the extensive travels, but she was afraid she'd sleep right through their next appointment, the most vital of all, as there really was no time to waste, especially considering the unpredictable Brinkman. . . .

* * * * *

As fond as Clara had been thus far of London's sights seen from train, carriage, and street, she was most amazed by the beautiful Gothic Palace of Westminster, its extensive spires rising with breathtaking splendor alongside the Thames, a most glorious riverside sentry.

The great vaulted Westminster Hall, which served as the base for the parliamentary expansion, led into modern, freshly built wings, though the Gothic sweep and pomp of its architecture made it classic and timeless. Designed by Prince Albert as a testament to his wife, the queen, it spoke of the grandeur of the Empire, and Clara found herself not nearly as fond of Capitol Hill in comparison. Perhaps it was the old soul in her that was so captivated by these halls instead.

The House of Lords was all done in red, the House of Commons in green, and Clara noted how dressed down the Commons was compared to the Lords in its lobby and halls, corridors, rooms, and appointments.

Black led them into the House of Commons, where the entourage was immediately accosted by various MPs in dark frock coats. Clara spotted the occasional decorative dandy-like cane, likely lords, a few peacocks among the gamut in bright colors or stripes, but most of the men seemed to prefer generally sober, functional attire.

In response to queries as to why those assembled had been brought together, Lord Black only smiled.

Just before a call brought the top of the first legislative session of the day to order, Harold Spire appeared at the top rear stairwell and offered a little salute to Lord Black. His men were ready, then. When they had parted, Bishop handed Spire a box of ample antidote for his men, and Clara hoped Spire believed them enough to have implemented it, along with her instruction that they mask their noses and mouths, as they could not be sure when and if Brinkman would strike.

A rush of nerves flooded Clara's body; suddenly her corset was too tight beneath her shirtwaist, her bustle chafed against her back despite its being modified for a work habit, her skin prickled beneath her muslin layers, the room was too warm, and she was terrified that everything would go wrong.

"Gentlemen of the Parliament," Lord Black said once the roll was completed, standing and seizing the floor.

There were a few calls of "Now what?" and "Don't you lords ever get tired of bossing us around?" before a horde of police officers, Clara glad to see all in powder-shielding scarf masks, entered the House.

"Do not be alarmed," Black said, speaking loudly to be heard over the complaints and concerns of the lawmakers. "I have been advised by a commissioner of the Metropolitan Police that a drill is being run today, a—shall I say— Fawkes-ian preemptive measure, hence the masks to protect from imagined fire and smoke. Let them do their job as you do yours, thank you."

There was a hush and then a hubbub of voices as the parliamentarians considered this, watching Spire and Grange as they led sets of half-masked Metropolitan officers into the upper gallery benches.

Lord Black continued from the Commons floor, Bishop by his side, glad that Lord Black invited a considerable contingent from the House of Lords to sit in for this special session. It seemed to Clara that Black had his own pull and mesmerism unto his colleagues. He was indeed an engaging, persuasive man. They were interesting complements to one another, these two contingents forced to become colleagues.

"Gentlemen," Black boomed over the hubbub, "if you value your lives and the fate of this country, you shall listen to this American."

At the word "American," the air erupted with infamous hisses, boos, and general reactive shouts that emanated from parliamentarians no matter, it seemed, if the sentiment being expressed was favorable or hateful. It was hard to tell, Clara realized, what the British liked at all. Disdain, or the love of noise, seemed the default here.

Clara felt the atmosphere of the room change as the senator began to exert his mesmeric qualities. The parliamentary rabble quieted the moment he opened his mouth. Just as in Congress, the reaction to his speech was magical. The men leaned in, a wave of murmuring creaks of leather seats and a sea of shifting frock coats.

"Gentlemen, there is a great threat at work in your city. I lead a commission that has been dealing with strange, paranormal matters."

The word "paranormal" broke Bishop's thrall and generated another round of boos and hisses. Undaunted, Bishop continued, and his eyes—his very presence—exerted complete authority over them and all fell silent. Clara caught Black's and Spire's looks of amazement, clearly never having seen such an effect before.

"I don't care whether you believe me or not, hell *is* coming home to roost on your banks, London," Bishop proclaimed. "Now you can either stand with us as we give you an antidote for a weapon that may be at any moment deployed upon you, or you can suffer the consequences of a mind-altering, recklessly endangering compound and vulnerability to dark forces.

"Take heart, whether you believe in the existence of ghosts and spirits, reanimated dead, or the power to transform a mind with a mere powder, this is not unfamiliar to us. In my city of New York we have already encountered and dealt with these pending threats. Take part in preventative care and we'll be a united front. If any doubt this, I'm sure you recall the Master's Society, and one Beauregard Moriel, one of your own citizens, the madman behind the plots our countries face. His work lives on. Join me here in protecting yourself. I will be the first to do so."

Bishop turned to Clara. She handed him an additional vial with a small bit of the powder, to which she'd added water to make it drinkable. Their team, including Black, Spire, and Rose, had all ingested the antidote the moment it was unloaded from the carriage outside. He downed it in a swig and worked not to grimace at the taste.

While it was hoped that Brinkman would wait until the MPs could make a choice to take the antidote willingly before charging in to detonate the drama, he did not heed anything but his own timetable. There was a flurry of movement at a mezzanine door, and Clara's nerves ratcheted to a new height, but as there were no spirits present, she was in no danger of seizing. She was nervous and alert, but in control.

All in black, collar and shirtsleeves undone, frock coat billowing, either the picture of a careless revolutionary or Mr. Rochester after one too many drinks, Brinkman burst into the room with antiquated blunderbuss of a gun.

"For the old ways and blood rights!" he cried, and the American team had just enough time to cover their own mouths with their kerchiefs—none wanted the offending substance in their lungs regardless of having ingested the antidote—before Brinkman fired the chamber, releasing a cloud of red powder into the air.

"Cover your noses and mouths, gentlemen," Bishop cried. "Don't breathe in, that's the very toxin itself! We have the treatment, keep the faith and hold on!"

The assembled MPs reacted to this in a variety of ways. Some did exactly as Bishop instructed and came right to him. Some panicked and went toward the doors, only to find them blocked from the outside. Clara wasn't sure who was responsible for that. Some just sat in the benches, stunned. Many turned toward Black and the rest of them and began shouting accusations of treachery, as if this were staged to hurt them.

They weren't entirely wrong.

For those who happened to take in a lungful of the offending agent, the change was nearly instantaneous—hideous and thorough. Bodies seized and hunched over, cries turned guttural and bestial, and the desire toward rage and violence was palpable.

Men lunged for one another like fighting bulls. Fists were thrown, insults from the most puerile parts of the mind were lobbed in unfolding volleys, and some just thrashed around on the benches where they had been sitting or where they collapsed. It was a terrible display of devolution.

At these first transformation signs, the Metropolitan Police deployed their designated response. They strode in files from the upper seats down to the Commons floor and pried apart members who were at each other like fighting dogs in a pit. Whatever Spire had said to these men had prepared them well. None looked daunted, some seemed surprised, and most, carefully dispersed among the throng, were perfectly able to keep these men from hurting themselves, others, or the parliamentary grounds itself as they flailed, wailed, and wrenched at their subduing officers.

The fits subsided eventually. Members who were overcome slumped to their knees and then to the floor, or over the green leather seats. Those who had taken the cue of the officers and the Omega and Eterna teams, and tied a kerchief or lengthened a cravat or ascot over their mouth and nose, had kept their wits together and looked on in wide-eyed horror at the scene unfolding. Some turned to stare at Lord Black as if he were either a savior or directly responsible.

Rose took to the House of Commons desks and rails with moist rags and began wiping up the dense powder residue. Thankfully, the stuff had weight to it so as not to be a continuously airborne threat. A few of the most sober of the MPs assisted her. Clara was busy tending to those who were horrified as they came up to her for an antidote, whether they had been affected or not. Her reassuring smile seemed to calm them.

Rousing those who had gone unconscious during the throes took about fifteen minutes, and as they came to, they stared around the Commons floor as the vague, hazy memory of their "fits" came back to them.

Clara grimaced. Even though a lot of these men were stubborn and arrogant, she empathized with what it was like to come to after being overcome, wondering what kind of scene one may have made. She knew that all too well from her condition.

Lord Black no longer had to shout to get anyone's attention; he merely spoke quietly into the murmuring throng. "Well, gentlemen, I'm sorry it came to that. I had word of an attack and thought we'd have time to better protect you. But we still can. Please comply with Senator Rupert Bishop of the great state of New York. Thank you."

Everyone turned sheepishly to Bishop as he stood, climbing atop the clerk's desk for better effect.

"My English friends," Bishop began, "if you do not work to protect yourself, all of London, perhaps the country, will fall. We are here to help you. Believe me or not, you are lucky that what just happened was not infinitely worse.

"If any of you are involved with the Master's Society, if Beauregard Moriel or Francis Tourney was an associate of yours, you will be found out," he stated.

Clara was not surprised to see Spire studying the lawmakers as Bishop spoke, taking note of who looked nervous. He was very good at picking up subtle clues and cues. While she could make an interrogation list based on clairvoyance and sensitivity, his abilities came from thorough study of human behavior.

"If you are guilty of such associations, come forward now and protect yourself. The longer you wait, the greater the likelihood your supposed allies will destroy you. You will be torn limb from limb and your body exsanguinated, as if the room in which you die has become a canvas for your blood. I wish that were an exaggeration, but it has happened with those involved in the Society that have invited in the purest evils. If you have aided or abetted them in any way, there is yet hope for your eternal soul to escape the jaws of hell.

"We are working on Wards that can protect you. We bid you to Ward each of your representative districts. Be cooperative with Lord Black and all will be given you. The Wards will be vitally important in the coming days, so please be amenable to them at Lord Black and Mr. Spire's distribution. If you have not already received the antidote for this toxin, please see my associate, Miss Templeton."

Terrified, quiet, affected men lined up soberly before Clara at the desk of the clerk. Vial by vial, she administered the antidote to each contrite member, if it hadn't been done already, bid them drink the contents, and collected the vials in the wooden boxes that carried the tubes as pegs in holes fit for their circumference. For the Wards, many MPs were discussing with Lord Black how to access and distribute them.

"Last," Bishop cried out to the room, in perhaps his most persuasive of reverberate tones. His powers of thrall still had the room by its throat. "Lord Black will give an account of these proceedings to local papers, on *our* terms and serving *our* purposes only. If any of you *are* involved and expect to report to Master's Society operatives about this little display, do so, but say only that dark aims gained a success today. Say nothing of intervention. That is for *us* to know. Is this entirely clear?"

There were murmurs and nods.

"People of the British Parliament, is your cooperation entirely clear?" The senator had raised up his arms, as if collectively holding the room.

A rousing "yea" shook the floor.

He lowered his arms slowly. Clara's senses allowed for the pull of his magnetism to shift and wane, his field returning to that of a mere enigmatic presence, not a whole dynamo in and of himself. He turned to find her gaze, and she was glad she was there waiting for it, so she could beam at him. He allowed himself a pleased smile in return and stepped down from the height upon which he had stood.

The next moment, she felt a presence next to her and turned to see the familiar face of Ephigenia Bixby. At the sight of her friend, she routed the remaining men to Miss Everhart, who was serving the line on the opposite side of the House dais.

"Effie!" she cried with a hug. "I'm so glad you received our wires. Did they give you hell trying to get in here today? Women don't seem to be much welcome."

"Mr. Spire saw me poking about outside as he gathered his men and showed me in, via Miss Everhart's secret passages," she said with half a smile.

"Tell me everything and help me prioritize what I need to know and do, and in what order," Clara begged.

"I've amassed a fairly good list, thanks to the help of Evelyn's friend Mr. Knowles. Apex took over the old Society offices in Earl's Court, as if nothing ever happened, evil begetting evil under new names. The Master's Society crest went out of vogue when Moriel was first arrested and Apex replaced all. I wired the offices not long ago with any American property holdings I could find listed here."

"Good, Franklin needs to be kept abreast of every detail."

"It's *bad,* Clara," Effie murmured.

Clara noted the dark circles under the woman's sharp eyes.

"You've not had an easy time of it, have you?" she asked quietly.

"No, and when I return home, I think I'll be resigning."

"Why? What have we done?" Clara said, aghast.

"Not you, Clara. I just . . ." She stared at the still milling members of the House. "Today, when a company I was inquiring about said of one of its workers who fell to his death that 'it didn't matter, because his skin color was brown' . . . I just . . . I can't do what I've been doing in the manner in which I have been." Effie stared at Clara with unmasked pain on her pale brown skin. Silently, Bishop had joined them and Effie folded him into the conversation. "What good is *passing* in your world if it's only adding more numbers to those who feel they've the right to visit injustices time and again on those arbitrarily considered lesser? I think Fred and I, once all of this is resolved, will move back to the Tenderloin."

Her anguished gaze found Bishop. "There, at home, if blood runs in the streets, *our* blood, not just that of the pigs and cattle, some seem unable to distinguish from human, at least it is blood I'm no longer pretending isn't of a lineage it is."

Bishop replied calmly, "I will support you and your family in whatever decisions you make. Just let me know how I may help facilitate, if at all."

Perhaps Effie had imagined Bishop would put some barrier in her way, for she seemed relieved at his response. Clara saw tension leach from her friend's body.

"Ah, one of yours, then, I see," Harold Spire said, approaching Clara and nodding at Effie. "This crafty young woman has a penchant for tracking me. First, when Lord Black and I attended the queen's parade, where she witnessed a rather unfortunate near assassination. I don't like such embarrassments to go by without making friends out of them," he stated. He leaned in. "I'm glad you found Everhart's passages earlier. I couldn't bear you skulking around outside any longer." Effie returned Spire's partial half smile.

"Effie Bixby, Mr. Spire," Clara introduced before turning to Spire. "Sir, your presence here today has been exemplary, and I hold you and Lord Black in high regard for trying to control this government, allowing ours to help and advise yours. A brave, bold step."

"I don't really have much choice," Spire stated, addressing both women. "None of this is as I, a mere policeman and detective, would have planned, believed, or hoped. But I appreciate friends above foes."

"I would like to consider you a friend indeed," Clara said, "and I hope our offices will continue to coordinate in a manner as effective as this."

"Whether it is effective is yet to be proved, but yes," Spire conceded.

At that moment, Spire's Metropolitan colleague Captain Grange, approached him.

"Sir, which of the MPs would you like taken in for questioning and possible arrest?"

Spire made a few subtle gestures around the stately room toward any he had deemed suspect during the proceedings. "And, while you're at it, Grange, ask Mrs. Northe-Stewart if she agrees. She's got . . . good instincts."

Clara smiled. The king of skeptics couldn't call it clairvoyance, but Clara didn't care. "Instinct" was a fine word for it if ability itself was respected and valued.

The kind-faced redhead named Grange nodded and approached Lord Black, who was consulting with Evelyn, likely advising him on the same suspects. Within the next few moments, with mere nods from Lord Black, policemen quietly led out several representatives. The redhead returned, bobbing his head to his superior. "Thank you, my friend.

Now make sure there's an increased presence around Westminster as a whole," Spire instructed.

"Grange, my good man," Lord Black added, "can you be the one to give an account to local papers? The Society will want to think their plan a success, but don't terrify the populace. Nothing sensational, but give a tale colorful enough to be pleasing to those wanting such news, and nothing of the antidote or our future distribution of Wards."

"Of course, sir, as the senator suggested, it shall be done." And the man was off with determination.

Effie handed several sheets of paper to Spire, at which point their company was joined by Miss Everhart. "These are the businesses' moving materials and properties from Master's Society to Apex locations, which your MPs and police forces will have to watch and Ward," Effie stated. "Now, if you'll excuse me, I must go get some rest, I've not slept in days."

"Noted, Miss Bixby, please do so, and thank you, this is exactly what I've wanted to get hold of," Spire stated with a bow of his head. Effie nodded, reached out to squeeze Clara's hand, and vanished into the vaulted Gothic arched shadows of an exit corridor.

Spire turned to address Clara and Rose together. "I am . . . uncomfortable with a . . . Warding process; I don't understand it. But I have seen what the toxin does, and I do believe in this antidote. I hope you can prove the Ward to me similarly, though I'm not sure I want to see another 'test' to do so."

"The next days will undoubtedly give us a chance, Mr. Spire," Clara stated. He set his jaw grimly in response.

Clara felt comfortable in the Omega team as a balanced initiative. Every team needed a skeptic, and Spire did his department no disservice in this.

Eventually, the teams filed out onto the green and into a waiting carriage belonging to Black, who insisted on hosting the group at his home. There was a second fine carriage beside Black's, Lord Denbury having arrived to rendezvous with them, the young man pacing in the courtyard, awaiting them. Evelyn volunteered to fill the lord in on the parliamentary proceedings, and the caravan proceeded en route to Knightsbridge, leaving Clara, Bishop, Spire, Rose, and Black to the larger cab.

It was only once the carriages hurtled *past* Lord Black's residence that they realized there was a problem. They tried to unlatch the cab doors, but they were jammed shut from the outside. There was no other explanation than that they were all being abducted.

"Sweet *Lord,* not again," Clara murmured under her breath.

"Lord Black," Spire asked, staring at every seam of the carriage construction, "did you notice anything different about your footmen today?"

"I confess, my friend, I didn't look up at them. I didn't notice," Black said mordantly. "That's the horror of how the Society seems to work its way into things, through those whom our positions of privilege have trained us not to see...."

Spire noticed that one of the windows was slightly ajar but before he could attempt to widen the gap, a black-gloved hand appeared and dropped a tiny open bottle into the cab. Smoke was issuing from it, and the air in the confined space quickly filled with noxious fumes. Coughing and gagging, the members of the Eterna Commission and the Omega department faded into unconsciousness. When they came to, sore and ill, they were in Greenwich.

The carriages stopped abruptly. The doors were thrown open and the passengers roughly yanked out and deposited onto the stone walkway of a grand estate.

"Of course," Black said bitterly, looking at the vast Gothic edifice looming before them. He explained to the others, "Welcome to Rosecrest, the Denbury estate. I assume it has fallen again into the dread hands of the Master's Society."

The group was herded up the walk by the burly, possessed guards. A separate envoy of two scarred men in besmeared workmen's clothes, their eyes sparkling dark and vacant with the tell of the possessed, dragged Lord Denbury and Evelyn up the walk, insult to injury, this disrespect on the young lord's own rightful property. He was fighting them tooth and nail, his fury entirely palpable, but with a third possessed body called up to help contain him, he was overcome.

Of Andre, Knight, Mrs. Wilson, and Blakely there was no sign. Clara hoped this meant they remained free, pursuing their Warding work at the Omega offices. Perhaps, she prayed, Louis would be called to her side to offer insight and then to warn and alert the others. However, as the spirit world was unreliable and operated on its own time, she could not count on this.

As she approached the manor, Clara's heart gave a sharp thump. She knew this place, had seen it in visions, of fire and chalices, shadows and earthquakes, broken justice and iterations of lives. . . . Her jaw sagged and she spun toward Rose, only to find Rose already staring at her, her face expressing equal shock. The visions or dreams must have been shared between them.

* * * * *

Was this it? Rose wondered. Would they, prophetically, betray one another right here in this very place? In trying so dearly to avoid it, would they fall catastrophically right into the very traps they wished not to? Rose was confident that Clara did not mean her any more harm than she did in converse. But what good would that be if they were compelled by forces beyond the average human will?

The house was fairly dark, save for an odd, disembodied glow that cast a deep bloodred light over the building's rough-hewn red sandstone exterior. One garish swath of moonlight illuminated the peaks of the estate's turrets.

The unnatural, ungodly stage, where unimaginable horrors would undoubtedly unfold, caused a pit of dread to yawn open in Rose's stomach. She glanced at Harold Spire. He was white as any ghost he did not believe in.

The British and the Americans were callously "escorted" down the hall by black-eyed, possessed footmen and ushered into a long, grand dining room.

A table was set for them. A last supper entirely spoiled, with more than a few insects having quite a time of the feast of turned turkey, spoiled jellies, fruits, and moldy puddings. This seemed representative of the Society's inversions of faith and power. Rose couldn't be sure when it had been left there, or if it was for them or for some other poor unfortunates, but it was disgusting nonetheless, and a sign Rosecrest had been in darker hands for longer than they knew.

A network of metal tubes crept up the walls and across the ceiling, culminating in what looked like vast metal showerheads. There was a sulfuric scent upon the air, under the smell of rotting food.

To Rose, their fate seemed very clear.

They would be gassed, collectively, a group execution. A death much like their teams' scientists, a horrid irony these dark forces seemed so fond of.

* * * * *

The guards shoved each person into a tall, velvet-backed seat and bound them to their chairs.

"Do have some supper before midnight," one of the guards said with a chuckle, his voice disembodied, low and animalistic in its growling, wet affect.

Clara stared at the moldering cutlet that had one bite out

of it from the last poor individual placed here before their sacrifice. A small insect crawled out from under the meat before miring itself in stale gravy. The dining knives were very dull. Not much use even if she could shift her chair to grab one.

Looking around, Clara watched her colleagues take stock of the room, looking for weapons and vulnerabilities. They would have to be crafty and clever in order to outwit those who had traded their souls for the darkest of powers.

A great deal could be done, but nothing that would be faster than a bullet, and each of the guards appeared to be armed. Where was Brinkman when they needed him?

The man of the hour himself soon joined them, and the fury on Evelyn and Denbury's faces meant this was, again, quite personal. Surely this was the man who was meant to have been executed.

Beauregard Moriel was short and balding, with beady eyes, fleshy fingers, and pale, pasty skin. He strode about the room, a caricature of regal comportment in a sash and grand vestments of arcane lineage.

Clara was sickened and fascinated. Her instincts were whirring at top speed, trying to hit upon a Spiritualist linchpin that could put a wrench in the grim proceeding's gears.

"Ah, my foils and foes," he began grandly. "It's been amusing having you poke about my enterprises. I thrive on opposition and conflict, but you're now getting in my way and I can't have that, not when the restoration is about to begin. I don't know what you managed to do inside Parliament today—I'm sure you tried to undermine me—but any loss I would have suffered I will now gain. Having you here further powers my engines at Vieuxhelles. By your very blood, life energy, and bones.

"In retrospect," Moriel continued, "all of you *titled* folk have caused me far too much *effort*. Years ago I should have sailed my ship entirely on the dead backs of steerage. Cargo, really. The world breaks down into first class and cargo, don't you think, Lord Black?" he asked in a conspiratorial tone,

"I could hardly disagree more, you mad wretch," Black fumed.

Moriel sighed. "Mad," he said with a snort. "How could a madman amass all that I have?"

"Now *that* I do want to know," Lord Black grumbled. "How you infiltrated two countries."

"You take so much for granted, you know," Moriel said, as if he were talking to a child. "Do you ever pause to think about the companies that provide you with basic services and goods? Really? About *where* they are, *what* they do, *how* they conduct business? You don't. That's how I've gained ground. I have, before your blind eyes and from under your upturned noses, created an industrial web, and now you and New York are mere flies to harvest."

"You can't have the loyalty you think you do," Spire spat, wresting against his bindings.

Moriel clucked his tongue and began a lap around the table. "It's amazing what opiates to the people can accomplish. Chemicals have been critical to overtaking dull minds of ordinary folk. Where that has failed, rending the soul from the body efficiently creates my dear drones. I have, as you know, many methods by which I craft compliance. Why, if I had time, I'd have you all painted on my wall of souls!"

Moriel whipped back a curtain Clara had not noticed before in the room's dimness. The wall thus revealed was hung with at least thirty oval portraits, each about half a foot wide. These were not mere images; Clara could feel that they were souls, banished into the frames. Their life force was undeniable to her heightened sensitivities. Undoubtedly, the Society's dark magic had given the victims' bodies over to those coal-black shadows.

This assault by the darkest arts pressed in on Clara, testing her limits. She felt the first trickle of symptoms of her condition, far off still but enough to be worrying, an itch between the connective tissues of her muscles and a slight shift of her vision. Pressing her eyes closed, Clara took a deep breath through her nose, catching a whiff of rotting food, which turned her stomach but grounded her firmly in her body. She mustered her will: She would not seize. *She would not seize.*

As if she had been touched, she opened her eyes to find Rose staring at her. The comforting, anchoring presence that had helped her weather City Hall Park again bolstered her here. Her muscles unclenched, and she allowed her soul sister to share in the burden with a knowing, appreciative look.

"It's a shame I won't be able to have you in portraiture for my coronation ceremony," Moriel stated. "But your bodies will do better service as sources for good parts with which to make up reanimated corpses. I want at least twenty for my procession to Parliament's doors. You'll tie nicely to the wires." He whirled to face Evelyn, adding, "The gifted ones *especially* do."

She spat at him and he spat right back with a delighted laugh. He looked around and sighed in contentment.

"I must go home, there are preparations to complete. Ah, but this place"—he sneered at Lord Denbury—"this dear, sweet, vulnerable, all too perfect place. . . ."

Moriel smiled with the kind of patronizing confidence that should have summoned hubris to strike him down like in tales of old, but no hand of God showed itself.

"You see, if a goodly place is *twice* overtaken," Moriel said, holding court at the head of the putrefying table, so joyous in having an audience for his horror, "hallowed, then sullied, then hallowed and then sullied again . . . why, it's *twice* as powerful a conduit!"

"Only because you've trapped all the good of the place," Denbury hissed. "Even the ghosts of my ancestral home cannot cross over this tainted threshold."

"Indeed," Moriel said delightedly. "No matter what happens here, this place serves as a feeding ground for what I've wrought at Vieuxhelles. If this place flourishes, or should it burn again, it all feeds the greater battery of my home estate. Death feeding my new life there, tied in the darkest of ley lines, from your home to mine," he sneered at Denbury.

It was horribly ingenious, Clara thought, the idea of one furnace of malevolent energy lighting and fueling the fires of a second, these dual crucibles of hell.

"The good of this place is banished outside," Moriel snarled. "I was able to Ward this house to *my* purposes, not your pathetic little solutions, because you *failed* the first time!" He snorted. "You all failed. I grew. I flourished in hiding. All my former colleagues are dead, their spirits added to my multitudes, enriching my energy and purpose by each death. There is always a displaced aristocrat ready to take up what he feels is his rightful mantle, and all of them will serve me. Eventually even the queen will have to bow."

"I'd not be so confident—" Lord Black nearly shouted, cut off when Moriel backhanded him. The fair nobleman's face went red with the strike, then redder with fury.

"I will be confident in what I already know to be true," Moriel insisted. "She is easily persuaded when her interests are served and her appetites are whetted. I will take advantage of any weakness and exploit it." His smile was a ghastly thing. "I am only allowing the true and right course of the world to unfold as it should, the Summoned shall pour forth." Here he turned to Lord Black to relish the man's discomfort. "And my triumph will culminate in demons tearing apart your cherished Parliament itself, that abomination 'of the people,' brick by rabble-rousing brick. A shame your living eyes won't see the glory of it."

He turned to the armed guard. "At the witching hour, close the shutters and turn on the pipes." The lackey nodded.

Moriel strode away, calling, "Now which of my slaves wants the honor of returning me to Vieuxhelles? I wish to feel its prowess surge with such fresh fuel."

* * * * *

The Guard of Six had been called, by their powers, to a formidable Gothic home in Greenwich. Arriving on horseback, cloaks and greatcoats whipping behind them, this secret cavalry of three men and three women slowed their thundering horses to a trot and then a huffing, shuffling, stamping mass a field away. In the air above, a large raven was hovering, squawking down at the company in a particular rhythm.

The tallest of The Guard, a fierce, brooding man all in black, dismounted and gestured for the others to do the same, tethering the whinnying, shifting beasts to nearby branches of the towering pines that marked the borders of the property. Horses easily spooked at the presence of the spectral world, and the Guard did not wish to have their transportation vanish while they dealt with it.

Between the moon and the ghosts, everything was eerily lit.

The Six strode up the winding slate walk, examining the scene that lay before them. The raven descended to perch on the shoulder of the most severe of the assembled women, tapping his beak upon her shoulder.

"Thank you, Frederic," the woman replied to the large black bird that bore one luminous blue feather upon its breast.

There were ghosts everywhere, concentric phalanxes of them, outside a looming castle-like manor that looked as if it had been built to be haunted.

Seven specters hovered directly before the house, luminous and gray, all bobbing and swooshing forward as if trying to get in. But each came up abruptly short, as if striking an unseen barrier. These actions repeated themselves as the Guard moved in careful steps closer to the edifice.

"Something is keeping those ghosts out," the man said, in a low rumble that carried farther than it should have given its volume. "That, my fellows, is odd."

Generally, in The Guard's experience, ghosts moved freely, wherever they wished. So to see a haunted house keep its ghosts out in the cold . . . that was unprecedented in their nearly fifteen years as secret arbiters of the spirit world.

It was The Guard's purview, granted them by an ancient, unquestionable force, to monitor the actions of the unquiet dead. When those spirits wished too actively to disrupt the living, it was duty to put them in their rightful place, unbeknownst to society.

"It would seem this place is having quite the party!" said a thin, flaxen-haired man in fine clothes who planted himself beside the group's leader.

A brute of a man charged toward them from the deep shadows near the estate's front portico.

"You haven't been invited," the brute snarled. "Who are you?"

The sharp-nosed blond held up a hand. The dim, burly man froze and stood, dazed, in his tracks.

"Wouldn't you like to know," the well-dressed man said. "People always want to know. Nosy bastards. We *should* be on retainer from Her Majesty," he added, "given how much we do for England—"

"Hush, Withersby," Alexi said with a slight growl. "Do your job."

"I did! It isn't as though he'll remember anything I say,"

Withersby insisted. The man still stood there, dark eyes blinking strangely. "You're a stubborn one aren't you," he added. "Move along now." He waved his hand again before the man's face, more insistently. The man growled.

"There's something quite wrong with him," said a man in a cleric's collar who crossed himself and murmured a quiet benediction.

"Look, he's now walking away," Withersby replied, reassured. "Though it does make me wonder what's going on in there. Can't be good if there's a guard at the door. That was no footman . . ."

"No matter," Alexi stated sharply. "To the Grand Work!" He raised his hands. A strange blue glow emanated from his palms. The gentle breeze coalesced into a wind.

As one, the seven ghosts shifted to face the man with the glowing hands and started gesturing wildly. The expressions on their grayscale faces changed from terror to anger to distress and back again. Some wore servants' uniforms; at the crest of the group was a beautiful woman in a fine gown. All alternately pointed to the house and clasped their hands together. Their mouths moved, but no one in the six knew what they were trying to say.

On the other side of Alexi, the intense woman spoke with crisp efficiency. "I do wish we could hear them after all these years of service. However, it seems clear they do not wish to depart and that something quite upsetting is happening in that house. Look at how desperate they are. Frederic has informed me there are a number of people trapped inside."

The company approached the house, surrounded by the ghosts. Occasionally, a specter swooped completely through a member of The Guard, causing unfortunate bouts of chills and a few French curses from the lovely brunette at the rear of the company.

The spirits directed the livings' attention to the beveled-glass windows of the dining room. The Frenchwoman clucked her tongue. "Well, that doesn't seem very nice. They're all tied up."

"The ghosts must want to help them, don't you think, Headmistress?" The priest asked the second-in-command.

The headmistress nodded in agreement. "But they are blocked. Is there some kind of Ward or spell keeping them out?"

Alexi made a face. "We don't deal in spells."

"Oh, no, we're powered by ancient holy fire and all sorts of entirely magical stuffs but, no, *spells,* that's right out," Withersby muttered.

The Frenchwoman, who seemed particularly attuned to him, elbowed him. "Some of them look familiar. Look, there." The headmistress pointed to one side of the room, where a scowling, broad-shouldered man was seated next to a grim-looking, lighter-haired woman, with an elegant blond man to their right. "Haven't we seen them before, Alexi?"

The leader nodded. "Government."

"Oh! I must be related to that one," the nobleman Withersby stated.

"The blond in colorful fashion?" the Frenchwoman asked. "Who else?"

"That one! He's the man who is obsessed with us," the headmistress stated, nodding in the direction of said colorful blond. "That's Lord Black. He's been on the hunt for us for years now. As I recall, he's got special permission from Her Majesty to look into the 'paranormal.' "

"The dear man," Withersby cooed. "Should we tell him the truth about us?"

There was a chorus of "no" as the Frenchwoman drove a second elbow into his side.

"But truly, Alexi, what do we do now?" the vicar asked. "We can't leave them in this state. The ghosts are having fits."

Alexi frowned. "I hate to say this, but . . . I do not believe this falls under our jurisdiction."

"It seems to be under the ghosts' jurisdiction, and by their engagement, must we not be as well?" the blond Irishwoman asked.

"Yes," the leader responded in a low, stern tone, "but the ghosts seem to want to help. In such cases, we always let helpful ghosts be, as the very action of their service will generally set them entirely to rest. Helping the living . . ." Alexi frowned. "While this is likely a matter of importance to mortal London, we have been told not to interfere in such matters."

"We should call the police," the headmistress said. Frederic the raven squawked once more and returned to the air.

"Ah." Alexi rubbed his chin. "Why, yes. Yes, we can do that. The police. Good idea. Let's send them by."

One particularly insistent spirit, the woman in the fine gown, perhaps a former lady of the house, was gesturing at the priest, toward his jacket, as if trying to reach an incorporeal hand into his pocket. The priest tried to shoo her away for a moment before making an exclamation of understanding.

"Holy water?" he asked the spirit. The shade of the woman nodded, exasperated. He withdrew a small bottle of blessed water from his coat pocket, and several spirits swooped in upon him and collectively floated the bottle out and away toward the house. From there, the ghosts hurtled it at the exterior of the house, and the bottle broke, the contents splattering across the front door and windows, causing a little shimmer of light about the perimeter.

"How very curious." Alexi stared after the spirits and their ritualistic actions. "Well, then. Let's see if the local officials like ghost stories. . . ."

The Guard returned to their horses and galloped off to alert the appropriate authorities that multiple government officials were being held captive in a grand manor house in Greenwich.

* * * * *

Clara's tie to Louis had been severed due to the spirit Wards set around the estate keeping the ghosts out, but she understood such bonds well enough now to break them. The spirits could help turn the tide enough for them to escape. She had to act cleverly, and if she broke that barrier, she'd have to then worry about a seizure, but she hoped her tether to Rose could keep it at bay. Her fluttering instincts ran through iterations of action.

"Lord Denbury," she said, "what's your favorite thing in this house? Is it still here? Something meaningful, powerful?" She leaned upon those last words enough to make his deadened blue gaze lively again.

He lifted his head, pointing with his chin at a painting mounted above the grand marble fireplace. "That portrait of Mother. The wretch Moriel was in love with her." With affection, Denbury said, "You can see she was a striking woman."

Denbury continued, his voice rising in conviction. "That is the one thing the bastard hasn't sullied in this whole dread place. *That* is meaningful to me. *She* is meaningful to me. In that portrait, she lives."

The change of tense from past to present seemed to charge the atmosphere as nearly everyone turned to study the painting of the beautiful Lady Denbury.

Clara, however, looked down. She'd felt something. To her left sat Harold Spire, who had subtly inched his chair against hers and used his fingers to loosen her bindings enough for her to slide one slender wrist free. Their eyes met for a moment before she turned to check the guard's gaze. He was glancing at a noise down the hall and she used that moment to slip Spire a dull steak knife from the table. He turned it in his palm to begin working on his own bonds.

Clara freed her other hand from the chair and jumped to her feet, darting behind Lord Denbury's chair. "This will hurt a moment," she murmured. Grabbing his hair, she pulled a thin clump free.

Following the motion, the guard turned back to the company, whipping his gun around to aim at Clara, but even as he did, a knife flew down the hall and hit him square in the throat, and the guard crumpled. Rose gasped in surprise. Spire managed to free himself and moved next to Lord Denbury's bindings.

Before the knife thrower could reveal himself, before Spire could move to cut another cloth binding, a dead-eyed, possessed man in a butler's dusty black coattails stepped into the doorway, training a pistol toward each of them alternately. When one possessed dropped, it seemed, there was an endless supply of replacements.

"*Sit,*" the guard droned at Clara and Spire menacingly. He did. Clara curtseyed. Lord Denbury remained as if still bound.

"I will, *sir,* don't worry," Clara said, playing a bit mad to the guard, spinning the jagged black lock between her thumb and forefinger "I'm just leaving Lady Denbury here a token to remember her son by, for when we're all gone!"

"I . . ." Denbury began with vague alarm.

"*She* lives, in essence. She remains . . ." Bishop murmured. A quick glance between them assured Clara that he knew exactly what she was doing; the subtle curve of his mouth spoke of his pride in her.

This was truly Louis's triumph, Clara thought. Without the token that had connected them, she wouldn't have known how to break the wall keeping the spirits out. There was comfort, at least, in that.

"Sit or I'll shoot," the guard droned. "Majesty wants you dead at stroke of midnight to stoke his fires, but *I* don't mind earlier. . . ."

"Sitting," Clara assured, moving toward her chair but not before she placed Lord Denbury's black hair on the thick frame around the portrait of his beautiful late mother, setting it down carefully so that the hair touched the canvas directly.

To Clara's senses, there was a palpable and immediate reaction, a ripple of air, a shimmer through the room. She *was* still here, right nearby . . . And she did *not* like being held back. . . .

Everyone in the room felt what Clara did, save for the guard at the door. But even he was aware of what came next, as the barrier fell.

At least seven spirits swarmed into the room, Lady Denbury at the fore.

Lady Denbury shrieked, sending a rending banshee wail of the whole spirit world, and the new guard at the door winced. Though it was not yet midnight, he moved toward the stopcocks on the gas pipes, but Spire leaped forward in an impressive bound, sticking the dull steak knife into the side of the guard's neck and tried to wrest the gun from his hand. The hefty man dropped instantly to the floor, a stray gunshot during the struggle lodging in the baseboard and bringing other guards running. More small knives flew down the hall and felled the fresh stream of guards, but the knife thrower remained unseen.

Spire picked up the gun and tossed his knife to Lord Denbury, who had been first unbound by Spire and was at present freeing the rest.

The entire house seemed to tremble, as if the spirits had unleashed an earthquake. Ten ghosts hovered before the wall of souls, facing their portraits. With a spectacular and unexpected strength Clara had never encountered in a ghost, Lady Denbury hurled a large candelabra at the wall. Paint, frame, and wallpaper went up in an almost immediate blaze.

Evelyn Northe-Stewart and Lord Denbury stood before the portraits, that part of the magic being of their particular experience, and recited a counter-curse in Latin, seeking to help reunite souls with bodies.

As the fire erupted, two guards who had rushed into the dining room, guns at the ready, stared as the paintings of their own likeness caught fire. Their possessed bodies crumpled in the instant, the magic tether that had been keeping them possessed now having vanished into the flames, the counter-curse bringing them to themselves again.

Everything was happening so fast that Clara barely had time to breathe, but she was aware that even with the help of Rose's fortitude and her own adrenaline, this much spirit activity meant a seizure was quite overdue. Her vision had begun to flicker and her muscles crawled under her skin.

Bishop grabbed her by the arm dragged her into the grand hall, followed by the other captives from Eterna and Omega. The dining room was being quickly engulfed in flames, which the ghosts were fanning furiously.

Running for the door, they were met by a host of police officers. Clara wondered if Brinkman or another Omega operative had sent word to them. Spire went over to the ranking officer immediately, introduced himself, and began giving directions on what to save.

"Let everything burn," Lord Denbury cried, interrupting Spire. "Let it *all burn*!"

"Wait." Clara reached out a shaking arm. "Won't burning it all . . ." she gasped. "Fuel him? Give Moriel more power?"

"No," Evelyn said, her voice full of wonder. "Thanks to

these brilliant, resourceful ghosts. Lady Denbury somehow blessed the place; she told me there's holy water around it, severing evil into the ley line. If it feeds anything at all, it will feed only light. She echoes her son; let it all burn. . . ."

Clara could feel the seizure coming. She managed to choke out, "Rupert," as her strength fled. Her legs gave way, and she fell as if she were an anchor dropped from the side of a ship, and then was caught, lifted by the lifeboat that was her guardian.

They were outside now, in the fresh air; Clara could hear everyone around her coughing. She could hear Louis murmur, finally reunited with her, "Hold on, Clara, hold on," before all senses faded entirely to black nothingness.

* * * * *

Each time Clara lost her sense of the tactile world, feeling that a bit of death had come to take her, she prayed she'd rise again whole. Each time she woke, her first thought was gratitude that if she was to die, thankfully it was not today.

She came to in a very fine parlor, sense by sense. Vision first: Bishop was standing watch over her, Louis floating against the wall opposite. Then hearing: a host of voices in a nearby room. Scent: a heady pot of tea steaming bergamot vapors right near the . . . ah, yes, touch: the sumptuous pillow upon which her head rested. She'd been deposited on a wide settee as lush as a bed and covered in a blanket. Last, she placed her location: Lord Black's mansion.

At a nod from Bishop, a maid in a simple uniform opened a door and ushered everyone into the parlor, where they milled about. Clara wriggled into a seated position; Bishop glided around behind the couch and stood sentinel. Louis wafted to her side.

In addition to her companions from their captivity at Lord Denbury's estate—save for Denbury himself and Evelyn—

Clara saw Knight, Blakely, and Adira Wilson, whom she hadn't seen since the voyage.

Lord Black strode into the parlor, his handsome butler close on his heels, and the nobleman fixed Clara with an intense gaze. "Hello, Miss Templeton. We've all managed to have some rest after our ordeal, and I'm hoping that includes you. We didn't want to deposit you in your guest room as we rotated watch over you for the past hours."

"I believe, for my part, I am, are we all, all right?" Clara asked in return.

Lord Black nodded. "We are all in various stages of recovery," he stated and then shared a long look with his butler, something passing between them that Clara found spoke of a deeper resonance in than mere master and servant. Black continued. "Lord Denbury has remained to see to the final and utter razing of Rosecrest so that nothing of the place survives. He is attended by the whole of the Greenwich police department, who know to act as though he perished in the blaze. Mrs. Northe-Stewart, remaining at his side, is helping to address any instructions from the late Lady Denbury herself."

"Where is Andre?" Clara asked Louis warily, suddenly aware that not everyone was accounted for.

"Still at the Omega department headquarters, helping Dr. Zhavia with Wards as he was instructed," Louis replied. "He has no idea of what has befallen us, so let's let him keep working. Mr. Blakely and Miss Knight, of course, wanted to come offer us support today after what befell us."

The rest of the company looked between Clara and the blank wall.

"To whom are you speaking, Miss Templeton?" Spire asked.

"Louis—his ghost floats there in the corner. I'm not sure I trust his twin any more than I would Brinkman, so I was asking his whereabouts."

"Of course," Spire muttered.

"It was your quick and clever thinking, Miss Templeton," Lord Black praised, "that gave us an advantage at Rosecrest. Thank you."

"It is my purpose as a Spiritualist to allow for the afterlife to aid our present life," Clara replied modestly. "A great deal of forces came together for our aid."

"We will need just such fortitude for the next battle to come, for the dread conflagration Moriel plans," Black stated. "I am ready to fight to protect those lovely bricks of Parliament, to protect the whole of our people, of every station. Are you?"

Everyone nodded, even Louis.

"Lord Black," Spire said, examining the weary nobleman before them, "if I may, at this point, you are not expected to fight further. You have been very generous. But you are needed in government and in the House of Lords, and we understand. You do not have to fight at our sides . . ."

At that moment, Lord Black turned to his butler and took the man's hand. Everyone in the room stared as the nobleman then lifted his butler's hand and kissed it. Twice. Lovingly.

The silence was deafening.

"Edward," the butler said, drawing away, trembling. His face was bright red with embarrassment but his voice was full of love.

Everyone stared.

Lord Black turned to everyone but aimed his words at Spire.

"You ask me, Mr. Spire, why I have been so passionate about these matters, why I helped with the Tourney business at all, why I have been so ready to fight." Lord Black's voice was thick with emotion. "This is why." He lifted the hand of his butler, who did not look up from the floor.

"My Francis here was a merchant, a hardworking man of business. He gave up a whole life of promise and purpose to live as less than he is, just so that we had a plausible excuse for him to be at my side. To live in hiding.

"Moriel would look at Francis, at his class, and try to wipe him and his like off of his feudalistic map, abuse him worse than they would me.

"It is hard enough to live as we have had to, for such a noble soul as his to have sacrificed as he has. . . ." Black clenched his fist as if looking for something to throw it at. All the cool, arch cleverness of his persona had fallen away, revealing an angry man in love in ways the world could not accept.

Francis gently patted his partner's arm. "It's all right, Ed." His quiet voice spoke of the pain they'd endured. "Don't work yourself up about this—"

Black caught Francis's other hand in both of his, clasping them to his bosom; the fair face of the blond lord was as flushed as his lover's but with the fires of justice.

"I would rather lay down my life, and all my privilege, than bend one inch toward a view that would usher in a new Dark Ages."

The shock of the social mores being broken was as sharp as if a glass had been dropped in the center of the room. Everyone had been struck silent. Miss Knight, Clara noted, was smiling, tears in her eyes as if a very personal chord had sounded.

It was impossible to ignore the police presence in the room. Spire had held high Metropolitan Police rank before being appointed to Omega. At his word, Black and Francis could easily be arrested for any number of offenses, including the acts Spire had just personally witnessed.

When Clara looked at Spire, though, she saw quiet admiration in his eyes.

"I can only imagine the difficulties of your lives, gentlemen," Spire said in a gentler tone than she'd heard from him in their short acquaintance. "But I am glad to have you as an ally in our fight, Lord Black."

Francis glanced at Spire, fear on his face. "You won't . . . report us . . . Mr. Spire?"

"I've better things to do and I care not a whit to be nosy in personal affairs," Spire declared in his usual brusque way. "I see no point in making enemies and sins out of love. One's private business is hardly a threat to me, to the city, or to the world."

Francis dropped his gaze once again to the floor, murmuring relieved thanks.

Perhaps it was a lovesick pain, or discomfort, or simply the need for business to take the fore again that had Mrs. Wilson step forward.

"I do not mean to interrupt, milord," she said quietly in her soft, Arabic-tinged English.

"No, no, Adira, please." Lord Black turned to the assembled team. "My friends, we owe Mrs. Wilson a debt of thanks. She did not take her prescribed time of grieving but instead tracked us to Rosecrest."

"I awaited you outside Lord Black's home after escorting Knight and Blakely to Dr. Zhavia at the offices," she explained. "I did not feel my place was with them in mysticism, but with you in action. When the carriages flew past this house after the appointed hour, it was clear something was amiss. I pursued on horseback. Thankfully, Reggie and I . . ." Her voice caught. "We're practiced at not being seen, and, of course, at ambush."

"It was *you* with the knives," Rose exclaimed, impressed. Mrs. Wilson nodded. Clara wondered what kind of international sensation the Wilsons had been in their time, as mysterious as they were dangerous.

"Thank you, Mrs. Wilson, we are indeed in your debt," Spire said earnestly before turning to Lord Black. "We need to find Vieuxhelles. Now. We've Miss Bixby's list of Apex-and Society-related properties, and I've read the whole list." He gestured to the papers on the console table before him. "None matches the description of an ancestral estate. Vieuxhelles seems to exist off record, and scouring the countryside would waste our time. If that damned Brinkman had *told* us—"

Blakely had come forward to peruse Effie Bixby's list, and his finger pointed to a name. "I know that name, Moore— it's a warehouse for salt and basic chemist's supplies, I order from them often. Must have been targeted, seized . . ."

"That warehouse marks the largest single property any-where on this list," Spire stated. "The building stood on my first police beat. I'll go and take a look. Let's take advantage of being assumed dead."

"I'll come with you," Clara said, sitting up. Senator Bishop made a noise of protest, which she turned to address. "I know what to look for when buildings have been tainted for Society use, Rupert," she assured. "We each have our areas of exper-tise, and fouled property has been mine since the Stevens case."

He sighed and held up his hands.

"What is the swiftest way there? As I assume it will be guarded, we need to be unseen and not followed there," Mrs. Wilson asked. Clearly she was coming along. Miss Knight had risen, too, and so had Rose. This would be quite the team effort.

"Well, the location in question is right near a Metropoli-tan underground stop," Spire told them.

"It's after hours, it will be closed," Blakely said, fluttering a hand.

"And that should stop us from using the tunnels how?" Spire asked.

Blakely did not mask distaste. "Ah. I see."

* * * * *

There were a great many rats in the underground tunnels after hours, Clara noted, trying to remain unemotional about that fact. She was a New Yorker and no stranger to vermin.

She tried to think of their route as a chance to see London in ways no tourist would. Recent events had truly inured her, and this present trip seemed more a stroll through a royal park than a descent into discomfort. She'd take rats over the horrors of that Greenwich estate any day. Her tolerance for the terrible had reached unprecedented thresholds.

At a particularly dark turn in the tunnels, Louis wafted to Clara's side in a flicker of gray and a breeze of chill.

"Steel yourself, Clara, darling, shield yourself from the effects and atmosphere of any Society building as they affect you. Stay close to Rose. I'll be with you."

Clara nodded and pressed the talisman he'd given her during their courtship in appreciation. He knew it was her habit to wear it beneath her layers and smiled at the gesture. He allowed her to keep silent, not wishing to make conversation for Spire's sake, speaking with the dead an additional discomfort to their unpleasant trek.

Miss Knight cursed quietly but colorfully as a sailor at each sighting of vermin. Spire and Adira Wilson were at the fore; the widow had donned a skirt that was actually split-leg-like trousers for more sensible movement. Blakely was at the rear, walking sideways so he could see if anyone or anything was creeping up from the shadows behind. Rose kept quiet pace at Clara's side, her presence helping her body not tense up amid recovery, a woman as undeterred from duty as she.

Spire finally led them up a ladder to an underground platform, turning to help the ladies, whose skirts and heeled boots were inconvenient on a ladder. It was Rose's turn to curse and swear that she'd come to work only in athletic costumes from now on.

Knight chuckled as she was helped onto the passenger platform. "I make no such promise to practicality in dress reform; my heart remains too devoted to fashion."

The lantern Mr. Blakely raised illuminated tiled walls of the station. Other than themselves, the platform was entirely devoid of light and persons and decidedly eerie in the swinging, shifting light of their several lanterns.

Spire gestured them out the gates, then into the black corridor of a service exit that he unlocked via the most impressive-looking skeleton key Clara had ever seen.

The warehouse that was their destination sat a shadowed alley away from the exit. They crept forward quietly.

"Give me five minutes," Mrs. Wilson said. "Wait here." She was off before Spire could give orders otherwise.

The group huddled in the shadows opposite the building while the lithe Mrs. Wilson hopped onto the sill of a first-floor window and launched her thin form through a gap in the hinged panes, disappearing for what was, indeed, five minutes. Then, with a groan on weighty hinges, a door ahead opened for them and they quickly filed in, Mrs. Wilson staring out at the alley behind them before closing and bolting the door.

"Good God," Spire muttered at the revelation within.

From floor to ceiling, the warehouse space was filled with rows and columns of glass jars filled with red powder. The maddening, expressive agent had indeed been mass-produced, with enough quantity before their eyes to poison all of London and the surrounding environs.

At the center of the floor was an elaborate, carefully positioned display of various horrors. If what the New York team had been construing was "Wards"—this was the antithesis— an obvious enticement of evil.

There were the same kinds of carvings Clara recognized well—texts from many different faiths, inverted, reversed, perverted from their once benign or hopeful messages into the grossest, basest apocalyptic threats, all lined in blood and tar. Numbers were carved in sequences that seemed to have no rhyme or reason until she thought of them as going forward, rather than backward. It was the golden ratio, used in paintings and ancient math, a divine sequence here done backward. Every negative opposite of a positive notion.

There was a fully disarticulated human skeleton with blood and gore still on its bones, which had been placed at four equidistant points within a circle, the scrawled words at the base of the dreadful display confirming the parallel to directional points on a compass.

THE SHADOWS COME FROM
ALL DIRECTIONS
ALL POINTS OF COMPASS POINT TO DIVINE RIGHT
ROYALS FEED FROM SUBJECT SUPPLY
LIFT THY LIFE TO THE RULING RITE

The matter inside the jaws of the skeleton was the pulp of a heart.

The stench of death was pervasive, and soon everyone had put a kerchief to their nose. Miss Knight fished into an embroidered drawstring bag attached to the double layer of her skirts and pulled out the small vial of incense oil she used in her readings; she offered to dab some on everyone's handkerchief. The men, save Blakely, were stoic and refused; the women universally accepted.

Rose, speaking past the linen square she'd bundled at her nose, gestured to the specimen jars. "I take it this is the bulk store of the chemical madness agent? One of the three tenets of Society destruction Mrs. Northe-Stewart outlined for us?"

"Yes," Clara replied. "Soul splitting, reanimation, and this, the toxin." She gestured to the floor, where everyone else's gaze was fixed in varying degrees of disgust, fascination, and horror. "What you see here in the center of the floor must be an escalation of what is known as their final phase, Moriel's dread revolution, as it were."

Rose noticed that Spire was not, in fact, transfixed by the implements of magic before them. Instead, he was surveying the larger space.

"What I want to know," Spire began, with careful caution in his tone, "is if this place is important to the plan, why in the world is it not being heavily guarded?"

"It was," Mrs. Wilson replied with cool nonchalance, taking Blakely's lantern and lifting it toward the north wall to reveal a row of four dead bodies with small knives squarely in the heads.

"Brilliant, Mrs. Wilson," Spire murmured. "You are *absolutely* brilliant." This caused the first smile out of her since her husband's senseless death.

"I don't know how long we'll have, so . . ." She gestured they take stock of what they could.

"I assume everything in this warehouse is meant to be carried along via the nearby rails," Clara stated. "Considering the cut and cover architecture of the underground, the particles would become airborne. This building is likely meant to be 'detonated,' as similar buildings were set up to be in New York, though that order, at the time, thankfully never came. In this case I believe Moriel would wish to send this airborne during his professed procession. Thankfully, Stevens tells me these compounds become inert after being flooded or burned."

"Finally some good news," Spire said. He fished in his pocket and pulled out a box of matches.

"It's going to take far more than logistics, you realize,"

Clara said. "More than burning or flooding buildings. He'll soon have all three wings of his army and capabilities at his side," she clarified. "We need spiritual weaponry as much as you need your physicality."

Her eye turned again to the bold declamations on the floor. The Society thrived on inversion, on taking sacred principles and turning them in on themselves. The compass struck her. She'd foreseen the concept in her dreams. Perhaps *they* could invert what *Moriel* considered sacred. . . .

"What is it?" Spire asked, studying Clara.

"I think I know the key here, taking localized magic to a new step and turning Moriel's tables against him," Clara began excitedly. "I've been musing about this since I woke, wondering why we have been brought together.

"Blood can be chosen," Clara said softly to Rose, reaching out to boldly take her hand. "I choose you, sister." She smiled, despite the pain it caused her bruised face, the seizure having taken its toll over her whole body. "I've missed you."

"I've missed you," Rose murmured, offering a squeeze of her palm. The women nodded to one another.

"This little session of bolstering is . . . warming my chilled heart and all," Spire said, pursing his lips between clipped words, "but would you get to the metaphysical point of whatever it is you ladies plan to *do*?"

"Not just the ladies," Clara said. "Right, Louis?" She turned to the disruption in the air that was her former love. Clara's eyes were focused on the team before her with a bright intensity. "Localized magic. It isn't just about the Wards, but also about the people. Together, we are the four corners of a compass." She pointed to the "directions" and "compass" proclamations on the floor. "More, we span between worlds. Ours is a bond that the Society's ilk, in their detached misery, can't possibly comprehend. We must combat horror with a more comprehensive humanity. Not science, magic, or faith, but life. That, perhaps, is the weapon of Eterna after all. *Life.*"

"But I'm dead, Clara," Louis murmured, his floating form bobbing near her.

"You are vital, Louis," she countered, "for your *connection* to life. It helps bolster the cause. We'll have to make sure Andre is with us as well. We must create something living and vital, the exact opposite of this travesty." She gestured to the sick corpse before them. "The Society loves turning the sacred into sacrilege, so we'll right what they've upturned. That's how we disrupt the forces around Moriel. He hasn't accounted for the dead fighting against him or the living harnessing their own invisible defenses.

"Ghosts helped us at Rosecrest. Louis taught me the value of tactile, talismanic, and personal magic. We must make a living conduit for that power, as if it was an electrical current. Just as that odd man Mosley untethered the ghosts with a charge, so must we disrupt evil's flow with the bonds among us. And we'll do so, right in the middle of his damnable *parade*. . . ."

"In your twin souls, all four of you, a unique capability, a unique chemistry," Miss Knight said, nodding in agreement and enthusiasm. "Two pairs of twin souls, too, all tied together through each other. Two brothers, raised together, parted by death but yet connected. Two sisters, separated in time and space, yet knowing each other as sisters the moment they met. And both pairs united *across* the worlds by the love between one sister and one brother, one living and one dead."

"Precisely," Clara agreed. "From the start it's been about the inversion of all we hold beautiful and meaningful. These forces derive power from ripping souls out from bodies, from disconnecting."

"So *connecting*, then," Mrs. Wilson said softly, "is the sole truth."

"The *souls'* truth," Blakely added. "Well done, Miss Templeton. Brilliant."

"I don't suppose any of you clairvoyants have a time for Moriel's obscene display?" Spire asked, clearly not as impressed by Clara's divination as the rest. "We know he wants his demons to disassemble Parliament, but at what hour?"

"Astrologically, I'd say two days from now," Miss Knight stated. "The stars enter a particularly volatile phase, it is the time of Ares, god of war, and the moon will be full." Clara nodded her agreement.

"Well, then, let's be sure all our operatives are agreed, and prepare," Spire said. "Now. For something practical."

He moved to where several oil lanterns sat on shelves and tables and threw them strategically across the room, shattering and spilling their contents across the floor and shelves. "Everybody out," he ordered, "back the way we came."

His tone was final and they hurried out. He brought up the rear, following with a lantern upended and a trail of oil out the warehouse door.

Without looking behind him, he lit several matches at once and dropped them over his shoulder and kept walking.

When the first small explosion sounded, he smiled. For the first time Clara noted genuine satisfaction on his oft sour face.

Returning to the tunnel entrance, the company turned as a group to watch for a moment as a second fire burst roared and the insidious outpost grew well and truly consumed. Thankfully, the building was not directly adjacent to others and the ground around it wet. Its toxins were disarmed without threatening the entire sector. If firemen were called, they would not be in jeopardy, the substance now inert, no one the wiser until word eventually get back to Moriel. They needed to get to safety well before that moment came.

* * * * *

Reconvening at Lord Black's residence, they were greeted warmly at the arched wooden door by the nobleman himself.

"You're back victorious, I hope?" he asked.

"If I need an arsonist, now I know whom to call upon," Rose offered with a chuckle. "Mr. Spire quite admirably set the horrific place ablaze."

"It would seem this work requires us all to . . . expand our repertoire," Spire replied and shared his colleague's smile.

"Well, then, good work, I say. You'll be happy to note nearly everyone is on hand tonight," Black continued, "save for Miss Bixby, who insisted she continue on her own beat, trying to persuade anyone she could find under Apex employ to quit, even if trying to convince desperate and hungry folk is futile."

Stepping into the gaslight of the front hall was a tired, unshaven, but neatly dressed Andre Dupris, who explained, "I'm here to update you on the status of the Wards."

"Good," Clara replied. Out the back garden window she watched Lord Denbury pacing in the dimming light.

"And there's someone else to see you all," Black said reluctantly, sliding back one of the carved wooden pocket doors of the parlor.

The moment Spire took one look at double agent Brinkman sitting in the pleasant white room, in the same all-black ensemble as he wore in the Parliament attack, Spire shook his head, pointing toward the door, crossing past brocade and lacquered furnishings to round upon the man with a heated demand.

"I want him out, Lord Black," Spire spat. "Can't possibly be trusted. Surely he would have known about our abduction and did nothing to help us—"

"Yes, actually, I did," Brinkman countered through clenched teeth, rising angrily to his feet, "and I have covered for and made 'assurances of' your deaths." Both men strode to stand nearly nose to nose, and if Clara wasn't mistaken, Spire was about to throw a considerable punch.

The tension shifted when Francis the butler drew a small silver pistol on Brinkman. Spire withdrew a step. Lord Black placed a supportive hand on his lover's back.

"Sit," Spire barked at the spy. "Say what you came here to say and get out."

"I'm here to help you plan your attack," Brinkman growled.

"No, you'll tell us where Vieuxhelles is for an appropriate raid," Spire countered. "You'll tell us what Moriel has there, what of his plans we can immediately disrupt, and then you'll leave. We can't suffer the *slightest* chance that you could undermine our plans, even accidentally under duress or to save your son."

"Out with it, Gabriel," Lord Black urged.

The spy sighed. "Machines to power reanimate corpses are being built inside Vieuxhelles, he'll use them in the procession. There are three times as many paintings on the walls of Vieuxhelles, all holding captive souls in their canvases. You must allow for two of his three prongs of evil to go forward, lest he cancel what he has devised. I know you've been to the warehouse storing the mood toxin. That I can cover for, but you cannot descend on Vieuxhelles too soon."

"Why let anything go forward?" Spire asked. "Why can we not round on him now, kill him in his lair, and destroy everything at once? Why indulge him and such risk?"

"He has too thick a magic built up around that manor to attack it or him in it directly," Brinkman said wearily, reaching into his pocket and procuring a piece of paper that bore the old Society crest upon it, a gold and blood-stained seal with dragons on either side. He held out his hand. Black placed a pen in it. Brinkman wrote an address and cursory directions as he elaborated. "Any attempts on his life there—and there have been a few from possessed guards that came back to themselves after the destruction of Rosecrest's paintings—only feeds the evil. I've seen bullets and knives repelled by the very air around him when he stands within those walls, it's *mad*.

"By all means torch the blasted place when you can, but take care. Mere fire won't solve a thing, and you have to do so when he's not present. He's too powerful there. Let him go into the city, let him try to tear Parliament down brick by brick in an ungodly show. In doing so, you can plan your counterattacks, place your Wards, more broadly bid the city protect itself, and allow for his vulnerabilities to be struck down when his armor is more widely spread and therein find the chinks."

"Has Moriel corrupted any of the local law enforcement within riding distance of Vieuxhelles?" Spire asked.

"Most of them, yes. I have only one contact who is any good," Brinkman replied, "but I'd rather have him arrive to a smoldering ruin than his department interrupt any attempts at sabotage. So you're on your own if you plan to attack the estate. I'll do what I can, and I'll see you amid the madness. For my part, during the procession, I will be trying to get close enough to Moriel to kill him with my own hands. Don't stop me," Brinkman declared and rose.

"Best of luck, ladies and gentlemen," he offered. "If we fail, see you in hell."

Francis followed him out, the pistol trained upon him until the front door boomed shut and the butler returned to the room in silence.

Spire had drawn a rough sketch of Victoria Embankment, ending in Parliament, and set it on the wide lacquered table that sat roughly at the center of their assembled company.

"Should we invite Lord Denbury inside to join us?" Clara asked.

Evelyn shook her head. "He's not well," she replied. The haunted young man was still pacing, as if trying to escape something unshakable. "He'll do his part and help, of course, but let's let him be for now. . . ."

No one questioned the medium's gentle advice. All eyes were on Spire.

"I have to think Moriel isn't so blind as to think he won't meet resistance in the Westminster precinct," Spire stated. "I'll have battalions make sure nothing gets past the bridge here." He pointed to the mouth of Westminster Bridge, under the shadow of parliament's great tower. "We'll create an outpost at Cleopatra's Needle," Spire instructed, putting a thumb at a square on his makeshift map a few meters east. He turned to Mrs. Wilson. "That will give you height for surveillance. We'll feign the obelisk is under construction."

"There will have to be a battery of Wards, all along the route," Clara stated. She turned to Louis and Andre across the room. "How many have you been able to work up?"

"Hundreds. If not over a thousand," Andre said, rubbing his eyes. Louis nodded to corroborate his brother. "I'm exhausted. Zhavia is made from sterner stuff, I daresay the old man hasn't paused for a moment. When not making a Ward, he's been out asking every rabbi—or priest—he knows to pray for us. I'm not a godly man, but you know, after spending so much time around such a wellspring as that man, I say that can't hurt."

"The brighter side of the spirit world," Louis added excitedly, "seems aware of the plight. It isn't only the darkness that has momentum." Clara smiled at the ghost, wishing she could take his hand through all this.

Adding onto Andre's point, Bishop stated, "We should have all clergy, of any faith, any belief system, of any age new or ancient, lending their particular strengths to a show along the route."

"I've many Anglican contacts," Evelyn stated. "I'll alert them first thing in the morning before traveling north toward Vieuxhelles."

"And I my imam," Mrs. Wilson offered. "From what I've seen of the way the Master's Society perverts a building, it insults all faiths in the inscriptions left within. Pushing back with more than one response to such blasphemy might constrain the demons."

"We'll convince those assembled along the Embankment to hold Wards in their hands as a part of the pomp and circumstance of a parade," Clara stated.

"And at a signal, light them," Bishop added.

"Like candles, but carrying within the magical impact of a firework. It could be beautiful," Clara mused.

"Even if only some of the populace does what we ask," Bishop offered, "I believe it can be enough to shield the bulk of witnesses and hold the Summoned at bay. I'll be . . . persuasive about the Wards," he assured, giving Clara a smile at the promise of his mesmerism. She smiled in turn, glad he was not conflicted about using such a force at such a critical time.

"There will have to be some kind of electrical devices to spur on the phalanx of reanimate bodies from the Vieuxhelles army," Miss Knight noted. "Lord Black, that device from your war room . . ."

"The coil? Yes. We might be able to use it to disrupt any flow of current and slow the machines, if necessary."

"Very good." Spire nodded. "Thankfully, some technology besides your intangible spells . . ." He turned to Clara. "No offense meant—"

"None taken," she replied amiably. "Magic isn't to everyone's taste, and belief isn't required for it to have an effect. The Ward will believe in you. It would be admittedly stronger if you returned its favor, but that is not for me to demand.

What will be most helpful as soon as possible is for the senator and me to meet with your Dr. Zhavia before distribution, to see if the Wards are ready and active or inert."

"Can we arrange transport for them, Lord Black, for the meeting and cargo distribution?" Spire asked. The nobleman nodded.

"For my part, considering all the paintings' at Moriel's estate," Evelyn said, "I can go there during the parade when the focus should be off the property. I will try to reverse the magic on those canvases, try to return those souls to themselves, at least in part. If some of his procession is made up of the possessed, I might be able to sow confusion, delay the parade, disassemble another of his prongs of attack, and hopefully save lives."

"We'll have two teams, then," Spire decided, pacing the parlor as he spoke. "The procession team and the estate team. Mrs. Northe-Stewart, what do you need to support you at Vieuxhelles?"

"Guards and someone with sensitivities. Since Clara has been instrumental with the Wards, she and Bishop should remain together and involved with parade implementation. Miss Knight, may I ask for your help?"

Knight nodded. "You have it gladly."

"Agreed," Spire added.

"Adira and I can take care of the guards at Vieuxhelles," Blakely stated. "With an aerial descent first, silent as a mouse and unseen. Reginald"—his voice caught as he turned to the widow Wilson—"taught me his ways well. I'll have help with new toys from the war room. I think a nerve gas I've been developing will serve to clear the rooms for us nicely. I will do you proud."

"I will of course take Jonathon with me," Evelyn added. "I promise he will be a focused asset there, and I must keep my promise to his wife not to let him from my sight."

"Good, then, thank you," Spire said to everyone confidently. "We have a plan."

Francis brought everyone tea, and the light, warmth, and crackle from the vast marble fireplace proved to be soothing in silence for some while.

That night, Clara had a chance to sit with Bishop and Evelyn and commune a moment before the teams would have to part the next morning.

"Clara," Evelyn said, "this is the test I have foreseen for you. You are the crux of the Wards, as you always have been the heart of this work. Stay strong." She turned to Bishop. "Shield her with more vigilance than you ever have, Rupert."

The senator reached out and placed his hands on the women's shoulders.

"We are more lit, all of us, than we ever have been. Bright as stars, bright as day. May we all reflect what we are."

Clara recalled, and rallied, that she had to be worthy of the squall, to see it all from the perspective of the storm, rather than be lost in it.

In a move bolder than she had allowed herself of late, Clara reached up to touch Bishop's hand upon her shoulder, felt its warmth, and kindled hope.

* * * * *

Gabriel Brinkman approached the once grand, now decaying ivy-overgrown estate of Vieuxhelles humming with turbines and the crackle of overloaded electrical wires, sick with dread about what and whom he would see there.

A small surprise offset the pending horror.

As he made his way up toward the formidable entrance, Brinkman noted a dull sparking in the shadows. He smiled broadly. Mosley had come after all, likely having followed the loud hum of the lines leading into the manor, hundreds more than were normal or necessary for the mere purposes of illumination. He carefully approached the shrubbery where he'd glimpsed the flash of light.

"Don't blast the place prematurely, my friend," Brinkman whispered. "Come to the procession tomorrow. You'll know when you can act . . . and by all means, I'm counting on it. . . ." There was no reply from the darkness, but he expected none and felt confident he was understood.

James, the tottering butler, let Brinkman in.

"Mr. Brinkman," James said softly. A flash of sympathy flickered beneath the cataracts in his eyes.

"How is he?" Brinkman asked, returning the quiet tone.

"The Majesty or your son?" James asked in his usual weary, matter-of-fact manner.

"Either, I suppose, or both."

"The Majesty is nearly ready to truly make his mark upon London, now that the Parliament has been appropriately shaken and the machines, and the stars, are ready. The Majesty is in the parlor, Mr. Brinkman. I'll be sure your son is brought around straightaway."

Brinkman nodded, steeled his stomach, and strode into the ostentatiously decorated room. He noted that the number of oval portraits on the walls had increased again, meaning Moriel had added to his underclass of the paranormally enslaved.

Moriel was sitting with slippered feet up on a leather ottoman, drinking a thick beverage that Brinkman had long ago learned never to ask about. Brinkman bowed his head in greeting.

The body of a small boy appeared at the threshold of the room. Brinkman forced himself to smile in greeting and said "Hello."

"Hello, Papa," said the body in a horrid, hollow tone.

Brinkman had unsuccessfully searched every holding of the Master's Society for the portrait of his child that would have held the soul ripped from this body and replaced by shadow. Now he knew that regardless of what anyone could do here to try to undermine the dark magic, he had to let go.

For one moment, the guard O'Rourke, the man who had seen Moriel through his internment, and Brinkman stared at one another. There was something so fleeting, and so subtle in their eyes, but they knew. They knew this was a good-bye and a last gasp. Behind O'Rourke's thick body, there were sparking eyes watching them from within the hedge just outside the window.

"Get good rest tonight, Gabriel," Moriel ordered. "I'll want your help whipping all my minions into quick shape and get them marching tomorrow."

"I will, Majesty."

"Good night, Father," said the demon disguised as his boy.

"Good night."

Brinkman walked up the grand, dusty stairs to one of the smaller guest rooms, where he lay atop the covers and gave himself his own last rite.

Clara was awake at the break of day, having rested deeply by the grace of some higher power, her seizures forcing the issue by exhausting her physically, despite the whirlwind of thoughts that hadn't stopped their rapid spin since arriving in England.

Lord Black escorted her and Bishop to a nondescript brick industrial building in Millbank, with an expansive view of the busy, noisy Thames, and held the door for them. As they stepped in, they heard a strange sound above them and a little pop, like that of a photographer's flare, and as the door closed behind them, they noted a contraption with a paper ticker above the door that recorded the time, the numbers, and the silhouettes of the three forms in the door frame in an unembellished overexposed print upon the thin strip.

"Not a bad idea for our offices," Bishop said to Clara, who nodded and took in the open, cavernous three-story space before them, a metal stairwell connecting the floors in simple, industrial grandeur.

Lord Black descended a stairwell and bid them follow him into a lower-ceilinged room with rows of long wooden tables and narrow windows looking out to the street, bars across the panes for protection. Not much light came in, but Clara deemed it a better work environment than a cellar—clearly better than the shuttered horror of the last Eterna work, and she marveled at the rows upon rows of small glass tubes, all layered with sediment, water, and various substances of provenance she could not determine.

At the back of these rows, on a tall stool, sat a man who seemed straight out of a fairy tale book, a sorcerer of ancient times, his dark hair offset by silver streaks and a long blue velvet robe draping from a thin body.

"Dr. Zhavia," Lord Black called gently. The man, so focused on his work, started but looked up with a smile. "I don't mean to disturb you, but—"

"New company? Who's this?" The man shuffled up the aisle between the tables toward them, youthful energy offsetting the wizened appearance. His accent was thick and seemingly Russian Jewish to Clara's ear, theirs being a prominent population of recent New York immigrants.

"May I introduce the heads of the American Eterna Commission, Senator Rupert Bishop and Miss Clara Templeton," Lord Black stated. "Dr. Zhavia has been working tirelessly since Miss Everhart wired us your Warding advice, Miss Templeton, and we're grateful to have had some time to prepare them."

The man studied the two of them with such scrutiny it would have been unnerving if he hadn't had such an excited look on his face.

"Oh, my friends," he said, nearly bouncing on his feet. "Gifted. Gifted, gifted." He lifted an aged hand to hover around Bishop's forehead, fingertips fluttering as if plucking strings of an unseen instrument. "Mesmerist, ah . . ." He then turned to Clara, hand hovering near her ear. "Hmm. Heart of the matter. Extrasensory talent attuned to more worlds than one. Ah, what a joy to see my people!" He withdrew his hand, and Clara and Bishop exchanged a surprised glance before the doctor waved them over to a nearby table. "Come, come, you'll understand this." He peered at Clara. "You will best. Your idea, the Wards?"

"Our commission's idea, yes," Clara replied. "The Wards were developed by Louis Dupris, Andre's brother, and we've implemented them. Speaking of Andre, where is he?"

"Warning friends of his who live in the city to take care today. Louis . . . ah, yes, the ghost twin. Brilliant man, brilliant. Localized magic—so simple and so effective with the right hearts."

"May I ask your recipe?" Clara asked, gesturing to the rows of glass vials.

"Oh yes!" He lifted a vial and pointed to each layer as he explained.

"Water of the Thames, of course, as every river is the heart of its city," Zhavia began. "Then dirt from as many different hallowed grounds that I and my associates could find. Thankfully, I have rabbi and Spiritualist Christian friends who helped gather all the various sacred sediments from around the city," he said with a grin, as if he were a delighted elf ready to shower the world with the good tidings of water and silt. "Mixing them, of course, as no one place is sacred for all people. Then a layer of dust from the stones of Parliament, as that is a throne of freedom we must protect from the deathly shadows," the wizardly man concluded with a bow of his head.

"Of course," Bishop agreed. Bishop and Clara couldn't help but share in this effervescent man's beaming smile.

"And," he said, gesturing to the little sprinkle of brown flakes atop the sediment, "tea leaves. Without them, this just 'wouldn't be a civilized affair,' " Zhavia added, affecting an upper-class London accent that roused a chuckle out of all of them, Black the most.

"Wonderful," Clara stated, "truly. Do you have any idea if it works? Have you been able to test it, perchance?"

Here the joyful man turned somber.

"I wish I hadn't such cause, but unfortunately, I did. Last

week, my rabbi had his small temple vandalized, and a member was killed there, out on the steps. An act of hate. The horror of the place had to be resolved." He gestured to a vial. "I set the Ward alight, lit by a temple candle, and it sent off lurking shadows. I left that candle with my rabbi, and I was told that candle still has not gone out!" He brightened. "I'll take any miracle I can get."

"So will we. Thank you, Dr. Zhavia. Your work is *vital*." Clara picked up a vial and studied it. "Hello, England," she murmured to its contents. She pressed it to her sternum, to the blessed talisman that had been a gift from Louis, the carved stone bird that flew below the layers of her clothing. At this, there was a small shimmer of light.

"Ah!" Zhavia exclaimed. "Look at that. You can simply light it by your breath, you are so full of life!" He peered up at her with his dark eyes. "Many lives."

"Yes, I'm aware I've had many," Clara replied.

"Bring them all with you!" he said with a laugh, tapping the vial she held. "Call upon them all!"

She withdrew an embroidered handkerchief from her sleeve, wrapped the vial tightly into its folds, and tucked it between buttons and behind a chemise layer to rest against her skin, armored by her corset bones, ready for the fight.

"Let's box it all up," Black stated. "I brought the largest of my carriages for this purpose. Trunks we fill here will serve as our distribution area near to Spire's lookout."

"If we want to be doubly protected along the route," Bishop added, "I suggest doses of the mood toxin antidote be distributed. In case Moriel has a second store other than the destroyed warehouse. There should have been a box of the cure deposited here."

"Indeed, a wise precaution." Black nodded. "We can mix it into that water barrel there," he said, gesturing to a metal frame over a basin where a banded wooden barrel trailed a small capped hose. "Bring along what we have here. We'll have the masses drink from a few tin cups, or pour it into their own flasks; it will serve as a bit of odd communion. Come, let's load it all and see how the lookout fares."

"If you don't mind, I wish to be with my congregation tonight," Zhavia said. "We will be in a group near Parliament."

"Of course." Black replied.

"Thank you, Doctor," Bishop said, striding forward to shake the man's hand. He bowed his head.

"We are, all of us, beholden and thankful," Zhavia replied, bowing in turn to Clara. "And you stay strong, madame, anchor that you are."

Clara nodded, not knowing exactly what he sensed, but her biddings from mysterious, gifted elders were similar enough not to question the prophecy.

* * * * *

Per Spire's plan, by midday, Grange's men had erected sturdy "construction" scaffolding around the base of the hefty Alexandrian obelisk. The "needle," which had been a gift that arrived only four years earlier, now overlooked the Thames rather than ancient Heliopolis, its twin having gone to New York the year prior. Once the structure was secure, Clara, Rose, Black, and Spire ascended to their stations. Below, Bishop was handing out the glass vial Wards to the crowd, flanked and assisted by Andre and Effie.

Bishop's mesmeric persuasion was working well, though Clara was not sure how much it was needed—the assembling bystanders seemed eager for any kind of souvenir. Those who did not have matches were given a box, and by the time an hour had passed, Bishop had given out a few hundred Wards.

As for the wooden-barrel station to administer the chemical antidote as a preventative measure, it didn't take long for a line to gather near the base of the needle for a free sip of "tonic" winkingly disguised as gin.

With these measures in place, to the best their team could manage, the bystanders were doubly protected from whatever offenses would appear. Clara hoped Parliament itself could withstand the next hours.

The sun had just sunk into that curious, golden hour when light appeared its most mysterious when the first noise alerted the crowd to the unfolding events . . .

The forthcoming display began with a low, long, deep horn blast. Looking down toward Waterloo Bridge, Clara could see nothing in detail, just the suggestion of a crowd moving in their direction.

At length, the extensive procession was close enough to be seen from those on the obelisk: ensigns and standards—family crests, but none from prominent London gentry. The banners were carried by dim-looking men, women, and children who didn't look fully awake. They were either drugged or possessed—perhaps both.

"Odd . . . I don't know any of those families," Lord Black stated.

A bright glow alerted Clara to the next phase of the display. "Oh no . . ." she said ruefully.

"What do you see?" Spire asked.

"Coming up to the crossing at Waterloo Bridge. Likely a host of ghosts," Clara replied. The two men squinted.

"I don't see anything," Black commented.

"Even my own spectral sight is limited and changes depending on circumstance. It is never consistent. However, that which is coming closer is an unmistakable horde of spirits," Clara explained.

"Will the crowds see the ghosts?" Spire asked.

"Some may, most will not," Rose replied. "This may be the same sort of display Clara and I saw in New York, on a far larger scale," she said. "And even there, while I doubted the populace all saw the ghosts, everyone was affected, especially as the ghosts were tied to dead bodies. That's what we can't see from here. It's the bodies that are the worst of it . . . But that's likely where the electricity will come in."

Black rummaged in a canvas bag, withdrew a wooden box, and lifted the lid. Inside was a sparking coil with a small buzz emanating from it. He shut it again promptly.

"Dreadful," Lord Black murmured, holding the box and watching as the next section of the procession came within a few hundred meters. "I don't see forms exactly, but there is a ghostly glow in tow, I am seeing a change in the light. A thought struck him and his eyes lit. "I wonder if this will lure out our most elusive department!"

At this, Rose and Spire sighed in tandem.

"There is, supposedly, a department that specializes in specters," Rose explained, seeing Clara's bafflement, "but we've found no actual evidence of them, just stories of a small band of men and women charged with spectral policing . . ."

"Like that small band of men and women there?" Clara asked, pointing toward Parliament. "They are mitigating some spirit onlookers. I can see them doing so."

"By God, that's them! Oh, look, Spire! I've got to meet them!" Lord Black could not contain himself. He set the box aside, dashing down from his post in a few gangly leaps and headed toward the long-rumored "hidden department."

"Lord Black, this isn't the time for—" Spire barked, then growled in irritation at being ignored. He turned to Rose. "I'll only be a moment. I can't let him get lost in this fray, I'll bring him right back." He darted after the nobleman.

* * * * *

The Guard had felt the pull toward the governmental heart of the city in unison during a shared pint or two at their favorite Bloomsbury pub. As a result, they came upon the parade from the direction of Westminster and positioned themselves at Westminster Bridge, among a battery of Metropolitan Police. The police were milling about in nervous efforts to keep the public from going past them.

The mouth of Westminster Bridge held a particular power for this group of six men and women: It was where they had first met, youngsters drawn to the heart of the city and to their collective fate. They always stood a little taller and more sure of themselves on Westminster.

"Ladies and gentlemen, we ask you to stay on the east side of this blockade; no one is allowed to watch the event from the Parliament side," said a uniformed young man, approaching The Guard.

The lean, ostentatiously dressed man with flaxen hair, Lord Withersby, stepped forward and with a wave of his hand shooed off the officer, who wandered away, dazed. The six men and women moved undeterred toward the throng of bystanders.

"Do any of those families mean anything to you, Rebecca?" Alexi, mounted on a black stallion, asked the tall, severe-looking woman walking alongside. She now and then patted the stallion's muzzle if he began huffing about having to plod along instead of keeping his usual speedy gallop.

"Not a whit," the headmistress replied. "To be fair, I don't know my heraldry very well, I haven't needed to at the Academy, but as far as I can tell, those crests are of lines long deceased or decried."

"Odd, but of little matter to us," the vicar said, standing at her side, a jovial-looking man with salt-and-pepper hair and a cleric's collar.

"Ah. But *that* is . . ." Alexi said, squinting ahead.

The raven familiar that followed them on their rounds was again circling their number from above, and at the sight of the oncoming light he gave up quite a cry.

Behind the heraldic pennants was a long stretch of metal carts, upon which bodies lay, with an odd gossamer glimmering around their forms. The Guard, watching, hoped that the stillness of the bodies was that of sleep rather than death. As the march drew closer, they could see that glitter was a vast network of wires. The filaments were connected to several taller carts that carried lines of turbines being hand-cranked by bent-shouldered laborers.

On either side of these supine forms floated a retinue of specters. Most of their transparent faces looked ashamed or horrified. Some seemed to be trying desperately to pull away from the procession.

"Damnable parades," Alexi muttered, glowering. His onyx stallion stamped, apparently echoing his sentiment. "Always kicking up spectral dust, inciting the ghostly rabble all over the city . . ." As he spoke, an ethereal blue fire, an offset of bright light against all his black layers, leaped into his hand as if summoned from above to land in his palm.

"What's all this for?" asked the Irish healer.

"By the look of it, it seems something to have to do with electricity," the Frenchwoman stated. "Look at those wagons."

"Anything for a stunt and a chance to make money," Alexi grumbled.

They heard a sudden, angry shout. "No, this cannot be," came an anguished voice. "This will. Not. Be!" shrieked someone in the crowd.

A small man with mousy hair that stood up around his head like a static-ridden halo, whose eyes were wild with light that seemed sparked from within, dashed out of the shadows. He ran right into the procession, nearly floated as it seemed his small feet barely touched the ground between two of the turbine wagons. Several burly guards on either side of the conveyances lunged toward him, only to be repelled when they got within a foot of him. There was a resounding smack like the crack of a whip and a fire started on one of the men's coats.

The Guard as a whole stopped and stared.

The turbines on each cart crackled with spun lightning. At first onlookers made noises of amazement and appreciation, but when the whine of the engines grew loud and shrill, when the collective hairs of the entire crowd rose into the air, they began to murmur in fear.

"No. More!" the young man shouted and flung his arms wide.

The sky was filled with a sudden arc of lightning, and everything that had been glowing went dark. Frederic the raven dove towards his mistress as silvery light threaded out in all directions. She held out her gloved forearm for him and once landed, seemed all too happy to tuck in against her.

The processional bodies shuddered violently on their platforms, then stilled. The turbines smoked, their belts and rotors turned to veritable dust. Smoke lifted into the air from singed clothes, from flesh and the rigging of the corpses.

In the stillness, The Guard looked for the strange young man, but he was nowhere to be seen.

"*That's* why we can't trust electricity," Alexi stated with satisfaction.

"But look," Withersby countered, "it rather did our job for us. Look. The ghosts are gone. They vanished with that surging strike."

"And people are left injured," said the Irishwoman, her hand lit with a soft white light of a powerful healer. "Let me go—"

"Not our purview, Jane," Alexi said softly. "I'm sorry, but we can't interfere further."

The healer folded her arms angrily.

"Come, let's course farther down the parade route and

make sure all has been put suitably to rest," the leader said, spurring his horse onward, faster now that the procession had stopped.

The headmistress turned to gather the others and follow, only to find Withersby toying with a couple of men who had stepped toward them out of the crowd. Two familiar faces, governmental operatives, the ones who had been in such trouble so recently.

"Lord Withersby, you stop that right now," she said as the nobleman made a man they knew to be Harold Spire raise his hands in the air and wave them about; Lord Black was frozen in place beside him, mouth open.

"Look, Rebecca, it's the government officials we saw held prisoner the other day! Hallo, old friends!" Withersby said, as if this assessment somehow justified his making the shorter of the two into a marionette.

"All the more reason *not* to muck about with them, Elijah," scolded the vicar.

"None of you have any sense of humor," Withersby pouted. "Very well, then. On your way." The snide, lean man wiped a hand over the faces of both men before him and darted off to catch up with his team, which had begun moving up the street, searching for ghostly residue.

They had not gone far when the quality of the day's light began to change, as if a bright dawn was coming toward them at breakneck speed and from all directions at once. . . .

* * * * *

Clara had been spared a seizure thanks to Mosley's arcs of lightning cutting the ghosts free from the dead bodies before she was overcome, and the tether of Rose's hand helped her stay cogent. She gasped anew from her vantage point at the speeding, brightening aurora ahead. . . .

As the wondrous light expanded and began to become more detailed, she noticed that the oncoming cloud was in fact individual spirits. But they were so bright, colorful, even. Brighter than the grayscale she'd grown accustomed to in Louis.

The luminous mob descended and swarmed toward the head of the parade, toward all the dull, dim-looking people carrying the antiquated crests. As the iridescent human forms reached those sleepwalking bodies, an odd separation began to happen. Something dark and cloudy peeled out and down from the bodies, slinking off onto the Embankment stones as if tar or oil were sliding off them onto the street to vanish or dissipating like smoke. The bright forms slid into the bodies as if putting on clothes.

"My God," Rose murmured.

"Evelyn must be successful, right at this moment," Clara gasped. "These are *living* souls reunited with bodies! The paintings must have been destroyed and the souls are returning to find their rightful homes. That's why all the forms aren't the grayscale color like my poor Louis . . . Oh, blessed, dear Evelyn . . ."

One by one, bright soul light snapped into place, like magnets connecting, and once whole again, each body began convulsing, doubling over, but after coughing or retching they came to, disoriented, and looking around for something familiar in an unfamiliar scenario.

For the most part, the souls found their bodies and began helping one another up. The Metropolitan officers, seeing them now to be persons in need of aid rather than a potential threatening mob, stepped in and began getting people to their feet, and a few families of dispossessed actually reunited, which allowed a few more bodies to regroup.

Clara and Rose, their own souls having already been reunited, stared with tears streaming down their faces at this moving display.

* * * * *

Rebecca explained to her important coterie what must be occurring, turning to Alexi. "My God, these are *living* souls and *living* bodies reuniting. They've been possessed, all of them, look at the pitch-black shadows oozing away. *What* kind of rite has gone on here on such a scale to have created this massive display?"

"Human interference like we've never seen," the imperious leader replied. "Our Pull didn't activate, meaning this was wholly human doing, not ghostly. There is no spirit here that wants to misbehave. They all want to stay alive in their rightful bodies and find their respective peace," Alexi stated.

His group nodded, feeling the truth of it in their interconnected hearts and the spiritual barometer that was their unique power. They watched in awe as egregious mortal wrong righted itself, soul by soul.

But there was one lost girl, small and slight, her body crumpled up to the side of the crowd near an Embankment parapet that shielded her from view of most of the crowd, but her soul was bobbing about, lost and confused.

Jane, the healer, broke free from the throng, and despite Alexi trying to keep her from interfering, she rushed forward to grab the unconscious body and placed the limp form across her lap. Lifting her lit healing hand, she slammed a jolt right onto the girl's heart. She stared up at the spirit separated from its body that seemed too confused to return and held out her other hand, reaching for the hem of the golden, transparent dress of the girl, even though her fingertips wafted right through the soul.

Jane turned her attention back to the corporeal body and bid it come back to itself with another jolt to the heart. The soul of the girl whipped her head around at last, as if seeing herself for the first time, and dove back into her body in a shimmering shudder of light. The girl convulsed once, coughed, and in a panic stumbled to her feet, leaning on Jane with a soft thank-you before turning to see her weeping mother, who flung herself into an embrace with her revived child.

The Guard beamed at their healer as she returned.

"All right then, *now* we can go," Jane murmured, shy as ever, but with a pleased, proud grin on her face that was exemplary of the reason they heeded their difficult calling day in, day out, entirely unknown and unappreciated by anyone but the forces that summoned them from ancient times.

* * * * *

After a long moment, Spire and Black shook their heads, as if fending off drowsiness.

"Mr. Spire," Black said slowly, "why are we across the street from our station?"

"I . . . I'm not sure, milord. What were we even on about?" Spire asked.

"I've no idea; perhaps some of that toxin got in our system. Let's not waste a moment more. Do I seem myself?" Lord Black asked, smoothing his light hair back in place.

"Yes. Do I?" Spire asked slowly.

Black inspected him. "Are you . . . generally irritated at the world?"

"Generally, yes, especially during parades," Spire replied.

"Do you think all our paranormal mumbo-jumbo is entirely that?"

"Yes. Entirely."

"All right, then, you're yourself," Black assured with a dazed smile.

"Where is our . . ." Spire looked around. He spotted the needle and the platform around it. "Ah, yes, that's right . . ." They turned toward their post, then took advantage of a slight break in the procession to rush back to the assembled company.

"Oh, thank God, there you are, we thought you must have

gotten trapped by Mosley's arcs of lightning!" Rose cried the moment Spire was within earshot below.

"The what?" Black asked.

"Did you see what happened with souls and bodies reuniting?" Clara exclaimed excitedly as Black climbed up to join them.

"No . . . I . . ." Spire scratched his head, remaining below, scowling. "No."

"No matter, come." Rose gestured to Spire. "We're just about to signal the lighting of the Wards. There's a lull, but we fear it's the calm before the storm, hurry!"

"I'm going to stay on the ground with the senator for his protection," Spire stated. "Give me a shout from your view."

The finale approached. . . .

What looked like nearly two hundred possessed bodies marched in rows surrounding a vast banner that bore the Master's Society crest—dragons eating themselves, rampant on red and gold. The red of the banner was too dark, likely blood in the paint. Clara assumed that Moriel, in whatever conveyance he had chosen, was behind that banner.

The procession stopped, and the possessed ones all turned at once to face the assembled spectators. In the fading dusk and tallow gaslight of the Embankment's lamps, the host of glimmering, tar-black inhuman eyes was enough to strain the resolve of any onlooker. The crowd, which had been stunned into silence by the electric display, began murmuring in refreshed fear.

The dread march was truly something to behold, and Clara was sure she and everyone near her would never forget the sight for as long as they lived.

From behind the banner, a phalanx of Summoned shadows poured into the air like ink in water. The crowd gasped, transfixed in horror at the sight of the roiling black cloud of vaguely humanoid forms. Coalesced malevolence floated toward them in the direction of Parliament's eaves.

There was another low, resounding note from an unseen instrument.

"London, you are ours," chorused the collected voices of the possessed.

The banner dropped and Moriel was revealed in an ostentatious robe and crown, standing on a golden calash like the one the queen had used in her recent parade. Guards stood on his every side.

"London, you are mine and I have come to collect your crown!" he cried, raising a dripping, blood-tipped sword in one hand. Clara surmised that fresh blood was needed in such dark rites as this, and enough of the guards wore bloodstains on their clothes that it could have come from any of them.

"For all that is right and good, hold your light aloft!" Bishop cried from within the crowd, affecting a common British accent. Moriel seemed surprised—and indeed offended—by this interruption.

"For London!" Black cried from atop their crow's nest, setting his Ward alight with a lit match into the vial, a shimmering light bubbling up from its contents, holding it up as if he was the embodiment of Lady Liberty's lamp, even though only the hand of that grand gift had been raised in Madison Square Park thus far. In this moment, Lord Black magnified just such a beacon of hope, and Clara's heart swelled afresh.

"For London!" The crowd lifted Wards high in a cascading ripple of light.

And then unrolled an incredible patchwork quilt of the plan.

The clergymen Bishop and Evelyn had invited began to

pray, as did the rabbis summoned by Zhavia. Vodoun practitioners Andre had located began drumming. A muezzin that Mrs. Wilson convinced to come began to sing a call to prayer in Arabic. Buddhists rang bells. Hindus of the Raj lifted hands in sacred dances.

Mediums channeled guardians and benevolent spirits. All across the Embankment, London and her people were being blessed and peace was being invoked. And, following Bishop's example, lifted Wards added threads of personal magic into the city's tapestry. Whether they shared any faith or believed in nothing but themselves and humanity in atheistic peace, all were a part of the fabric.

The cloud of onyx shadows, the horde of demon forms, halted, wavering, a street away from Parliament's doors. Moriel looked confused, unsure of himself or perhaps just how to command his silhouette army in response.

"For London!" Black cried again. Another wave of Wards lofted into the air with a resounding response: "For London!"

And then came gunfire. While some onlookers had fainted during the previous acts, now, many fled at the sound of shots.

Seemingly from out of nowhere, Gabriel Brinkman was racing toward Moriel, shooting as he went. Every guard around Moriel, all of them sporting the blackened eyes of the demon possessed, stepped into the path of a bullet as the calash proceeded, bodies falling away in an increasing wake.

"Metropolitan!" Spire shouted. Two hundred men whipped off a top layer of nondescript worker's clothes, revealing their uniforms beneath. All leaped at the possessed guards. The officers were wearing padding and carrying various weapons, ready to face the brute force of the demonically possessed. Moriel kept the weaker bodies for flag bearing, the stronger for his personal guard.

Many of the recovering standard-bearers, having been returned to themselves, were eager to battle the still possessed. The police guarding Westminster did not stand in the way of victims adding their numbers to the good fight.

"Stand strong! Hold your lights aloft, London!" Lord Black shouted, his voice towering above all. "Help our brave policemen by holding your light so they might see!"

Those remaining did so.

Black, Clara, and Rose clambered down to street level; Spire had already gone to take command of the Metropolitans. Bishop was weaving through the crowds, his mesmeric forces keeping them strong of will and heart, Andre and Effie still at his sides.

This secondary rally scattered lightless Summoned shadows like roaches scurrying from a blaze. Brinkman continued to fire his multichambered gun, taking down the guards closest to Moriel.

Moriel screamed, swiping his blood-drenched long-sword toward Brinkman; the Summoned swept over the double agent immediately. There was a horrible cry, followed by the even more horrible sound of a body disintegrating. Brinkman suffered the same fate as Tourney had, his blood and body splattered over the Embankment's stones.

The police officers did their best to shield the crowd from that horror, but there was no hiding it entirely, and a wave of fear and terror swept through the onlookers.

Clara fervently prayed for the souls of Brinkman and his young son, hoping they would be immediately reunited in heaven and rewarded for all their trials on Earth.

The Wards were holding despite the wavering of the crowd. The Summoned silhouettes could not get closer to the bystanders or to Parliament's stones.

Moriel descended from the calash, closely shadowed by

a large, bald man Clara assumed was his primary personal guard. Moriel lifted something golden from within the calash—a wide-mouthed chalice.

Clara shuddered at the chalice, another item from her dreams coming into vivid focus. Holding the large goblet in one hand, he struck at the Embankment stones and then at the air with his bloody sword—whose blood that was she could not guess—then splashed liquid from the chalice onto the ground in a vague line, creating a threshold. The crimson fluid was garish even in the light of the gas lamps.

Clara wondered if he was trying to call forth more Summoned or join them in their nether state. She had barely completed the thought when a hazy, uneven trapezoid—a wavering doorway—flickered into existence.

Her hand flew to her mouth as she saw Louis standing on the other side, along with Barnard Smith and the dead Omega scientists. They stood shoulder to shoulder, blocking the passage, holding their hands out to show Moriel that he was not welcome in the world they had been driven into.

Clara rushed toward that portal, drawn by Louis, their bond magnetizing them in the moment. Rose was dragged along in her wake as if by a rope, as was Andre.

Their compass held, their four corners never so much a concentrated power until now. The quartet's bonded magic had catalyzed into an elemental force beyond blood, body, or timeline.

Moriel tried to move, but Clara, Rose, and Andre spread out, keeping him rooted from behind, while Louis and the scientists blocked him from in front, a dark mist rising behind them in this gray otherworld as if a ghostly fog were rolling in.

As the three living "corners" approached Moriel, Clara noted that his cruel, bloodshot eyes no longer looked human.

Clara tried to focus, but her vision swam. No! Her body couldn't fail her now. She stared at Rose, rallying.

"O'Rourke!" Moriel cried.

"I'm here, Your Majesty," the enormous Irishman replied in monotone, his eyes vacant. Not possessed, Clara noted, as the guard's eyes were not blackened, but he was not to be trusted. "Not to worry."

Acrid smoke, that rising tide of fog, poured then from the portal Moriel had opened, going right for his throat and making the attempted usurper choke and gag, smothering whatever orders he had been about to give as he gasped and writhed in his place.

Though Andre and Clara had stopped moving, Rose kept going, approaching the portal where Louis floated.

"Rose, what are you doing?" Clara cried. Rose turned to her with such conviction it was like a flower had been dipped into molten metal and turned steel in the instant.

"If we are the points of a compass, Clara," she said, looking at her, Andre, and Louis alternately, "we aren't properly balanced. We have to hold Moriel in place, and there's only one way to do that."

"Rose," Clara cautioned.

"You've led so many lives, Clara," Rose explained. "Maybe I'll do the same. This was destined. Don't you remember what I first told you? It was prophesied that you would be the death of me, dear sister, and I forgive you for it." And with that, Rose stepped over the bloody line into the next realm, and her living body crumpled at the threshold.

Within the portal, another Rose now stood, grayscale like Louis, who reached out for her hand . . . the compass between worlds balanced.

Blinking rapidly, the sights before her spinning, Clara felt herself begin to seize, this threshold was too much, and with her dear tether Rose, now . . . dead. . . .

She looked over her shoulder, seeking aid, and found Bishop a few feet away, trying to reach her through an invisible barrier. The forces she and the others had created in their compass had stopped him in his tracks, and she despaired, feeling her knees give out.

Even as Clara faltered, Bishop dropped to his knees as if falling for her. His hands were upraised, palms toward her. She felt a veritable wave of light and harmonious reverberations surround her, felt him shield her like never before. The first symptoms of the seizure eased. He'd bought her another few minutes, perhaps, and Clara knew he would keep bolstering her as long as he, giving over the whole of his life force, could remain conscious.

"O'Rourke, shield me, I cannot move, I am pinned to this fulcrum," Moriel gasped in panic, still struggling.

"Yes . . ." O'Rourke moved closer to Moriel.

A flash of light caught everyone's eye.

Spire strode toward the usurper with a ball of something fiery held in one raised hand. Clara could just make out that it was four Ward vials tied together. He would have only a moment, and nothing could stand in his way. . . .

The visitor's words about her lives and their relationship to time rang in Clara's ears, along with Zhavia's bid to bring all of her lives with her. She responded to that call to arms and drew upon every life she'd ever lived. The representations of them peeled away from her like ghosts given color, like all those souls she'd seen earlier, transparent memories representing the threads of her soul's tapestry.

Spooling around her in a widening circle, spilling centuries into this single, modern moment, time slowed, expanded, and all of Clara Templeton that had ever been was all around them, every life culminating to the breathless *now*. . . .

As if moving through mud, O'Rourke slowly stepped aside, giving Spire clear aim. "May you burn, *Majesty*," the guard hissed, the words elongated by the stretch in time, "and may the saints forgive me."

Moriel shrieked, Spire cried out in fury, and the vials arced into the air, heading straight for the horrid little man.

"Go whence you came," Spire growled as the projectile landed squarely on Moriel's chest.

Upon contact, the Wards exploded in a coruscation of light and sound. The intensity, Clara imagined, was exacerbated by the monstrousness of the evil Moriel had perpetrated. Time returned to its normal flow as Clara's lives folded in on themselves and returned to their histories with a loud tearing sound.

The madman went up in flames.

O'Rourke was immediately beset by the jet-black silhouettes of the Summoned. With an ungodly cry, the guard was instantly reduced to nothing but crimson pulp slickening the stones.

The horde of shadows then pounced upon Moriel, who disappeared into their black tumult. A fresh burst of acrid smoke rose from the spot. Louis and Clara both murmured prayers while Andre and Rose stared at one another across the dimensional doorway.

An instant later, the pitch-black Summoned that remained floating in parade form rose, hovered, then scattered to the winds, no longer a coalesced mass oozing toward Parliament but thin dark lines losing focus.

"London, I beg once more for your light!" Lord Black yelled. His cry was taken up and echoed through the city's streets, and people everywhere lifted whatever fire they had unto the darkening night. Effie had joined Lord Black at his vantage point, holding two Wards high and bright.

The portal that Moriel had opened by blood wavered. Some of the remaining Summoned slipped into that strange corridor. Others became wisps of night sky. A few sank into the Embankment's stones. In seconds they had all vanished, their mission having disappeared with Moriel himself.

The moment there seemed to be peace, Clara turned to
Louis, still floating in that precarious space, her own body
still clenched on a precarious seizure precipice. "Can you
help Rose?"

Spire, thinking Clara was speaking to him, rushed to
Rose's body and knelt before her, lifting her torso carefully
onto his knees. He blinked at the air before him, past the line
of blood and toward the threshold it demarked, as if trying
to focus on something he could not quite see.

Louis lifted Rose's hand, grayscale transparencies able to
make contact on that other side. Her spirit stared about, taking in her dim surroundings with wonderment. "No, Miss
Everhart," Louis declared, "this purgatorial place is not yet
for you. You may cross through here one day, but not today."
He led her back across the threshold with a gentle push
toward the living.

"Now, Miss Everhart," Spire said with a mounting urgency teetering on desperation, taking her pulse at her wrist
and leaning over her to watch for breath, "do come back, we
need you here. *I* need you here. . . ."

Rose's spirit stepped back across that mortal line and re-
connected with her body in a shimmering ripple of light, two
Roses superimposed and then just one limp body that suddenly gave a spasm. She gasped and coughed, curling inward
against Spire, who held her tightly. He murmured, "There,
there, oh good, *very* good . . ." in a tone gentler than Clara
had ever heard from him. She felt confident they would both
be quite all right indeed.

And so would she be. As Rose was restored, so, too, did
the threat of Clara's imminent seizure lessen, with the additional help of Bishop rushing up to her, engulfing her in
a joyful embrace, invigorating her with a rush of energy that
allowed her fraught muscles to relax against his tight hold.

Over Bishop's shoulder she saw the final images of the portal. . . .

Louis's grayscale form stared at his twin across the threshold. Andre stood with his hand upraised to the doorway, as if trying to take the sprit's hand.

"No, don't reach through, Andre," Louis warned. "I wouldn't try Miss Everhart's stunt if I were you."

Bishop noted Clara's gaze and released her, letting her have a moment with this scene, as always respecting her loss even though he'd been wounded by her secrets.

"You've been so good to me, Louis," Andre murmured, tears streaming from his hazel eyes. "We've never been closer, and all since you died . . . This, Brother, isn't fair . . . You've made me a better man—"

"And for that my afterlife is sweeter, Brother," Louis assured. "Do not grieve. I would not trade a day of this, and indeed, had I done so, I doubt we'd have been successful."

"Louis . . ." Clara rushed up too close to that same perilous line. Her former lover held up another halting hand.

"I'll try to come again, Clara, one last time, but for now, this door has been open too long to be safe," Louis said. "You're brilliant, you know, my forever muse, what incredible work you've done to save the day!" He beamed, blowing a ghostly kiss to her and then saluting his brother before turning into the gray mist behind him and vanishing in the murk. The hovering trapezoidal shape between worlds snapped into nothingness.

Clara willed back tears and turned back to Bishop, stalwart. He was there with a hand on her shoulder. "Thank you for your help, Rupert. You are my rock."

"He was right, you know," Bishop said. "You saved the day, you brilliant woman. I'll never let you forget it." He held out his arm and she took it with a wide smile.

Captain Grange appeared, seeking Spire, and launched into his report even as Spire gently helped Rose to her feet.

"Sir, madam, pardon me please," Grange said breathlessly.

"Yes, my friend," Spire replied. "Go on."

"I have received a report via wire from precinct to precinct that your colleagues, Mrs. Northe-Stewart and the rest of your team, are safe. They had to remove the portraits from the estate to finish their work because of an electrical fire that blew out the entire place." Grange paused, then said hesitantly, "They described a man as . . . standing directly in the middle of a lightning blast. There was no evidence of him after."

"You will say that man died in that fire," Spire said.

Clara was glad to hear Mosley would get his freedom after all.

"Yes, sir. Understood. Mrs. Northe-Stewart and the rest of your team have been taken to an inn north of the city to rest."

"*I* am headed home for a stiff drink," Black announced, having descended to join the group on their level, Effie quiet behind him, still looking around warily, and Clara wondered what of the proceedings she had seen, and what she could only have sensed. "Where you're all invited to stay the night," Black added. "I think it might be best if we stay close, considering."

Rose nodded. "Yes, sir, that would be best." Still holding on to Spire for support, she reached out a hand to clasp Clara's.

"Can your men coordinate cleaning all this horrible mess up, Captain Grange?" Black asked. "In addition, perhaps ask some of the various clergymen to . . . help people with whatever they saw?"

"I'm wondering what the hell *I* saw—" Spire said, almost under his breath.

"'Hell' being the operative word," Grange stated. "But yes.

Our men will handle cleanup. Go in peace, friends. I believe, if I may, that the worst is over, but I'll have to be more sure of it when I wake up in the morning and the whole world hasn't gone *more* mad than it did tonight."

"Tomorrow will be a brighter day," Bishop assured him. "The momentum is in our favor now."

Lord Black's residence had been such a pleasant safe haven before, and so was it again, for those who took Black up on the invitation. Effie and Andre wished to stay with other friends, and no one took offense at anyone's preferences.

The embrace between Black and his lover at the front door was long and fond, and after a moment, Francis pulled back with a blush and ushered everyone in. "There's a roaring fire for you to shake off the horrors of the day," he declared, "and a vat of spiced rum."

"Don't mind if I take a cup or two of that." Spire chuckled.

"May all my lives be praised we survived to see this night through," Clara murmured, collapsing onto the settee before the welcome fire.

"I feel like I've lived several lifetimes today, and I don't even believe in more than one," Spire said, eagerly accepting a mug of liquor from Francis with a warm thanks before leaning toward Clara. "I ask now not for your mysticism but for your opinion. Is our age doomed? Is there more of this to come?"

Clara thought a long moment before speaking with very careful words.

"At the beginning of this century the world presented itself as more innocent, full of incalculable possibility. We were a hopeful, optimistic people with the possibility to be generous. Now, for all the powers of the modern age, all the free-doms and conveniences, there are so many more complications as each mechanization comes with a cost. Innovation is necessary across every front, but there are times when I long for simpler days.

"If that's what Moriel had advocated," she continued, "simple peace rather than an absurd return to feudalistic dictatorship, who could have argued against simplicity? But simplicity should not come at the cost of modernity and broader societal freedom."

"Certainly not," Black agreed, and bid Francis sit on the arm of his chair by the fire. He did so, and Black folded his hands over his beloved's knee.

"You speak so clearly about the early part of this century, Miss Templeton," Spire said with a bit of awe.

"Because I remember it," Clara replied. Spire blinked at her. She continued. "Memory, experience, emotion, evocative details, the finer points of a past life, and the contexts in which it was lived all mix in the air like sensual fog. Those of us skilled enough can pluck out distinct moments from our elder mists. Sometimes we cherish what we've found in the gloam, as all such lost heirlooms should be treasured when they find a safe heir."

"That's beautiful," Rose said.

"She is," Bishop agreed.

Clara blushed.

"Our next task is to be sure our country is similarly protected as we have tried to do here," Clara continued. "The Society has holdings in America, so we must systematically disassemble any remaining framework that exists. Those from the Eterna Commission who remained behind should have things well in order, but this trip has proved full of terrifying new insights."

"Do let our department know how we can be of service,"

Lord Black offered. "I believe we have felled the beast today, but tell me if other death throes in your country need any of our resources."

"Thank you, milord." Bishop nodded.

There was a long silence before Clara felt the weight of the day collapse upon her and she rose to her feet. "Whether nightmares and constant replays of the horror and loss we've faced tonight will allow me any rest, that will be as yet determined, but I must try. Shall I take the same guest room, Lord Black?"

"Yes indeed, and consider it yours whenever you wish to visit us," the nobleman said cordially.

"Come, I'll escort you up," Bishop replied, going to the stairs. Clara moved to him. She could feel Mr. Spire staring after her as she crossed the room, as if wanting to say something else, his skeptic's mind likely straining harder than hers after a day like today, fumbling for sense and purchase. She turned at the landing.

"Good night, Mr. Spire," she said. "Thank you for your work in keeping us alive today. Thank you all."

"And thank you both for yours," Spire replied.

At the top of the landing, Bishop's room directly across from hers, he stood at the threshold, his tall frock-coated figure elegant in the gaslight. "I'm here if you need me," he said softly.

"As am I," she replied from across the hall. The two shared a smile and closed their doors.

Alone in her white-walled guest room decked in blue, this was the first time Clara had a moment to breathe, to process, to grieve for all the horror she'd seen.

The inevitable question for Clara was, What to do next? Where was she called to be?

Clara was not alone with her thoughts for long when a chill draft pervaded the room. Louis's presence, while welcome, caused a feeling of dread, as the look on his face spoke of something they'd been ignoring since his first appearance . . .

Louis's ghost had traveled great lengths to be at her side this day, to fight the demons whose unwanted presence had cost him his own life.

In essence, his purpose had been fulfilled.

"Clara, my dear love," Louis began cautiously, wafting close, trailing a ghostly breeze of a fingertip down her blushing cheek. "I am so proud of you for all you did today."

"As am I of you. Your magic saved the day," she replied.

"Only thanks to your implementation and your actions, as the anchor of our compass and impressive wielder of time and lives."

They stared at each other for a long time, solid and shade. Finally, Louis breached the silence. "You and I both know our states cannot remain connected indefinitely."

That truth hung in the air as his incorporeal body did. This was not a state that could last forever, even if the spirit was an eternal concept.

"This is good-bye then, I suppose, darling . . ." Clara whispered.

Her grief over Louis had taken many odd turns since his death. His current, albeit hollow, existence was a great comfort to her, and she'd have accepted it over nothing at all, but it was selfish of her to deny him the peaceful journey she hoped for all spirits.

"Can we make a promise?" Louis asked.

"Of what, my love?" Clara said, forcing her voice not to break.

"To find one another again . . ."

"In a future life?"

"Yes, in a future life. We know these truths now."

"Oh, yes, please do. Please come find me," Clara exclaimed.

"Good, then." Louis smiled and his translucent form seemed a warmer shade of gray than before.

Clara rose from the bed to face him. She knew it was time. There was no prevaricating, no lingering. Only corporeal tears and the faint hint of vapor.

"Good-bye, my dear," Louis said with a sigh. "You're not alone, you know, Clara. Someone who loves you very much is with you, alive, in the here and now. You have loved him before and are beautifully suited now. I will love you in our future."

Tears poured down her face as she nodded. "Good-bye, Louis Dupris. Rest well. . . ."

She lost him for the third time.

It was no easier than the first.

There were no words to capture the particular pain of saying good-bye to a loved one multiple times, and the finality of this last moment.

It was difficult to believe, even for a Spiritualist, that they would meet again. It was hard to believe anything while grieving. Hard to see any light through the hot, silent tears of loss.

She clung to Louis's last words, knowing that he spoke the truth. A love waited for her, a devoted, patient, pining love. Love that was, despite all, meant to be in this life.

Her beloved senator.

* * * * *

Every year, on the anniversary of David Templeton's death, Rupert Bishop performed a solemn ritual. That he was far from home this year did not mean he would shirk this duty. In fact, the anniversary falling on such a day of import made this rite all the more important.

In his white-paneled guest room, the furnishings and draperies in the complementary colors of russet and orange, opposite Clara's room, he lit a tallow candle that made the whole room glow autumnal.

He rang a small bell, letting the delicate note linger in silence.

He placed his palms flush upon a sturdy oak desk.

Then he asked the same question he'd been asking for the last several years on this day.

"David, my dear friend," Rupert murmured to the air. "Do I have your permission to ask for her hand? I cannot and will not proceed without your blessing."

For years, the only answer had been silence.

But tonight . . .

Tonight the candle went out as if snuffed. There was a faint trembling in the air.

A quiet voice whispering in his ear . . .

In the darkness, Rupert Bishop smiled.

He quietly moved across the hall to Clara's closed door.

He knocked.

"Come in," she said. She was sitting stock-still on the end of the bed, fully dressed, looking as if she'd just seen a ghost. Perhaps she had. She looked up as the door opened. "Hello, my dear . . ."

Rupert approached Clara slowly. She rose to her feet, searching his gaze intently for clues to his mood, why he was here. If there was fire in his eyes, for the first time he did not hide it.

His hand protectively cupped the back of her neck, then his fingertips trailed up her ear. She shivered and allowed a small breath to escape her mouth, soft and sensual.

He pressed his lips to her forehead, prompting her to lean even nearer, closing the last distance between their bodies. Rupert loosed a gamesome huff of contentment at this now covetous embrace. He kissed her temple and was thrilled when she tilted her head to increase the pressure of his lips.

After an aching moment, he shifted slightly to place his lips against her ear.

"Tomorrow, we go home, my darling, to further protect our country," he whispered. "And then . . . a future awaits us, one that we've not allowed ourselves to think about, but should."

"Yes, my dearest," she replied in the same quiet tone. "It is time to go home."

* * * * *

Black and Francis retired, leaving Rose and Spire alone in the parlor, staring out at the sloping garden behind Lord Black's home, a quiet spot of green, a little oasis of verdant life against so much dark death. "Shall we retire, too?" Rose asked gently.

"Retire? Can I?" Spire said with a little chuckle. "Can I be done with this dreadful business for the rest of my life and live out my few remaining days on a quiet beach in Suffolk? Tell me, Miss Everhart, that you are a messenger of the angels come to promise me a future of the blessedly silent absence of humanity!"

"It will hardly be a 'few' days, Mr. Spire. You're full of health and vigor. Well, venom, at least. Full of health and venom." She grinned. "You're not fond of people, are you?"

He snorted. "Truthfully, I have found that most people are hateful. I like a great many of them better when they're behind bars."

Rose scowled at this extreme statement. Spire looked at her steadily, then allowed the corners of his mouth to turn up.

She laughed. That felt good. Spire stared at her. She held his gaze and did not look away.

"Suffolk, you said?" she asked quietly.

"Suffolk, yes, Miss Everhart. Do you like Suffolk?"

"I do."

"Well." Spire seemed surprisingly contented. "That's good."

"However," she cautioned, "Suffolk or no, there's a *great* deal of work to be done before any such future rest."

"Pragmatic, Miss Everhart," Spire said, amusement in his tone.

"Would you expect anything less?"

"Promise me you'll never be anything but."

They shared a smile that Rose sure was the happiest she'd ever seen on Harold Spire's face. She was fairly sure she was returning a similarly unprecedented expression, life far fuller with such blossoms of possibility on the horizon.

FOURTEEN

The queen demanded an immediate report, of course. The papers were full of incredulity.

Black invited Spire and Rose to come along, and they agreed, if nothing else out of support and respect for Black and all he'd done, risking and fighting at their side.

They met over tea in one of the very finest receiving rooms of the palace. Black offered a relative account of what occurred, with Spire and Rose contributing the occasional detail. That it wasn't a full account was for the best.

"And what of Moriel's estate?" the queen asked. To Rose's chagrin, she seemed to be somewhat titillated by the story, as much as Rose could tell given her generally dour mien. "Do tell me your department has seized it and purged it of all foul magic, that it can never be resurrected."

"The estate burned to the ground the night of the procession," Spire assured her.

"Electrical fire," Rose added.

"Electrical . . . that reminds me," the regent said, eyes lighting. "That Mosley person, did you have any luck with that man?"

"No, Your Majesty," Rose said quietly. "He is presumed to have started the fire and most certainly perished in it."

"Oh . . . that's a shame." The queen clucked her tongue and took a sip of tea.

"It is," Black agreed.

"I hear electricity may prolong human life," Victoria said airily. "There are sparks of it within our bodies, you know. I had hoped that Mr. Mosley might be a *healthier* key to the Omega initiative toward immortality."

Rose noticed Spire's grip tighten upon his saucer and prayed the delicate china would not shatter.

"Don't worry, Your Majesty," Black said, "we'll still chase immortality for you." His companions knew full well they would not, but they'd be happy to put on a show of it as long as their honest work would keep true evil at bay.

"It isn't for my vanity, you know . . ." the queen said coquettishly.

"Of course not," Spire confirmed. Only Rose, and perhaps Black, could detect the undercurrent in his voice, and Rose would commend him later for his tact.

Rose kept her smile to herself and thought of Suffolk.

Soon dismissed, the three were off to meet the Eterna team at the bustling grand train station that marked the beginning of their journey home.

* * * * *

Evelyn and Lord Denbury were already assembled in particular finery when Clara and Bishop met them at the station, Clara rushing up to embrace her mentor.

"Yes, my dear," Evelyn began before Clara could ask. "I promise to tell you everything about our wild time at Vieux-helles in vibrant detail. After a drink or two."

"Or four," Denbury added. He looked exhausted, but a weight was off his shoulders, and his striking blue eyes had regained some measure of sparkle.

"Lord Denbury," Clara said, "I'm relieved to see you looking healthier than I've seen you in some time."

"Thank you, Miss Templeton. I'm desperate to get back

to my wife and child. The news of Moriel's death has made me feel like a new man. Thank you also for your work. I know what you did yesterday was nigh impossible."

"I'm so proud of you *both*," Evelyn exclaimed, hooking a satin-decked arm around each of their necks.

Effie and Andre were there on the hour, with trunk and carpetbag, talking animatedly together like old friends.

They were interrupted jovially by the arrival of Spire, Rose, and Lord Black.

"This is not the last our teams will see of one another," Spire stated as hands were shaken and hugs exchanged. "If I may be so bold, I would like to suggest a biannual meeting between our commissions, in addition to a free and regular flow of communication."

"I couldn't agree more," Clara said. "After all, one cannot separate siblings indefinitely." She smiled at Rose, who beamed back at her. "Neither of us has blood family to claim or tend to us, so you and I, Rose, must build the one that magic brought together. Write me every week. Promise?"

"We must," Rose agreed with a nod and a smile. "And also we must make sure that long after our tenures, our respective offices do not take what we've done in vain, or become something they should not. We've made some very important promises, to very important forces and figures."

"I'd rather take magic right out of the equation," Spire said, shaking his head, "regardless of the inexplicable things we've dealt with. If I never see the like again, it will be too soon. Omega's purpose remains to make sure what we killed remains entirely dead, no further resurrections. Otherwise, you're all on your own, and I go back to blessed, bloody police work."

Lord Black held up his hands in no contest.

Clara moved forward to embrace Spire. He seemed taken aback but did not withdraw. "England needs you just as skeptical as ever, Mr. Spire. Keeps us 'damnable mystics' on our toes. May your skepticism prove ever a fruitful challenge to the great mysteries of the world, my friend."

"Why, thank you, Miss Templeton," he said, seeming moved.

"Be blessed, my friends," Senator Bishop said.

Just then, a harried letter carrier in a telegraph company uniform rushed up to them.

"Are any of you Senator Rupert Bishop?"

"I am." Bishop stepped forward.

"Thank goodness. The office that sent this didn't know where exactly you'd be, only that it was an emergency and to try and find you here." The young man thrust an envelope at him and darted away.

Clara's sensitivities allowed her to feel everyone's heart jump to their collective throats, hers included.

Bishop opened the envelope and read the wire. His face was grim. Clara felt her heart begin to sink from throat to stomach.

"It's from Franklin," he stated, and read the message aloud. "'Today: The torch borne by the hand of Lady Liberty burst into a green, inextinguishable flame. Trinity Church graveyard emptied of bodies. Columbia College overrun with the reanimate. Request your return. Request help.'"

Everyone stared at Bishop. The train whistle screamed.

"Bloody hell," Lord Black whispered.

Evelyn, stone-faced and all business, made sure porters got all of their things on board. Clara wrung her gloved hands.

"Well?" Bishop stared at his British compatriots. "There was that offer you made, Lord Black, about requesting—"

"Bloody hell," Black moaned again and stepped on to the train, turning at the compartment door to look expectantly at Rose and Spire.

"I . . . but I don't have my things . . ." Rose protested meekly.

"We've a safe house for these kinds of emergencies, Miss Everhart," Black declared. "And I'm rich. I'll get you what you need, and we'll wire everyone with news of our plans from the port. After these Americans bravely risked their lives for us on our soil—"

"We'll do same on theirs," Spire muttered. *"Bloody hell."*

The train whistle screamed again, louder and higher, the unbearable sound the only appropriate underscoring for the mood and moment.

"It . . . it won't be long," Clara said with a shaking smile, trying to sound hopeful as they all filed onto the train and Lord Black procured tickets for his team. "Think of all we've learned. It'll just be a quick few . . . supernatural fires to snuff out!"

"How many states in your country?" Spire asked, taking a seat across from Bishop.

"Thirty-eight," Evelyn replied, next to him, her elegant face as angry and fed up as Lord Denbury's across from her, whose gray pall had descended once more with sickening swiftness. Effie and Andre's bright conversation had fallen into silence as they stared out the windows past plumes of steam.

"That's a lot of fire," Rose murmured. "Across a vast lot of space."

"But we'll be fighting the conflagration *from* a thin island just over thirteen miles long that beats with the heart of the world," Bishop rallied. "With our connected powers, we've all the weight of the heavens on our side."

Andre had procured a newspaper from a trolley in the next aisle and dropped it into Bishop's lap. The headline asked the question on everyone's mind:

**HEART OF CITY BESET BY MADNESS
AND MONSTROSITY.**

DAY SAVED BY WHOLE OF LONDON'S PEOPLE.
BUT IS THIS THE END?

Clearly, it wasn't, and Bishop's optimism hung in the air in such harsh contrast to the last curdling scream of the train as it chugged them out from the station and on toward the port in a hypnotic rhythm, this band of inextricable souls falling into a silence with a weight as heavy as their value was priceless.

Clara pressed a hand to the talisman below ruffled lace, blessed with an old magic that rested at her sternum, and prayed she could creatively whip some new tricks up her sleeve. As industrious a spirit as her country claimed, so might the capacity for horror be matched. Noticing her hand to her heart, as Bishop was increasingly attuned to her movements, he leaned close for an additional reassurance.

"Do not worry," Bishop added, just for her, a whisper into her ear. "You were brilliant here in England, in a country not your own, with borrowed magic on another soil. Just think of what you'll do on yours. You were born for this fight, Clara Templeton, and I'll not have you doubting yourself. You've proved you are the heart of what Eterna was meant to become. Our commission has saved lives; *you* have saved lives and will do so again."

She stared up into the senator's luminous eyes steel bright with conviction and knew he was right.

This whole ordeal had forced her to stop cursing what had gone wrong with the commission and embrace its innovations instead. It was her rite of passage, and now she could be the sort of spirit-warrior she'd always wanted to be, like her idol Evelyn Northe-Stewart, staring determinedly out the train window, inexhaustible after having led the demise of Vieuxhelles to gain victory of soul and bodily reunion.

Clara had grown into what her mentors always expected.

The visitor would be proud, she thought, courage swelling within her, the energy enlivening the Ward still tucked into her corset.

She had become the storm, and the storm was headed home.